OCEAN

of

SILVER

Editor: Nancy Kohutka
Proof Editor: Mary Benjamin
Cover and Interior Design: Mallory Benjamin
Cover Art: Shutterstock

ISBN 979-8-9868674-4-3-4 (paperback)
ISBN 979-8-9868674-4-1 (hardcover)
ISBN 979-8-9868674-5-8 (ebook)

To Anthony—for helping me find my strength.

THE LIGHT KINGDOM OF LUX

SUNINDAYA RIVER

LUXIAN CITY

BAY

PUBLIC BEACHES

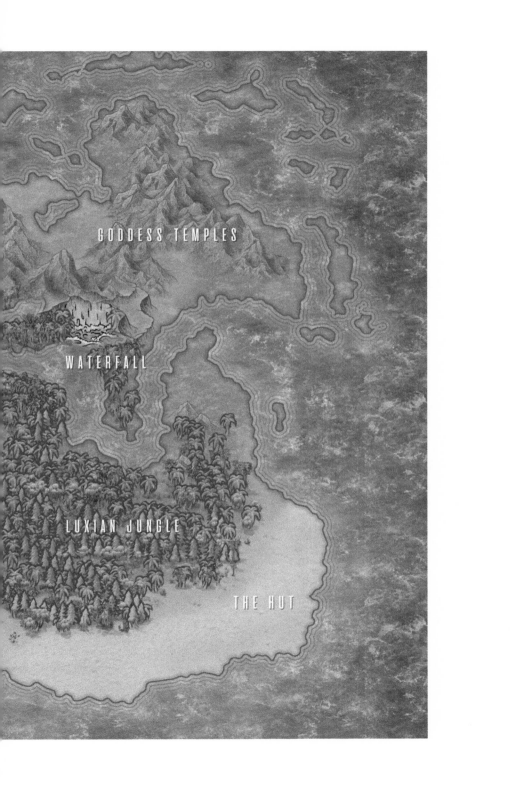

PROLOGUE

Princess Dovelyn

I HATED TENNEBRIS. The cold and darkness of the Kingdom seemed to have seeped into my bones and lingered long after I'd left. And now, my father was forcing me to go again. Only this time, it wasn't for a celebration. We were going to collect a prisoner. It was bad enough that I had to meet Scotlind when she married the Dark Prince, but now, we were bringing her back to Lux.

I visited the Goddess temples on the outskirts of the island multiple times, praying to Pylemo that the girl would turn up dead before we were due to retrieve her. She was supposed to be dead. Only when my father got the message regarding the trade, everything had changed. His greed for power outweighed any rational thought. He couldn't stand to see a Luxian without their abilities on record. He wanted to know what her powers were and if he could use them—use *her*. She would have been better off dead.

I looked up at my two brothers. The King was forcing all of us to go. He wanted to present a formidable front. Everything was calcu-

1

lated with him, every single painstaking detail. My youngest brother met my stare. For a moment, I saw the hard gaze that most of Lux saw. The look that set his reputation ablaze as the Fire Prince. But then it softened. An unspoken understanding flowed between us. He was dreading this as much as I was, just not for the same reasons.

My older brother, Arcane, moved to sit next to me on the underwater monorail. We were waiting for our father to board before we would start the dreaded journey to the frozen Kingdom.

"What are you planning?" he whispered to me. He looked so much like me that sometimes it seemed like I was staring at my own reflection.

I spoke at a normal volume. It didn't matter anyway. Our younger brother could hear everything we were saying no matter how softly we spoke. "It's none of your business."

"It will be my business if Father catches you." He gestured toward the corner of the monorail where I was hiding Kallon under my invisibility. "You shouldn't have brought her."

"Relax, Ar. He won't find out." All I had to do was keep her hidden until we entered the Dark Kingdom. There she'd create a portal that would take her back to Lux. The only Advenian who'd be able to sense what I was doing was my father's second, and I knew he wouldn't risk bringing him. He needed to leave someone in charge while all the Luxian royals left the city.

"I pray for your sake, sister, that he doesn't." He stared at me for a long moment before sighing, "Wipe the sweat off your forehead before he arrives." Then he moved back to his original seat without another word, leaving me alone to my reckless fate.

I did as he said, but felt two more beads of sweat already forming over my brow. Of course that was what tipped Arcane off and how he knew I was actively using my powers. My older brother was meticulous with detail. He missed nothing.

I just hoped that my father would be too preoccupied with his success of getting Scotlind Rumor that he wouldn't notice the friend I was hiding.

ONE
SCOTLIND

I WAS GOING TO DIE. I just didn't know if it would be from the cold or lack of food. They were both vying for first place. The guards stationed outside my cell didn't seem to notice or care. At first, I pleaded with them, begged for water, food, a blanket, a toilet, anything, but I'd since given up. I could barely lift my head now, nonetheless speak. And it didn't matter how much I screamed, they never acknowledged me.

I didn't know how long it had been since I had woken up in the dungeon cell. I remembered Peter's words when I first arrived at the castle. He told me during his tour that the dungeon was located below ground, which meant no windows. Only a lone torch broke the darkness from the room. There was no way of telling if it was night or day. No way of telling if I had been here for hours or weeks. The last thing I remembered was being taken away by Sie's father and a sting radiating up my thigh before everything went black. He had injected me with something. I expected Sie to put up a fight, to try and stop it, but he didn't.

When I awoke, I was hurled onto a damp floor. Chains were clamped tightly around my wrists, covering my zeroes from view. I knew the rusty metal contained Alluse as I tried over and over again to move water into my cell. A small puddle was located by the door of the dungeons just out of reach from me. I watched every single guard walk through it as they switched rotations. Their muddy boots splashing and spraying droplets, but it never reached me. I tried relentlessly to draw upon my abilities, to will the water to move and glide toward me. My throat was scratchy and raw, and I honestly didn't care if the murky mess was just mud brimmed with filth. I needed water.

But I was left with an emptiness whenever I tried to use my ability, a void that was hard to explain. Even though I had only just discovered it, it felt like a piece of me was missing—my power was gone. Completely and utterly blocked. I hated Alluse.

All I could do was wait. Wait and think and think and wait. Every time the dungeon door groaned open, I perked up in my cell. A newfound wave of energy bolted through me like electricity as I scanned the guards who passed, searching for black or green eyes. But they never came.

I fantasized about Sie or Peter barging in and freeing me. Sometimes it would just be one of them. Sometimes they'd both come. They would explain to the dungeon guards that this was a misunderstanding—a terrible mistake. Then, they would whisk me far away from this wretched place, and everything would be fine. But that was only in my dreams.

Whenever I didn't see either of my would-be savior's eyes, I sank further into my desolation. As time went on, I stopped believing in fantasies, and my mind drifted to darker places. Places I didn't think I would ever come back from.

Was this Sie's plan all along? I told him about my past, about being from Lux, and how I ended up in the Dark Kingdom. I told him *every-thing*. And then, the next morning, his father showed up with High Council members and Tennebrisian guards. At first, I didn't connect the two, but with nothing to do but let my mind wander, I started to believe it couldn't have been a coincidence. Sie barely protested as they led us to the monorail and then drugged me. He *let* them do this to me. And where was he now?

I tried to push those thoughts away because they hurt more than the gnawing ache in my stomach and the emptiness in my veins. I didn't want to think about how the one time I opened up to someone —to him—he abandoned me. So, I focused on the cell. It was larger than the previous one from the warehouse that Kole had stuck me in. I could stand up and walk about five steps in each direction before the chains went taut.

A nudge tapped my knee, and I looked down to see Scarlet, a mouse that had shared the cell with me since I got here. *I don't even have a crumb to offer you,* I thought as I pet the top of her head. I'd truly gone crazy as this mouse was the closest thing to a companion I had these days. I had no idea why I decided to name her Scarlet, but it felt wrong for something to go through life unnamed.

Whenever the nightmares were gone long enough for me to dream, it would be about what my life could have been—if I had never been kidnapped from Lux and I'd been able to live a normal childhood with my parents. If I never had to pretend to be something I wasn't. If my life wasn't the shit show that it currently was—I always imagined that I'd have a pet. I guess this was some sick way of the Goddesses giving me what I wanted.

Scarlet scurried away to her corner as the door to the dungeon rasped open. I could just barely make out the figures through the cracks in the bars. Lifting my head, I squinted in the dark to see who was approaching. Even though I told myself not to, to save myself from the impending disappointment, I searched for black and green in the sea of eyes.

"Hey, little nix."

My body revolted at the words, at the voice. *No, no, no.* It couldn't be him. I sprang to my feet too fast, only to lose balance and fall back onto my knees. His laugh focused my vision on two brown eyes. Eyes that haunted my nightmares.

Kole.

"Did you miss me, little nix? Because I certainly missed you. We have some catching up to do, but I'm afraid it'll have to wait until later." He looked me up and down before turning his attention to the guards that accompanied him. "Bring her up."

Kole looked different since I saw him last. He looked older, stronger, more tenacious. He no longer donned the black uniform of the Tennebrisian guard with the twin pink moons over the chest, but instead, he bore the outfit of the High Council. I toppled over myself and threw up bile all over the cold floor.

The guards that flanked Kole didn't seem to notice as they unlocked my cell door and grabbed the chains that connected to my wrists and ankles. My bare feet scraped against the stone as I was dragged out.

My eyes squinted shut on instinct, blinded by the sun pouring in through the stained glass windows of the castle halls once we exited the dungeon. Was this going to be my last time seeing the sun? Were they going to kill me? Surely Kole being here wasn't a good sign. He was marked as a traitor when he tried to kill me, but now... now, he was a member of the High Council.

I could do nothing as the guards pulled me behind him. Kole occasionally glanced over his shoulder at me and smirked. He'd won, and he knew it. I knew it.

They halted outside an oak door. "Leave us," Kole ordered the guards. The authority in his tone, the way the guards cowered to him... This wasn't good. They dispersed immediately, leaving me alone with the male I hated more than anyone else.

He leaned forward, grabbed a lock of my brown hair, and started twirling it around his finger. My body locked, unable to do anything but stand there and gawk at him. Letting my hair fall back down over my shoulder, he leaned in closer, his breath hot against my own.

"I can't believe, after all these years, you aren't even a nix. If I had known..." He paused as his gaze roamed over my body. "I wouldn't have tried to drown you."

Before I could respond or even process what he had just said, he pushed the doors open with me in tow. My mouth gaped as I finally took in the black and green I'd been dreaming about.

Peter. My heart stopped beating. Sie.

They were waiting across the room. I glanced over at him. He looked good, better than good. He must have seen a healer again because there wasn't a scratch on him. The same couldn't be said about me. Finally in the light, I could still see bruises across my arms and legs, turning from purple to yellow. The only indication of how long I'd been stuck in that cell.

Sie sat next to King Lunder with Synder flanking his other side behind a thick table. His father, the Commander now, was also in the room. Braven Bask stood behind them all. I searched Sie's black eyes, trying to find a small glimpse of the guy I knew back at the lake, but his cold, blank mask was back on. The door slammed shut behind me. A second later, Kole pushed me toward the center of the room.

Sie didn't do anything. He barely reacted to my presence. I bristled at him. I couldn't understand how he could have left me there for so long. He was also trapped in Kole's cage—how could he not understand what that would do to me? How, after everything we had been through, could he act like I was a stranger? I was his *wife*.

"Thank you for bringing her to us, Kole," King Lunder said before turning his attention to me. "Do you have anything you would like to say before the we start, Scotlind Rumor?"

I blinked. Once. Twice. *Rumor* not Noren. "I'm not sure what you mean." My voice was hoarse and rough. I barely recognized it as my own. How long had it been since I last spoke? Days? Weeks?

King Lunder met my gaze for a moment before turning toward Kole. "Strip her. I need to see it for myself."

Kole didn't hesitate as his body lit up with his golden markings. It took me a moment to realize what he was doing as he used his telekinetic ability to remove the dirty slip I was wearing. He was leaning against the wall, hands still in his pocket when I heard the fabric tearing. I looked down in time to see my torn dress falling past my shackles. I was naked before I could so much as blink, my clothes in shreds around my feet.

I tried to cover myself with my hands, but the chains met resistance leaving my body exposed. Peter flinched. He stood in the corner, away from the men who were domineering the table before me. Sie wouldn't even look at me.

"Turn her," King Lunder ordered as he twirled his finger in a circle. I felt a tug on my chains as Kole spun me with his ability so that my back was exposed to everyone else. Then, one of the guards poured a bucket of freezing water over my body, revealing my black markings. Proof that I was Luxian.

Lunder gasped. "So it's true. She really is from Lux—a traitor."

Kole turned me back around to face the councilmen, this time using his hands to do it instead of his mind. Bumps rose all over my body, and my teeth began to chatter. I was already numb from my time in the cell, but now, without clothes and soaked in water, I could feel myself stiffening, my blood thinning. Out of the corner of my eye, I saw movement. A black swoop, then a blonde head of hair stood before me as Peter wrapped his long coat around my shoulders.

"That's not necessary," Kole said. I hated how I cowered at his tone of voice and the authority it held as he looked at Peter.

Peter didn't return Kole's stare. He barely acknowledged him as he responded, "We need her alive, so having her freeze to death is not an option." He cupped my shoulders, only for a split second, as he clasped the ends of the coat together, his green eyes boring into mine, before returning to the corner of the room.

"For now," Synder murmured under his breath, or at least I thought that was what he said. I couldn't feel my fingers and toes, and a quiet ringing noise reverberated in my ears as I started swaying where I stood. It felt like forever since I stood on my feet, and my body was dizzying from the effort. But I couldn't stop replaying Peter's words in my head, *we need her alive*. So they weren't planning on killing me, then why was I here?

As if reading my thoughts, King Lunder spoke again, "Miss Rumor, I do not know how you infiltrated our Kingdom, but we will surely get to the bottom of that in due time. We have contacted King Arcane the Seventh of Lux, and he was willing to make arrangements for you. We will be returning you to him as his prisoner. Seeing as you belong to the Luxian society, he will deal with you accordingly. From this day forward, you are the property of the Lux King and belong solely to him."

No. My eyes snapped up to meet Sie's, but he still wouldn't look at me. This couldn't be happening. Sie couldn't send me to him. He warned me against the entire Luxian royals at our wedding. He told me to stay far away from them no matter what. He wouldn't do that to me. And the Lux Prince—the Fire Prince—the youngest son who I hadn't met yet. I couldn't. He wouldn't force me to go. I was still his wife... but they kept calling me Rumor.

King Lunder spoke again, "For now, no one outside this room will know the truth about you. As you will be a prisoner of Lux, we will not be telling the Tennebrisians about this predicament. Our people will continue to believe that you're Tennebrisian and that you are a rank zero. That being said, we cannot allow you to continue to be wed to Prince Noren. Sie, would you care to elaborate on what is to happen."

I looked at Sie again, and this time he met my gaze. I shivered as I didn't recognize the man I had trusted before. The man that I was beginning to develop feelings for. Now all I saw was a stranger. A shiver went down my spine as he spoke, and I fought to hold back the tears that threatened to spill.

His voice was cold and distant as he finally acknowledged me. "As part of our agreement with the Lux King, your true Kingdom will be kept hidden. They are going to have a broadcast where you will admit to being unfaithful. The Council needs a reason to end our marriage without revealing that you are Luxian. We will annul our marriage publicly and our people will believe that you are imprisoned for adultery against the crown. Once the Lux King arrives, you will leave with him immediately and discreetly."

I went to open my mouth, but Synder stopped me. "It will be wise for you to accede. If you do not, I will have no issue sending Kole to dispose of you for good. Or maybe I would give Prince Noren the honor of killing you. But mark my word, if you do not admit to having an affair, or if you alter what we order you to say in any way, you will regret it until your last dying breath. Do I make myself clear, Miss Rumor?"

"Yes," I gritted.

"Good," King Lunder remarked with a wave of his hand. "Get her out of here, Kole. Throw her back in her cell until it's time."

Kole smiled as he pulled on my chains, and I had no choice but to follow him as he led me back to my damp, dark prison.

TWO

SIE

ANOTHER TWO WEEKS HAD PASSED, and I was still at a loss for what to do. The Lux King would be arriving tonight to collect Scotlind. That meant that today we would be forced to annul our marriage, and she would no longer be my wife. I didn't want to think about what those extra weeks did to her. She was skin and bones and withering away before my eyes when I last saw her in the council room, and that was only from one week in the dungeons.

It was killing me slowly. My mind kept replaying the expression on her face when I told her that we were annulling our marriage. Then, her horror as King Lunder told her the news that she now belonged to the Lux King. I could barely stomach looking into her sapphire eyes, pleading with me, willing me to step in, to defend her like her husband should. But instead, I did the opposite. I just let it happen.

I wanted to murder everyone when Synder had Kole fetch her. How he stood possessively over her. How he grabbed and pulled at her chains, and how his gaze kept roaming over her naked body. I wanted to kill him then and there. It was made worse seeing how his presence affected Scotlind too. She hated him—feared him. Our time in the warehouse haunted her just as much as it haunted me.

A knock sounded on my bedroom door. Peter cracked it open before I could mutter a word. "Hey," he said as he stepped inside, shutting the door behind him. He leaned against the frame. "You ready?"

"Am I ready to destroy my marriage with the girl I was falling in love with? Am I ready to willingly send her to be King Arcane's prisoner?" I snapped. I knew it wasn't Peter's fault, but I couldn't help it. Peter frowned but didn't say anything. "What are we supposed to do, Peter?" I started pacing my room. "We are playing a dangerous game. We can't let them take her."

"You know what to do, Sie. Send me," he answered flatly.

My head snapped up. "I can't ask that of you. I won't."

"You aren't asking," he said. "I'm volunteering. Send me. I'm half the reason that she's being sent to Lux in the first place. I want to do this for myself as much as for you. She's my friend too."

"I know," I admitted as he pushed off the frame and walked toward me. Peter and Scotlind spent every day and night together leading up to our wedding. I knew the two of them were close. I knew this was hard for him too. "But Lux is stronger than us. They've been breeding warriors for centuries, and King Arcane and his children are no different. If you get caught..." I shuddered. "You know what the royals would do to you—"

"Then I won't get caught," he cut me off. "Think about it, Sie. You know my ability. You know I'm capable. I will look out for her. I can try to uncover what Lux is up to while I'm over there. I can finally get to the bottom of their connection to what happened with Scottie. You and I both know that whatever is happening here isn't over. Someone from Lux is working with someone from Tennebris, and we need to find out who and why. We only have guesses. We know it's probably Synder, maybe even your father, but we need proof. The only conclusive thing we know is that Kole is involved, and now the Council welcomed him with open arms."

I looked over at my only friend as I contemplated his words. I didn't want to send him. I didn't want to think about the fact that the only two people I cared for would be on Luxian soil. But Scottie would be safer with Peter there. He would make sure she didn't get hurt. And if he could figure out Lux's connection to all of this… Why Kole had Alluse, and who he was working for… "Don't get caught." I finally said.

He flashed me a wicked grin, his usual warmth gone from it as he replied, "Never."

———

A CAMERA CREW was hovering around Scotlind as I walked into the throne room. She had been cleaned up since the last time I saw her, and that pissed me off even more. Had they forced her into a tub? I couldn't stop seeing her fear of it after the warehouse, how she refused to go near one. She was dressed in a plain gray dress that didn't hide the weight she'd lost since spending the past three weeks in a cell. She was still chained, but this time, the shackles only claimed her wrists.

A male I didn't recognize stood by her side. The male, I was told, had relations with someone from the rebellion, and no one survived once they were linked to the rebellion. Both Kingdoms feared what would happen if the lower ranks fought back, which was exactly what was starting to happen. If they didn't comply with the jobs given to them at their Trials, our system would crumble.

The male was sweating profusely, probably aware they weren't planning on letting him live after today. He was told if he kept his mouth shut, his wife and child would go unharmed. Once someone from the rebellion was caught, their entire family was found guilty and slaughtered. It didn't matter how many generations back it went. It was the only time that Advenians didn't honor and protect the youth. It didn't matter how old you were or how rare children were to our kind. If you threatened the way things were, there was no going back. I hoped, for this male's sake, that the High Council would stay true to their word and let his loved ones live.

I stole a glance at Scotlind. Everything about her was paler, except for the color of her eyes, the blue hue from the stained glass windows illuminated them. They were so bright I had to question how no one recognized them as Luxian before. But even the shape of her eyes had changed. They seemed sullen, sunken in. Black circles had developed under them, so dark it looked like ink had splattered and was spreading as it slowly took over her face. It was like the darkness was draining her of life, slowly consuming her from the inside out.

King Lunder informed me that this event would be turned into a broadcast and mandated for all of Tennebris to watch. A lot of citizens from Palm were seated in the audience, but anyone from the other fives villages would be forced to watch from a monitor screen.

They mostly kept me in the dark about what they wanted Scotlind to say during the broadcast. But whatever it was, it would have required her to do exactly as she was told. I didn't trust her. I couldn't shake my gut feeling that she'd mess up on purpose. That she'd use this as an opportunity to say Goddess knows what about our ranking system. It terrified me. I couldn't stop thinking about what they would do to her, or worse, make *me* do to her if she messed up. All I knew was that if I was forced to kill her, I wouldn't be able to. Like Scotlind, I would go down as a traitor. I would forfeit my life, my title, everything. I couldn't do it.

Which was why I suggested to Synder that Kole should compel her. That way she couldn't mess up, and they couldn't kill her for not doing exactly what they wanted. It was another thing she'd hate me for, but I didn't care. I had to keep her alive.

King Lunder and Synder stood on the dais as Braven gestured for me to join them.

"Good evening, fellow Tennebrisians," King Lunder bellowed, ushering the crowd that had gathered into silence. "Thank you for tuning in today for this mandatory announcement. It displeases me as to why we are meeting today. Our Princess has betrayed and deceived us all. We call her forward today to speak the truth as to why our Prince has been absent recently."

King Lunder gestured to where Scottie stood chained. All the cameras turned their attention toward her. To my surprise, she held her head up high. Her sapphire eyes met mine and pinned me to my spot above everyone else. Her expression held a promise of revenge. But she didn't say anything. She just kept staring me down to the point where I felt like I would crumble beneath those eyes.

I held my breath as I waited for her to say something, anything. I knew the general gist of what they planned. They wanted her to admit to having an affair with the male next to her. It was some stupid, elaborate story that Synder concocted in order to keep her identity hidden while still meeting the Lux King's demands. But Scotlind didn't speak. She didn't do anything but stare straight ahead.

Shit. Was she trying to get herself killed? Would she really choose death over being sent to Lux? I thought about speaking to her over the past couple of weeks to explain why I agreed to send her away. To explain that I was doing this in order to keep her alive, but I knew it was cowardly. I was willingly sending her to the worst Advenian alive. I was sending her somewhere she would probably get treated far worse than she had been here, all because I selfishly couldn't let them kill her. I needed her alive. I knew deep down that this sentence was probably far worse for her than death, but I couldn't help it. I couldn't let them kill her. *I couldn't be the one to kill her.* It would break me.

Did they not compel her? Or did they only compel her to say condemning words once she started? Maybe keeping her mouth shut was her only way of fighting it. Maybe Synder changed his mind and didn't want Scotlind to speak at all. I should have compelled her myself. I shouldn't have left her fate up to fucking Kole. Then I wouldn't be standing here worried sick about what she was going to do.

Once Synder noticed that she wasn't going to speak, he stepped forward. "Your Princess has betrayed our Prince and, in turn, our Kingdom. She has been having an affair with this male." A few gasps echoed across the throne room from those in attendance. "Some of you may recognize him as a former ranking evaluator. Many Tennebrisians were confused as to why a rank zero was selected for our Prince. To be honest, the Council felt that having a zero on the throne would be a good thing. At the time, we hoped to separate the divide and rift that has been growing amongst our ranking system, but Scotlind has proven us otherwise. It has been discovered that Joshuan Carithin," Synder continued as he pointed to the male, "has been working with Scotlind from the beginning to tamper with her results in order for her to be selected as the Princess."

He paused as he looked over at Scottie, then turned toward the camera crew panning over him for a better angle. "Our system was designed to help our people thrive. It is needed in order to keep things fair, to keep things functioning. If our society doesn't abide by their Trial outcomes, everything will go into chaos. Which was exactly the motive that Scotlind and Joshuan were seeking. They wanted to over-throw the system, the Council, and Prince Noren himself." Synder paused long enough for whispered murmurs to echo throughout the throne room.

"It is made clear now that a rank zero will stop at nothing to get what they desire. The greediness amongst the lower ranks is amplify-ing, and as such, we will be investigating the ranking system further after this incident. A rank zero will stop at nothing to move up in our society, and we simply cannot allow them to do so. We will be working closely with King Arcane Xandrin of Lux to look into modeling our system more closely to theirs. More will be coming in the next couple of weeks about what to expect. But many changes will be made in order to protect ourselves from something like this ever happening again."

"Do you admit to these charges, Scotlind Rumor?"

My own breathing hitched. This was it. They must have compelled her to only answer this one simple, condemning question. I could tell she was struggling. It looked like she was fighting as her entire body started to shake, but she couldn't win against compulsion. Her teeth gritted as she whispered, "Yes."

Scotlind paled after she said it. Her face drained of all color before she went to open her mouth, probably to protest, to protect rank zeroes, to plead that this had nothing to do with them, but a gag was strapped over her mouth before she could utter a word. Tears pooled and poured down her freckled cheeks.

I caught her looking at Peter, her eyes pleading with him. Peter shook his head slightly. To others, it appeared that he was just shaking out his messy, blonde locks that had gotten too long and in his eyes.

Damn. They didn't tell me that they were planning on using her as an example to help their goals for changing the ranking system. My mind was whirling on how in the hell I could spin this otherwise, on how I could convince the High Council to not change it, but the damage was already done. Everyone would be looking at zeroes with disgust. Everyone would see this image of Scottie—chained and gagged, fighting desperately against the males holding her. She would never forgive me for this, for letting this happen. She wanted to change things for zeroes, and now she was being used as an example to demolish their rights further.

I was too lost in my own thoughts that I missed the rest of what Synder had said until he turned to speak directly at me. "It is because of this that we have brought everyone here today to annul the marriage of Prince Sie Axel Noren for the treason and deception that Scotlind Mae Rumor has committed against the crown."

Before I knew it, the priest that wed us came up to the dais to end our marriage. I tried my best to maintain a blank face as they pulled Scotlind next to me. I tried to remain calm as I was now mere inches from her. Seeing her chained and gagged brought me back to the warehouse. It haunted me every second of the day. I wanted nothing more than to pull her toward my chest. To hug her and kiss away her tears. I wanted to grab her and teleport her somewhere far away. But if I tried anything, they'd kill her without hesitation.

I flinched as I took in her expression. One of hurt and abandonment. I knew how this looked. How *I* looked to her. She had finally opened up to me and told me everything, and the next day my father imprisoned her. And now, I was standing here, agreeing to send her to Lux, agreeing to this stupid facade that she had an affair so that the High Council could spin this on the fact that she was a nix seeking power. That they could mold this to their advantage.

17

Even if she made it out of Lux alive, there would be no way in hell she would forgive me. No way she would forget a minute of this.

The priest's voice felt like daggers embedding into my heart as he brought me back to reality. He'd just cemented the end of our marriage, taking away the only good thing that had ever happened to me. Scotlind was no longer my wife.

THREE
SCOTLIND

HEAT ENGULFED my entire body as everything lit up in flames. I tried to move, to run, to do anything, but I couldn't. I was paralyzed, and all I could do was stare at the fire dancing toward me, licking the oxygen of air. Sweat coated every inch of me as I stared at each flicker of the orange hue. I prayed for the heat to leave my body. I prayed that the flames wouldn't reach my skin. I knew what it felt like to have my flesh burned off.

Then I was shivering. I recognized the warehouse. But this time, there wasn't an array of men—just two. Kole stood before me, his brown eyes blazing as two black ones came into view. Sie. Unchained. Unharmed.

Then I noticed the tub looming in the distance as Kole closed the gap between us, a wicked grin plastered on his face. I looked toward Sie. "Please, help me. I'm your wife. Please, Sie, don't let him do this to me." Tears sprang from my eyes as I took in his cold, detached expression.

"You're not my wife anymore."

Then there was darkness. Kole plunged my head into the tub, but when I opened my mouth to breathe in the rushing water, it clogged my throat. It burned worse than the flames as it filled every space left in my lungs. I tried to fight him, but no matter how hard I fought, the burning grew. Laughter echoed throughout the empty room as I struggled. I knew that laughter. I seldom heard it, but I knew it. It belonged to Sie, and he was laughing as Kole drowned me.

You're not my wife anymore.

My body grew lifeless as the laughter grew louder and louder. Soon it was the only thing I could hear.

I WAS DRENCHED in sweat despite the draft. This was how I awoke every day since I was brought here—the Luxian dungeons. I glanced at my right forearm, where I used the ragged, sharp end of my fingernail to tally the number of times the moon rose from the small window in my cell. Twenty-seven.

Twenty-seven bloodied tallies. Twenty-seven days of torture. Twenty-seven days of little food and water. Twenty-seven days of being questioned for information by different Luxian guards. Then, when I didn't—couldn't—speak, I was thrown back into my cell with my skin flaming red. I thought so many times I was going to die, that I'd bleed out before they could finish, but somehow they stopped precisely at my body's breaking point. The blood from each session continued to cake on me, layer after layer, until it became a part of me. I knew I had black and blue splatters of bruises beneath the running crimson because everything hurt.

Next came exhaustion, and sleep usually found me. Every night was the same. It was a nightmare where I couldn't tell if it was worse to be sleeping or awake.

This place was hell and made the Tennebrisian dungeon seem like heaven. Everything about my situation now was so much worse. Everything I'd ever known was left in Tennebris. I was completely and utterly alone. The only time I saw anyone was when the Luxian guards made their daily rounds and tortured me. Most of my time spent in the cell was in isolation, my only company was the writhing agony I was left with.

I didn't know how much more of their *questioning* my body could handle. My mind was already letting go. The only thing that was better about the Luxian prison than the Tennebrisian one was the lone window. It was smaller than my fist, not big enough for the taunting sun to reach my flesh and provide the warmth it tempted each day, but I often stared up at the sky.

I knew what the window resembled. It gave the prison dwellers a sick form of hope that would never come. It felt like the Goddesses were playing a sick joke on me. Like they were reminding me that I should be grateful. I'd prayed and prayed to return to Lux. I longed to see the sun set and rise from the island, to be able to see the ocean and feel the sand beneath my feet. But that wouldn't happen. I wasn't getting out of here. The small window was a reminder that everything I ever wanted was within my reach, but I was chained to a different, crueler life.

But at least the window meant light, and that glimmer of the sun was my only salvation.

The cloudy nights when the moon didn't appear became the times I prayed for death. When my cell was drenched in blackness—the soggy floor, the distant dripping of water, the small enclosed space—it felt like I was drowning in the tub. Endless. All over again. I couldn't breathe those nights. I couldn't break the surface of my perceived water prison to reach the light. The darkness surrounded me and trapped me down, and once again, my head was pressed against the tile beneath Kole's menacing grip.

Once the sun rose, I would wake up shivering as the cold air hit my damp skin, drying my sweat. My body would shake uncontrollably as I waited to be fetched for my daily *questioning*.

Like clockwork, a Luxian guard would open my cell and drag my drained body into another room. In the beginning, they only asked questions. But it changed once they realized I wouldn't speak. I dreaded that room and what it meant. It made me long to be curled up again on the floor of my drafty, cramped cage. But they never asked me why I was sent to Tennebris. No. They asked me questions about Sie— his weaknesses, his abilities, his family.

21

No matter how angry I was at him for leaving me to this fate, I could never give in. I could never tell them what they wanted to hear. I'd die soon enough anyway. All it would take was one guard to forget to call a healer after my session and then peace would finally find me. I could leave my body and this agony behind.

The door creaked open, and I sat up in my cell. It wasn't large enough for me to stand. I couldn't even stretch my legs out fully. All I could manage was to sit with my legs crossed or curl up into myself like a ball. The latter was my preferred position. I squinted at the blinding light breaking the darkness to see who my intruder was. It was too early for them to fetch me for the questioning. Stars still peppered the sky.

I managed to curl my lips in a small smile when I recognized the guard that entered. He had bright green eyes with a hint of brown in them. They reminded me of moss growing erratically on a tree trunk. It made me wish to be outside, to be anywhere but where I was. The guard reminded me of Peter. Except instead of a mop of blonde waves, his hair was Vallie's firecracker red.

He was the only nice guard in the rotation of the men I saw. He bent down with bread and water in tow. My eyes were fixated on the food like a moth seeking damnation to flames. My mouth started to salivate uncontrollably. My dry lips cracked. This green-eyed guard was the only one who brought me food that wasn't rotten or moldy. Most days, he was the only one who bothered to bring me any food at all.

I knew I shouldn't eat it. If I stopped eating, my body would fail me. This agony would be over. That was what I wanted, right?

My stomach grumbled as I grabbed the small loaf before he could change his mind. He lingered by my cell, watching me as I inhaled the food in seconds. His eyes darted to my mouth as I licked my hands for any lingering crumbs. I didn't think about the layers of dirt embedded into my nails as I slid each finger between my lips.

"Thank you," I mumbled as I gulped down the small amount of water too fast. The bread stirred in my stomach and threatened to come back up. He gave a curt nod before turning back around, leaving me entirely alone. He never spoke and half of me was happy for that. I sometimes pretended he was Peter when all I would focus on were his eyes. And I was too scared that his voice would ruin my delusion. That as soon as I heard the guard speak and it wasn't my friend, I'd have to admit that he wasn't coming for me, that everything wouldn't be okay.

When Kole drug me back to my cell in Tennebris after I first found out my fate, I was elated. I felt the curled up piece of paper that Peter had left for me in his coat. *Hold on.* That was all it said. Those two little words. But it gave me hope. It made me believe that he'd come for me. That he was going to save me just like he had in my dreams.

But then I was brought out in front of everyone to annul my marriage with Sie. And the next thing I knew, I was here in Lux, and it was too late. I woke up in a new prison with a new outfit on. Peter's coat and note were gone along with the dream of escaping. Peter wouldn't get me out of here. So whatever comfort I found in the Luxian guard was my own doing. It was the small part of me that wasn't giving up.

I didn't know how long I dozed off after that, but voices stirred me from my restlessness and when I forced my eyes open again. The sun was beginning to replace the night.

"Tezya, you're here. We were just about to take her for another session," one of the guards on rotation boasted proudly.

"Session?" a low voice growled.

"Yes, sir, per the King's request. We have been trying for weeks now to coax any information out of her regarding the Dark Prince, but she won't say a word no matter what we do to her," the Luxian guard responded, but now he had a slight quiver to his voice. He sounded petrified, and in the twenty-seven days I'd been here, I had never encountered a Luxian guard who was scared before. They were all callous and merciless.

I couldn't bother to tilt my head up all the way as the stranger came into view. I glanced slightly to see tanned, muscular calves hovering behind the bars of my cell. I was sure they would hurl me to my feet soon enough. I was curled up in my usual fetal position, but I didn't care. It was all the space would allow for anyway. All I cared about was keeping the bread in my stomach down and not throwing it up.

The stranger spoke again, "This is her?"

The guard scurried over to my cell. "Yes, this is the prisoner from Tennebris." I sat up then, finally taking in my surroundings and who the owner of the deep voice was.

The guard by my cell had the sun symbol of Lux over the center of his leathered uniform. I recognized him from my *torture* sessions. He liked to smile as he flayed my back open until he was forced to call upon a healer to keep me from the brink of death. But his usual smug grin wasn't plastered on his face this time.

Another guard stood toward the back of the room by the door. Squinting, I looked closer and saw the flash of red, then the green eyes. A worried expression flashed across his face as he glanced between the stranger and me.

That was when I noticed him. The owner of the calves. He wore loose-fitting black pants that stopped halfway down his legs. The material bunched up like it needed to go further down but couldn't fit past his massive calves. He wore a baggy white shirt that fell over his pants, tucked in only on one side. And he was tall, about a head taller than the other two guards in the room. Every inch of him was corded and defined in muscle. I couldn't help but notice how the guards recoiled slightly in his presence. My torturer was cowering, his previous arrogance and cockiness gone. But this stranger didn't wear the Luxian guard uniform. He looked disheveled, like he had just gotten out of bed.

His hair was bone-white and shaved around the base of his skull, with long, thick strands falling at the top of his head, just covering his eyes. The messy locks favored his right side. He was attractive, as far as my jumbled brain could tell. But I couldn't take my eyes off of his face. A thick, jagged scar went from the bridge of his nose to behind his right jaw past my view. I briefly wondered how far the scar continued until I realized I was gawking at him.

"If you're here to beat me, you are going to have to get in line," I spat at the stranger. Something about the way he assessed me made

24

me unnerved. He opened the cell door and stepped inside. Well, squatted inside. He didn't fit.

He was eye level with me now as my attention veered from his scar to his crystal blue eyes. He shook his head, causing his messy white mop of hair to spring clear of his vision. They were so clear and light that I swore I saw glimpses of silver in them.

Up close, I could really look at him, and he was the most striking and haunting male I ever saw. I stiffened as his pale stare pinned me to my spot. He clearly did not like my tone, and now I was worried that he really was going to beat me. And judging by his broad shoulders, thick muscles, and the way he composed himself—I might actually cave.

I averted my attention from his face as my eyes darted across his defined chest and strong arms. He must be in the guard with the amount of scars that covered his body. A five was branded onto his wrist, indicating that he was powerful and strong within Lux. I was getting used to seeing a lot fives.

The stranger spoke again but didn't turn his attention away from me as he said, "You are no longer allowed to torture this girl. Tennebris finally sent over a compulsion user. I'm here to bring her to the King."

———

THE TWO GUARDS dragged me down the dingy hallway as they followed the stranger up the stairs. I should be happy that I was finally leaving the dungeon, but instead, I was filled with dread. Why did they need a compulsion user from Tennebris? During my torture sessions, they always questioned me about Sie. His weaknesses, his strengths, his abilities, if we had sex, which was the weirdest question of all. But I never gave up any information regarding him or my time spent there. Would they now compel the answers out of me? Would they force me to betray him?

I was brought into a room brimmed with wires and monitors. There was a mirror that took up the length of the entire back wall that

I refused to look at. I was filthy and hadn't bathed in weeks. I knew every inch of me was either covered in dirt, dried blood, or my own secretions. I didn't want to see what my reflection would show.

The stranger bowed slightly, and that was when I noticed the Lux King. His gaze flicked over me. He was just as intimidating as I remembered. Prince Arcane and Princess Dovelyn were also in the room. Shivers ran down my spine as I searched for the youngest prince, but luckily I didn't see him. Was he still in battle?

The two eldest royals seemed more like twins than siblings. The only difference between them was their height. They were both slender, the Princess slightly more petite. Their matching sleek, pale hair flowing past their waists would have looked ridiculous on anyone else but the two of them. Dovelyn wore a silver dress that matched her striking eyes and hair. She was impossible to miss as she was covered from head to toe in diamonds. Arcane wore a fitted blue attire, not as flashy, but still managed to display wealth at every thread. They both looked regal and *deadly*.

"Hook her up to the monitors," the King demanded. The green-eyed guard was hesitant. He flashed me an empathic look before ushering me toward an empty chair and started placing sticky squares attached to cords all over my body. By the time he was finished, I had twenty or so black wires spiraling out of me.

The multiple screens flared to life before my eyes like a mirror. But it wasn't a mirror. I turned my head toward the Lux King as he appeared on the screen. Then I whipped my gaze toward the green-eyed guard whose eyes were blazing at me with uncertainty, like he wanted to step forward. Then the stranger appeared on the screen as my eyes settled on his affixed gaze.

It dawned on me then. These wires were revealing what I saw and was somehow displaying them on the screens. I started to shake as I attempted to stand, wanting to rip the cords from my body, but the other guard from my cell held my shoulders down. He then swiftly tied my hands behind my back, strapping them to the chair before I could attempt to flee again. I fought against the restraints, but it was no use, they weren't budging. I had no muscle left on me anyway. The beautiful stranger shifted from where he stood.

"What is this?" I demanded at no one in particular. My voice didn't sound like my own. It was scratchy and raw as I only ever used it when I was screaming. The screens shifted from person to person as I looked around the room.

The Lux King smiled slightly, but it didn't reach his eyes. His gaze was unwavering as it locked in on me. "I was warned that you were feisty, Miss Rumor," he said, taking a step closer. Everyone else in the room remained silent. "I was also told that you refused to give up any information regarding Sie Noren, regardless of my soldiers' efforts. I do not take it lightly when people don't obey me." His voice dropped for a moment, holding a threat. "But lucky for you, Tennebris has finally sent a compulsion user to Lux for me to use at my disposal. So I'll finally be able to get the information I want from you."

On cue, Kole stepped out of the shadows. Shit. Shit. Shit. I struggled more. Tears spilled down my cheeks so fast that my vision blurred. My heart hammered against my sternum to the point where it hurt. I couldn't breathe. I couldn't think. *"No, no, no,"* I think I screamed the words out loud, but I couldn't hear them over the ringing in my ears.

Kole approached me, his steps were heavy and daunting. He kept going in and out of focus, and all I could see were white tiles submerged underwater. The room around me disappeared as my head was pressed into the bath all over again. I could feel the burning in my lungs. My eyes were seeing spots as the dizziness was taking over. I couldn't breathe. Couldn't think…

"This is Kole Sanders," the King's voice broke through my thoughts. "He's a Tennebrisian Council member and will be stationed here at Lux for the time being with a work visa. I was told by Synder that you two are quite familiar with one another," the Lux King said as he gestured toward Kole, a smile blossoming on his face. "Here is how this is going to work. He'll compel you to reveal your past memories, and thanks to our advanced technology at Lux, we will be able to see everything that is in your mind once your memories start to unfold."

My gaze whipped around the room. Half in awe, half in an absolute panic.

"How?" My voice was breathless, but I managed to get the word out.

"You will find that Lux, unlike Tennebris, isn't as transfixed in the olden ways of traditions from Allium. As you might know, Miss Rumor, Lux oversees the mortal territory of this planet. While Tennebris has focused its efforts on the space program, we monitor and study the humans and their way of life. We learn from the mortals. Then, we recreate more powerful technology. Better. Stronger. More adaptable to our needs. So there's no use in struggling as you cannot resist. We will get the information we want from you."

He didn't give me a chance to retort as he turned toward Kole and commanded, "Begin." Kole hadn't stopped looking at me since he came out of the shadows. His expression was just as dark as the version of him I concocted in my nightmares, just as cruel and menacing. He nodded as the King continued to bark orders. "Start the memories from when she first arrived in Tennebris. I'll tell you to skip as needed or rewatch anything if it's not clear."

"With pleasure," Kole took one last step toward me as he cracked his neck from side to side, his arms turning from his tanned skin tone to golden as he prepared his ability. Then, he compelled me to reveal every single awful detail of my life.

FOUR
TEZYA

I HAD no idea the Luxian soldiers were torturing her daily for information and that the King granted them free reign to do so. I thought this entire time we were just waiting for Tennebris to send their compulsion user. But judging from the way I found her today in that cage, the way she had been treated... I wanted to beat the living shit out of Lansting once he admitted to torturing her.

I stared at the girl chained to the chair before me. She looked terrified of the compulsion user. They must have had some sort of past. And based on her reaction to him, it couldn't have been a good one.

She clearly had been through hell in the month that she'd been in Lux, and she smelled like death to prove it. I inhaled once, reaching out my heightened senses to her. Fear, agony, and desperation were radiating from her.

She might have been pretty if she wasn't covered in her own piss, blood, and vomit. If she wasn't withering away to nothing. She barely looked Advenian. Her thin gown was shredded in the back, revealing old and fresh scars that I was surprised the fabric stayed on her skeletal shoulders. Her joints were too large for her failing body. Like the weight of each prominence was a struggle for her to hold upright.

The Tennebrisian male began speaking his compulsion, forcing the girl to reveal her life. I watched the large screens as she started reliving her past for us to see. A terrified little girl hacked up her lungs on a beach in Tennebris. She was crawling away from the crashing waves, a raw burn covering her entire right calf as she favored her left side.

The screen flashed and the girl was in a school, pleading with a counselor that she was Luxian. The counselor dismissed and threatened her. She cried herself to sleep over her presumed dead parents until she was out of isolation. Then a beautiful red-headed girl gave her a lollipop. A younger version of the male in front of me tormented and compelled her for his own amusement.

The screen flashed again. She was older but not by much. She started training, waking up early every morning, even during the dark winter months of Tennebris. She enlisted in Tennebrisian Guard classes. Her classmates made fun of her, teased her, and attempted over and over again to persuade her to stop, but she only trained harder. She woke up earlier and earlier until she learned to fight back.

The screen flashed again, and she was older—gorgeous now. Her bright sapphire eyes were striking against her pale brown hair and freckled, pointed nose. Her body was nothing like the one chained to the chair. She was still small and too short for our race, but she filled out her uniform, and I could tell she worked hard for the lean muscles hidden beneath it. She looked alive.

She fought in the Tennebrisian Trials against the same male compelling her now. I felt pity for her as she was forced to rewatch him beat the shit out of her while she was pinned against the walls of an arena. She took every blow, never giving him the satisfaction of surrendering, even though she used no abilities to fight with.

Another flash, and she was running into Prince Noren, and he was flirting with her. My gut twisted as I watched them together. I watched her cheeks turn bright red as she tried to run away. Then her name was called to be his bride, and I could see the dread and fear written all over her expression.

Another flash, and she was drinking with a red-headed pair. Then, she was stumbling, laughing, and slurring her words. The Dark Prince carried her home.

Flash. Prince Noren gave her a Complete Alluse necklace. He knew something was off about her being chosen. I looked toward the Lux King to gauge his reaction, but he revealed nothing as he glared at the screens on display.

I watched her first kiss with Prince Noren. The passion and lust between them were evident. I turned away from the screen until it changed again.

She was now in a room full of people who were compelling her to do awful things. Prince Noren lounged on a leather sofa with two girls positioned on either side of him. I watched her crawl on the floor toward the same man she had been kissing prior. I watched as her lips pressed into his boot. Then she was forced to sit on his lap as she whispered, "I hate you." The Prince did nothing as she was forced to strip naked in front of him—in front of *everyone*. Mercifully, before everything came off, a blonde male whisked her away. My fists clenched at my sides. I knew that the Dark Prince had a reputation with females, that he was known to be a dick, but to treat his own fiancé that way was unacceptable.

Flash. Her wedding night to the Dark Prince. Out of the corner of my eye, I saw the King stiffen. I knew he wanted to know about the blood bond—if it took after their consummation, and more importantly if she was with child.

Knowing what was about to unfold, I took a steadying breath and forced myself to look back at the monitor screen. The last thing I wanted to do right now was listen to her moaning over him, but I knew the King wasn't planning on skipping over this. I had no idea why it bothered me so much. Lux didn't shy away from sex and nudity like Tennebris did, but this felt wrong—to go into her mind like this, to force her to display this memory.

But then the Dark Prince took off her necklace, and a conversation played out in her head, revealing more of his powers, and holy shit, he was strong. He could compel anyone from both Kingdoms. And on top of that, he possessed telepathy and teleportation. I could see why the Lux King viewed him as a threat if he ascended the throne.

I expected them to have sex, but they didn't. They were pretending. I was shocked as I stared at the girl. Mortification and shame were painted on her face, but she could do nothing to stop the images from playing.

The next flash was of the compulsion user again. He kidnapped, gagged, and bound her. She fought against him, but he ripped her necklace off and compelled her to surrender. She woke up in a warehouse where she and Prince Noren were tortured. Then he was drowning her. I could sense her panic stirring in the chair as she was forced to relive this memory. This clearly left more of a scar on her than the physical ones scattered across her body. I ground my teeth together, trying to remain calm. This was a different level of fucked up to have the male who attempted to murder her force her to replay the night it happened for all of us to watch.

The last flash was her and the Prince training at a beautiful sapphire lake. She was using water abilities of Lux. The Dark Prince and a blonde male were trying to figure out what her markings meant. The screen showed Sie replaying her back into their minds. It was covered in Luxian symbols. Every element had a place amongst her flesh. I had never seen anything like it.

"You can stop it there," the King interjected just as she was dragged onto a monorail and injected with some serum. "I'm aware of what happened after that." My blood boiled as I recalled Lansting stating that he was ordered to torture her. She had been through more trauma in her short years of life than most Advenians saw in centuries. Hell, most of our kind lived a sheltered life, never knowing what it felt like to wield a blade, never-the-less, what the sting from one felt like.

The screen showed my face, and it took me a moment to realize that she was staring at me. I looked toward the girl. Her emotions were overwhelming and all-consuming. Shame, humiliation, rage, and fear were mixing and radiating off of her in waves, crashing into my ability. Once the compulsion ended, she sagged into the chair, her restraints pulling taut.

She'd been through hell and back, but the King should have no more use for her. He had what he needed. Sie clearly knew she was from Lux and still wanted to be with her. From this footage alone, Prince Noren could be declared a traitor and off the Tennebrisian throne before he was even crowned, just as the Lux King wanted. He defended her, very poorly, but he knew she was Luxian. It also proved she wasn't carrying his child, which eliminated *that* threat.

My mind whirled at everything that had been displayed on the screen, at everything she'd been through. I couldn't help but think what other horrors she faced that weren't displayed. What tortures she endured on my own soil by the same soldiers I fought alongside with. She was shaken from being compelled and coerced into reliving every humiliating and wretched thing in her life. I was shocked to find her with her head held high as she looked up at the Lux King. Her eyes narrowed and focused solely on him now. Most Advenians cowered in his presence, not daring to look him in the eye.

The King turned his attention to me, a broad smile plastered on his face like he'd just won something. I guess he did. "You will train her. She clearly can manipulate water, but I want you to find out what other abilities she possesses of Lux, and figure out how strong her water powers are. Her back markings are quite unique, which leads me to believe there is more to her than meets the eye. You have ten weeks to train her. Then depending on your reports, we'll see if she can enter our society."

The King stalked toward the girl and placed his fingers under her chin, forcing her to meet his gaze. The room was silent as he peered down at her, smiling while casually rubbing his thumb over her dirty cheek. She tried to pull away, but his grip only tightened, cupping her jaw.

She snarled and bared her teeth at him, her blue eyes flaring. "Such a fiery one," he chuckled. "If only you had answered our simple questions before, it could have saved you a lot of pain. We wouldn't have had to resort to such methods on you." He tsked before adding, "It is rather quite amusing, though. While we were *questioning* you for the Dark Prince's weaknesses, it seems we were staring at it this whole time. All you had to do was tell us that he cared deeply for you."

"You're wrong," she said softly as if she didn't quite believe it.

He paused as his fingers made another long stroke down her cheek. "You will behave, or I will send you back down to that cell to finish out your days." She fell silent at the threat. With a smug smile plastered on his face, the King turned away from her to address the room. His fingers still clamped under her jaw, forcing her head to twist with him. "No one outside of this room will speak of what we saw today. To anyone in our society, she is just a Luxian nix, as that was part of my arrangement for her with Tennebris. She is not to talk to anyone or give any indication that she was the Princess of the Dark Kingdom. The people of Tennebris believe she's imprisoned on their soil as we speak, and it's better to keep it that way... for now." He turned back to face the girl. "You will train with Tezya as he is accustomed to working with the new recruits in our army, but I don't want anyone finding out what happens between the two of you. You will train in secret and only come out in public if he or I deem it necessary. I won't hesitate to kill you, so don't break my rules. I don't show mercy for those that cross me."

He finally dropped her chin and said to the two soldiers, "Show her to her chambers and give her a bath. She can learn the details of this arrangement later."

I didn't wait to see if Lansting or the other soldier unchained her as I stormed after the Lux King. I made a quick mental note to myself to scold Lansting later for his treatment regarding the girl. I didn't think the other soldier tortured her, not from the longing and worry that lingered in his gaze as he watched her, but I did want to look into the ginger-haired male. It was unusual for me not to recognize someone from the army. He must have been a new recruit who hadn't come to training yet. Maybe he never saw how Luxians regarded their prisoners and couldn't stomach her treatment. He would have to get used to it. Being in the army, we were forced to witness many abhorrent things.

"What is this about?" I asked the King once we were alone in the hall.

His silver eyes whirled on me. "I don't trust anyone else to train her. She has to be special in some way. Her back markings are identical to the ones shown in your sister's visions. Make her trust you. Do whatever you have to do in order to figure out what her abilities are."

"I know what you ordered me to do," I said through gritted teeth. "What I want to know is why? You have proof that the Dark Prince knew about her. Why do you have to keep dragging her along? She's been through enough."

His smile reached his inner cheeks as he looked over at me. "Why do you care what I do with her? She's my property, and I do not owe you any explanation." He paused for a moment before adding, "But you're wrong. Regarding the Dark Prince, we don't have enough to charge him. Her memories could have been tampered, and if we try to go after him with that alone, we'll lose. So we have to catch him in the act. What I sought from her today was to gauge how much he knew of her. What we discovered was even better. The young fool is in love with her."

Realization hit me as I guessed what the King intended for her. There was no way he would ever let her go. It was more than just a curiosity of what powers she might possess, more than just his obsession to find powerful and rare Luxian abilities. He wanted to use her in every way possible—for her powers and for leverage against Sie...

"I also want to know if their blood bond took, and if they are with child for obvious reasons," he continued. "I don't trust her memories. She might not remember sleeping with him, or for all we know, the Prince could have compelled her to forget about it, so I expect testing to be performed to confirm it."

My gut twisted. "This is about that damn prophecy, isn't it?" When he didn't respond, I added, "And what will you do to her if she is with child? Will you kill her?"

"Mind how you speak to your King, boy. All you need to concern yourself with is making the girl trust you and figuring out her abilities." He turned to leave. "And Tezya, no one is to know about her. Tennebris is using her to keep the lower ranks in line, so keep the training a secret and keep her and that marvelous back of hers hidden from the public. I might just kill her and *you* if you fail in that."

FIVE
SCOTLIND

I WAS BROUGHT into a small room with a bathing chamber off to the side. The entrance was just big enough for a small table with two chairs tucked into it and a bed that took up the majority of the space. The frame was a light, ashy wood with a soft pale comforter tucked tightly into it. The checkered white and pale gray floors were cold against my bare feet. A small window was carved into the far wall with the curtains pulled shut and a chair positioned in front of it. Everything was light and airy and, to me, seemed like heaven. Anything was better than that cell. No, not a cell—cage. That was what I'd been living in since I got here.

The green-eyed guard disappeared the moment the King left the monitor room, so I was led up here by my previous torturer. "A maid is being fetched for you. You are to bathe before you meet with Tezya."

"So I'm not a prisoner anymore?" I had to ask. I couldn't believe that after all that time spent in the dungeons, I'd just be let out.

He looked at me with disgust. "You will always be a prisoner, Tennebrisian scum."

I turned to him, ignoring his comment, and swallowed down my pride, my hands pressed against my throat. "Please, can I have water and food?" My stomach turned in on itself. The bread I got from the nice guard had long left me, and my throat was so scratchy it burned with each inhale.

He scuffed. "Just be thankful I'm not throwing you back in that damn cell. You don't belong in our society. Your blood is tainted with the Dark."

He turned and slammed the door in my face, leaving me entirely alone. But at least I wasn't surrounded by darkness anymore, and the cool draft from the dungeon was no longer hugging my skin. It was warm and comforting in this room, despite my body crawling with a sweeping sensation of danger.

It was strange to be in a normal room after so much time locked away. Just being able to stand again felt foreign. Chandeliers illuminated the space, filling the room with buzzing electricity. There wasn't a candle or torch anywhere. There wasn't even a fireplace.

I knew that Lux contrasted greatly with Tennebris in most ways. While Tennebris clung to the dark and olden traditions, Lux conceded to the new. They embraced technology and electricity and didn't seem to have any sort of shortage with either, but it was still a shock to see it in person.

I slowly walked over to the only window in the room, my legs aching and cramping with each step. I had to sit down, just standing felt taxing on my body, nonetheless walking. I sank into the off-white chair that was perched in front of it.

My fingers curled around the ivory curtains, and only then did I notice myself—how out of place I was. My fingers were covered in dirt and looked wrong against the cleanliness of the fabric. I pulled the material aside abruptly, not wanting to stare at any part of my body any longer than I had to. I just wanted to look outside, to see Lux for the first time. A scream of surprise escaped my parched, cracked lips as I was blinded by the light now streaming in. I slammed my dirty hand over my eyes to shield them.

The sun. I'd seen glimpses of its rays every day, but to have a full, unshielded view of it... I didn't know how long it'd been since I had felt its warmth. Even through the thick window, I could imagine how it used to feel running under it in Tennebris each morning. I inched

38

closer to the window, wanting to feel its warmth on my skin, wanting to know if it'd be different here than in the Dark Kingdom. My fingers trembled around the edge of the window sill, feeling for the latch to open it, but there was none. It was glued shut. Still closing my eyes, unused to the brightness, I pressed my forehead against the cool window pane and sighed heavily.

"Good morning, my dear," a thick female voice sounded from behind me. I lifted my head and noticed a brown smear imprinted on the glass from where I was leaning into it.

"H-hello," I said hesitantly, taking in the older female before me. She was slightly plump, which was a bit unusual for an Advenian, but somehow still came across as frail. Her black hair was peppered with gray, and a few wrinkles were etched around her eyes and the corners of her mouth. She must be ancient to be showing signs of aging.

The woman curtsied awkwardly in a way that made it appear like she'd never done it before. "I will be your maid while you're at the castle." That was when I noticed the zero branded onto her left wrist.

I suddenly felt awkward that she was bowing to me. Did she not know why I was here? That I was a prisoner? She clearly must know something was off by my appearance alone. "Please, that's not necessary," I said softly as she rose from her curtsey. A loud pop resonated in her knee. "My name is Scotlind, but you can call me Scottie."

I quickly covered my mouth as I let out a small gasp. The words had slipped out of me before I could stop them. Was I supposed to tell people my name? Did the people of Lux know anything about me? That a nix named Scottie used to be the Dark Princess? All I knew was that the King said *no one* should know who I really was. I assumed that meant not telling people my real name. He also said that I was supposed to train with that beautiful stranger from earlier, and no one was to know about that either. I prayed to Pylemo that I didn't just condemn this woman for revealing a part of me.

I internally groaned as I came to the realization that I still had to pretend I was a nix. That yet again, I had to hide who I was. At least it was better than rotting in that cage.

The woman gave me a knowing smile that seemed genuine as it

reached her eyes—her green eyes. I never knew I could find such comfort in a single color before.

"I'm Patricia," she started as she hobbled over to me. "And there's no need to worry. I am aware of who you are, my dear. I would have had to be informed of you if I'm to care for you, wouldn't I? Now, let's get you cleaned up. You are to meet with Tezya to learn of your new arrangements."

I kept staring into Patricia's eyes as she slowly made her way across the shiny floor. If she fell, I think her bones would snap, even with the extra cushion surrounding them. She noticed my assessment and halted. "What is it?" Patricia grumbled, and I swore her voice sounded deeper, huskier at that moment.

I brushed it away. "Nothing," I replied. "It's just... your eyes... They remind me of someone from my hom—" I paused, stopping myself mid-sentence. I almost called Tennebris my home, and to be honest, I didn't know which Kingdom I belonged to anymore. I don't belong to either of them. "They remind me of someone that I miss," I settled on saying.

A half smile grew on her wrinkled face as she winked at me. "A cute boy, perhaps?"

"Yes," I laughed, knowing that Peter would be smiling to hear me say that, "but it's not like that. He is... I mean... he was a friend."

"Once a friend, always a friend. Come on, dear. We don't have much time." She finished her way across the floor and stopped mere inches from me as she gently reached for my arm to lead me toward the bathing room.

I planted my feet on the ground. "Could I have some food?" I choked out. I felt disgusting in every way possible, and to be clean again sounded like a fantasy that would never come true, but I needed food, or I was going to collapse.

She looked sympathetic as she said, "I'm sorry, but there is no food in your chambers. I was given instructions to clean you up. The sooner we do so, the sooner you may dine with Tezya."

Dine with Tezya. I couldn't hide the disappointment from my face as I let her lead me toward the bathing room. I didn't want to *dine* with anyone from Lux, but I figured this person would be informing me of my training with the white-haired stranger. Whoever he was, he better have food, or I would throw a fit or pass out. Whichever happened first.

I froze once I saw what awaited me inside the bathing room. A tub. A beautiful white bathtub with silver faucets. The bath was large enough to fit two people but still felt too small. Too suffocating.

It was still an enclosed, circular prison that would be filled with water. Patricia bent over, grasping the side of the bath for support as she turned the faucet to its side. Water poured out in a heavy stream. Steam and heat instantly spiraled and twirled around the water, clinging to it for life. I didn't have time to be impressed that the heat of the water was immediate.

I stepped backward, hitting the wall so hard that the mirror above the sink clamored. My throat closed up. I wanted to scream. I opened my mouth to do just that, but nothing came out. I couldn't. I couldn't relive that horrid memory. It was bad enough that a version of it came into my nightmares each night, but this... I couldn't face it.

Patricia turned to face me, noticing my panic and hesitation toward the bath. Her brows furrowed. "Is something wrong, dear?"

"I can't," I started, my voice thick, "I can't get in there."

"You must wash. I mean this with all the respect in the world, but you smell so horrible that even the rats would flee from you."

A tear escaped my eye and slowly ran down my cheek. I hated how this affected me. How Kole affected me. It was stupid. I knew I had to bathe. It was just a tub anyway. I could *breathe* underwater. The water wouldn't get me. It wouldn't kill me. *He* couldn't kill me.

I went to take a step closer to Patricia, closer to the looming white doom, but Kole's brown eyes flashed in my vision. His laughter filled my ears. The burning in my throat felt all too real.

I scrambled back again, hitting the wall harder. "I... I can't. I'm sorry."

"Hmm," Patricia turned the faucet off, stopping the flow of water in an instant. "I'll fetch you some rags then. If you won't get in the tub, you at least need to scrub your body. I'll help you with what you can't reach."

I nodded, unable to say anything else. Shame and embarrassment lingered. Who was scared to bathe? Patricia hobbled out of the bathing room, leaving me alone with the tub of death. If I wasn't so frightened by it, I would have leaned over and drank the water that rested at the bottom. I looked toward the sink to avoid the thought but immediately regretted it.

I caught my reflection in the mirror, and I hardly recognized myself. The girl staring back at me was hollow and empty in her body and soul. Black sunken bags were painted under her eyes so deep I would have thought they were permanently there like the Luxian markings. Her cheekbones were prominent against her sullen face, and her freckles were undiscoverable under a thick layer of crusted dirt. Her body was worse.

I lifted the gown I was dressed in, the material almost breaking as it was held together by threads. I could count my ribs. My stomach dipped, and each joint stuck out at odd angles. I didn't fit my body anymore. The muscles I worked for every day of my life were gone as if that part of me had dissipated before my eyes. That part of me was dead, and I didn't know what that left me with or who I was anymore.

Patrica came back into the room with a pile of white rags in her arms so high that I couldn't see the tip of her nose. She set the material down and added soap to the water that collected at the bottom of the tub. Then, after dipping a cloth and lathering it with soapy water until it was foaming, she placed it in my hands.

"I'll prepare the rags and wet them. You scrub."

I didn't know how long Patricia and I worked on my body. I knew it would have been much faster if I had just gotten in the water, but she didn't complain as the minutes turned into hours. My body was pink by the time we were done. The white material of the cloth turned black. It still felt like a layer of grime lingered on my skin, a layer that only a bath could cure, but I didn't care. It felt amazing to finally clean myself.

I normally would have been embarrassed to have someone help me wash. It was something I had never fathomed before with having to keep my back markings hidden. But something about Patricia seemed familiar. She was patient and kind, and I truly needed the help. I barely had the energy to scrub at the filth, and there would have been no way of getting to certain areas without her assistance. She distracted me as she cleansed me gently, careful of the many still-healing wounds. They were all over, and the soapy water stung as it met with each open area, especially my back. Patricia cursed roughly when I turned around, and she saw it for the first time—saw what they did to my back. It was the one guard's favorite method. He'd sneer that I didn't deserve to lay down comfortably ever again.

"Here you are," she said gently as she handed me a pile of clean clothes when we were done. "It's the latest Luxian fashion. I was told to dress you in this. Change quickly. I will wait outside your room and then walk you to Tezya's chambers."

I wanted to ask more about Tezya. Did this person know about me too? Was I supposed to tell him my name? Who was he? Was he one of the guards that tortured me? I couldn't remember any of the names I heard during my time in the cell. Everything was jumbling together.

I wanted to know why I was supposed to dine with him and if he was going to tell me what to expect from the white-haired male, but Patricia left before I could open my mouth. I stared after her, puzzled. She was hobbling and wobbling around earlier, but now she moved with such grace and agility.

I shook my head and looked at the clothes in my hand. It was a silky, tan slip that seemed too thin and too delicate to actually be an outfit. The dress, if you could call it that, looked more like my old nightgowns but much more elegant. Sighing heavily, I pulled the material over my head and tugged down. It clung to my body, exposing every bone and prominence. I would normally be abashed, but all I could think about was food, and the sooner I met with this person, the sooner I could eat... or so I prayed.

———

NERVES RACKED my body as Patrica stopped in front of two silver doors. "Here we are, dear. I will see you afterward."

"You aren't coming with me?" I choked.

She shook her head. "No, dear. The instructions were for you to go alone. Now hurry, he's waiting."

I hesitated for only a moment, but the thought of food was what moved my hands into motion and had me reaching on the door. It opened on the second knock. The person was the stranger from the interrogation. I had no idea why that shocked me or why I never thought of it. I just assumed that there would be a middleman, that the stranger wouldn't waste his time dining with me.

He was looming over me, staring with such curiosity and intensity that my cheeks reddened at the appraisal.

"You're late," he said by way of greeting and opened the door further, gesturing me inside. I found myself staring up at the most handsome male I ever saw. Now that I was mere inches from him and with a slightly clearer mind, I finally got a good look at him. Each of his features suited him like they were molded and only existed for him. Every inch of him was wholly crafted into a beautiful warrior. A warrior. That was what he was, what he had to be. *He trains the new recruits for the Luxian armies.* He had to be powerful and high ranked within the army itself to earn that title.

Sie was an amazing fighter, lean and muscular, and he knew how to take out an opponent in seconds, but as I studied this male, I didn't know who would walk away from a battle between the two of them. Sie was agile, but this stranger seemed powerful, stronger. He seemed —more, like he was crafted for the art of killing, shaped by death itself. Like he could kill you with his eyes closed and come out without a scratch on him, despite his array of scars scattered over his skin. And there were so many on him that it just seemed to be a part of him. Like he was born into this world with the scars, as if they always belonged to him, just like the stars belonged to the night sky.

The thick, raised scar over his right cheek kept grabbing my attention. I traced it with my eyes from the bridge of his nose as it crept past his jaw. I wanted to know how far that scar continued and if it reached the back of his scalp. I knew it was rude to stare, but I couldn't look away. I wanted to know how he got it. I was surprised that anyone was able to make a cut on him during a fight, especially, one that brutal.

My head reached the height of his collarbone as I stood before him with nothing to do but ogle at his sculpted chest, visible through the loose-fitted shirt he wore. The top button was undone now, revealing a bit of tanned skin beneath. He looked as if he had spent much of his time outside under the golden sun.

He folded his arms and crossed them over his chest, causing his muscles to flex beneath him. "Well," he spoke, his voice coming out low, deep, and rough that I startled. "Are you planning on standing there gawking all day, or were you going to come inside and sit down?"

I met his light blue eyes again, trying my best to avoid staring at the scar. His dark brow, such a contrast to his moonlight hair, was raised at my inquisition. That broke me from my stunned, creepy assessment.

"You're the one from earlier. You brought me to that interrogation."

His eyes narrowed at my arms, which were now crossed against my own chest. "And you're the prisoner that I am stuck training. Now that that's settled, come inside."

"No, I'm not going anywhere with you."

He paused to study me for a moment, then said, "You will if you want to eat." I hated that he was using food against me to get me to do what he wanted. I hated it more that it worked. I was being led by my gnawing hunger right now. It was as if he could sense that I would do anything for food.

"Fine," I grumbled and pushed past him, trying my best to appear nonchalant. I scanned the room in a blindly obsessive and fascinated manner. It felt like I was seeing things for the first time. Everything in Lux was so different from Tennebris. Everything was... well, lighter, more extravagant. I'd never seen so much silver scattered throughout the walls and trim of a room. But it was more than just the burnished metal. Everything seemed to actually glisten. It reminded me of a diamond sparkling under the sun.

The things inside the room—the furniture that filled its space—seemed less imposing, like it didn't belong. The door I walked through opened up to a greeting area that held multiple brown, worn-in leather sofas. A dark desk sat in the corner with books and papers scattered across the oak, making the wood barely visible under all the clutter. The chair was pushed out like he had busied himself in the work moments prior.

I followed him as he led me through another set of double doors. My eyes widened as I realized it was his bedroom. A beautiful allotrope chandelier hung low over the center of the ceiling, illuminating white walls and porcelain floors with more of that silver-diamond trim. My head spun as I took everything in. His bed was massive and spread across the room. The silver comforter briefly piqued my interest as I wondered what it felt like to lie in its silky embrace. A large monitor was displayed before the bed, and I frowned slightly at what that could be used for. Did he interrogate people in his bedroom?

"It's a television," he said, eyeing my curiosity. "Come." He gestured toward the small table on his balcony, already set for two. "I thought you'd like to eat outside." He pulled the metal chair out, dragging it across the balcony floor before he took a seat.

I stepped outside and halted. His balcony overlooked the bay. I gawked at the setting sun, casting hues of pink and purple across the glistening water. For years, I'd longed to see the sunset, and it was more beautiful than I could have imagined. I could almost hear the waves tumbling and crashing against the light brown sand in the distance. A warm breeze swept the hair off my shoulder and down my back. I closed my eyes as I inhaled the salty, citrus scent.

Home. This was home. If nothing else in Lux was, I at least belonged to the waves. This was the bay and the ocean that I longed for. The scent filled my nose, engulfing me as it entered my soul. With my eyes closed, I saw images of me playing in the surf. Kicking up sand as a musical voice laughed. Then, I was laughing with the voice, coloring waves onto someone's forearms.

I couldn't convince myself that my mind was playing tricks on me. It felt too real. It was as if being in Lux brought back what I lost. As if I stayed here longer, I might be able to uncover more of my childhood, more stolen memories of my real parents. The thought alone was intoxicating. And the sun. It was better than I could have imagined, so different from the rays in Tennebris. The sun here seemed to melt off the numbing cold I'd felt since the dungeons. It felt like a warm hug, completely engulfing me—

"It's beautiful, the bayside," he said, breaking the tranquil moment that took over me. My eyes flew open, and I stared into a different intoxicating blue. His irises were almost translucent, rimmed with silver, where the light blue color filled the rest. A striking contrast next to his thick, brutal scar. The one that kept drawing my attention. I looked closer, and I thought I saw a smaller scar, the top of it just barely visible through the messy mop of his sun-bleached white hair cascading down his face.

A sudden urge to run my fingers through his hair came. I wanted to feel the buzz of his shaved head on the bottom as I moved up his scalp to the thick strands that surrounded his face. I wanted to know if his hair was smooth or coarse...

I shook my head. What was wrong with me?

He nodded subtly toward the open chair across from him, and I realized I was still standing awkwardly in the doorframe. I slipped into it, careful to avoid his now outstretched legs before me.

"What do you want with me?" I spoke for the first time since coming outside. My voice came out scratchy from the lack of water.

He leaned back in his seat as he assessed me further, a relaxed arrogance radiating off of him as he sipped slowly from a crystal glass filled with amber contents. "I'm going to train you."

I perked up in my seat. "Train me for what exactly?" I was trying to remember what the Lux King had said to me back in the monitor room, but everything was blurring together, and my mind was fuzzy.

He gave me a half smile, noting my excitement. "I will be helping you access your Luxian abilities, to discover what and who you are."

"Why?"

He shrugged. "As you heard earlier, it was requested by the King of Lux. I don't know what he has planned for you. I'm just a soldier, doing as I'm told. You are to discover your abilities over the next couple of weeks with me, and then you will be granted a private ranking assessment where he will decide then what he will do with you—where you will belong in this society."

"So I'm not to be kept your prisoner then? Why the sudden change of heart?" I asked.

"Unless you want to be a prisoner? I can arrange for you to return to the dungeons. It would save me a lot of time and effort." I thought I caught a glimmer of humor in his expression, but I couldn't tell.

I narrowed my eyes as I glared at him. "So I'm really going to be allowed to rejoin your society after everything that has happened?" I didn't need to say the details. He saw everything about my pitiful life on those monitor screens. I was an ex-princess, a traitor to them, and as far as anyone was concerned, a liar. No one had any explanation as to why I was in Tennebris.

His dark eyebrows furrowed beneath the white locks that flowed down his face. "I don't know. It depends on how well you prove yourself. If the King finds use for you, then maybe he will grant you that. This training will not be easy. *I* will not be easy on you. You will be expected to master what most Advenians do over years in just ten weeks."

"Fine," I said through gritted teeth. Anything was better than that cell. I didn't want to go back there ever again. "What does this training entail?"

"You won't go anywhere in this castle without the maid that was assigned to you or me. You won't be allowed to. You will wake up at dawn, train with me, and do exactly as I say. Then, once we are done, you will return to your chambers to eat and rest. You will eat a healthy diet and sleep regularly to keep up with the training regime. You should try to build some strength back into your body too. I'll train you in both. Physical training as well as your ability training."

"Why?" I couldn't help the question. I wanted it. I wanted to get strong again, but I couldn't help but wonder what would be the benefit to him. What the benefit to any of this was? Why was the King even going through all this trouble?

"Why what?"

"Why train me in both? The King only said to train my abilities?"

He took a long sip from his drink before setting the glass back down on the table. "Because no one should be as weak as you."

I bristled at that. I wanted to snap back that I wasn't weak. That I was strong. That I could defend myself. But right now, I knew it would be a lie. I was so weak that walking to his chamber was exhausting. I *needed* to retrain my body. I *needed* what he was offering me.

He looked me over as he added, "And because no one should treat you the way you have been treated in the past. You should make yourself strong so no one can... repeat what has happened to you."

I heated slightly as shame crept through me. I hated that he saw everything on those screens. I hated even more the pity in his eyes as he looked at me like I was some pathetic, helpless being.

But in reality, what he was saying didn't sound all that bad. I could finally figure out what my Luxian abilities were. Something I'd wanted to do my entire life. Something I only started to do with Sie. I could eat regularly, sleep in a warm bed, bathe, or half-bathe with the rags. And I could train again.

I hated feeling weak. I hated the feeling ever since I was taken from Lux at a young age. But unfortunately, that feeling kept following me my entire life. It seemed like every turn I made, someone stronger kept overpowering me. Like no matter how hard I trained, how hard I worked, it still wasn't enough. I wasn't enough. Maybe he could train me to be better. Maybe I could finally become as strong as I always wanted to be. The only part I didn't like was being confined to my room, but considering this morning I never thought I'd make it out of the dungeons, I wasn't going to complain.

"You work for the King then?" I pried. If I was going to be

spending my days with him, I wanted to know who he was and what he did for the Lux King. His room wasn't overly elaborate, although the view was amazing. The walls and trim seemed more grand, with mundane furnishings inside. But the five on his wrist and the fact that he trained the recruits for the Luxian army seemed enough proof that he was high up in command.

Before he could answer, two servants opened the balcony doors and emerged with trays of food. The food filled every inch of our small table. I was almost drooling from the smell of it. The sight alone was intoxicating.

My stomach growled loudly in protest, knowing what awaited. I hadn't had a proper meal, other than stale, moldy bread, in weeks. In fact, thinking back, I didn't think I had eaten a feast like this since the breakfast after my wedding day. I tried not to think about that, about my time in Tennebris, especially about Sie or our wedding.

The male nodded his head toward the servants in thanks as they left us alone again. Then he dug into the food. "Eat," he ordered, not bothering to look my way. "You're too skinny, and if you're going to train with me, you'll need your energy."

Not caring how desperate I looked, I obeyed, gouging myself with food, stuffing my face with fruits, cheeses, meats, anything I could get my hands on. I even sipped on some sparkling fluid in a crystal glass that I assumed was some sort of wine after I guzzled two glasses full of water.

I moaned loudly, unable to help myself, as I bit into a delicious strawberry-filled pastry. The male stiffened in his seat at my moan, and I immediately flushed. I forgot he was even there, too submerged in my hunger.

He smirked. "Was the food in Tennebris not good?" My cheeks heated as I set the pastry back down. I definitely wasn't going to eat that anymore. My stomach rumbled at the assortment of foods already working their way down. My chest felt heavy and tight.

The male laughed as he noticed my movements, noticed the way I refused to eat it now. "Oh, by all means, don't stop on my account. It's just not every day you hear a female make sex noises while she eats dinner. Is this customary in Tennebris?"

I gasped, then composed myself as anger took over. "Wouldn't you like to know," I heard myself say before I could think better of it.

"I have better things to do than know what turns someone of your youth on." He resumed eating. I wanted to slap him across his gorgeous face right over his thick scar but instead thought it better to change the subject.

Youth. It made me wonder how old he was. Most Advenians aged slowly, except for my new maid, Patricia, it seemed. It made it difficult to tell anyone's true age.

"I will not apologize for enjoying food when all I've eaten in the past twenty-seven days was a moldy piece of bread. If I was given any food at all, that is. And before that, at Tennebris, it wasn't much better. So I may be skin and bones, but it is because of your people."

He tensed. His tan hand paled and tightened around his utensil. I caught him glancing at my forearm. My last tally was still bloodied and raw, indicating just how many days I had spent in that cage. The other marks faded to various states of healing. He seemed to notice that I paid attention. That I was aware of how long I was kept a prisoner. That I was aware of everything they did to me and that I would not forget it, and even if the Lux King offered me a place here, I wouldn't belong.

"They are your people now too," he said softly before he resumed eating.

I scuffed. I didn't belong anywhere anymore.

"And what is it that you do?" I asked, remembering that he never answered my question about working for the Lux King. He seemed to take orders directly from him, so I wanted to know just how close they were.

He kept eating, ignoring me wholly now. I could feel the anger boiling up inside me. I hated the fact that he probably knew everything about me, and I didn't even know his name.

"Who are you?" I asked. I knew Patricia had told me a name, but it was unusual, and I couldn't remember it.

He still didn't reply as he plopped a piece of meat into his mouth. I repeated my question, this time more sternly, causing him to glance up at me just once. *"Who are you?"*

A quick flash of shock registered on his beautiful, cold face as if he was taken aback, as if he was surprised that I asked him that. Like I should have known who he was.

Probably being a powerful warrior and by his good looks, he was used to people whispering his name everywhere he went. Most likely people were either afraid of him or wanted him. But he was definitely not accustomed to people not knowing who he was.

"My name is Tezya," he finally answered, setting down his fork and resting his strong forearms on the table.

"Tez-yeah?" I attempted to pronounce.

He chuckled softly at my poor attempt. "No, it's Tez-uh, and you are Scotlind Mae Rumor. Eighteen years old. Former Princess of Tennebris and previously married to Prince Noren. You're from Lux, deemed a traitor found and married in a different Kingdom, which is illegal. You studied to be a guard in Tennebris but didn't qualify, and if you weren't selected to be the Prince's bride, you would have been a servant."

A piece of cheese dropped from my lip as my mouth gaped open. Not all of that information was displayed on the monitors. How did he know so much about me?

I quickly recovered. "And Tezya, what about you? Do you work for the Lux King? Are you a member of the Luxian guard?"

"Everyone here works for the Lux King in one way or another. And I'm a member of Lux's *army*. We don't call it the guard like Tennebris does. We are warriors and soldiers, not mere guards. That's all you need to know."

"So you get to know everything about me, and I don't get to know anything about you? Only your name?" I said, my voice rising.

"No. I also told you that I am a member of the army. That's two things you now know about me."

I huffed. "I could have answered that on my own, judging from the looks of you."

"Oh, how so? How do I look to you?" He asked, amused, meeting my gaze as he leaned back in his seat.

I looked away and stared at the pears and apples to my left. I wanted to say: because every inch of you was covered in muscle and scars. Because you look like you are ready to kill me at any given moment. Because you completely and utterly scare me. And because there was no denying that you must be a part of Lux's army. Because Sie told me stories of your brutality, stories of how the army fought and how they killed. Then, the Lux King admitted that you alone trained the new recruits, and now I'm going to be trained by you. Instead, I said, "Well, you said training, so I assumed as much."

"Right," he smiled, settling back into his chair. "And I don't know everything about you. I only have the files Tennebris sent with you. What are your Luxian abilities? How skilled are you at using them?"

"I don't know," I admitted softly.

"Have you ever used your abilities?"

"Once," I said too quickly. He stared at me with a blank expression as I continued. "I was too nervous about being discovered, so I never was able to find out or practice them before. I only trained once when —" I cut myself short, thinking back to Sie and how he risked everything to help me. How he spent days with me at the lake and tried everything to help me discover my powers, even though he knew nothing about it. My heart broke in two as I thought of the last time I saw him when he annulled our marriage with a detached, emotionless expression. How he sent me to Lux after he warned me to stay clear of them. How he gave me up to be a prisoner to the very man he said was dangerous.

Anger threatened to boil at my surface whenever I tried to understand what had happened. How he was so caring, how he rescued me from Kole, saved me, protected me, trained me, only to abandon me. Then, as soon as I was discovered by the High Council, he stopped fighting for me entirely. He gave me up like I meant nothing to him. He didn't look sad or hurt or affected in any way as I was brought to the dais before him in chains. He wouldn't even look at me, not once, as they...

Tezya was watching me, analyzing me, probably wondering why I stopped talking. "I was able to move water once," I said, "that was it."

He ran a hand through his hair at the top of his head, exposing the fullness of that scar and a thinner one that hovered over his temple and slashed through the corner of his right eyebrow. Embarrassment ran through me as he looked generally disappointed, like he expected me to be further along. Like I should already know whatever abilities I possessed.

I felt stupid being here. I knew little about their ways. I knew nothing about Lux besides the bit we learned at LakeWood. What was worse was that I knew nothing about myself.

His tone turned harsher as he said, "You are not allowed to go anywhere without me. If you aren't training with me, you will stay in your room and be kept hidden. You will do exactly as I say and when I say so with no questions asked. You will tell no one your name. You won't speak to anyone unless I am there with you and give you permission. This is important, so do not forget it. Now, leave and go to sleep. We start training at dawn tomorrow." As he spoke, the same two servants emerged from the balcony doors, ushering me to come with them.

I just exchanged one prison cell for another.

SIX

SIE

I'D BEEN STARING at the same four damn walls for hours now, pacing my bedroom, waiting for Moli to arrive. We'd been meeting like this for the past two weeks after King Lunder was *murdered* at a dinner banquet. And since Synder was his second, he automatically became the King of Tennebris until my coronation—that was if I lived that long.

Moli was there after Kole cut Scotind's thigh. Hell, she was there after Scottie and I were tortured by the prick. She was the only healer I trusted. I'd known her since I was little. She frequented my childhood home many times due to my father's incessant outbursts. She was only a couple of decades older than me, still extremely young in the eyes of any Advenian, but she had a way about her that always seemed more mature. She found me shortly after the King's murder and informed me of the real cause of death.

Poison.

The people of Tennebris were led to believe that King Lunder died choking on his food. They were all a bunch of idiots for believing Synder so easily. For a species that rarely died of such trivial things, they didn't question the notion once. But I did. And so did Moli. He was murdered.

Fucking murdered.

And now the man who attempted to orchestrate Scotlind's death—who tried to get me to kill her—was on the throne.

I looked forward to my visit with Moli because, regardless of how short they were, they were minutes that I stopped worrying about my wife. Ex-wife now. Fuck. I hated that. I hated being away from her. I hated knowing she wasn't mine anymore. I hated that she was in the Light Kingdom's territory as King Arcane's prisoner. I hated even more that she might come across the Fire Prince, the youngest of the King's children.

Was she okay? Was she still kept a prisoner, or did they welcome her into their society? I prayed every day for the latter. I couldn't stomach thinking about her rotting away in a prison cell. But that was all she would have done here. Or worse, I would be burying her like we did Lunder. At least this gave her a chance at a normal life, even if it meant a life without me.

And Peter. I hadn't heard from my friend, and I should have by now. The silence was concerning. It's been a month and nothing.

A faint knock turned my attention away from my thoughts. I walked over to the door with a slight tremble in my hand, sweat already pooling at my forehead, down my temples, and onto my neck.

"Hello," Moli said sweetly as I swung the door open. She frowned once she realized I was leaning too heavily against the frame. "Are you sure this is a good idea to keep doing this? You don't look well, Sie."

I gestured for her to enter and quickly shut the door. A healer technically shouldn't be visiting my chambers, and we both could get in a lot of trouble for this. The stakes were much worse for Moli.

She eyed me hesitantly before taking a seat by the fire. The flames gave way to a beautiful glow of her rich dark skin. Her coily black hair was tied up in a bun that I was surprised it managed to stay on the top of her head. The girl had a lot of hair.

"I don't like this, Sie," she said as she eyed me suspiciously. "This could kill you before anyone else even gets the chance. I know you believe that someone will try to do something similar to you as they did to Lunder, but what if we are wrong... I just... I don't like it."

I huffed as I slumped into the seat next to her. The hours of pacing were taxing on my body. "I know," I said as I grabbed the poison from her bag and swallowed it in one gulp before she could protest. Her coral eyes narrowed at my throat as I choked the contents down. It took every effort not to throw up the putrid liquid.

I didn't care if doing this would kill me. I didn't particularly like the nasty side effects of the poison or the thick taste of it as I forced it down, but I would rather die from my own actions than from Synder. I wouldn't let him beat me. I wouldn't give him the satisfaction of winning.

Silence followed, and then, "In another week, you will be at the max dose," Moli said as she grabbed the empty vile and shoved it back into her bag. "Then your body should start adjusting. *Hopefully*. If all goes well, the sweats and body shakes should leave within the following week or two."

"And if it doesn't?"

"If it doesn't, Tennebris will be burying another King."

I grabbed her hands in mine, startling her. "Thank you, Mols. I know what you risk by helping me."

My vision blurred as the strongest effects of the poison started to take hold. All I saw was coral pink as I attempted to focus on her large eyes. She pried her hands away briskly, then strode toward the door. "Just don't die. Our Kingdom needs a ruler like you, Sie." Then she was gone. Every morning was the same. Moli brought my poison, slowly upping the dose, then disappeared before the healer's quarters realized she was missing.

I normally soaked in an ice bath to try to compensate for some of the side effects as heat flared throughout every inch of my body, but I didn't have time today. Synder called an emergency Council meeting, and there was no way in hell I was going to miss it.

All the seats were filled by the time I arrived. The room hushed and halted its murmurings the moment I entered. I had to shoulder the door open, and it took every effort to hold myself upright.

Synder looked up and studied me, noting every movement I took as I immediately slumped into the only empty seat left, not able to stand much longer. "You don't look well, my Prince."

"I'm fine," I grunted, not meaning to sound so wounded. His mouth curved into a cruel smirk as he noted my flinch, the beads of sweat that rolled behind my neck, and the way my hands shook slightly. I held them together, placing them on my lap under the table. He noted it, and fucking smiled. "I just got back from training. I didn't get a chance to bathe yet," I lied, but I needed an excuse as to why sweat was pouring out of me. Winter was fast approaching. In another couple of weeks, the constant darkness would be here. The servants were cleaning most of the fireplaces and torches in preparation, and I couldn't even blame my perspiration on the fires—not that the constant flames were even a good excuse for how I looked.

"I'm glad to hear it. One part of this meeting was called to actually discuss your well-being."

I held my breath, waiting for him to continue, my gaze never breaking his stare. The males of the High Council looked between the two of us. The stirring of heads was dizzying. My heart was pounding too fast. I could feel each thump and tick it made against my chest. My skin grew clammy as my body heated more and more. Shit. I needed ice.

"It's regarding you taking a bride," Synder said.

"No," I snarled too fast to be casual.

Synder bucked. "Surely you don't plan to spit on tradition and not take up a wife when you are crowned."

"Let me remind you that I did have a wife. I am not going against tradition. I took one that you and the men in this room unwisely chose, so I'm not eager to take up another, especially by your hands." I loosened my jaw, not realizing how tightly I was clenching it. I hated talking ill of Scotlind, but I had to keep up the ruse in order to be believable. I had to convince them that I didn't care for her. I had to act like it wasn't eating away at me that she was gone, worse than any poison. She was in the heart of enemy territory, sent there because of me. Weakness was what caused this downward spiral that was my life.

I wouldn't show Synder any more of it. I wouldn't let myself have any more weaknesses.

"Ah yes, and she, unfortunately, cheated on you. My sincerest apologies, Sie. We can assure you that this next one will not disappoint you, though. She will be faithful."

Right. Scotlind *cheated* on me. That was the story that was told to the High Council and to all of Tennebris because they didn't want the truth to come out that she was from Lux and wasn't really a nix. Not when Tennebris was using her rank zero status to their advantage. Only a handful of people actually knew the truth. Not even the entire Council realized where Scotlind really was right now.

Instead, the entire Kingdom believed that Scottie was rotting away in the dungeons somewhere below the castle for her indiscretions. Synder was using her as a ploy to sabotage the current ranking system, manipulating the Tennebrisians into compliance about the changes being made, and it was fucking working.

Ever since the incident, the Council passed laws that eliminated the basic Advenian rights for rank zeroes. *They are too closely related to the mortals to be trusted. It is human nature to have greed and to always want more, and that is what Scotlind Rumor proved. She wasn't satisfied with what we blessed her with. She wasn't satisfied with her Trials. She wanted more and more, and no amount of power would placate the cravings of mortal avarice. Rank zeroes won't stop until our society is in ruins, so we must take action and stop them before it's too late,* he announced to the general public a week ago. And now, rank zeroes lost their right to participate in the Trials at the end of their education. If they got a zero during the ranking evaluation, that was it. They'd automatically become servants.

He was milking every aspect of Scotlind being a known nix to his advantage. Spilling lies about how she manipulated the Council in the first place by sleeping her way into power. The amount of fabrications he twisted about her felt like a punch in the gut. He painted a bad picture for rank zeroes, and the Tennebrisians were starting to believe it. Gossip stirred that they were more closely related to humans than Advenians.

And it still wasn't enough. Synder was currently working on a law that would pull every rank zero out of school—they wouldn't even get an education—they'd all just become servants. If you couldn't prove you had powers, you'd be banned from school and forced to work—at *six* fucking years old. He planned to make it mandatory to go up against compulsion in order to start school. All children would be compelled to cut their forearms. Anyone that made the cut, that was forced to obey, forfeited their right to an education.

He wanted to make them illiterate, to solidify their future even more. Rank zeroes would have a harder time fighting against the new laws if none of them could read them. It was sickening. I tried to not think about what Scottie and Peter would make of the situation. I was just relieved that the laws didn't pass... yet.

I knew that Scotlind would be appalled if she knew what was happening. I also knew that Peter would be heartbroken. Thinking of his little sister, Lilia, working at such a young age, of never attending school or laughing with her friends, would break my friend. She deserved better than that. I knew that. I knew zeroes deserved to be educated. They deserved a life. Synder's visions were wrong. He only wanted to cast Advenians to the bottom of the food chain to secure his power. And I could do nothing to fucking stop it, at least, not yet. Not until I became King.

It was why I had been slowly consuming the poison every day. I would not let Synder win. I knew that was his plan, to get me off the throne. I was the real threat, not King Lunder. If he got rid of me, he would remain King. Peter was nowhere to be found, and the next King's Tournament was a decade away, and a lot could happen in a decade.

I knew I was next, that probably every male in this room wanted me dead, except my father, who was so fucking oblivious to it all and just wanted to make sure the family name remained in power.

I willed my thoughts back. I just had to stay alive long enough. Once I was crowned, I would figure out what to do next. Starting with bringing Scotlind and Peter back. I didn't care if she really belonged to Lux. *I was going to get her back.*

Synder peered up at me through a thick stack of papers. "You will be wed again, Sie. That's an order. We will not stray from our tradition. The future King must have a Queen. You will marry one of our own."

"And who is that, may I ask?" There was no chance of me talking my way out of it if they already had someone in mind.

"Reagan Baker. Her father is on the Council, and you have known Reagan since you were little. She is the obvious choice."

"Forgive me, but I only just had my previous marriage annulled a month ago. I do not see why I need to marry again for a mistake that the Council had thrown at me. I willingly gave up my right to choose a wife that all Tennebrisians get. I gave that to you, to the High Council, and you selected Scotlind Rumor. It's not my fault that you have chosen unwisely, so I don't think you should be able to force me to—"

I was cut off by Synder raising his hand. "It is not our fault that you were unable to satisfy her in bed and that she sought pleasure elsewhere."

I bristled.

My father, now the Commander, spoke up for the first time during this horrible meeting, "How about a compromise? You will marry Reagan, son. Your betrothal will be announced immediately. However, given the nature of the shortened timeline, you do not have to marry her prior to your coronation. As long as you two swear before the Goddess that you will be wed, I do not see why you can't have a longer engagement if that pleases you."

"Here-here," someone else chimed in.

"A vote then," Synder said tautly. This clearly wasn't part of his plan. "All in favor of our Prince marrying Reagan prior to his coronation as our tradition demands, raise your hand."

I watched as hands flew in the air. I counted thirteen.

"Now, all in favor of Prince Noren marrying Reagan after his coronation with the agreement to become engaged immediately." The rest of the hands shot up. I sagged in my seat, happy that I didn't have to marry Reagan right now. I couldn't go through another wedding. The thought made me sick, not when Scotlind's and mine still haunted me.

Whatever speck of relief I felt about not having to get married immediately was washed away. I was furious that they were still forcing me to remarry at all. Some sick, twisted part of me clung to the idea of getting Scotlind back. But this… marrying Reagan, made that dream seem like it was already dead.

My sweaty hands clamped in fists under the table. When I didn't have the poison working through my veins, when my head was clear, and I could think straight, I'd figure out a plan to get out of it. I'd worry about it later. Just one thing at a time, and right now, I needed to stay alive.

"It's settled then," Synder said. "Sie Noren and Reagan Baker are to be engaged and will be wed at his coronation. I'll arrange for an engagement banquet right away to announce the good news." Synders words didn't pass by me. He said our wedding would be the day of my coronation—when he still held power and had a say. And my coronation was fast approaching. Fuck me.

"Now, for the other matter at hand. Where is your claimed second?"

I tensed. "I gave him time off since he doesn't officially become my second until I am crowned."

"Be that as it may, but if he is still missing at the time of your coronation, I will name your second for you."

"He will be there," I replied, and I fucking hoped it was true.

SEVEN
SCOTLIND

I woke up to high pitch screaming. My body shot upright as I covered my ears from the bleeding screech. My voice grew raw and hoarse, taking me a moment to realize it was coming from my own throat.

As I adjusted to the morning light, I noticed Patricia staring at me, eyes flaring with concern.

"Sorry," I scratched out once I recovered and remembered where I was. A bed. I was in a bed, in a room. I was not shoved and pressed into a tub, unable to breathe. I didn't wake up with my neck bent and my legs stiff. I wasn't permanently forced into a fetal position in a cage. I was out.

I stretched longingly.

"No apologies needed, dear," and I swore Patricia's voice became hoarse before she cleared her throat and then continued, "Tezya had breakfast brought up to your chambers. You are to eat here and then I am to bring you to the training center. You don't have much time, so hurry up."

I slowly peeled myself out of the soft bed and shuffled toward the small table and chairs that Patricia had set up. Everything hurt, and I had to remind myself that the pain was temporary. That the worst was hopefully behind me, even if it didn't feel that way.

I looked down at the meal, and my stomach curled and flipped inside itself. I was starving. I still had nothing in my stomach after I threw up the dinner I ate with Tezya last night. I spent the night bent over a bucket once I was escorted back to my chambers.

But despite my hunger, the thought of eating now made me nauseous. I wasn't used to eating so early in the morning, so soon after my nightmare. I wasn't used to eating at all anymore. I looked at the spread of meats, oatmeal, eggs, croissants, and bread. My gaze flickered over a massive amount of pastries—the same ones I moaned over yesterday.

"I'll eat this later," I said as I reached for a banana, tucking it under my side. "I'm ready to go now."

Patricia eyed me closely, then looked longingly at the flakey croissants.

"You can help yourself to anything. I only want this." I raised the fruit for emphasis. My maid hesitated for only a second before scooping up the croissants and shoveling them into her mouth. I swallowed down a giggle as crumbs peppered her thin lips.

"Follow me, dear," she muffled between bites.

My stomach turned in knots just thinking about the training and what was expected of me. I was grateful and excited even. Anything was better than that cell. I knew I couldn't pass up the chance to build my body back to health and become strong again. Especially now that Kole was on Luxian soil. I didn't have a choice.

As Patricia led me through the winding halls, I realized it would be a miracle if she knew where she was going. She kept muttering to herself and repeating turns out loud like she was memorizing a pattern. Maybe it was her old age that made her mind slowly decay. I never knew that could happen to Advenians, but I also had never seen one who looked as withered as she did.

"*Shit.*" My eyes widened at the curse coming out of her mouth. She seemed to realize it too, then added, "Wrong turn. Sorry, dear, follow me... um..." She put a finger to her lips as she longingly searched the hallway, "This way."

I turned my head in the direction she was pointing, but my eyes kept wandering all around. I didn't mind the detour. I couldn't stop staring at everything we passed. I knew I probably looked like an outsider, but luckily only a few Luxians crossed our path. I was slightly disappointed when they didn't even look my way. I wanted to see their eyes, to see what colors they had.

The castle at Lux was unlike anything I'd ever seen. Such a contrast to the cold darkened one in Tennebris. Lux's castle was bright and cheerful and full of lights and ornate decorations. Paintings framed with silver swirls filled every inch of the walls, consisting mostly of Advenians with silver eyes or drawings of the ocean. It added color and life into the space.

The entire castle held the extravagance that the single Throne Room had in the Dark Kingdom, making me feel like I was living inside a diamond. The only similarity between the two castles were the excessive amounts of windows. But unlike Tennebris, Lux's windows had no glass, making it open to the elements. I could feel the warm breeze as I walked. The curtains flapped against the wind as wafts of briny and citrus scents filled my nose. Sunlight dripped through the open panes, adding a glow and shine to the speckled floors.

After what felt like forever, we arrived in front of a pair of alabaster doors. Gauging the distance we traveled, it seemed like we were somewhere toward the back of the castle. Either that or my maid had me walk in circles. I cursed my body as I already felt drained. The walk alone was taxing, and I didn't know how I would make it through whatever training with a Luxian meant.

"Tezya will be waiting through these doors. I will be outside after your training is finished to walk you back to your room," Patricia said with another awkward curtsy. I honestly thought I had just as good of a chance of finding my chamber as she did.

"Thank you," I attempted a smile but failed miserably. I stole a steadying breath before pressing into the door and opening it. I took one step inside, allowing the door to shut behind me, and froze. The banana fell from my sweaty hand and dropped onto the floor, but I didn't notice—didn't care—because the largest bath I'd ever seen was directly in the center of the room. The tub was carved into the floor, making it so that if you took a wrong step, you would fall right in. I'd never seen a bath that was built in the ground, nor a bath so grand and large. It was the size of the bedroom they had me staying in.

Then my eyes caught sight of the floor. White tile. The same tile that my head was pressed against in the tub. The same tile that was in my childhood bedroom. Flashes of that night peppered my vision. The masked men, the smoke wafting into my room, the flames looming just outside. Then of Kole drowning me, of everything that happened in that warehouse, of Sie.

My back slammed against the door as I retreated further, wanting to put as much space between me and this place as I could. I couldn't do this.

Tezya appeared from a door I hadn't noticed before. When I finally looked up, I saw that there were three doors toward the back of the room, all the same, leading to other areas. He stalked over to me, assessing my appearance. He was either oblivious to my apparent distress or didn't care.

"You need to change," he spoke firmly. That was when I realized what I was wearing. I was in such a rush to leave my room this morning that I never changed out of my nightgown or even washed off the sweat from my nightmare. I felt disgusting and was sure I looked worse. With my sweat plastered to my skin, the nightgown was even thinner and more constricting than the tan dress I was forced to wear last night.

"I... I don't have clothes," I said softly as he closed the gap between us. I didn't have it in me to be embarrassed, not when all I could see was that bath. I tried to focus on his form and not the room we were in. He bent down to pick up the banana I had dropped and extended the fallen fruit out to me.

"The last door to the left is the changing chambers. There's workout and swimming attire for you there. I want to start on your abilities, so put the swimsuit on."

"No," I blurted as I grabbed the banana from him. "I'm not going in that bath."

"That's not a bath. It's a pool, and yes, you are," he ordered.

"Please, I can't swim." I stuttered pitifully.

"Can't or won't?" When I didn't answer, he sighed before adding, "I'm here to train you. In order for this to work, you need to be honest with me."

"Won't," I admitted, my voice barely audible. To my relief, he didn't ask me why. He just looked at me like I was some mystery to uncover or some experiment to be tested.

"Fine. For now, change into the workout gear, but you will be getting into that water."

I scurried to the third door before he could change his mind. I walked embarrassingly close to the edge of the wall, avoiding the looming doom of sinking water in the middle of the room.

A crystal chandelier hung over my head in the changing room, illuminating the pale blue walls. A set of gray clothes were folded on one of the light wooden floating cabinets. I reached for it, not even bothering to look at whatever swimming attire was acquired for me as I stripped out of my sticky nightgown and threw it over the bench. I left the banana untouched next to my clothes, knowing that there was no way I could stomach to eat it now, not with that bath just outside the door.

The pants that Tezya left for me were the exact same shade of gray as the shirt, and they were both skin-tight. I had to pry them over my legs which surprised me as my legs were basically twigs now. They left little to the imagination, which I was gathering was a theme for Luxian fashion. The shirt, luckily, was slightly looser and not as constricting, but I could still make out the swell of my breasts through the material in the mirror. I was just thankful that it didn't show my ribs through the fabric. I didn't dare look at my face as I moved my hands to braid my hair down my back. The effort from just holding my hands up for that long was taxing. I hated the reminder of what I'd become.

Tezya was watching me as I emerged from the changing room. "We are going to do both physical training and ability training. You are too weak right now, so we'll work our way up to the harder stuff…"

Frustration coursed through me. I couldn't stand to hear him talk about how weak I was, even if he was just stating facts. He pointed toward the first door. "There's a private gymnasium inside there."

"What's a gymnasium?"

He looked at me, puzzled, before he answered. "Think of it as a training ground, but it's purely designed to build strength instead of just fighting people. Different machines target specific muscles, so you can focus on any weak spots you might have in your form."

I nodded, not really sure what he meant by machines, but I guessed I would find out soon enough. The athletic arena in Lake-Wood was just a large, open room with mats, and when I trained with Peter, we were always outside.

"This entire space is closed off to the public, so only you and I can enter. We will be able to practice here without fear of someone seeing us or noticing that you have abilities or recognizing you as the Tennebrisian ex-Princess."

"Goddess forbid our kind knows the truth for once," I grunted under my breath. His lips tightened into a thin line, but he didn't comment or give any other indication that he heard me as I followed him through the door. My eyes widened as I took in the *private gym* he was referring to. It was massive and had two stories. An open stairwell gave way to a circular loop on the top level. I recognized some of the free weights and weapons that were scattered across the bottom level, but there were a lot of things I'd never seen before. It must have been the machines he was talking about. It was all foreign, except… my eyes snagged on the fighting arena in the far corner.

Tezya didn't give me time to fully ogle. "Go to the upper level. It's an indoor track. Run until I tell you to stop."

"Running inside?" I'd never heard of that before, and I desperately wanted to go outside again after I was on his balcony. "Can't I run outside?"

"No." He nodded toward the staircase, and when I didn't move, he sighed. "You can't go outside because one, you aren't allowed. And two, your body can't handle it right now. Even if I were to let you, it's too hot, and you'll give yourself a heat stroke. You're too malnourished and dehydrated."

I glowered at him but did as I was told. My thighs felt heavy by the time I finally climbed the stairs and made it to the track. A bead of sweat had already started to drip down my forehead, and I didn't even begin yet. I glanced down at Tezya. He hadn't moved from his position on the lower level. His arms were crossed over his chest, exposing bulging muscles. His head was tilted slightly up as his clear eyes pinned me to my spot. He arched his brow, and I realized that I was staring at him. Again.

With that embarrassing thought, I started to run, or I tried to. I was slow, too slow, but I kept moving my legs. I doubted anyone would call it a run. I was pretty sure that Tezya could *walk* faster than my poor attempt at it.

I huffed in frustration. I used to fly across the ground. Running was my escape every morning back at LakeWood. I loved feeling the breeze on the back of my neck, although I always wished it was a warm breeze instead of the harsh winds of Tennebris. And here I was, finally in Lux, running—walking—but I was stuck inside. In here, it was too stuffy, and I was all too aware of the pale, blue eyes that kept following my steps.

Just when I almost made it one lap around the track, I tripped over my own feet and stumbled forward. Stretching my arms out, I tried to catch the fall but landed flat on my stomach. My face planted into the weird texture that made up the floor.

Scolding myself, I slowly peeled myself off the ground, that was neither hard nor soft but still managed to hurt. A quick glance down at my knee told me that I had landed hard. I ripped a hole through the ridiculous pair of too-thin pants I was wearing. Red started to bubble around the hole. A subtle burning sensation spread across my forearms and cheek, and I was sure without looking that I had abrasions growing there too.

I shook my head and started running again. *Smooth, Scottie.* When Tezya finally ordered me to stop, I was embarrassed. I was wheezing from the effort and completely drenched in sweat. My clothing clung to my body as I walked down the stairs, gripping the railing with all my weight. I sat down on one of the benches on the lower level as Tezya handed me a glass of water.

"That was pathetic."

"Yeah, well, I couldn't exactly go for a run in my cell, so I would really, really appreciate it if you stopped with the comments," I snapped back as I gulped down the water in one go. Most of the contents missed my lips, adding to the watery mixture of sweat over my shirt.

"You didn't eat breakfast."

"What?" I replied, startled. How did he even know that?

"You're starving."

"How do you know that I'm starving or that I didn't eat?" I seethed.

"One, I can hear your stomach gargle, and two, your entire body is shaking. Besides not being able to workout in your previous condition, you shouldn't be *that* weak. I told you that you needed proper nourishment and rest to keep up with my training. So you need to eat. You are in control if you remain weak from now on, but your body needs fuel." He paused for a moment, seeming to think something over before adding, "And besides, I just know. I have a sense about that sort of thing, so don't question me again. You have to eat, then we will continue."

"You have a sense for when people are starving?" I snapped, unable to hide the sneer in my voice. It pissed me off that he was mocking me for being weak when his people and his King made me this way. And I really could have used his *senses* when I was locked in the cage with nothing to eat for twenty-seven days.

"I have a sense about a lot of things. Let's go," he said as he stalked out of the gym. I stumbled after him on shaky legs, my mind puzzling over what the heck he meant by that, but I was too tired to ask. He led me toward the middle of the three doors in the main area. It was the smallest room yet. It held one table with six chairs tucked around it. Along the wall were cabinets that made up a miniature kitchen.

Tezya opened one of the doors and grabbed an apple out of it before tossing it over to me. I bit into it. The crunch and my chewing seemed too loud for the awkward silence that followed. Neither of us took a seat, and he just watched me eat. His weird, unrelenting gaze gave me the chills and would come off as creepy if he wasn't so attractive. I hated to even admit that in my head. He was just here to train me, so why did I keep staring at his muscles, his eyes, his scar... and worse, he was a Luxian soldier. This man probably killed the Advenians who fought for a fair and just life. A soldier who, according to Sie, fought *against* the rebellion, against everything I wanted.

An ache formed in my gut as I thought of Sie. His abandonment felt worse than my time in the dungeons. It left a huge gaping hole in my heart. It hurt me more than I'd like to admit. I took a breath and pushed him from my mind like I did many times before when my thoughts drifted toward him.

After I ate the apple down to the core, I followed Tezya back out of the kitchen, but to my dread, we stopped there and didn't go into the gym again. He halted in front of the large trap of water.

"I told you that I'm not getting into that bath."

His mouth quirked into a half smile. "And I told you that it's not a bath. It's a pool, but to be honest, you could really use a bath."

I rolled my eyes and crossed my arms over my chest. I noticed him following the movement before he met my gaze.

When I didn't answer, he added, "If you can give me an honest answer as to why you won't go in there, I won't make you. For today, at least."

I thought about just telling him. There shouldn't be anything wrong with what haunted me. That was what my counselor said to me when I was little and I wouldn't go near a fireplace or refused to burn a candle. She told me that it was just the stress from the trauma, and it was normal for some things to trigger it, that it would take time to heal. Was this the same thing?

No, it wasn't. It was pathetic that I couldn't even properly bathe. He probably thought I was stupid for being scared of the element that I possessed. I should be able to control water, but yet, it was controlling me.

If I just told him, I could avoid this panic rising in me. We could go back into the gym so I could work on training my body. But I couldn't get myself to admit it. I couldn't form the words to say that I was scared of the water. He should know anyway. It was cruel of him to make me speak it out loud. He was there when Kole made me show my memories to the King. When I was forced to relive the night he drowned me.

"You can't make me go in," was all I said in return.

He eyed me carefully in that annoying analytical way of his that made me uncomfortable. I shifted on my feet. "Yes, I can, but I would prefer not to force you to. I report to the King, who instructed me to train you and help you discover what your abilities are. All we know right now is that you possess something of water, but you are scared to death of it. In order to master your ability, you have to let go of that fear. The first step to that is admitting what your fear is. You shouldn't be ashamed of it."

"I'm not ashamed..." I started to say but stopped mid-sentence because I realized I was. It frustrated me that Kole affected me. It bothered me that I couldn't function normally because of what he did to me.

"And," Tezya said with a half smile, his scar rising slightly, "I could always just pick you up and throw you into the water."

My mouth gaped open as I took a step back from him. "You wouldn't dare."

"Oh, I would," his smile grew, and I couldn't tell if he was serious or just messing around with me, but I wasn't about to stick around to find out. "It's just you and me in here, Rumor. No one will help you. No one will stop me from doing just that. Not even you."

I ran.

72

I didn't care that I looked absolutely pathetic and crazy. His expression made it seem like he was completely serious, and there was no way I was sticking around for him to throw me into that water.

I darted for the gym door and slammed it shut just as I saw his massive body sprinting after me. I fumbled for a lock and cursed loudly when I realized there were none. He was at the door before I knew it. I darted toward the stairs, knocking over weights, balls, mats, anything I could get my hands on to try to slow him down.

I made it up four steps before callused hands gripped my ankles, and I started to fall. He caught me around the waist before my face landed on the edge of the steps. I yelped as he swung me up against his chest. My legs draped over his arm while the other pushed open the door. He was only carrying me with one hand—one hand. I bristled as I struggled to escape his grasp, annoyed and disappointed in myself that I was utterly helpless against him. He didn't seem flustered at all, yet I was breathing in air like I had just learned how.

He slowed as he reached the water. My body tensed up in response. "Please, don't," I begged.

"Why," he pushed.

"Because," I started and stopped. I took a deep breath. "Because I haven't been able to go in the water... since that night with... with him... when he..."

"Tried to drown you," he finished for me.

"Yes."

"But he won't ever do that to you again. No one will. You have water abilities. Learn them, master them, and no one will be able to harm you with it."

When I didn't answer right away, he added, "You need to overcome your fear."

"Why do you even care? I thought you were only training me because of the King's orders."

"It doesn't matter why I'm training you. I am. The King wants to know your abilities, yes, but you can use this to help yourself. Take advantage of the situation you are in. And in case you weren't aware,

Rumor, we can't really practice your water abilities without being in the water."

"It's Scottie," I said softly as he slowly set my feet back down on the ground. I was still standing too close to him, too close to the water.

"I like Rumor better," he said. When I rolled my eyes, he added, "Well, *Rumor*, let's see what you can do."

EIGHT

TEZYA

THE GIRL HAD BEEN SITTING by the edge of the pool for the past hour. Her legs were crossed and curled into each other as she stared at the water. I'd instructed her to see if she could manipulate the water like she did at the lake from her memories, but so far, all she had done was gawk at it or at me when she thought I wasn't looking. I was pretty sure she didn't even try to access her abilities once.

It seemed odd to me that she could practice so freely at the lake with the Dark Prince but was terrified by the pool. Was it the fact that this was an enclosed space? Or was it the company?

I would have to try taking her to the ocean in the next couple of days once I secured a private spot to practice. Maybe being outside in the open air would help her feel more comfortable. I prayed that was the case because if Sie was her grounding point and the only reason she could practice her abilities, I had no idea how to help her with that. She wouldn't be getting back together with him.

"You should try putting your feet in the water," I suggested as I slowly, cautiously approached her, trying my best not to startle her.

"What?" she cocked her head to the side and glanced up at me as I took the seat next to her.

"You aren't trying because you're scared."

"I'm not scared..." she started, but I held a finger over her mouth to silence her. I quickly drew it away, feeling the exact fullness of them beneath my touch.

"You are scared. I told you before that I have a sense about certain things. You can't hide your emotions from me, so don't bother trying."

"Is that your ability then? To know people's emotions?"

"Something like that, but there's more to it," I answered. I caught her eyeing my left wrist, where my rank five brand was burned into my flesh. She audibly swallowed before looking back at the pool.

"Fine then. I am afraid. I don't know what you want me to do about it."

"I want you to learn that this water won't hurt you. That the water will, in fact, do the opposite. It will help protect you when you call to your ability. I want you to learn that it won't harm you ever again."

"And I am supposed to do that by putting my feet in the water?"

"Yes," I said, looking down at her. Even sitting cross-legged, she was small in stature. I had not seen such a small Advenian, other than my sister, in a while.

I tried to hide my smile as she slowly peeled her shoes off and rolled her pants to her knees. It was a good start if she was willing to try so soon. My eyes snagged on her right calf as she shimmied closer to the edge. Her skin was mutilated there, a permanent burn. I remembered seeing her leg raw and incinerated crawling on that beach, but the King started her interrogation in Tennebris. He didn't show how she got that, how she was taken from her home. It made me curious about what unfolded that night and why the King wasn't concerned about it.

"I won't let you fall in," I said to her because I think she needed to hear it.

She nodded, then slowly lowered her legs. A soft gasp left her lips as her toes hit the water first, then her breathing turned ragged. Slowly, she closed her eyes and sank her calves in, submerging the mangled area of her skin from my view. With her eyes still closed, I took the opportunity to study her face. Her lips were pressed tightly

76

together, her eyebrows were thick and scrunched so close to one another. Now that the grime from the dungeons was mostly washed off, I noticed she had freckles scattered across her nose.

"Good," I coaxed softly, not wanting to cause her to sink further into a panic. "The water won't hurt you. It's a part of you. Think of your ability as a connection. It's an extension of yourself. You are one and the same. In order to master your ability, you need to master your fear. If you are scared of it, it will control you. If you can overcome it, you will control the water."

Her eyelids gently fluttered open. Her lashes elongated around her bright sapphire eyes. The reflection in the water made them appear like they were glowing. Even with the bruises beneath them and her hollowed cheekbones, she was absolutely stunning. I could see glimpses of who she used to be.

"Now what?" she asked hesitantly.

"Now nothing. I want you to sit here until you no longer have a pained expression on your face."

"I don't—"

"You do," I interrupted. She was the most stubborn person I'd met, and I barely knew her. This training was going to be a lot harder than I thought. "I want you to sit here until this feels comfortable for you. Until you are no longer scared of just soaking your feet in the water. That's your assignment. No more training today. I'll send for your maid and have her wait outside. When you are finished, return to your chambers, eat, and then get a good night's rest. Tomorrow we have to do some testing before we train again. Meet me at dawn."

She nodded her head nonchalantly, but I could see the fear shining in her eyes. This was difficult for her, but she didn't seem like the type to shy away from a challenge.

———

"You're late," Brock said when I finally made it to the training grounds.

"Yeah, I know. Sorry, mate. Did anyone give you a hard time?"

"Only a few." My friend shrugged, but I could tell he was hurting. His body was stiff, and his knuckles had a layer of dried blood on them.

I hated that the soldiers liked to challenge him when I was gone. I knew it was a lot worse than he let on. I scanned the group before us. They were hours into their training for the day, but not nearly finished. It was my job to train all the new recruits, and from time to time, make sure the seasoned soldiers knew their place. I honestly hated it. I hated everything about the army, but the only saving grace I felt was when Brock and I brought the men off their high horses.

"Polaris?" I asked as I nodded toward him. His brown hair was pulled into a tight bun, exposing blood dripping from both of his ears.

"Yeah," Brock admitted. "The prick doesn't know when to quit." As if he knew we were talking about him, he glared Brock's way, but quickly got back in line when he saw me next to him.

"He hates that you're better than him. I hope you gave it to him good."

"I did."

"Good." I smirked. We only had another six weeks with him before the King recruited him to his personal guard. He took all the strongest soldiers for himself, and Polaris was a lethal rank five. One of the worst I'd seen in a long time. He was too similar to the King for my liking, just as sadistic and power hungry.

"So, where have you been?" Brock gestured toward the field ahead of us. "What's been occupying your time that's more important than all of this?" It was meant to be a joke. Brock and I both hated being soldiers, having to spend every second of our day with men we despised. There were a few soldiers that I admired, Brock being one of them, but most of them were brainwashed by the King. To make it into the Luxian army was a rite of passage. It became a stamp of approval to Lux, making it known that you were better, stronger than the rest of society. I found it to be a vindictive cult.

"The King ordered me to train the Tennebrisian girl." If Brock was shocked he didn't show it. He always held his emotions back, mastering a blank expression was crucial to survive. We'd both learned that the hard way.

"Dovelyn told me about her. She said that you were there when they got her from Tennebris."

"I was." I didn't add more. I didn't want to talk about it. It'd been a long time since I'd let my emotions get the best of me, and seeing how the Dark Prince treated his so-called love of his life made my blood boil. It was the cherry on top when I saw everything else he'd done to her during her interrogation.

"Dovelyn also told me that the girl looked one second away from death."

"She wasn't wrong." I blew out a breath. "She's even worse now. The King's men tortured her for information about the Dark Prince."

"I hate them." Brock's voice was bone-chilling. He had every reason to hate them, sometimes I thought, his reasons were worse than mine.

"You and me both." The King's men were hand selected and they were some of the most vile Advenians I knew. "Speaking of them, I've arranged for Lansting to come back to training."

Brock nodded. He knew what I wasn't saying—make sure he pays.

"I'm going to be missing a lot of practices," I added into the silence, after a minute of us watching the soldiers train.

"How many?"

I looked over at him. I felt terrible knowing that he would suffer from my new task too. Whenever I was around, no one dared to act out of place. I wasn't sure if it was from my appearance—the only good thing that came from my array of scars—or my reputation and status with the King. My friend, on the other hand, never caught a break. He was second in command and was one of the best fighters I knew, but men like Polaris liked to prove they were better than him. "Almost all of them," I answered. "I'll try to make it to most of the evening sessions, but I'll be missing all morning and afternoon ones for the next ten weeks."

He nodded. "What does he want with the girl?"

I sighed. "What he always wants. What this is all about," I

gestured to the half beaten men scattered across the open field. They were drenched in sweat and covered from head to toe in bruises. "The King wants to know how strong she is. He wants to know what her powers are."

"And what are they?"

"She has water abilities, but I'm not sure how strong she is with them as she never practiced. The King believes that she has two abilities though."

"What do you think?"

"I think he might be right."

"And you only have ten weeks to find out if she has more?"

I nodded.

"And if she comes up with only water as her ability after the ten weeks, you'll be punished?"

I nodded again. Brock and I both knew the brutality of the King firsthand. "He threatened as much," I said, "but I think the girl's punishment will be worse."

"Does she know that? Maybe it will help motivate her."

I sighed. "It's only been a day. I'll see how it goes." But I knew I was damned. It took Brock nearly fifteen years before he discovered his second ability, and the Tennebrisian girl had only nine weeks and six days left.

NINE
SCOTLIND

I REMAINED at the edge of the pool until my toes wrinkled and turned to prunes. I stared at the water, repeating the mantra in my head, *"I am not afraid of you,"* over and over again. I thought about what Tezya said to me, how my ability could save me, not harm me. How my ability was a part of me, an extension of my soul. I tried to think of the water like I would a limb. I wasn't afraid of my arm, so why would I be afraid of this? But whenever I thought I was making headway, the tile would flash under the surface, and I would be right back at square one.

By the time Patricia finally came into the private training area, night had fallen. I wasn't used to the sudden change in light during such a small time span. When the shadows came out each night to steal the sun away, it felt like a reminder that I had failed. I definitely hadn't mastered my fear of enclosed water. The only thing I could say I accomplished was that, by the end of the day, I stopped hyperventilating *every* time I looked at it—I only did it *sometimes*.

When I got back to my chambers, I still opted for the washcloth bath. Then, I stuffed my face with dinner, begging Patricia to stay and join me, offering up my rolls as enticement. I'd been alone for so long that it felt nice to have someone to talk to. I enjoyed her nonsense and her kindness. It felt like I was tempting fate by having her assigned to me. I was surprised that the Lux King gave me someone so nurturing. I'd never known a mother's love, or at least I couldn't remember it, but I assumed it would have been similar to Patricia. The King of Lux didn't seem like the type to notice or care about that sort of thing.

But maybe they gave me her because of her age. She talked in riddles and seemed just as confused by the castle and Luxian traditions as I was. Maybe they didn't even pay heed to their servants or their tasks. In school, we learned that all zeroes were servants here. I didn't doubt that they weren't treated fairly. Either way, I was thankful for her. Her company felt like a gift from Pylemo—it felt like the only thing that went my way in such a long, long time. I was almost scared to like Patricia or my current situation. I didn't want to get too comfortable only for it to be taken away from me like everything else had. I knew better than to believe that whatever treatment I was getting, that whatever this was, would last.

But for the moment, I was happy to be out of that cage, happy to have a bed I could sleep in, happy that I could stretch my legs. All I could do was live for one moment at a time, and right now, my focus was captured by the fact that when I went to bed that night, I didn't remember dreaming. I was too exhausted from my training with Tezya to even recall if I had a nightmare. I woke up sweat free for the first time in months. It was exhilarating.

I rushed out of bed, only to sag slightly as I stood. My legs were wobbly and sore. All I did yesterday was run, well, walk-run. That was it, and yet I was *this* sore.

My face scrunched. I used to run for miles on end every morning back in Tennebris. I ran for fun, and now I couldn't even run a couple of laps around the track without my body aching in protest. But at least I'd slept, really slept.

Patricia forced me to eat something small before she let me leave my room. I didn't really want Tezya saying that I needed food and watching me while I ate again, so I obliged. We walked in silence. I still didn't know my way to the private gym, so I was surprised when we approached Tezya in a random hallway. He was leaning against the wall with one leg pressed against it, and his arms crossed over his chest.

I briefly recalled him telling me that I had to do testing beforehand, but I thought that was a part of the training. Now I didn't know what he meant by it. I cursed myself for not asking.

Tezya regarded my maid for a moment longer than I thought was normal, then said, "Leave us."

Patricia's fists clenched at her sides, and she looked like she was about to say something to him. But in a split second, she changed, her wrinkles smoothing as her face went blank. She glanced at me once before waddling off. It wasn't until we were alone that he turned to me. "Good morning, Rumor," he drawled, pushing off the wall. "Did you sleep well?"

I nodded my head, still surprised that I had. "What are we doing?"

"The King ordered physical tests for you. You spent almost two months in different dungeons, so he wants to make sure you are healthy. He also wants to confirm that you aren't carrying Prince Noren's child."

"What?" I snapped, appalled at what I had just heard. "Wasn't going through my memories proof enough that I'm not?"

"He was a compulsion user, Rumor. He could have slept with you, then compelled you to forget it ever happened. The King only went through *your* memories. There's a lot that's up for interpretation when doing that."

"*I. Am. Not. Carrying. His. Child.*" I seethed, making sure to enunciate each word slowly. The fact that he even thought that could be a possibility—that Sie could do such a thing. I already felt so violated. They had already taken everything from me—had *seen* everything on the monitor screens—but it wasn't enough.

"Rumor, I'm sorry, but you have to get the testing done."

"Sie would never do that to me. He's not..." I stopped myself from saying that he wasn't a bad person. I was in Lux's territory now. I had to be careful with what I said. I wasn't sure how close Tezya was to the King. For all I knew, this could be the test. I also didn't know what I believed anymore. I didn't think Sie would do such a thing, but then again, I had never imagined he'd do what he's already done. I didn't know what he was capable of anymore. He sent me to a prison when I thought he was the one person I could finally trust. He got me to open up about my past—about *everything*—and then he handed me over to the Lux King as his prisoner, to the very person he warned me to stay away from.

"It doesn't matter. The King won't trust your memories alone. Like I said, it's not foolproof. Your memories showed that you two didn't sleep together on your wedding night. That's not to say that you didn't on a different night. The memory compulsion can't pull up every memory you have. The user has to have specific dates in mind. The Lux King went over the dates with Kole before you were even brought into the room. And even if you don't think the Dark Prince is capable of compelling you, the King won't believe it. If we take his compulsion out of the question, you still could have been drunk one night and forgotten about it. Or it simply could have happened on a night they didn't look into. There could be numerous reasons as to why you two sleeping together didn't show on the screen or as to why you don't remember."

"Why I don't remember? You talk as if you are so sure we had sex and that I simply can't recall it. Last I remembered, you weren't involved in our relationship," I snapped, then internally crawled inward on myself, trying hard not to dwell on the fact that I said *relationship* like it was still a present thing. I hoped Tezya didn't pick up on it. I also tried not to think about the fact that if we did have sex that night, that entire room of Advenians would have watched us on those screens. Another kind of mortification started in my stomach as my gut twisted.

"Rumor, you two were married. It's abnormal to be wed and *not* have sex. Plus, you two performed the blood bond, and in your memories from the night at the warehouse and at the lake, Sie admitted to having his ability heightened when he was around you. That only happens to people that are soul bound by the blood oath. And in order for that to happen, you would have had to have had sex to lock the bond in place."

84

"So? Why does the King even care if I'm pregnant?" I asked. I knew that it was illegal, and that should be an answer in-and-of-itself, but it seemed like a big ordeal to go through all of this just to find out. According to ancient texts from Allium, a child conceived from both Kingdoms would die immediately upon birth. If the King wanted, he could just wait for that to happen, or he could have continued to let me rot in the cage I was in. I couldn't comprehend why he wanted to know so badly or why he even let me out in the first place.

"It's his order. We don't have a choice but to obey them. It should be a simple test," he diverted, not answering my question. I was just about to respond when the door swung open.

A tall, slender male with dark onyx hair stepped forward from a darkly lit room. As he came into the light, his eyes blood-red eyes met mine. "I presume this is Miss Rumor?" he asked Tezya, his voice rattling.

"Yes," Tezya replied casually, like we weren't just yelling at each other moments before. "Rumor, meet Semadar. He is the head healer in Lux and works for the King directly. He will be completing your testing today." Tezya turned to look at me. "I'll pick you up here after you're done so we can train."

Semadar nodded in respect toward Tezya, his head angling down just a fraction. Tezya glanced down at me one more time before turning away and leaving me utterly alone with the healer. I watched his figure disappear as he walked and rounded the corner.

When I glanced back at Semadar, any indication that this testing would go pleasantly vanished. "This way," he ordered tautly, his voice rattling deep as he opened the door to the darkly lit room.

———

HOURS LATER, I was finally allowed to leave Semadar's exam room. He poked and prodded at me more than I thought physically possible. Sampling my blood, collecting my urine, and hooking me up to more monitors that I didn't understand. I watched as lines and numbers appeared on the screens in pure fascination, having no idea what they meant. At one point, Prince Arcane came to collect the blood vials Semadar took. I had no idea what he planned to do with them. His cold, silver eyes assessed me once, but the quick gaze was so critical as if he knew everything about me from just one look. He pocketed my blood and left without uttering a word.

Tezya met me outside the healer's door as promised. He walked me to our private training center in silence with a thick, tan folder pressed into his side. I couldn't stop staring at it. Were the results from whatever tests the healer performed already back? And if so, what did they say? I didn't recognize any of the tests he ran on me. I had no idea what other information he collected beyond finding out if I was pregnant or not and giving my blood to the heir of the Luxian Kingdom.

"Well, do you believe me now?" I asked when we finally made it to the pool area. I purposely avoided looking at the water sunken into the floor, but I didn't shudder at it either.

"Believe you about what?" he asked as he set the folder aside. Everything in me tingled, wanting to rush to that folder and read what it entailed.

"About me not being pregnant?"

"Oh, that," he laughed. "The results should hopefully come back by the end of the week."

"I'm glad you find it amusing. I bet if I shoved a long silver object up you to test if you had sex, you wouldn't be laughing."

"Long silver object?" he asked, looking perplexed. He stopped laughing immediately once he met my hard, tightened gaze.

"Whatever object he shoved inside me to do the *tests*. I have no idea what he called it, something like a *specul*—I don't know. It was long and looked like a duck's beak when it opened up, and it had absolutely no business being inside of me. I can assure you that you would not be laughing if it was done to you." I cradled my lower abdomen thinking about the stupid device. It seemed more for torturing than to determine the nature of someone's virginity. My pelvic area gave way to an immense round of cramping afterward.

"Did Semadar hurt you?" he asked, his tone turned serious. His eyes flicked down to my stomach.

"Forget it," I said, not wanting to discuss it further and trying to hide my blush from his assessing gaze. "What are we working on today?"

He brushed it aside but worry still dotted his face, which I couldn't understand. "Running first. Then, I want you to start weight training. After lunch, we will work with your water abilities again."

I nodded as I made my way toward the door that held the gym with the track a floor above. My legs still ached from yesterday, and I couldn't imagine how added weight training would amplify my soreness, but I didn't complain as I climbed the steps this time.

I was drenched in sweat by the time I finished. Even more than yesterday, and I didn't think that was possible. The running went slightly better than the day before, and by that, I mean I still ran at the speed of a turtle, but I didn't fall flat on my face.

The weight training was the real embarrassment. It was made worse when Tezya decided to train with me. "What?" he smirked when he caught me staring at his now drenched shirt as he began working out alongside me. It was sticking to his abdomen, exposing ripped muscles beneath. "I figured if I'm stuck in here with you all day, I'd at least workout."

I nodded and tried my best to focus on the whopping five pound weights I held—and struggled with—while purposely not looking at what he was doing. After our workout, when we were both covered in sweat, we moved to abilities training.

The rest of the week followed in a similar manner. Physical training in the morning, lunch, then ability training in the evening. Afterward, Patricia and I ate dinner together in my chambers. I usually asked her about her life, and I swore that she had a different story every single night and stuttered every time I asked her to elaborate. But I enjoyed her constant presence.

Then, I would dreamlessly sleep from pure exhaustion. Which, in turn, made me train harder and harder every day. I pushed my body to its breaking point, thoroughly exhausting myself with every single training session both physically and mentally. The thought of not having a nightmare kept propelling me to dive headfirst into my training with Tezya. If I kept exerting myself, if I kept pushing, I could escape what haunted me. I could outrun the shadows that crept into the crevices of my body and clung to my existence.

The first week was only focused on discovering the extent of my water powers. Tezya claimed there was no use finding out what other abilities I had if I couldn't even control the power I already knew about. I still refused to go in the pool, so it limited what I could do. Tezya hounded over and over that he wanted to see how long I could hold my breath, how deep I could submerge myself, and if I swam faster than normal. Which, due to my still current fear of the water, we could do none of those things.

At least by now I managed to feel *alright* sitting by the edge of the pool, and on some days, I created a small wave or moved the water into the palm of my hand.

By the end of the first week, Tezya remarked, "You know this would be a lot more enjoyable if we actually went in the pool." I couldn't deny that cooling off in the water sounded appealing. We were both drenched in sweat from our workout this morning, and the room was growing sticky, but every time I thought about jumping in, my lungs would burn, and Kole's laughter would fill my ears.

I shook my head, trying to get Kole out of it. "You can go in if you want. Don't let me stop you."

I expected him to refuse my offer, but he didn't. My mouth gaped open as he reached up and pulled his shirt off, then shrugged off his pants, tossing both to the side. Cool water splashed me as he jumped into the pool. I watched as he dove under and waited with my breath held until he re-emerged on the surface.

He shook out his hair, some water droplets spraying off him before he ran his fingers through it, pushing the wet strands out of his eyes, revealing the full extent of both scars on his face. The one was a small knick through his right eyebrow, stopping just above his pale eye. The other was all consuming. I had to force myself not to stare at it. I wondered if he got that a lot, people gawking at his face. I wondered if he hated it in the same way I hated when people stared at my zero brandings—I was the only Advenian with two.

I forced my eyes away from his scars as they drifted down his body still submerged in the pool. I'd never seen another Advenian of Lux in water before. I'd gotten glimpses of his markings during training from the sweat clinging to him, but this was different. His black markings were scattered across his body like paint, so vivid and purposeful. A mixture of thick black flames and spirals expanded over his broad chest, entwining up his neck, and crept over part of his face, covering the bottom half of his beautiful scar that continued past his jaw.

"It's nice. You should come in. Wash off some of that sweat," he smiled when he noticed me staring.

I swallowed once. Twice. Then shook my head and tried to focus on manipulating the water again. I asked Tezya earlier what Sie had said about my water abilities—how he thought I could only manipulate water that was already there and not create.

Tezya remarked that most Luxians could only manipulate if they possessed one of the elemental powers. He said that if someone could *create* an element, it automatically placed them at a rank four or five for how rare and powerful that was. So the likelihood that I could only manipulate was looking more and more prominent. Especially because every time I tried to create water without using the pool, I failed miserably.

So I continued to stare at the sunken tub, and now, actively trying to avoid staring at the half-naked male swimming in the water. But it didn't work. I could barely think straight, nonetheless concentrate on manipulating the water.

"Do you mind? I'm trying to practice." I finally said by his tenth lap.

"You were the one who gave me permission to swim." He smiled, his scar sparkled with the water.

"Right, but I didn't think that meant you would do so naked." I didn't mean to blush when I said it, but I could feel my cheeks heat.

"First off, I'm not naked. And secondly, you are going to be in for a rude awakening if you are this embarrassed about seeing me in my boxers." He laughed at me again. Then added, "Actually, this will be rather enjoyable for me."

Frustrated, I stopped concentrating on the small drop of water I moved from the pool and turned to look at him. The water made a small splash as it landed back into the depths of the surface. "What's that supposed to mean?"

"It means that most Luxians prefer to not wear much of anything. It's blistering hot here all year round. And they especially don't like wearing anything when going for a swim. Many of our beaches are clothing optional."

"And that will be enjoyable for you, how?"

He swam up to the ledge I was sitting crossed-legged at and placed his thick arms on the outside of the pool. The water spanned out and traveled past where his forearms now rested. "I think it will be fun to see your reaction to the people of Lux."

"I thought I wasn't allowed to go out in public."

He frowned slightly. "You aren't for the time being. But when you are allowed to, Rumor, I fully intend to be there to witness it."

TEN
SCOTLIND

THE NEXT MORNING, when Patricia woke me up at dawn, I noticed a small bag packed by the edge of my bed.

"What's the bag for?" I asked sleepily as I stretched out my sore, stiff, newly forming muscles. A long yawn followed shortly after. I was starting to recover more quickly since I was actually sleeping.

"I was instructed to pack a bag for you, dear."

"A bag? As in sleeping stuff?" I swallowed. Patricia didn't say anything but merely shook her wrinkled head, yes, her bright green eyes blazing into mine.

"Why?" I asked as casually as I could muster. Were they sending me away? The thought of leaving the castle thrilled me. I didn't want to be anywhere near the Lux King or his three offsprings, but I also didn't know where that left me.

"As part of your training," my maid answered, "Tezya is taking you somewhere."

"Where?"

"I don't know," she said as she gestured for me to get out of bed. "Come, dear. Quickly eat and get dressed, or we'll be late." Worry lingered in her eyes, which only added to my growing unease of the situation.

But she said *we*. "Are you coming with us then?"

"No," she snapped with enough of a bite to make me realize she wasn't happy about it either. "You and Tezya are going alone. Apparently, my presence would be a distraction from your training." She huffed, then grumbled lower so I barely heard her, "I'm not even allowed to know where you're going. *It's confidential,*" she mocked what I presumed was Tezya as she finished stuffing the bag.

I didn't want to stay anywhere alone with Tezya. My thoughts were jumbled enough with everything that happened with Sie. I needed to accept that I would never get to see him again, that I would never get closure for why he sent me here. I needed to accept everything that would never happen with him, and the one thing that did—he betrayed me. He didn't want me.

But Tezya... I couldn't deny that he was attractive, unholy attractive. I hated that I was drawn to him, that my eyes would always drift toward him while we were training. It was like he was made and crafted by the High Goddess herself in the exact image of everything that captivated me.

But I didn't need a distraction. I didn't *want* one. I couldn't afford one. I needed to focus on my training, focus on getting stronger, focus on staying alive. And I did not see how spending a night *alone* with him was going to get me any closer to that.

Why he thought my old, haggard maid would be a distraction over him was beyond me. Had he seen himself in a mirror? My maid, oddly enough, felt like a comfort, like someone I'd known for a while. I would never call her a distraction.

But if it would help me discover my powers, I had no choice but to go through with it. I didn't really have a choice in anything that was happening to me. I wasn't a fool. I knew I was still a prisoner. The King himself threatened to shove me back into that cage if I didn't obey him. It was enough motivation to get me to do whatever he wanted because I would rather die than be back in the Luxian dungeon.

What would happen if I didn't have a second Luxian ability? Or worse, if I couldn't even control the elemental power I did have? What if all I could do was move small drops of water at a time? Was my freedom banking on me being able to do more? I had grown up knowing that Lux was the stronger Kingdom. That they lived and breathed in high ranks. Would I only be free if I was strong enough? I tried not to dwell on it, but it was hard not to, especially since I was getting nowhere with my training.

When I finally finished eating with Patricia and completed my quick cloth bath, I stood by the door outside of my chambers, my jitters fermenting and festering into something stronger.

I managed a small smile as Tezya approached me. An overnight bag was slung over one of his broad shoulders. He had on his usual pair of black pants that didn't quite fit over his calves, and I wondered if he owned a pair of pants that did fit him properly. But what caught my attention was his tanned chest, completely exposed, as he opted for no shirt today.

"Is that necessary?" I asked as I nodded my head toward the direction of his sculpted abs. Yup. He was definitely a distraction.

His smile grew like he knew it. "We're going outside today and it's *hot*. Plus, I find it amusing how uncomfortable you get around not entirely clothed Advenians, and I wanted to see you squirm."

I rolled my eyes at him, but my breath hitched in itself, and I couldn't hide it. Outside. I was going outside today. Other than eating on Tezya's balcony on my first night out of the cage, I hadn't been allowed to leave the castle. I hadn't been allowed anywhere other than my own chambers, our training area, and the one time I went to the healer.

Excitement coiled inside me right alongside my fear and nerves. I wanted to see Lux. I wanted to see what everyone called the Golden City. It was ironic that the only thing that slightly resembled gold here was the sun. I envisioned the castle to look like the Tennebrisian Throne Room. Gilded and glistening.

But everything was varnished with silver and diamonds—at least the parts of the castle I had seen so far. I guess it made sense. Gold resembled the Tennebrisian markings. I shouldn't have been surprised if the castle was decorated in black to resemble the markings of Lux. But it wasn't. The King's cold, silver eyes flashed in my forevision, so clear and vivid that I thought he was actually staring at me. I half wondered if he had the vanity to adorn the entire castle to match them.

"You're taking me into town?" I asked, my voice rising, trying to push thoughts of the Lux King from my mind.

"Not exactly."

"Where are we going then?"

"Follow me, Rumor," he said with a grin, raising his scar, "and you'll see."

———

TEZYA WALKED me toward the back of the castle by the gardens. As soon as I was outside with the sun beating against my neck and the breeze blowing my hair, I sighed heavily. Closing my eyes, I tilted my head toward the yellow rays and spun around in circles, flaring my arms out.

I didn't care how I looked. Everything felt so fresh and open. The confinement that haunted me from the cage and the tub was in the far back of my mind. There were birds chirping loudly, all with different melodies and tunes. My nostrils flared as the briny, citrus scent invaded my senses.

Free. I felt free.

"Beautiful," Tezya breathed.

I opened my eyes and realized he was staring at me. Heat crept along my cheeks as I turned from his gaze. "I've dreamt of this. Of being back here. The warmth of the sun, the heat radiating from it, the breeze cooling everything off and the smell…" I inhaled deeply again, somehow unable to resist. "I wanted this when I was over there. Everything was cold and dark and just different. But this feels like… being *alive*."

He was still staring at me when I turned back to face him again. I didn't really know why I admitted all that to him. It sort of just blurted out. He was easy to talk to, and we'd made tons of small talk during the first week of training, but I still couldn't believe how easily I opened up. Even though his looks were daunting, he wasn't for some reason.

Tennebris made me reserved. I was constantly worried about people finding out about me. But being here, I felt the freedom I longed for with every scorching beat of the sun. I knew I wasn't really free, not even close. But in this moment, I could close my eyes and almost taste it.

And Tezya practically knew everything about me anyway. I didn't have to hide my back or fear him finding something out about me that would be detrimental. He'd seen it all that day on the monitors, so I didn't bother with pretending. I didn't have the energy for it anymore. And right now, I didn't have to be something I wasn't. I could just be me, even if all I was were broken, shattered bits.

"Being alive suits you," was all he replied before walking away. I didn't have time to analyze what he said as I scurried to keep up with his long strides. I could barely take in the sights around me as he moved at record speed.

I wanted to see it all. The beautiful garden we were in with its lush grass to the gorgeous pink roses and large sunflowers. I assumed all of it was manipulated by ground users, but it didn't take away from the uniqueness of it or how everything seemed to fit so perfectly together. Tall skinny trees were scattered everywhere with no branches or leaves on their thin trunks until they feathered out like a green fan at the very top. As I looked around, the nickname for the city clicked. It wasn't dubbed after the castle at all, but rather the town... the outside part of the Kingdom. There was color everywhere and the sun painted it all golden.

In the distance, behind the open, ashen castle, I caught a glimpse of the city. It was daylight, so I couldn't make out any of the lights that claimed to brighten the place at night as much as the sun, but I stopped and gasped as I took in the height of the buildings. They seemed to reach the clouds. Endless looming towers were scattered around the paved brick roads. It wasn't the boring, ugly bricks either that lined LakeWood or the jagged sandstone castle of Tennebris. No, this was something else. It felt like a different world.

Pink, red, and orange flags were sprinkled throughout the buildings with the Luxian symbol of the sun printed in the center. It added life and color along with the strange, narrowed trees and vibrant colored flowers that bloomed at every corner. If I squinted, I could just make out the bay in the distance, but I wanted to see the ocean. I *needed* to see the ocean.

Tezya came up behind me. "We have to keep moving if we are going to make it to the hut in time."

"The hut?" I repeated. He nodded his head once as he looked out onto his city, not meeting my eye.

"Come on, I want to be there before the sun sets."

Right. The sun sets each night. I kept having to remind myself that this place had a ticking clock for the hours in the day. I felt like the moon was laughing at me each night it rose in the sky, reminding me that I, yet again, didn't accomplish anything with my powers. Another day gone, wasted.

"I really want to see the water," I said as Tezya started walking again. "Please," I added a tad desperately as I tried to keep up.

"Where do you think I'm taking you, Rumor?" he asked as amusement caused his scar to rise.

"I honestly have no clue," I admitted reluctantly, turning my gaze from the unusual city to stare up at him. "All I was told was that I needed a bag and that we're training."

"You have water abilities so of course I'm taking you to the ocean. Clearly the pool isn't cutting it. While I might admire the small waves you manage to produce, it won't be enough to impress the Lux King."

"Thank you," I smiled, ignoring the jab about my abilities or the hidden threat to try harder to figure out my powers. I already had a sinking feeling that his King would make me regret it if I came up at the end of this training with nothing. I didn't need him to remind me.

But nothing could ruin my good mood right now. I couldn't believe it. I was finally going to see the warm beaches I dreamed of. I would finally be able to see the waves and feel the sand. I couldn't stop thinking about the memory of the ocean that came to me when I was on Tezya's balcony—of coloring in blue on someone's arm.

Then, my smile faltered as I recalled his words, and confusion overtook me. "You said we had to make it on time. Isn't the ocean close since the bay is right there?"

He laughed. "Yes, the ocean to the city that is accessible to all Advenians of Lux is just past the buildings on the other side of the Luxian bay, but I'm not taking you there."

"Why not?" I frowned, wanting to see more of the city. This small glimpse wasn't enough. "Where are you taking me?"

"Rumor, as much as I would *love* to take you to the city's *nude* beach, we can't practice your abilities with so many civilians around. The King has required me to keep you hidden for now, so we're going to a private beach. It's a half day's walk, and we need to start now if we want daylight left to practice."

Only now did I notice the looming forest in front of us and realized that Tezya was planning to hike through it.

The forest was lush, green, and vibrant. It was hard not to compare it to Peter's eyes and somehow thinking of him hurt worse than Sie. He was my friend, and the last time I saw him was when I was brought into that room by Kole. I tried not to think about him, about how I would have done anything for him if our situations were reversed...

The trees were different from the odd, bare ones by the castle. They were more dense and entirely covered in moss, leaving nothing of the brown bark on display. Light barely peeked through the top of the leaves. It created a thick canopy, blocking the sun like an air user's shield could block the rain. But it did nothing to quench the heat. I felt sticky and wet and every inch of the clothes I donned became drenched. I understood why Tezya opted to not wear a shirt.

Neither of us spoke as I trekked behind him, following his bare back. I was starting to memorize the patterns of the scars that covered every inch of his skin. And when he became slick with sweat, I studied the markings that materialized overtop of them. It felt good to see another Advenian with the black Luxian markings after so long of being surrounded by the Tennebrisian golden designs.

I didn't mind the silence either. The further in we hiked, the more the animals overpowered my hearing. We were slowly leaving behind the bustling city. I could no longer hear any voices or chatter coming from the town. All that greeted me was the wind gently howling against the leaves, the crickets singing, distant hooves stomping, and the occasional bird chirping. With each step we took further into the green fested forest, the more fear and worries I left behind with it. It was calming.

My shoulders were aching from the weight of carrying my pack, and I desperately needed a break to rest. Trivial things that used to seem like nothing to me were still taxing on my body. My legs were shaking, and I knew Tezya was walking slower than he normally would have because of me. I was thankful that the terrain was mostly flat, unlike Tennebris' mountainous landscape.

I jumped when Tezya spoke for the first time, "We're here." He looked back at me as he pushed a tree branch out of the way. The view through the greenery was small, but I could just make out a small brown hut with a wrap-around porch that was larger than the building itself. Then I heard it. The sound of the waves crashing against the shore, lapping against the sand. It filled my ears, mixing with the dense sounds of the forest behind me.

I pushed past Tezya and ran, probably faster than I ever did on the track. I missed running outside—of being surrounded by nature. I ran toward the ocean, throwing my overnight pack onto the sand. I didn't stop until I was knee deep in the rushing water.

I inhaled longingly and scanned the horizon. The sun was high in the sky and blistering against my skin. Tezya came up behind me, and with his pants halted at their normal spot halfway up his calves, the water didn't soak through his clothes like it did mine. His eyes were wide as he took me in.

"What?" I asked, a little breathless.

"You're actually in the water. I mean, I hoped that you would go in the ocean, but it was wishful thinking. I thought maybe the openness of the sea would be enough to get you to swim. I just didn't know if it would work."

I looked down at my feet. They were still visible through the clear aqua water below. I probably looked crazy to him. Running into the cresting water, the waves lashing up to my thighs when they crashed. I knew, without touching it, that my hair was a tangled mess from the humidity of the hike, but I didn't care. I was happy for the first time in a long time. I wanted to soak up this moment and paint it into my memory so I would never forget it.

I wiggled my toes inside my shoes, wishing that I had stopped to take them off. I wanted to feel the sand beneath my feet.

"Why don't you change? Then we'll go in the water."

"Change?" I asked, turning around to face him as a large wave crashed against my back. I was further out than him, the vastness of the water behind me.

"Your maid was told to pack swimming attire for you. Unless you wish to try out that whole nude-beach-swimming-naked thing. I'm fine with that too."

"No," I blurted before I realized he was only joking. His heavy laughter joined in with the sound of the waves. "I'll go change," I said shyly, turning away from him.

"There's a room in the hut if you want privacy. I'll wait for you outside." He was still smiling.

"Don't you need to change?"

His smile broadened. "I'll change out here once you leave."

Oh-OH.

I hurried past him, picking up my bag as I went. The image of him naked on the beach was fresh in my traitorous mind. The wrap-around porch only took one step to climb, then it stretched out into a flat deck before I came across two wide doors made of glass. I tried to open them, but they wouldn't budge. I tried harder. There was no way I was this weak that I couldn't open a door.

Then laughter sounded from the beach. "The doors don't open like that. You would be doing that all day. Try sliding them instead of pulling."

Huffing softly, I slid the one door on top of the other, only to realize that there was only one bed—one.

The hut was a deep brown color, even on the inside, the wood seeming to make up the walls, ceiling, and floor. Matching rows of cabinets lined the far wall above the *too-small* bed that sat in the center of the room, demanding all my attention. Thankfully, I saw many bedrolls tucked into the cabinets. An emerald green sofa aligned the other side. The only thing that was large about the hut was the table and six chairs that sat opposite the couch. I pushed past the room, hoping and praying that the door led to another bedroom, but it didn't. It was a small bathing room. I was thankful there was no bathtub until I realized that the only thing the room had was a hole carved into the wood. There wasn't a lingering stench, and I wondered if it was the work from an air user, and I prayed to the Goddesses that I wouldn't have to go to the bathroom while we were here.

I'd been through worse. The cage I was in had no bathroom, not even a bucket, but somehow this felt more degrading.

I quickly realized that there wasn't any resemblance of electricity in the hut, but I also didn't see torches or a fireplace either to light the space.

This was it. This was the entire hut. I could walk the length of it in fifteen, maybe twenty, steps. It was nothing like the luxury of the Luxian castle, but I liked it better—minus the no toilet thing. The hut was simple and to the point. It was charming.

I looked back through the glass doors. Green curtains to match the sofa could be drawn for privacy, but the door was the only window in the whole place. Above it, etched into the wood, were the words, *For when you can't pretend anymore.* My breath halted. The words sank deep into my soul as tears filled my eyes. Did someone else feel the same way I did?

I stepped closer to the quote without meaning to and noticed, even smaller was, *You are enough.* It looked like it was carved into the wood from a knife, not nearly as eloquent as the larger quote, but I somehow loved it more. I smiled, needing to see those words, needing to know that I wasn't the only Advenian struggling, that even if I felt alone right now, I wasn't really.

Setting my pack down on the bed, I opened it up to see what swimming attire Patricia had packed for me. My eyes widened as I took in the black strappy undergarments. I searched the bag again. Then a third time just to be sure. She must have forgotten it. She seemed to forget everything, not even able to remember how to navigate through the Luxian castle. It shouldn't have surprised me that she didn't pack what I needed.

Sighing, I walked back out to Tezya, who had already changed. His pants stopped mid thigh and were tighter than his usual loose attire, and I tried not to notice his corded muscles showing beneath them.

"What's wrong?" he asked once he saw me still in my half wet clothes.

"Um, my maid didn't pack any swimming attire for me."

"I'm sure she did."

"No, she didn't. There are only undergarments. I checked the bag three times." My face reddened. I didn't even have another outfit to change into.

He laughed again, but this time it was deeper as his scar inched higher on his face. I was growing sick of him mocking me. "Rumor, if a person from Lux decides to wear anything at all, it does tend to resemble undergarments. It's hot in Lux year round. Really fucking hot. Things are different here than in Tennebris. No one is going to swim in a bodysuit."

"I'm not wearing that," I gasped as I realized that the thin black piece of material was, in fact, my swimming attire. "It... it won't cover anything."

"Well, unless you want to swim in your clothes and walk back to the castle in that barely-covering swimming attire, I would suggest you put it on. I doubt your maid packed you another outfit as we're supposed to leave tomorrow." He paused, probably knowing full well she didn't. "Besides, I want to look at your markings for myself, and I can't do that with all your clothes on."

My mouth hung open as I gaped at him. But I didn't dare move. He seemed to sense my unease. I was getting deja vu from the lake with Sie. It felt so similar, yet completely new, and I couldn't pinpoint why.

"Rumor, I'm here to train you because of the King's orders. That's all. I can promise you that I don't care whether we do it naked or in your suit, but we are going to train today, and that's *all* we are going to do."

Slowly, I turned away from him and stalked back toward the hut. Point taken. Not that I wanted to do anything with him. I honestly didn't know if I could say I hated him or liked him. No. That wasn't true. I didn't hate him. I enjoyed being around him, but I wouldn't consider him a friend. He was just someone who I was stuck spending my time with. So why was I so disappointed with what he just said?

I was probably just feeling this way after not having any Advenian contact in months. I would like anyone that was around me right now after being so lonely for so long. That's all this was. I craved not being isolated because whenever I was, it brought me back to all the things Kole had done to me. It brought me back to the nights I'd spent alone in the cage, to the darkness.

When I was training with Tezya, I didn't think about all the things that haunted me, at least, it wasn't all consuming like it was at night. And Tezya just happened to be easy to talk to. He also happened to be super, unnaturally attractive. And he was the only male in my life at the moment. He was the only person I even talked to at Lux, besides Patricia, and she was definitely not a guy.

I wanted to be near Tezya as much as I wanted my maid around, and for the same reasons—I didn't want to be alone. Ironic how at LakeWood, being alone and soaking in a bath was my release, and now they became my nightmare.

I would have asked Patricia to spend each and every night with me if I knew I wouldn't sound so desperate. I'd thought about asking her many times to not leave at night, but I bit back the plea with my pride.

Once I was back inside the hut, I pulled the velvet curtains closed enough to give me privacy while still allowing some light to flow in, knowing full well the black suit did absolutely nothing to cover myself. It would have been almost the same as if I was swimming naked because it barely concealed anything.

I took a deep breath before sliding the glass doors open and walked back to where Tezya waited in the water. I was thankful the hut didn't have a mirror because I probably would've run back inside out of embarrassment if I had seen myself. It didn't matter if Tezya made it clear this was just training. I felt as ridiculous as I knew I looked, and it did nothing to quench the lingering self-consciousness.

When he saw me, his eyes widened for a brief moment. It was so fast that I thought I had imagined it. I probably did. Instinctively, I covered as much of my stomach as I could manage with my hands, which wasn't much.

He swallowed. "Do you think you are able to go all the way in?"

I nodded my head and slowly waded out further into the water. It was cool against my bare skin. Everywhere the water hit me felt refreshing to the contrast of the blazing heat. When the water lapped at my hips, I dove under as a large wave came barreling toward me.

The salt water stung for a moment as it met with my still-healing flesh on my forearm and back. My tallies were almost all healed except for the newest marks closest to my wrist. But my back was worse. The healer who had visited me in the dungeons kept me from death, but she never mended me fully. I could still feel the bite of the whip when I moved a certain way, and I still opted to sleep curled up on my side rather than flat on my back because of it. The salt dug into the crevices of the wounds and cemented itself there. I pushed past the burn and swam deeper.

Opening my eyes underwater, I was surprised that I could see clearly. Just as vividly as if I was looking on land. Better even. I opened my mouth to breathe. It still startled me when I felt the immediate relief in my lungs as the water filled and poured into every inch of me. It was nothing like my nightmares.

I didn't want to risk having a flashback from being in the tub, so I kept my mouth open as I swam, not wanting to hold my breath at all.

A sense of calmness overtook me, similar to how I used to feel taking baths back in LakeWood before everything happened. The water finally started to soothe. I swam around, studying the various sea life with fascination. I dove further, deeper out, surprised I was at ease swimming near the bottom. The sand looked nothing like tile. I searched for shells and rocks along the seafloor. A crab inched its way past me as I wiggled my toes and looked up. A pair of legs were hovering far above me. I could make out the slight glimpse of the sun through the deep blue.

When I finally broke the surface, Tezya was smiling softly at me. "You were under the water for a while."

"Sorry," I replied as I swam over to him. "I didn't realize how far out I swam."

"Don't apologize. I'm glad you did, but water isn't my specialty, so if you don't mind, let's practice closer to the shore."

I followed his gaze and realized we were at least a mile off from the hut. I started to make my way back before he grabbed my arm to stop me. "What?" I asked.

"Race me."

"What?"

"Race me," he grinned. "Consider it part of your training. I want to see how fast you are in the water unless you're scared of losing."

I took a moment, pretending to think it over. "And if I win?"

He arched his brow. "What do you want?"

"I want two things," I said, surprising myself.

He chuckled. "Greedy thing," he joked as he ran his fingers through his hair. I couldn't help but notice how he bobbed in the water. Sinking too low for his muscular body. He spit out some water that had entered his mouth. I loathed the fact that my eyes darted to his wet lips. What would it be like to taste the water on them? I bristled, furious that the thought even crossed my mind. I had to remind myself that he was forced to train me. We weren't two friends hanging out by choice.

"I want to know something about you, something that I don't know. No. Tell me something *no one* knows about you." He still felt like a stranger to me, and even though I'd been spending my entire days with him, I found myself wanting to know more.

"Done," he laughed. "And the second thing?"

"I want you to answer whatever question I ask, and you have to answer honestly."

He was silent for a moment before agreeing. "Okay, but only *one* question. If I win, you have to do whatever I want."

I didn't get the time to respond or even process what that meant before he was gliding toward the shore. I dove under the surface and stroked as fast as my body could take me because I did not want to find out what he'd want me to do. I didn't feel as weak in the water as I did on land. I didn't notice that my muscles weren't what they used to be or that I was still slowly recovering from months of being starved. In the water, everything was different. I felt lifeless and alive all at once. I just swam, becoming one with the ocean. I could see Tezya swimming at an unnaturally fast speed above me, which only made me pump my arms and kick my legs harder, putting everything I had into this race.

When I finally reached the shallow end, I stood up and sprinted the rest of the way toward the hut. The waves were pushing against my back, egging me forward. I stole a glance behind me as I felt Tezya's fingers graze my arm. He was trying to grab me, probably to throw me behind him. "That's cheating," I squealed. I could hear him mumbling something in return, but I didn't pay attention as I focused on my target ahead of me.

I stopped abruptly as I finally made it out of the water. Turning around, Tezya nearly tumbled into me. "I win," I grinned and realized that I was actually laughing, that my cheeks hurt from smiling.

"Next time we do that, I want to time you."

"Why?" I asked breathless. Now that I was standing on the hot sand, I realized my entire body was shaking.

"Because I've never lost a race before." He was smiling back at me, which only made me grin wider as a feeling of triumph washed over me.

"What would you have made me do if you won?" I asked because if he never lost a race before, it dawned on me that he went into this fully confident that he'd win.

"I'm only answering that if that's the question you want to ask me."

"No," I blurted a little too fast. There was no way I was wasting my question on curiosity. And as much as I wanted to know, I needed to use it wisely. I needed to learn something about my situation, but I had to be careful and make sure it was something he could answer.

"What's the question you want to ask me then?"

"Hmm, I'll think about it," I said, dramatically putting my pointer finger over my lips. "We never agreed to a time that I could call in my win. But you also owe me one too. You have to tell me something that no one knows about you."

"Okay," he laughed as he walked to catch up with me on the sand. "I absolutely hate strawberries. They're the worst fruit ever."

A high pitch squeal escaped me. I was not expecting that. "That is sacrilegious. Strawberries are the best fruit. Next to bananas, of course."

"Bananas I can get on board with," he grinned, and we both laughed.

"That doesn't count. I'm sure somebody else knows that you hate strawberries. I said it has to be something that no one knows about you."

His smile faltered. "You're right. I'll think of something."

"What? No. I want to know something now."

He smirked. "How did you just phrase it? *We never agreed to a time* or something like that..."

"That's not fair," I frowned, realizing he was using my own words against me.

Tezya shook out his hair, water spraying onto my face, before he suddenly became deathly serious. "I forgot to tell you, but your results are back. I brought them with me. They're in my bag. I'll have to give them to the King tomorrow when we make it back to the castle. He's been waiting on them. But... I thought we'd look at them together first."

I shuddered thinking about that test. "You didn't look at them?" I asked.

"No, I waited for you. We can do it now if you want."

"Okay," I agreed, my voice a little shaky. I had no idea why, but as I followed him into the hut, I suddenly became nervous.

ELEVEN
TEZYA

THE WORD *virgin* stared back at me through the paperwork as my mind whirled in a thousand different directions.

Unexplained relief.

Confusion.

Shock.

I wasn't an idiot. She was married to the Dark Prince before coming to Lux. I felt reprieved that she wasn't carrying his child because I didn't know what I would have done if she was. To be honest, I hadn't opened her file when I first got it from Semader because I was terrified. I'd been sitting on the information for days. I knew the King was planning on killing her if she was pregnant, and I didn't know where that left me or why the thought of her dead bothered me so much. Maybe it was because I'd seen all she'd endured and believed that she deserved to be happy, at least *alive*, after all of it. Maybe I was projecting my own past onto her, that it was what I hoped for myself and knew I would never get.

I was more shocked though that she never had sex with the Dark Prince. Sie must have had one hell of a willpower because I could tell from the little bit I glimpsed that he was crazy about her. During her interrogation in the monitor room, through her memories, he mentioned that he felt a pull through the blood bond, that his powers were amplified around her. That could only happen if the bond was completed, or so I thought. It didn't make sense.

I looked up at her. She was perched on the green worn-in sofa, a frown forming on her face. She said how it wasn't necessary, that she couldn't be pregnant. I didn't think she was lying to me... I just thought Sie compelled her to forget. Not that it mattered if I'd believed her or not. The King wanted it done, and there was no denying him, not unless you wanted to be publicly murdered.

Her eyebrows furrowed even further into themselves, and I couldn't help but notice how her nose crinkled and her freckles drew closer together. Her skin had a slight burn to it from the hours spent under the sun today. She'd been so pale and on the brink of death when I found her in the dungeons that it was odd seeing her like this.

"Now do you believe me that I'm not pregnant?" she scowled as she crossed her arms across her chest. I quickly drew my attention back up to her face and tried not to notice the way her arms were pushing against her breasts. I really wished she had changed out of that black suit. Despite me brushing it off, it was distracting and revealing, and I couldn't concentrate with her in it. The Tennebrisian bodysuit would have been much better.

"You're a virgin?" I stupidly asked as if I couldn't read the words on the paperwork. "But you were married?" I realized I was beating a dead horse by asking her, the proof was right in front of me, but I couldn't help it. I somehow needed to hear it.

"I told you as much before, but you didn't listen to me. Unlike some people, Sie's a gentleman."

I couldn't suppress my laugh. "Sie is *not* a gentleman when it comes to this. Even I have heard of his reputation in his short twenty-something years of life. He gets around." I thought of the memory of her crawling across the floor toward him, of his friends laughing, and the two girls draped around his neck, kissing him while she was forced to watch. I clamped down on my jaw until it hurt.

"Well, he didn't with me."

"Clearly," I snorted. The man was an idiot for letting her slip through his fingers. Although I was relieved he had. She wasn't who the prophecy spoke of. She was safe, and for some reason, that meant something. Relief flickered through me, and a small part of me was screaming that it had to be more than just relating to what she'd endured. I barely knew her, but she was slowly getting under my skin.

"What about you? Are you married or in love?" she asked. I could tell she was trying to change the subject as her cheeks turned slightly pink, and her scent radiated toward me. Embarrassment clung to her. She clearly didn't want to talk about her virginity or her past with Sie.

"Marriages are different here in Lux. It's not about love. It's about who will be the best breeding partner to create a strong rank offspring. We don't have a choice, and we only get paired within our rank anyway."

"You can only marry someone of the same rank?"

I sighed heavily as I sat down next to her on the worn sofa, the paperwork still in my hand. "Yes. All rank fives get arranged marriages by the Council. Anyone of a lower rank can marry whoever they want, but it has to be within their own rank. Eventually, I will have to get married. It will be arranged for me with someone from Lux who is also a five. Until I am forced to take a wife though, I will keep delaying the inevitable."

"So you don't believe in marriages at all?"

"Not when they are forced upon you, and neither party has a say in the matter." I turned back to face her, realizing that she had gone through the exact thing. Even though most of Tennebris allows you to marry whoever you want, they didn't give her a choice because their High Council declared it when Prince Noren won the tournament. She probably understood more about Lux than she thought.

The news of what happened in Tennebris spread like wildfire. Although no one here knew what she looked like, the Luxian civilians knew the gist of what had happened in the Dark Kingdom. I remembered the moment I found out that a rank zero Tennebrisian flat out refused when she was announced and said no to the Council in a public manner. She only agreed when she was threatened with treason if she didn't comply. I'd been intrigued by her ever since. I loved the idea of some girl standing up for herself, of fighting the system without even realizing it.

I was also envious of Tennebris. When I was younger, I wished I had been born into that Kingdom instead of Lux. I hated the ranking system, and I hated the Luxian Council to my core. I like that the Tennebrisian King changed every decade, that it wasn't one fucked up family ruling and making the decisions over everyone since back on Allium. I also loved that they had more freedom than us. They could marry anyone of any rank. It wasn't the exact freedom I wanted, it wasn't like what the humans of Earth had, but it was something. A step in the right direction.

"Can you see now why I'm not in a rush to get married?" I said, forcing myself back into the conversation with her. I didn't want to dwell on all the reasons I hated the Advenian Kingdoms. "Yours lasted a whopping two weeks and you didn't even have sex, which is probably the only good part to it."

"I don't appreciate you joking about my marriage or my sex life."

I looked her up and down, noting the seriousness in her tone. "You truly cared about him, didn't you?"

"No... yes... I don't know. I don't think he's as cruel as he wants people to believe he is. I hated him at first. He did a lot of messed up things to me. I might hate him forever for some of the stuff he did, but he also looked out for me... until he didn't, when he—"

She stopped talking. I didn't know what went down between them at the end, but I could sense the resentment radiating from her. I thought it was messed up when I learned that the Dark Prince was handing over his own wife. I'd been following them ever since I learned about her. But from what I saw of Sie, I had to believe there was more to it than anyone knew. It wasn't an excuse though. I don't care what corner he was trapped into, he could have found another way than to hand her over to the Lux King.

I was about ready to travel to Tennebris when I found her in that cage and saw the state she was in. I wanted to murder the Prince myself for letting it happen. How could he leave his supposed lover to that fate? How could he do absolutely fucking nothing to help her? I could sense she was feeling the same conflicting emotions toward him, that she was questioning everything. I didn't care to defend the Dark Prince, but I wanted to give her some of the clarity she sought. "For what it's worth, he did care for you."

"How do you know that?" she asked. A bit of her wet hair hit my shoulder as she whipped her head in my direction.

"I was there in Tennebris the day Lux brought you here," I admitted.

"I don't remember seeing you though?"

"You wouldn't." I tensed as I remembered the state she was in even then. I briefly saw her being transported from the castle to the underwater transport. She was in shackles, covered in dirt, and barely alive. I knew the Tennebrisians guards treated her like shit. I just didn't account for the Luxian soldiers being worse. The King, I didn't doubt, but not the soldiers. "You were starved and out of it. Plus, they sedated you after the broadcast. I would be surprised if you remembered anything from that day."

She shook her head as if trying to wipe away the memory. "What does that have to do with you knowing that Sie cared about me?"

I fiddled with the crinkled piece of paper I kept in my pocket before deciding to give it to her. Her eyes widened as she took in the two words *hold on*.

"How did you get this?" She reached up and snatched the paper like it was the most important thing to her.

"It was found on you the day you were captured. One of the soldiers gave it to me."

"You kept it?" She looked up to meet my gaze, her blue eyes swimming with tears. "Why?"

"Sie must have slipped this into your pocket the day you were taken," I said instead of answering her questions because I had no idea why I decided to keep the ratty paper this whole time. I had it before I even interacted with her.

The tears finally fell from her eyes as she wiped her cheeks. "This note wasn't from Sie."

"Who's it from then?" I asked, puzzled.

"It doesn't matter anymore. I won't ever see him again."

That made me even more confused as to who she was referring to. "Regardless, he still cares about you."

"Right," she half laughed. "That's why he left me in the dungeons and sent me away."

"I could smell the emotions that were fuming off of him that day," I admitted. "He was pissed that you were being taken to Lux. I still think he should've done something though. It doesn't excuse his actions for allowing you to be treated that way. He was even more pissed when he saw all the Luxian Royals escorting you out."

Her eyes flared to life. "The Fire Prince was there?"

"The Fire Prince?" I chuckled at the nickname. But my laugh stopped short as soon as I saw her face. She was scared. My eyes trailed down her thighs and halted at the mangled flesh of her calf. It made me wonder what other horrors she faced.

"Yes, he was there. What do you know of him?" I asked, genuinely wanting to know. It was surprising how little she knew of Lux.

"Just that he's powerful. Sie told me that he's the Commander of the Luxian army and that I should stay away from him and everyone in his army."

"Well, you're doing a terrible job at that. I am in the Luxian army, after all," I grinned, thinking about all the time we had spent together. I caught her eyes darting toward the scar across my cheek.

"First off, me spending my days glued to your side is not my doing. But I'm serious, Tezya. Why would I be warned about the army? Are they really that bad? Is the Fire Prince really that bad? Have you met him?"

"I guess it depends on who you're asking. Everyone in the army is strong and dangerous to some degree. It's harder to qualify for than the Tennebrisian Guard. They only allow rank four or fives in. But I am dangerous, Rumor. Sie wasn't far off in warning you to stay clear of me, the army in general, I mean. I've been alive for a long time, and I've been in the army almost as long. I've seen a lot, done a lot, killed a lot. But I also think that Sie's warning wasn't just about Lux's soldiers. I think it has to do with my reputation. He wanted you to stay clear of me, probably of every Luxian male."

"What do you mean? Stay clear of *you*? Why would Sie warn me about you? Does he know you?"

"I didn't mean me specifically. All the men in the army, hell, all the men in Lux for that matter."

"And why would he be worried about a soldier's reputation? You lost me."

I sighed, contemplating how much I wanted to tell her. "I've been alive a lot longer than Sie. Most of the soldiers that make up our armies are the same. So I've had more years to do what should have happened on your wedding night. I'm assuming that is part of why Sie warned you away. He's probably jealous as hell, thinking of another male being with you."

"Oh," she whispered, turning bright red. "How old are you?" She looked me up and down as if just now wondering about our age gap.

"Rumor, I'm old enough to be your father or grandfather, maybe even your great-grandfather if it was during Lakimi," I said, flashing her a wide smile.

"I'm serious, Tezya. How old are you?"

"I'm a hundred and twenty-one." Awkward silence filled the room. She nodded her head but didn't respond. I looked down at my hands, realizing that I was still holding her folder with all her information in it. I grabbed the paperwork regarding her virginity and ripped it in half before using my flames to burn the paper. Nothing was left of it but ash.

She rose to her feet. "Your ability is fire?"

"Yes," I said slowly, forgetting for a second that she had a traumatic history with, not just water, but fire too. I cursed myself when I remembered her right calf and the mangled skin that remained there. I was just staring at it moments before, along with the long gash that went from her hip to her knee. I wanted to murder the Tennebrisian compulsion user when I realized it was him that gave it to her. It was a whole other level of fucked up that the Dark Kingdom's High Council sent the compulsion user they tried to kill her with to us.

"I thought... I thought that you just had a way of knowing people's emotions?"

I laughed. "Well, first off, I told you that my ability is more than just knowing people's emotions. A lot more than that. And secondly, I don't just have one ability. I have two. I don't think I would be in the army if I didn't. Fire is one of mine. Elemental abilities are really common here. A lot of people have water, fire, air, or ground abilities. I figured you knew I possessed fire when you saw my markings in the water."

She nodded, a small shudder working its way through her. "I just never saw you use it before. I hadn't thought about it." She paused, then looked around the hut. "But there's no fire in the room. That means that you can create the element, not just manipulate it."

"I know. It's why I'm a rank five. Along with my other ability that you can't seem to figure out."

"Tell me then," she said as nonchalantly as she could muster. I could tell she was attempting to calm down. She took a seat on the sofa again, this time curling her legs under her.

I grinned as I realized it bothered her, not understanding why I could gauge her emotions. I also realized I liked making her flustered. "Rumor, I'm not just going to offer up the knowledge of my ability for nothing."

She rolled her eyes before they focused on the ash that was now scattered across the floor. "I thought you said that the King forced you to have those tests done on me? Why are you destroying them? I'm not going through that exam again. That duck-beak-thing is not going back up..."

"Relax, Rumor. I won't let that happen. The King just wanted to make sure you weren't pregnant. I kept the paperwork stating just that, but he doesn't need to know about your virginity."

"Oh," she said, playing with her thumbs and looking down at her knees. She asked even more softly, "Why?"

"Because I don't want to find out what he would do with that information," I said through gritted teeth, knowing full well what he has done in the past. "Everyone thinks that you have been touched by someone of Tennebris. I think it's better that everyone continues to think that."

"Why?"

"No male will try to approach you if they think that you are…" I struggled to find the right word to say without insulting her. "Tainted by them."

"So no one would want to touch me? *Ever?*"

"It's better that way. Trust me."

"What right do you have to say that?" she snapped. "What if I don't want that?"

I arched my brow. "I can introduce you to males once the King declares your fate if that is what you wish."

"I don't want that. That's not what I meant. I just…" she paused, sucking her bottom lip between her teeth. "I'm sick of people looking at me like I'm a freak. In Tennebris, it was because they thought I was tainted with human blood, and now this. I'm sick of lying and not being able to be myself. I'm sick of people thinking I'm something I'm not."

I was all too aware of what she was feeling.

"You are going to have to trust me, Rumor. I know it's not ideal, but I am doing this to protect you from the King. Even though you were born here and you are Luxian by birth, you aren't a citizen, not yet anyway. You need to be careful and not draw any attention to yourself. Only a few Advenians will know who you really are, will know about your past, and it's best to blend in as much as possible."

"I guess." She started twirling her wet hair around her finger, and I found myself unable to look away.

"Rumor," I said before I sucked in a breath. "I have something that no one else knows about me."

Her blues eyes met mine, her hair was still around her finger, but she momentarily stopped twirling it.

"But you have to promise me that you won't tell anyone."

"I won't."

"I'm serious. No one knows this for a reason, Rumor," I said, trying not to second guess this. "I could get in a lot of trouble for saying this out loud," I added, which was an understatement. If she were to tell the King or if he used the compulsion user to go into her memories again, I'd be killed for what I was about to tell her. But there was something about her vulnerability that made me want to open up, made me want her to know everything.

"I won't tell anyone. Besides, the only person I know on this island other than you is my maid, Patricia, and she is so old, and I'm pretty certain senile that no one would believe anything she says. But I promise I won't say anything to anyone, even to her."

"Okay," I swallowed as I watched her track the bob in my Adam's apple along my throat. "I don't agree with the ranking system."

Silence followed as we stared at each other. I watched her face go through waves of emotion as she processed what I'd just revealed. I didn't even have to use my abilities to know how she felt about it, it was written all over her face.

"Why?" she finally asked. Her voice was barely audible and came out breathy.

"It's not right to judge someone's worth based on a number. I believe that everyone in our society is important regardless of what is burned onto their wrists."

She nervously looked down at her own wrists and started rubbing her zeroes as I continued, "I wish that our people could marry whoever they want to, that they can do anything they desire instead of being told what to do at some Trial. We have the Trials too, like Tennebris does. After graduation, everyone takes them, but the difference with ours is we don't even get to decide what we want to try out for. We don't have any say at all. We are just told, and we have to accept it. All the rank zeroes are servants no matter what. You will never see a zero rank do anything else here. It's not right. I've known many rank zeroes who are just as talented and pivotal to our society as someone who is a five. If you're a male who has a rank four or five, you are almost always placed into the army, even if you have no desire for bloodshed. There's a rank four that I fight alongside with who is the strongest male I know, yet he doesn't get the respect he deserves because, to Lux, he isn't considered the best. He's a four, not a five.

Here, if you don't have this on your wrist," I lifted my arm, exposing my brand, "you don't matter."

I looked at her, meeting her gaze before continuing, "Did you know that back on Allium, it wasn't like that? It was a free world. They didn't have a ranking system until the very end. The ranking system was the catalyst that started the Ability War. Everyone worked and lived and loved alongside one another. It was free until the current bloodline took over the Luxian throne. They turned it into the dictatorship that it is now. That's who caused the war that destroyed our planet. The current King that sits on our own throne, his prior bloodline, through greed and wanting control, caused a civil war that soon spiraled into the war against Tennebris as well."

"I didn't know," she said quietly. "They told us about the war between the two Kingdoms, but they never went into detail. They just said that they fought for power, and I thought that meant land. I didn't realize that they didn't have a ranking system. I didn't know things were ever different before."

I shook my head, pissed at the manipulative way our school systems taught our history. "Tennebris fought back at first. They saw what Lux was doing. How they were controlling their people and manipulating them. They tried to fight for what was right. But it wasn't enough and eventually Allium was destroyed, and we were forced to come here. And now, the same bloodline still rules in Lux."

"Do you not like the current King? You talk of his bloodline with such hatred."

"Is that your question for me?" When she nodded yes, I answered, "You're right. I don't like him, Rumor. I *hate* him."

"Why did it matter if I was pregnant and if the blood bond took?" she asked after a moment. "I'm not so naive to think that the King was only concerned if I broke the rules. There had to be something else."

"There's a prophecy," I said, deciding that she needed to know. It would be more dangerous for her if she didn't. "Back when the Ability War started, this prophecy arose that a boy would be born of both races. Every Advenian that worshiped the Goddesses spoke of it until one day the King had their tongues cut from their throats. The boy is claimed to destroy the two current governing systems as they stand, bringing either complete annihilation or uniting our kind once again. How things pan out is still up to fate. The Lux King thought that you and Sie would fulfill it. That you would bear the child the prophecy spoke of. That's why he wanted to know if you were pregnant."

"But that's impossible. Even if I did fall pregnant with Sie, a child wouldn't survive. Everyone knows that any inter-kingdom offspring would die immediately."

I shook my head. "Is it?" I questioned. "Our kind hasn't tried to reproduce since on Allium, and the records dated back to that time are far and few between. They could have been tampered with. Plus, maybe Earth is different. Maybe a baby born from both would survive, could survive here. Or maybe that was all a lie to control us, so we obeyed and didn't question the current governing system. Think about it, neither King would truly want the prophecy to come true. Either it will annihilate the Advenians completely, wiping us from existence, or destroy the Kingdoms' two rulers. Neither of them would want that. They both want to keep their crowns."

"What would the King do to such a child?" she asked.

"He would murder it without hesitation. And it wouldn't matter if that child was born or still in the womb. If you were pregnant, Rumor, he wouldn't have hesitated to kill you."

She shuddered. "Why are you telling me any of this anyway? I mean, I'm glad you are, but the prophecy clearly isn't about Sie and me since we aren't having a baby together. You saw for yourself that I'm not pregnant, so why tell me?"

"Yet. You and Sie didn't produce an offspring *yet*. You could still fulfill the prophecy. And with the King now knowing that you are Sie's weakness, I'm certain that you two will be forced to be together."

"So," she questioned, her voice starting to rise. I could sense that my words bothered her. She probably thought she'd never see the Dark Prince again. "I didn't sleep with him while I was married to him. What makes you think that I would do it now that we aren't together?"

"I'm not saying you will," I struggled with my words again, trying to figure out how to explain this to her. "But even if there was suspicion that you did, the King would kill you for it. He won't risk an offspring actually being born that would threaten his rule. I'm just warning you to stay clear of him. Plus, everyone in Tennebris thinks you two completed the blood bond. If they find you two in a room together, they would think it's because of the side effect of the bond. Did your Dark Prince happen to mention that to you?"

Her cheeks grew redder, a shade so deep I didn't know it was even possible, but I found myself memorized by it. It made her look alive, so unlike the skeleton she was when I first saw her. I also loved the fact that she couldn't hide her emotions, that she wore them on her face without knowing it, despite the fact that I could smell them on her anyway. It made her seem more pure and honest.

Her now developing blush also told me that Sie did, in fact, tell her about that part of the oath, where the newly blood bound couple wouldn't be able to keep their hands off each other.

"But Sie and I... we didn't... the blood bond isn't..."

"Rumor, I know now that you two didn't fuck." She cringed at the word, and I realized I probably shouldn't have used that phrase. "You don't need to beat around the bush. It's just odd that Sie felt something toward you. I think that's another reason the King believes you are the one in the prophecy because a blood bond has never occurred before between the two different Kingdoms. Sie said that his powers were stronger with you, so clearly you two are a match. Even if you didn't consummate it, everyone still thinks you did. So you have to be careful. Don't be alone with him, don't do anything with him. No matter how you two might feel about one another."

"I don't..." she stopped mid thought and shrugged it off. "Fine. I won't talk to him if I ever see him again."

"Good. Now let's get back in the water. We still have a couple more hours of daylight left, and I want to look at your markings."

She nodded her head but didn't get up yet. "Tezya, why did you tell me all of that?"

"I thought you deserved to know why those tests were done to you and why you need to stay away from the Dark Prince."

She shook my head, cutting me off. "No, not that. About your feelings toward the ranking system and the King. That was..." She stopped mid sentence, but I could sense what she didn't say. I revealed way more than one simple fact that no one knew about me. I revealed enough for her to blackmail me with. She could use it against me, but somehow I knew she wouldn't.

I met her electric sapphire eyes and decided on the truth. "Because I thought that you would understand. I saw on those screens how you were treated because they thought you were a zero. I hoped maybe that you'd feel the same as me because you lived through it."

She nodded her head. "Thank you for telling me."

I stood up, brushing some sand that was still on my black shorts. "You're welcome." I started to walk toward the sliding doors.

"Tezya?" She said my name in question. I turned around to face her and saw that she rose from the sofa, but hadn't move toward me yet. "Why did the King think it was me? That Sie and I were a part of some prophecy? Why was I kidnapped and brought to Tennebris all those years ago?"

"I don't know, Rumor. Just make sure it doesn't come true. During your interrogation, the King learned that you are Sie's weakness. Once he finds out that you aren't pregnant, I wouldn't put it past him to use you until he has completed what he wants with Sie."

"Which is what?" She swallowed again, bracing herself for the answer that, deep down, she probably already knew.

"He wants him dead or locked away. He doesn't care which one happens first as long as he's off the throne. He doesn't want Sie to rule the Tennebrisians. Luxians breed and control who their citizens reproduce with. It makes for a strong Kingdom. We have tons of rank fours and fives because of it. But in Tennebris, you are still free to marry for love. Rank fives marry rank twos and so forth, which in doing so, dwindles and lessons their abilities in future generations. Tennebris is seen as weak because of it. Sie is the first rank five born from Tennebris in a long, long time, and he's strong. The Lux King is threatened by him, by what he could do as a leader."

"So he wants him off the throne before he takes it."

"Yes," I nodded. "And I think he is now going to use you to accomplish it. I'm not sure how yet, but he will probably force you and Sie to see each other during the annual meeting, which is only two weeks away. The date is still to be determined, but it's coming up. You can't be left alone with him. Even though you two aren't married anymore, if you were to fulfill the prophecy, if you were to conceive a child, he will kill you, and he won't wait for a baby to be born either. He'll murder you on the spot just for sleeping with him."

"I'm not going to sleep with Sie," she said in a rush. "The last time I saw Sie, he wanted nothing to do with me."

I hesitated before saying, "Rumor, I saw your memories together. He cares for you. You have to be careful." I could tell she didn't fully believe it, that her feelings were conflicted and full of confusion when it came to him.

"I'm not going to do anything with him," she said again. This time her voice came out louder, more determined.

"Good," I said in a flat tone, trying to hide the fact that her statement relieved me. "Because you need to be careful. Especially with him."

———

RUMOR'S TEST results weighed heavy in my pack when we finally returned to the castle the next day. I knew the Lux King would be paying me a visit shortly to review them. He was probably pissed that I hadn't handed them over immediately.

We did one more training session in the water this morning before we headed back, and I was finally able to look at her back markings. Last night, it was too dark to even attempt to see all the peculiar designs. And when I finally saw her back, I was livid. Her back was still mutilated. It was hard to see exactly what her markings were through the scars from the lashings. A few of them were still open and in various states of healing. She had too many scars for such a young age. Most of the Luxian soldiers that had seen battle weren't as covered as she was.

She did a good job of hiding what was done to her. I hadn't realized that she wasn't fully healed. I was pissed at myself for not noticing it during our swim. I was too preoccupied with other parts of her... I thought Semader would have healed her. I thought that was what had taken so long during her visit with him. I forced her to train every day in that state when the average soldier would have barely been able to stand with the same amount of wounds, yet she didn't complain. Not once. I hadn't even known she was in pain. My senses were confusing any physical pain for emotional ones whenever I got a read on her.

I called Brock the moment we returned to pay her a visit. I hated asking my friend to use his abilities, I knew what it would cost him, but he was the only healer I could trust with her. Brock, being who he was, didn't hesitate when I asked him. He didn't even ask a question. He just nodded and made his way toward her chambers. I owed him.

I had to rely on my memory from what Sie revealed of her back when the King forced it out of her. What I could make out of her markings baffled me. I'd never seen anything like it. She had to have more than just manipulating water. I just had no idea what else she possessed. Her markings were so unique and had so many elements entwined in one. But yet, she couldn't manipulate fire, air, or the ground like her back would suggest. I had her try all of them over a fire I made on the porch last night. Then during our hike back through the jungle, we practiced with air and ground powers, but nothing came out of it. She didn't possess another elemental ability. It had to be something else.

I walked toward my desk with her file in my hands. I'd worry about her markings later. I just hoped that her other ability would manifest itself soon. Maybe she's been using whatever this ability is the entire time without even realizing it? It took me a while to figure out what my second ability was as a child. But we didn't have the luxury of time.

Slumping into my chair, I opened her file again and started to read through it for the hundredth time. After being imprisoned for two months, she was fairly healthy. She was still severely underweight, and her iron levels were too low, but those were easy fixes. I flipped some pages, skimming the rest of her file. I froze when I saw her blood type was listed. It made me wonder if she knew who her family was and if they were still alive. Were they missing her and looking for their lost daughter who was stolen years ago?

During her interrogation, the King hadn't gone that far into her past. He didn't look into who captured her that day and brought her to the Tennebrisian soil. A pang of unwanted guilt was bubbling in my stomach because I knew I could have spared her from all this pain. Deep down, I knew who probably orchestrated it. After meeting her, I started to doubt more and more that the prophecy was about her. At least, her involvement had nothing to do with producing the offspring. I had to start accepting the truths right in front of me.

Almost all of her memories were laced with pain and fear. I hated that. I hated that I might have been the cause of it. It was one of the reasons I was determined to train her, and not just in her abilities like the King had requested. I would train her like I trained the soldiers. I wouldn't stop until she was back to the girl who stood up against the Dark Kingdom's Council. She wouldn't remain weak.

Hell, she hadn't seemed weak last night. She actually smiled and laughed. Seeing her in the ocean... like she belonged to it, or rather the ocean belonged to her. It was hers to live and breathe in. Hers to control. I was surprised by how much I wanted to see her smile, how I wanted to hear her laugh as we raced in the water.

The corner of my mouth twisted and curved into a grin as her image flashed in my mind from last night. I couldn't stop replaying her rose colored blush when she thought we'd have to sleep in the same bed. Her innocence was amusing. It was refreshing to me compared to Luxian born females I was used to. I couldn't decide if I liked her blushing and flustered or happy and laughing more. Laughing, I realized.

My grin faltered once I saw who was lounging on my sofa across the desk. Her legs were propped up on the table adjacent to it, resting on a stack of my books. She materialized out of thin air.

A high pitched voice echoed from across the room. "What has you smiling like a pup?"

"How long have you been there, Dovelyn?" I sneered at the Princess.

"Long enough to see that handsome face of yours go from brooding to that disgustingly lopsided grin."

"You know I hate it when you use your ability like that. Just because you can make yourself invisible doesn't mean that you should use it to trespass into someone's private chambers."

"But that wouldn't be any fun," she pouted as she flicked a silky, silver lock of hair over her thin shoulder. "Plus, I recall a certain someone who always asks me to spy and snoop for him."

"What do you want, Dovelyn?"

Her feet thumped on the floor as she sat up straighter on the sofa, her nose wrinkling. "Do I need a reason to check up on you? You haven't been around much lately, and I wanted to know why."

I sighed. "I'm fine, Dove. I've been training the girl. You know that."

"Yes, I was made aware, but what I don't know is why you are spending *all* your time with her. Last I checked, a getaway beach trip wasn't in your job description."

A low growl escaped my lips. "It was not some getaway trip. I took her to the hut to train. That's all."

She rose now but still managed to glower at me even though I towered over her. "Tez, I know you. I just want to make sure that you don't get invested. You know whatever the King has planned for her won't be good. It's better if you don't get attached. Plus..." She paused as she surveyed me. "She still has something to do with the prophecy, and we don't know what that means yet. We can't lose focus on what's important."

My abilities lashed out toward her without meaning to. I found worry and concern lingering through her scent. She did a good job masking her outward emotions, making it seem to the world that she was the spitting image of her father. She cared for me, I knew that, and she didn't want me getting hurt. But I was fine. I was only training Scotlind. I wasn't about to fall in love with her. Dovelyn was too overprotective.

"Dove, I'm fine. You need to leave. Your father is expected to pay a visit today, and you shouldn't be here when he does."

She scuffed. "Right." She started to make her way toward my door but halted with her small fingers curled around the wood. "You are coming tonight, right, Tez?"

"Of course. I wouldn't miss it. But you know Brock is going to hate every second of it."

Her smile was serpentine. "That's exactly the point." Then she was gone, disappearing before my eyes.

A knock sounded on my door seconds after Dove vanished. The Lux King sauntered in without waiting for me to respond.

"Well, let me see it," he snapped in greeting, his hand outstretched, gesturing toward her files on my desk. He tsked as he skimmed the pages. "Well, it looks like our feisty prisoner gets to live for now. How is her training coming along? What are her other abilities?"

"Her training is going well," I said cautiously, careful of my words. I longed to reach my senses out to him, but every time I did, they came back blank, probably from some object of Alluse he kept with him to protect himself. "So far only her water ability is present. I do not know if she possesses anything else. I may need more time to figure it out."

"You have until the Dark Prince's Coronation. I want to know what her abilities are." He paused as he regarded me with cold eyes. "I expect you understand what will happen if you don't deliver and you disappoint me."

I nodded my head. I fucking did.

TWELVE
SCOTLIND

I WAS in my room for all of five minutes before a knock sounded on my door. Without thinking, I opened it immediately, expecting to find my maid. But a tall brunette male stood before me. Tall wasn't the right word for him. He was a giant.

"Hello," he said. His voice was deep but not as rough as I would have expected. I stared back at him, blinking, not able to do much else. I didn't think anyone else knew I was here. They told me not to mention who I was. I didn't know what to do or how to act.

"Can I come in?" he pressed gently.

"No." I attempted to shut the door, but he caught the frame immediately.

"I'm a friend of Tezya's. My name is Brock," he said slowly. "I'm not going to hurt you. I'm a healer."

"I think you have the wrong room," I said back, attempting to shut the door again. "I don't need a healer."

"I don't have the wrong room," he smiled softly. "Tezya's been training you. He said you have open wounds still all over your body, the worst being on your back."

I halted, confused that Tezya noticed or cared enough to send for a healer. He didn't say anything when he scanned my back this morning.

He was deathly quiet for what seemed like minutes before he finally told me that we were heading back to the castle. Then he stormed out of the rushing waves, leaving me with a new insecurity about my back. I honestly hadn't seen it for myself. I tried not to look too closely at anything on my body since I came to Lux. But it did ache, causing me to sleep on my side because of it.

"You can trust me," the male urged. This time his voice was even softer, lighter, and I found all my worries floating away until I was left with nothing but trust for the brute, and I couldn't understand why, but I found myself opening the door wider, allowing him to pass.

He nodded thanks as he stepped inside my chambers and closed the door behind him.

"Let me see your back, please."

"I..." I started, having no idea why I was listening to him. Not an inch of his skin was turning golden, and even though he had brownish eyes, the coloring suggesting that it could be Tennebrisian, I knew he was from this city, that he possessed Light abilities. I looked closer at him, inspecting his eyes more closely like I'd find all the answers I wanted there.

"What are your powers?" I asked him.

"I told you I was a healer, didn't I?" He smiled again. "And didn't anyone ever tell you that it's rude here to just blatantly ask someone what their abilities are?"

"No, I didn't know..." I started. I had no idea what the Luxian customs were, what was acceptable, and what wasn't. I still wasn't convinced that I would get to find out. I didn't trust that my current situation was real. It felt too good to be true. Yes, I was Luxian, but I was still considered a prisoner. I still grew up in Tennebris. I didn't know if I would ever fit in here. I didn't know where I belonged anymore.

He interrupted me with a softer grin. "It's okay. Let me heal you now."

I had no idea what had me agreeing, why I was now lifting my shirt over my head, so he could see my wounds, but I did.

I swore that the male was hiding a grimace as my cuts healed one by one, but he never said anything. He continued to work on me, healing each and every wound.

I rolled my back and was surprised by how good it felt. I turned to look at him. His eyes looked more golden now that the sun was shining on them. I didn't know why I thought they were the Tennebrisian brown. Beads of sweat coated his skin, and I caught a glimpse of black markings on his chest, exposed through his shirt.

"I can't take away your scars," he gestured toward the long gash from my knee to thigh that Kole made twice and the mangled skin on my right calf. I fisted my hands and still felt my scar on my palm from my blood bond with Sie. I didn't know if it made me happy or upset that I would be keeping that scar. "I can only heal recent wounds."

"Thank you. Thank you so much," I said and meant it.

He only offered me another smile as he walked out of my room, leaving me alone. But as he left, I felt a glimpse of my old self coming back for the first time in a long while.

———

I HAD to get out of the castle. It was starting to drive me crazy only seeing the same four walls, whether it was the walls in my new chambers or in the training area. I needed fresh air.

I wanted to explore the city beyond my small window. Going to the beach with Tezya was agony. Not because I didn't love it but because I did. I loved the ocean and the feel of the sun warming my skin. It was agony because now I was stuck inside and not allowed to leave. It was a small taste of freedom, and I wanted more. I *needed* more.

I also was growing bored. Dangerously bored. Tezya said we weren't training in the afternoon once we returned because he had to meet with the King, and I was absolutely restless. My entire existence lately had consisted of going full force into training, and I didn't like to sit idle and let my thoughts haunt me. My maid Patricia stayed with me for a little bit, but now she was gone, claiming she needed to perform other duties around the castle, whatever that meant—I honestly had no idea where she went when she wasn't with me.

And with nothing to do but think, I kept replaying over and over again what Tezya had admitted to me. How someone who was a high rank in Lux didn't agree with the system. Someone who probably benefited greatly from having it in place too, judging from his five branded onto his wrist and his position within the army.

I had always wanted to hear those words. I had always wanted someone else to agree with what I believed in, and Tezya just offered up the information for nothing. He was a member of the Luxian army. He worked with the Fire Prince, who had murdered every rebel that disagreed with the King and with the system. He was probably forced to fight them, to kill them. I shuddered, thinking of what would happen to him if any of the Royals heard him voice what he had told me last night. And yet, he still told me, still trusted me with it.

I dreamt about Sie saying that to me, about him telling me that he would help me change things. And although Sie wasn't completely in agreement with the system, he never wanted to discuss it. He never wanted to take action about how rank zeroes were treated. He only cared about keeping me safe. It bothered me that he was going to be the King, and he didn't want to act to change things for his people.

You aren't a nix anymore, Scotlind. You aren't one of them. His words at the lake clanged through my head. *One of them* like they were some-thing different than the rest of the higher rankings. Another memory flashed from our conversation at the lake. *They want to kill you. This isn't the time. Maybe afterward, when you are safe, we can talk about how they are treated and try to come up with better a solution, better conditions for them. We can make it so servants are respected.* Did Sie truly believe that rank zeroes belonged as servants? Did he not think that they could do better? Be better?

I needed to stop thinking about it. Mainly because every time I thought about Sie, either tears threatened to spill down my cheeks or I tried to break something. Either way, neither reaction was a good one.

Coral and fuchsia mixed with the deepening blue as I watched the sun set through the one window my chamber had. But the city didn't fade into darkness. It wasn't swallowed up by the sky as the moon and stars would soon take over the clouds. It glowed.

I watched as light after light lit up every window. An aura seemed to hover over the colorful sun-symboled banners, luscious flowers, and strange trees. Many of the buildings were made of glass, making the skyline reflective.

My window wasn't nearly good enough. Mainly because it didn't open, which I could understand why, but I wanted to smell the sea. I wanted to explore it with all my senses until it engulfed me, and I could think of nothing else. I had to see it for myself.

I sprung to my feet and trekked my way across the room toward my dresser before I could think better of it. I shoveled through the thin clothes of Lux and tossed them aside until I found what I was looking for. A long coat. The material was thin, not made for warmth like the Tennebrisians coats were, but designed for fashion.

It was tan, which I didn't know if it boded well for blending in, but I guessed it would do just fine in a golden city. I pulled the thin coat over my shoulders, happy when I noticed there was a hood. Not even my eyes and freckles were exposed through the fabric. No one would recognize me.

To my surprise, no one guarded my chamber door or even bothered to look my way. It was odd. I technically was still a prisoner here, yet I wasn't trapped. In Tennebris, I couldn't go anywhere alone. A guard had to be with me everywhere I went. That was until Kole tried to murder me. Then Peter or Sie stayed by my side. But I was never, ever alone. I wasn't allowed to be.

But this was easy. Too easy. No one paid attention to me as I walked through the resplendent halls. The last rays of sunbeams were floating through the open windows, reflecting off the chandeliers that were cast into a dim light. The curtains billowed in the breeze, taunting me, begging me to go outside. The briny smell of the ocean rippled toward me, my nostrils flaring. I wanted to see the water again, but I also didn't want to see anyone naked tonight. Tezya made it clear that the oceanfront by the city was clothing optional, and I would definitely stand out with every inch of my skin covered if that wasn't the norm.

I wasn't sure what to do from here. I didn't plan this out well. I honestly didn't think I would be able to make it past my bedroom doors so easily.

It took me longer than I thought it would, but I finally found the castle entrance and walked through the archway leading outside. The city spiraled out before me. My feet laden with excitement and antici-pation as I descended down the massive sandstone steps.

I was thankful for the thin material of the coat as soon as I made it outside. The humidity clung to my skin like morning dew, embedding its way through the fabric. Somehow inside the castle, despite all the open windows, there was a draft, but outside was blistering.

I pulled the ends tighter around me when I noticed men with the Luxian sun symbol plated on their chests guarding the front gate. I pivoted on my feet sharply, wanting to avoid the soldiers. Remem-bering the forest Tezya and I trekked through, I slowly made my way toward the back of the castle by the gardens. There had to be a path that led toward the city, I hoped.

My newly formed plan was to find the forest path, stroll around the city, maybe visit a few vendors, walk to the bayside, and avoid the nude beach no matter what. Then, I would track down a library before heading back because I needed a book or two. I would figure out the no-money-thing later.

Excitement settled into my core as I neared the edge of the forest. One bush separated me from the woody escape. I shouldn't have to hike too long until I came across a pathway.

"You know," a low voice drawled, "I didn't take you to be a fool, Rumor." I halted with my leg half raised in the air, about to hop over the bush. "You shouldn't be out here. You're not supposed to leave your chambers. Not to mention gallivanting through the jungle *alone* when dusk is approaching, in a place you aren't familiar with, with no weapons, might I add." Tezya tsked, and I could feel his gaze assessing me from behind. "Very foolish."

"Give me a weapon then." I lowered my leg but didn't turn to face him yet.

He let out a throaty laugh. "Definitely not going to happen and even if I did, it still doesn't help with the whole *you're not allowed to leave your chambers* thing."

"If I'm not allowed to leave my chambers, then why didn't you have any soldiers guarding my door? If I'm still a prisoner, why taunt me with such freedom?" I finally culled the courage to turn and face him. It was breathtaking the way the sun set behind him, his white hair reflecting and catching in the glows of the sky. His eyes were shining as he watched me. His lips were twisted into a half grin, amusement flickered across his face, across his scar.

"Soldiers aren't guarding your door because I ordered them not to. I figured you didn't want random males gawking outside your chambers while you slept, and it wasn't necessary anyway."

"And why wasn't it necessary? Clearly, it was if I was able to get out of the castle without being caught."

"Who said you weren't caught?" He laughed again, the other side of his lip pulled upward into a full grin now. "I don't need anyone guarding you because I know your whereabouts. I've been following you since you left your room."

"H-how?" I gaped. Humiliation ran its course through me. I actually thought I got away with it.

"My other ability, besides fire, is summa sensibus."

"Summa-what?"

He laughed again. "I'm assuming by that reaction you aren't familiar with all the powers of Lux." I glared at him before he continued, "It's called summa sensibus."

"And what is that exactly?"

"It means I have heightened senses, Rumor. When your maid leaves your room, I take notice of monitoring you."

"Heightened senses? What does that mean exactly?" I asked, biting my bottom lip. "What *senses*?"

"All of them."

I swallowed. Patricia never stayed in my chambers while I slept. Did that mean he was monitoring me throughout the night? Could he hear my screams when I had nightmares?

"I have heightened everything. I feel things harder. Agony hurts more. I feel the sting of a blade tenfold to what anyone else would. The touch of a female is more euphoric, the pleasure is better. I can see miles beyond anyone. I can hear you even if I'm not next to you. I can smell you. Your fears, your desires, your emotions, they radiate off you as easily as light leaves the sun. Like right now your panic is laced with mild curiosity and a little bit of embarrassment."

I swallowed again. The lump in my throat was now bulging. "I... I get it." I stammered. This is what he meant by *more*. He definitely was right. It was more than just knowing someone's emotions. The fact that he could sense whatever I felt made me uncomfortable. Could I hide anything from him? Holy Pylemo.

"Why didn't you stop me then? If you were listening and monitoring me, why let me leave at all?"

"I was curious. I'm honestly surprised that it took you this long to leave your room. I wanted to see what you would do. I wanted to see where you'd go and if you'd try to run away, which clearly you are." He cocked his head toward the dense trees looming behind me.

"I wasn't running away," I said tightly. "I just wanted to explore the city."

He arched his brow. "Last I checked, the city wasn't in the jungle."

"I know that. I didn't want to go in there exactly," I said, gesturing toward the woods at my back, "I just figured that I wouldn't be able to walk past the front gates, so I hoped that the trees would eventually lead me to the city. I just wanted to leave. I had to get out of that room."

"Why?" he asked, scanning me, and his assessment took on a whole new meaning now that I knew what he could do.

I figured there was no sense in lying to him if he'd just know I wasn't telling the truth, so I said, "Because my room was starting to feel like a prison, a much bigger and nicer one, but I couldn't stand the confinement. I couldn't stand the... I just wanted to be outside for a little bit."

He stared at me for a moment with deathly stillness. I shifted on my feet, uncomfortable with his gaze and how it seemed to penetrate right through me. His silence was growing more paralyzing, so I rambled more as I awkwardly twirled my hair. "I just wanted to walk around. Just for a little while. I wanted to go to the bayside and then maybe the library. There's nothing to do in my chambers but to think and think and think, and when I'm alone with my thoughts, they linger on..." Kole's brown eyes crept into my vision. I roughly shook my head, trying to shake him away.

"I'll make a deal with you," Tezya finally spoke. "Train with me and I mean *really* train with me. Work through your fears. Let me help you overcome both fire and water. Be able to go in the pool or bathe like a normal Advenian. Do that, and I'll give you more freedom."

I was stunned for a moment. My brain kept snagging on how he knew about my fear of fire. I never told him, and even my memories from the monitor room didn't show how my childhood home burned down. "What kind of freedom?"

"You still can't go anywhere unattended. Not until the King declares it. It's too dangerous to go against his orders, but I'll let you come out with me as long as the King's not around. We can start tonight. I'll take you somewhere. You don't have to go back to your room right away."

"Why do this? What's in it for you?" I asked, confused, not fully believing there wasn't a catch. This bargain seemed more beneficial to me than to him. I would be a fool not to take him up on it. Although I recoiled at the idea of being near fire or going into the pool. I knew I needed to. It was a weakness that I had to get over. I wanted to overcome it. But I didn't see how that benefited *him*. I didn't see how anything he did for me benefited him.

He said that he'd take me somewhere tonight and the thought of not going back to my room was too appealing. I wanted that more than anything. It was enough to get me to agree on the spot, but I forced myself to wait for his answer.

"Let's just say it's more convenient."

I crossed my arms, refusing to accept that as an answer. I needed to know why he was so willing to help me. It seemed too good to be true, and my guard was in full force, my walls built so high I didn't know if they would ever crumble. I didn't know if I ever wanted them to after trusting Sie and seeing how that turned out for me. "Why is it convenient for you?"

He smirked when he noticed I wasn't budging. "I was tasked to train you, and I can't take you to the hut every other day for you to actually go in the water. So training you is kind of challenging if you keep refusing to go in the pool. Plus, if I'm forced to be around you all the time, I would prefer that you bathe."

I went to open my mouth to protest that I did wash but stopped myself. How much could he overhear in my room? Did he listen to the conversation I had with Patricia on my first night and knew that I refused the tub? I bit back the remark as I thought of how I actually smelled to him. I hadn't washed properly since before Kole kidnapped me. After that, it's been only the ocean, lake water, or my cloth baths. And I was training hard every day, sweating profusely. On top of that, he said he had a heightened sense of smell. Humiliation coursed through me, but I didn't want him to sense that too, so I tried to brush it off.

"I... I won't be able to right away. I can't just turn it off," I said, trying to deflect, but it was the truth. If he was expecting me to get into the pool tomorrow morning just because I went out with him tonight, he was crazy.

"I know that, Scotlind. I'll help you. I'll be there with you the whole time. You just have to trust me."

I swallowed hard. The shock of him actually using my real name hit me. I couldn't explain why. But he was serious, that much I could tell. He wasn't joking around or toying with me. But could I trust him?

"Okay," I said slowly. "I can't make any promises, but I'll agree to try."

"Good enough. Now let's go, I have somewhere to be, and I'm late because of you."

"Where are we going?" I stammered as I hurried to follow after him.

A wicked smirk appeared on his face, contorting his scar upward. "To a party."

THIRTEEN
SCOTLIND

I WAS INSIDE one of the towering glass buildings a few blocks from the castle. Tezya said that one of his friends lived in it, along with many other Luxians. It supposedly was called an apartment complex. The building itself was high, too high for my comfort. I counted seventeen flights of stairs before Tezya finally said that we made it. My breath was embarrassingly ragged by the time we stopped. I'd never felt so frustrated with my body as Tezya smiled at me from above the landing. He was leaning against a white door frame, breathing perfectly normal. He looked casual and relaxed, like walking up all those steps was as easy as rising out of his bed. I, on the other hand, was in rough shape.

"Whoever your friend is, they are crazy for having to walk up that every single day," I huffed. My body was bent over as I pressed my hands into my knees.

"His name is Rainer, and while he is crazy, he doesn't take the stairs. He's too lazy for that."

"How does he get into his house if he doesn't take the stairs?"

"He takes the elevator."

"The what?"

Tezya laughed. "Sorry, I forgot they don't favor electricity much in

Tennebris. It's basically a box that moves up and down the flights for you. We can take it on our way out if you would like."

I glowered at him. "That would have been nice to know before you made me climb up all those stairs."

"Consider it part of your training," he grinned. "Come on, Rainer's place is around the corner."

I followed Tezya down the hall that was lined with too many identical doors to count. He stopped at the furthest one, positioned at the end of the building.

"I hope you like to drink," he said as he pushed the door open without knocking. The space was small but comfortable. We entered into a tiny gray and white kitchen. A small table was set off to the side, and at the end of the room were two deep purple sofas and a large monitor screen mounted to the wall. A slate door was closed off to another part of the home, and a set of sliding glass doors by the sofas led to a balcony outside.

When Tezya said he was taking me to a party, I didn't expect *this*. I pictured that it would be similar to the one Vallie took me to on our last night in LakeWood, or the one I walked in on with Sie when Alec compelled me. I thought it would be crowded with strangers and blaring music. But this was quiet. More intimate and private, but I still felt like I didn't belong.

There were only four people occupying the sofas. I was shocked to see Princess Dovelyn among them. She was perched on the armrest, leaning into a broad male. "You're friends with Princess Dovelyn?" I whispered to Tezya as he dragged me further into the room.

He stole a glance back at me, a half grin on his face. "Something like that."

A gorgeous female with long, silky black hair on the left side of her head noticed our presence first. The right side of her hair was a light blue, a shade darker than Tezya's eyes. Her hair was split directly down the middle across her bangs that went straight over her forehead, covering her eyebrows. I'd never seen anyone with hair like that or as captivating as she was. I couldn't look away. She was slender and looked dainty despite her height. Her features were just as acicular and delicate.

"Tez, you made it!" she said as she set a large amber filled cup down on the table and stood up. She glided over to him, pulling him into a massive hug. His body flung toward her despite the girl's narrowed frame. She was tall, coming up to the tip of his nose. Her beautifully slanted eyes noticed me as she pulled away from him. The color was striking—a bright neon yellow. "And who did you bring with you?" Her eyes lit up with excitement, making them look like they were glowing.

"Kallon, this is Rumor. Rumor, Kallon." Tez said as he gestured to me.

The girl didn't hesitate as she took a step toward me, engulfing me in a hug like she'd known me her whole life. Jasmine and rosewater wafted my senses as her soft hair fell forward and covered my vision in a sea of black and blue. "It's so nice to meet you, Rumor," she beamed as my face pressed into her breasts.

"It's nice to meet you too," I said with a smile when she finally pulled away. I desperately wanted to correct her on my name and tell her to call me anything except Rumor. I had no idea why Tezya insisted on calling me that, but I never asked him what I could call myself. The King made it clear that no one was to know about me. And yet, Tezya didn't lie about my last name.

"Hey, Rumor," a smoky male voice sounded. "You must be why Tez here hasn't been around much." The male looked me up and down, making a point to do it very, tauntingly slow.

"I can't believe you kept a beauty like this locked up all to yourself," Kallon chimed in as she too assessed me, her bottom lip pouting a little. I'd never seen anyone so uniquely beautiful before. It made me slightly embarrassed by her compliment. I couldn't even bathe properly, and I had no idea what I looked like anymore. I was too scared to find out, so I avoided mirrors.

The male's smile widened as he took me in again. "Well, at least now I can see why he's been so *occupied*."

"Shut up, Rainer," Tezya laughed as they clamped hands and then patted each other on their backs. The male that was sitting on the sofa next to Dovelyn stood now. My eyes widened as I recognized him. He was the healer from earlier.

"You—" I started to say.

He smiled. "Nice to see you again, Rumor." Princess Dovelyn narrowed her eyes at our interaction.

"This is Brockwich," Tezya said as the brunette male finally made his way toward me, and I realized that I had never thanked Tezya for sending a healer. "It's his birthday tonight."

"Happy Birthday," I said, my voice coming out weaker than I intended.

"Thank you," Brockwich said roughly. "I go by Brock. The only person who calls me Brockwich is Tezya, and that's only because he knows it annoys me." I offered a smile. Brock and I seemed to have that in common as Tezya wouldn't stop calling me by my last name.

He halted next to the male named Rainer. Brock was a good head taller than everyone in the room, including Tezya, and seemed twice as big as the guy he was standing next to. They seemed like polar opposites. Brock was a mask of calm, while Rainer seemed wild and unpredictable. Rainer's amethyst eyes were striking against his dark skin and black hair. Brock's golden eyes complemented his chestnut hair that he kept short and cropped against his head, while Rainer seemed to favor a more untamed look. He had a mess of curls that he tied back in a bun that I was envious of. My hair was straight and only held a slight wave if it was braided or curled.

Rainer was the smallest male in the group, even smaller than Kallon. He was also the leanest. Brock was broad and built more like Tezya. His features were sharp and angular, while Rainer's were soft and light. Rainer couldn't stop smiling as he leaned into Kallon to whisper something while Brock kept a serious and composed expression on his face.

It seemed like an odd group of friends. They were all so different. The only similarity they shared was that they were all attractive in their own unique way.

"Damn straight. I'm not going to stop calling you Brockwich,"

Tezya said with a smile, then looked over at the Princess, who was still settled on the sofa, silently taking everything in. "What? Are you too good for us now, Dove? You can't even get off your ass to say hello?"

My eyes widened as my ears couldn't believe what he was saying. He was talking to the Princess like that.

"Now you want to see me, Tez? You weren't this happy to see me when I snuck into your room this morning," Dovelyn said as she pretended to inspect her nails. She still hadn't moved from her spot on the sofa or even bothered to look at us. She was in his room this morning?

"Key word is *sneak*, Dove. No one likes it when you show up uninvited."

Kallon seemed to notice the question on the tip of my tongue as I looked between Tezya and the Princess. "Oh, Dove and Tez are—"

Tezya cut her off. "She's my *friend*." Dovelyn looked up at that, a smirk on her face.

"We're just friends now, Tez?" she asked innocently as she finally hopped off the sofa. She was still wholly ignoring me. She came up next to Brock, who was looking down at her with adoration in his eyes.

Dovelyn stood a few inches smaller than me and looked too petite and dainty next to Brock's large frame, but I knew not to be fooled by her appearance. I remembered Sie telling me that she was just as strong and cunning as the two Luxian Princes. She crossed her arms as she finally glanced my way. "You shouldn't have brought her here, Tez. The King won't be happy when he finds out."

"I can do whatever I want, Dovelyn," Tezya snapped. "And the King does not need to know about it, got it?" He glanced around, making eye contact with each one of them, challenging them.

"I'm sorry if I interrupted. I can leave," I said, all too aware of the thick tension radiating throughout the room. "I was going to go for a walk anyway,"

Tezya grabbed my upper arm. "Oh no, you don't. You're not leaving, Rumor."

"She should leave, though," Doveyln challenged as she met my stare. "I'm sure you don't feel like partying tonight anyway. Not with the news we received today from the Dark Kingdom."

"What news?" I asked, hating myself for falling into whatever trap she was setting, but my curiosity was getting the better of me. I had to know. Were Sie and Peter okay?

"Dove, stop—" Tezya warned, but the Princess cut him off. His grip on my arm tightened as she continued.

"We just received word that your husband, I'm sorry, ex-husband, is remarrying."

I took an unsteady step backward on instinct as two things became utterly clear. The first was that everyone in this room knew who I was and seemed to know everything about my past. The second was that Sie was getting married.

"W-what are you talking about?" I barely registered that I had backed up into Tezya.

He gave her a stern look, his hand still gripping my upper arm, which was the only thing holding me upright right now. "Are you serious, Dovelyn? You couldn't keep your mouth shut for one damn night."

Then another thing hit me. Tezya knew. He knew, and he didn't tell me. Not that he was required to, not that he owed me anything, but he was so open with me last night at the hut that the shock of it hit me.

"Well, she deserves to know," Dovelyn replied. Then she shrugged, grabbed a glass of wine, and walked back toward the sofa. I just stood there, dumbfounded, not sure what to do next. Sie was remarrying. Sie was actually going to get married *again*.

Tez looked down at me, noticing the anguish on my face. "Come on, I'll get you a drink."

"No, I'll do it," Kallon said as she pried my arm out of Tezya's death grip and ushered me away. "This calls for girl talk."

"Here you go, babes," she said as she gently placed a glass of wine into my hands and led me through the sliding doors, which opened to a beautiful view of the city. I wordlessly followed her, staring up at her blue and black parted hair. I sat furthest from the ledge, not wanting to know what seventeen stories high looked like from up here.

She took the seat opposite me as I pulled my coat tighter around my arms. The night air had chilled, or maybe I just felt numb now. "Sie's getting remarried?" I asked her, unsure why I felt so comfortable being vulnerable and exposing that Dovelyn's words affected me. She was a complete stranger, and I knew nothing about her. Maybe I was just done wearing a mask and pretending. It was too exhausting, and I barely had any energy left.

"Yes," was all she offered. She was being careful not to upset me.

"How... how do you guys know about..." I couldn't finish the sentence. I couldn't get the words out.

"The Royals are always made aware of the happenings in Tennebris. The two Kingdoms stay informed about each other. Dovelyn found out the news first and told the rest of us this afternoon."

"Do you know who?" My voice was a whisper. I was surprised she heard me.

"I don't know much about her. I heard that her father is a part of the High Council there and that she has known Sie since childhood. Ugh, why can't I think of her name..."

"Reagan," I said with dread, knowing before she answered that it was true.

"Yes, that's it!" Kallon exclaimed before she looked over at me. I don't know why it bothered me so much. It shouldn't. Sie and I were never really married anyway, at least not in the kind of way I would have wanted to marry someone. We never loved each other. Maybe I would have loved him if time went on. If he never betrayed me—hadn't hurt me.

The thing with Sie was that I never understood my feelings for him. The only thing that was clear was that I found him ungodly attractive, but I couldn't decide if I liked him or hated him after that. He was confusing and twisted. One second, he would do awful things to me or not stop his friends from tormenting me, but then the next, he was protecting me, jumping head first into saving me.

I was starting to trust him. I had finally opened up to him. I told him everything, only for his father to imprison me the next day. It broke something in me when Sie annulled our marriage and sent me to be a prisoner here.

It hurt worse than any cut or scar on my body. I dreamt of Sie being my savior, of him swooping in and taking me out of the dungeons. I dreamt of him changing the ranking system for me—with me. Of him and I changing our society for the better. But that was all it ever was. A dream. Because he never would be that guy. Sure, he didn't completely agree with the ranking system, but he didn't seek to change it either. He never admitted to wanting to change it.

There had been plenty of opportunities for him to talk to me, to at least explain what was happening while I was left to deteriorate in the Tennebrisian dungeons. But instead, I rotted in that prison cell while he what? He got closer to Reagan. Was that all a part of Sie's plan? Did he want to marry Reagan all along? Was he really only using me to seek his own answers with the Council and always planned on this outcome? Reagan flirted with him all the time. She was there the night Sie didn't stop Alec from compelling me. She lingered by his side and had leaned into him as they both watched me humiliate myself.

"I'm sorry about Dovelyn," Kallon said softly, breaking my train of thought. "She is nice once you get to know her. She's just overprotective of Tezya to a fault, and you being around him worries the living shit out of her."

"Why would I worry her?" I asked.

"It's a long story. They've just always had that kind of relationship. Once you get used to her overprotectiveness, she'll eventually warm up to you."

I really didn't know what kind of relationship she meant, but I nodded my head anyway. It was strange yet comforting that Kallon was speaking as if I would be around for a while. I wanted to belong somewhere. I wanted to just live. But that was just another dream that wouldn't come true.

"Look. I know you cared for him, for Sie, but don't let him ruin your night. Males have a way of trying to do that, and I say *F* them all. Tonight we're celebrating Brock's day of birth. He just turned a hundred today. Don't let what Dove said to you get under your skin. Come drink with us. Forget about your Dark Prince for the evening."

"I don't care for him. Not anymore."

"Well," she smiled lightly, raising her own glass in the air, "the best way to get over a man is to drink."

FOURTEEN
TEZYA

I WAS GOING to strangle Dove for telling Rumor that Sie was engaged. I brought her here to have fun, not to make her feel like shit. I saw the haunted look in her eyes when she was talking about feeling trapped, and I just wanted her to forget about everything for a night. I'd known enough about a soldier's trauma to understand that mental healing was just as crucial as physical recovery. And whatever happened to her was deeply rooted now.

I kept watching her, trying to gauge her reaction. But she seemed fine ever since she re-emerged from the balcony with Kallon. I had no idea what Kal said to her, but I'd have to thank her later. Maybe she didn't care for the Dark Prince as much as I had thought. Hell, I really didn't know a thing about their relationship.

Rainer and Kallon were both hovering over Rumor like some prized possession, chatting her ear off. They were probably grilling her about every mundane detail of her life, about what it was like growing up in the Dark Kingdom. But she looked happy enough. She slowly sipped from her wine, but I couldn't help but notice her grimace after each one. She was listening intently to the two of them talk. Rainer and Kallon were over the top and both dramatic. Brock always said that they had a knack for engaging in conversation with everyone and anyone and somehow making them feel appreciated. Scottie was more reserved, smiling slightly, laughing softly, while my friends' laughs were barreling toward me.

Brock came up behind me. "So her, huh?"

"What's that supposed to mean?"

"You like her."

"No, I don't. You know the Lux King gave me orders to train her. That's all this is."

"Right, and training her means bringing her to meet your friends?" He gave me a half smile as he took a sip of the ale Kallon had made. "You are always closed off, Tez. You never let anyone new get close to you. Well, besides the four of us, but that's only because you're stuck with us now."

"That's not what this is. She isn't getting close to me," I said, growing frustrated that I had to explain myself. "I caught her sneaking off. We made a deal that I would get her out of the castle if she agreed to the kind of training I needed her to do. You know King Arcane won't be satisfied until he knows all her powers."

"Right. You keep telling yourself that. And what kind of training do you need her to do again?" Brock grinned, slowly shaking his head as he followed my gaze to where Rainer casually threw an arm over the back of the sofa to position himself closer to Scottie. "You and I both know that an Advenian doesn't need to be healed physically in order to access their powers."

I don't know why I didn't just tell him about Scottie's fears. If I explained the extent of her trauma, how it was hindering her from using her abilities, Brock would stop pestering me. Out of everyone, he would understand the most. He had seen horrors that I couldn't even imagine and had learned to deal with them. He had been with me through all my hell, in and out of the army. And besides Dovelyn, he was the only one who knew how my father treated me in private, about how I got the scar across my face. How I got all my scars. Hell, he would probably be a better trainer for her than me anyway.

"She isn't progressing like she should be, and I'm running out of time to figure out her abilities."

"Interesting," was all Brock said before taking a sip of his drink.

"What?" I snapped.

He held his hands up in the air, feigning innocence. "Tez, I've worked with you for over eighty years and have been friends with you just as long. I'm just saying that I know you. Plus," he added as he glanced over at Scottie. "You were given orders to train her, but the only thing I see by bringing her here is an excuse to be around her more."

"Stop being an ass and mind your own business. Just because you finally reached a century doesn't mean that you're all knowing."

Brock huffed a laugh. "You don't have to be an ass to see what I'm seeing. You haven't stopped gawking at the girl since you brought her here."

"I don't like her like that," I said coolly.

As if this conversation couldn't get any worse, Dovelyn snuck up behind us.

"You don't like her, huh?" she crooned as she inched her way in between us. "Then you wouldn't mind if Rainer takes his shot with her? You know he has a thing for brunettes, and I heard him tell Kal that she was pretty. They would make a good match, don't you think? Or maybe she is only looking for a rebound after Sie. Either way, I'm sure Rainer would be happy to oblige her in whatever her needs are."

I walked away from her, not wanting to listen anymore. With my heightened senses, I could hear Brock yelling at Dovelyn to stop, but I zoned them out.

"Tez, come here," Kallon said, gesturing toward her. Scottie looked up, her doe-like eyes burning cold flames into mine, the blue the hottest part of the fire.

"I'll be right there," I said as I nodded my head toward her. I opened another bottle and poured a glass of sweet wine before making my way toward them on the sofa. I placed the sweeter wine in Rumor's hand. "I think you'll like this one better," I said as I took the bitter wine from her. Our fingers lingered on each other's for a split second, and I could have sworn I felt a jolt of electricity shoot through me, entwining with my senses. Did she possess electricity? Was that one of her powers?

She hesitantly took a sip and, to my satisfaction, didn't grimace afterward. "Thank you."

Kallon arched her brow at the gesture. I ignored her as I slumped into the seat across from them. She and Rainer were both still hovering over Scottie like a newborn baby.

"We were just discussing our favorite pubs. The Hilting is mine and by far the best in Lux... We *need* to take Scottie there. Did you know, Tez, that she's never been out drinking in a pub before?"

I did know that, or I had guessed as much from her memories. She was always training during her time spent at school, and the only two revels she went to didn't end well. The first, the same compulsion user that was in Lux tried compelling her while someone else tried kissing her against her will. The second, Sie just fucking sat there on a leather sofa, watching as his friends did fucked up things to her. I'd seen people go through worse. I'd seen and lived through more abuse, more messed up shit that should have killed me. So why did her past bother me so much? I seemed to have no self control whenever I thought of her memories.

I didn't answer and took a sip of what remained of Scottie's bitter wine instead, finishing it in one gulp.

"So," Kallon continued, completely unaware of the tension building in me. "I was thinking that we should take her!"

"Yes," Rainer added delightedly, then turned to face Scottie. I noticed the way his knee pressed into hers, the way she pulled slightly back. "You have to come dancing with us. It's so much fun."

"She can't," I said and hated myself for it. Everyone turned to look at me, even Rumor. "She could be recognized. She can't go into public places like that yet."

Kallon slumped down into her seat. "Fine, then I want to take her to the waterfall."

Scottie's eyes lit up. I assumed that she used to love water. Most Advenians favored the element they possessed, and whenever the King had Kole shift through her memories at school, she practically lived in her dorm room bathtub. At the time, I couldn't process the sadistic look on the compulsion user's face when he noticed it too. It wasn't until I saw the memory of him drowning her that I realized what it was. I'd never been so livid in my life.

"A waterfall? Here in Lux?"

"Yeah, it's not too far from here," Rainer said, noting her excitement. "It's one of our favorite spots to hang out, and it's private, so it's perfect."

"I've never seen one," she started to say, meeting my eyes. I could see the lingering question there. She wanted to go.

"We can go in a couple of days. I already had planned on taking you back to the hut to train at the end of the week. There's something I want to try that we can't do in the pool. The waterfall is not too far out of the way."

Kallon clapped her hands together. "Perfect, I can't wait." Then she turned to Scottie. "You're going to love it."

"Can't wait for what?" Brock asked as he joined us again. Dovelyn was trailing by his side.

"We're going to take Scottie to the waterfall," Rainer said with a grin. Dove let out a hiss as she rolled her eyes but managed not to comment.

Rainer wrapped his arm around Scottie. "Let's play a game."

Everyone groaned.

"Rainer, come on. I know you're still a child, but no one likes to play drinking games," Dove said smoothly.

"Just because I'm not ancient like you doesn't mean I'm a child. I am thirty-three years old, thank you very much."

Dove huffed. "Exactly. A child."

"Come on, don't be a party pooper, Dovie. We can play truth or dare. It'll be a perfect way to get to know Scottie better." Rainer flashed Dovelyn his award-winning puppy dog eyes.

"It's Brock's birthday. Let him decide," Dove replied, then looked longingly up at my friend.

Brock shrugged. "Sure, why not." Dovelyn frowned, clearly annoyed that Brock didn't side with her. I didn't particularly care for the game, but if it made my friends happy, I wasn't going to stop them.

Rainer started, "Okay since it's Brock's birthday, he can go first. Scottie, the rules are simple. You either have to answer something honestly or do something that we say. If you refuse, you drink. Brock, truth or dare?"

"Truth."

"Hmm," Rainer made a point to tap a long, dark finger to his lips, pretending to think. "Do you have a crush on someone in this room?"

Brock didn't hesitate to take a sip from his drink. Everyone knew he liked Dovelyn, but he would never admit it. Brock was a rank four, and she was a five. They could never be together.

"Lame," Kallon and Rainer both grumbled.

"Tez, truth or dare?" Brock asked.

"Dare."

"I dare you to chug an entire cup full of Kallon's ale." Brock grinned.

"Are you trying to kill me, Brockwich?" I asked as I poured myself one of the infamous ales Kallon made.

"What is that supposed to mean, Tez? My ales are amazing."

"Kal, your ales are disgustingly strong, and we all know it. It would knock anyone out. Except you," I said as I chugged the drink. It went down smooth enough. Her ales were usually thick and heavy, great for sipping casually but vile to chug. It would have been easier to just take a sip, but I didn't want to offend her.

"Okay, Kallon, truth or dare."

"Dare always," she said with a wink.

"I dare you to not drink ale for the rest of the night."

Kallon scuffed. "Absolutely not," she glared as she took a massive swig from her drink.

Kallon turned to Scottie. "Truth or dare, babes?"

"Um, truth," Scottie replied.

"What do you think of Tezya?" Kallon smiled as she pushed the blue side of her hair out of her face, revealing a thin, arched eyebrow.

Rumor's eyes went everywhere but to mine. "He's... uh... nice."

"Nice?" Kallon almost spit out her drink. "Come on, Scottie. You have to give us more than that. Do you find him attractive?"

"It doesn't matter what she thinks," Dovelyn snapped. "He's betrothed."

Everyone stopped. "Seriously, Dove, what is wrong with you tonight?" Kallon asked, her yellow eyes flaring.

"Nothing is wrong with me. I'm the only rational one here. All of us except Brock will be betrothed by the Council at some point or another." She turned to look at Rumor, her gaze lingering on her two zeroes. "And I'm sure she'll get to marry whoever she wants within her own rank if my father decides she can live," she said as she rose from the sofa. "And this game is stupid. I'm going home."

Dove arched her back, and with a snap, two beautiful white wings appeared. She fanned them out, drawing attention to herself as she made her way to the balcony. "Happy Birthday, Brock. I'll see you tomorrow." Then she slid open the balcony door and leapt off, flying into the night.

I stole a glance at Rumor. She was gazing out the balcony after Dovelyn, completely mesmerized. I wanted to know what she was thinking but stopped myself from using my abilities to reach her. If she was shocked by the fact that I was engaged, she didn't show it. She seemed more intrigued by Dovelyn's wings than anything else. With a grunt, I walked toward the doors and slammed them closed after Dove. "Come on, Rumor, I should get you back before someone notices."

FIFTEEN
SCOTLIND

THINGS WERE AWKWARD the next morning. Tezya and I didn't bring up anything that happened last night, especially the fact that he was engaged. It was none of my business anyway. We started our training with our usual morning run then workout. It wasn't until after lunch, when he told me we were going to get into the pool, that I started to regret my decision to make our deal.

Tezya was half way down the wet stairs, the pool water hitting his knees when he turned to look at me. "Come on, Rumor. I'll be here with you every step of the way. Nothing will happen," he said as he held out his hand for me. Black flames wrapped around his ankles where his thick calves were already submerged under the water. I knew that as he continued down the stairs into the pool, the flames would travel up his entire body, not stopping until it reached right over his scar.

I stared at his outstretched hand for a long moment before I finally placed mine in his. His fingers wrapped around mine, and I became utterly aware of every callus he earned. Tezya never took his eyes off me. He gently tugged on my arm as I slowly, very slowly, made my way down. His hand was like a vise grip, locking me to my own stupid, reckless decisions.

My breathing was ragged by the time I made it to the same step as him. I glanced down at my feet, noticing the water circling above my knees. "Don't look down," he said as he gently tilted my chin up. "Look at me."

I exhaled heavily as I stared at the blue and silver in his eyes, focusing on it.

"Good," he said. "It's just like when we were in the ocean. This water won't harm you. You are in control." I closed my eyes, listening to his words, letting his voice soothe my fears.

His fingers tightened around my hand while his other hand lightly touched my lower back. "You can do this, Scotlind." Hearing him say my name, my real name, made my eyelids flutter open. I didn't realize how close I was to him. With each ragged breath I took, my breast just barely grazed his bare chest. I started breathing heavier, but not from the water. Being this close to him felt... I don't know how it felt. It was like I was drawn to him. I felt a tug pulling me closer to him. I couldn't get close enough, like completely pressing every inch of my body into his still wouldn't be enough. It wasn't the same desire I felt when I was around Sie. That was pure lust and exhilaration, but this was somehow different... more...

He let out a deep breath and took a step back, removing his hand from my back in the process. "Sorry," he said. Cold lingered where his touch had been. The lack of it was disappointing. "Are you up for going all the way in?" he asked.

I nodded my head, but I wasn't so sure of my answer. Never letting go of my hand, Tezya sank into the water with me in tow. He waited patiently for me, the water now resting around his abdomen, while I slowly descended the rest of the way in. My feet came in contact with the cracks on the tile floor. I could feel the slipperiness of it on my toes. I knew how it felt against my cheek, how it felt to have my face pressed against it.

He pulled me into his chest as soon as I started hyperventilating. "I got you," he cooed over and over again as he gently tucked my hair behind my ears, leaving water dripping off my face. "I've got you."

"The tiles—"

I didn't need to finish my thought. He gently lifted me up, picking my feet off the ground. I wrapped my legs around his body without thinking. "Is this better?"

I couldn't speak but nodded my head. I found it surprising that it was true. With my feet no longer feeling the crevices of the floor and with his touch, I felt protected, safe even. The feeling of his body against mine was distracting. His hand kept caressing my hair, pushing the strands out of my face.

His other hand shifted as if he had only just realized where he'd grabbed me when he picked me up. He fanned his fingers out, resting them over my hip instead. I gasped at the feel of him, his wet body against mine. I meant to push away from him. I wanted to prove to myself that I could swim on my own, but I couldn't, not yet. It was too overwhelming, too much for right now, so I just stayed wrapped up in his arms, letting him hold me.

"Do you want me to let go now?" he asked softly.

"No," I panted, my voice breathless. "Just... distract me."

He halted with his hair tucking for just a moment to peer down at me. "Alright," he said slowly, "tell me about yourself."

I frowned. "You already know everything. You saw all my memories."

"No, I only know what the King forced you to reveal. I want to hear about your life from you. What do you like? What do you hate? I want to know who you are from *you*, not from a screen," he said as he gently started to move around the pool. My body was still pressed against his, my legs wrapped—probably too tightly—around his muscular back. Despite the cool feel of the water, I was flushed, and every place his body met mine felt like it was on fire. I didn't know if it was from his abilities, if a fire user's skin reflected some of that heat that was hidden beneath them, or if it was from something else entirely...

"I... I don't remember anything from my time in Lux before I was taken. I can't even remember my parents, but I remembered the ocean. I remembered it so vividly that sometimes it was the only thing that kept me sane. I missed it when I was over there. Everything seemed so dark. Except for my friend, Vallie. She and her twin were the only ones who were nice to me growing up."

"The redheads?" he asked. My heart ached as I thought of them, especially Vallie. Goddess, I missed her so much. I missed her relentless teasing every time I came back late from training. I missed the way she so effortlessly threw her hair up in a perfect messy bun. I missed how miserable she was whenever she tried to spend time with Miles and me when we were reading. She hated it. Her ability allowed her to power through and memorize every detail about any book she ever picked up. She always said that reading was boring, and she would finish her book in a matter of minutes. But she'd sit with us nonetheless, just to keep us company.

"Yes."

"Tell me about her." He made another lap around the pool.

I sucked in a deep breath, focusing on Vallie. "She is kind to everyone she meets, probably the kindest person I know. She's also the bossiest and doesn't take no for an answer. Kallon would love her. They remind me a little of each other."

"What? Is she dramatic and loves to drink?"

I grinned as I thought of Vallie. "Exactly." Then my smile faltered as I remembered what Dovelyn had said last night. Tezya was engaged, and I was letting him hold me. I had my legs wrapped around him, my chest flushed against his.

I pushed away from him, my fingers gliding over his abdomen as I slipped out of his grip. "You shouldn't touch me like that."

"Like what?" he asked as he arched his brow. His grip slackened on me, but he didn't let go, and I didn't exactly push him away either. I didn't know if I was ready to swim in the pool without him holding me, and we were at the opposite end of the stairs. I wasn't ready to feel the bottom of the floor.

"You're engaged. Why didn't you tell me when I asked you about it at the hut?"

He kept his expression blank as he responded. "I honestly forget that I'm engaged at times. My marriage has been arranged ever since my powers manifested, and I was declared a five." He let out a heavy sigh. "I'll be forced to marry eventually, but until then, I'm just trying to postpone the inevitable. Remember when I told you that the people of Lux don't get to choose who they marry—at least anyone that's a rank five—that it's only about who can breed strong offspring?"

"Yes."

"That's all it is. That's all it ever is in Lux."

"So people never fall in love?"

"No, they do," he said slowly. "Sometimes people are lucky enough, and they fall for someone within their rank. No one is allowed to marry outside of the one they're in, but it's only rank fives that are forced into arranged marriages. As long as a four marries a four, a three marries and three, and so on, it's fine. However, most Luxians aren't that lucky. Most fall for someone outside their rank, which is illegal. Some still take the risk and try to hide it. But if they're ever caught, it's not pretty. The King doesn't take mixing within the ranks lightly. That's why many people have very long engagements here."

"And your fiancé wouldn't be upset if she saw us?" I gestured between our bodies. My legs were still wrapped around him, although much looser than before, and my hands were on his chest, pushing back so that we were further apart. He stopped playing with my hair. His hands now rested lightly on my hip and lower back.

He laughed. "No. Neither one of us wants to get married."

He eyed me for a moment before taking me on another lap in the water. The air was cold on my back as we emerged in the shallow end. "Are you still doing alright in the water?"

"Yes," I said, realizing that my breathing had returned to normal. "I think the distraction is helping, thanks."

"Can I ask you something now, Rumor?"

"Sure."

He paused, making another lap before he finally asked, "Why didn't you ever sleep with Sie? Was it because you were from Lux, or did you not like him in that way?"

"I um..."

"You don't have to answer if you don't feel comfortable," he interrupted.

I bit my lip and watched as his eyes followed the movement. I quickly stopped. "No, it's okay. I don't mind answering. Growing up I never planned to get married or ever be with a guy because I knew it was treason. It's one of the reasons I chose to be a guard, but then my name was called, and everything happened. I felt like I was waiting to be discovered. I felt like being selected was my death sentence, so I didn't want to sleep with him because I was so scared that I'd be discovered sooner, and I realized…" I paused. "I realized I didn't want to die. No guy was worth that. I found him attractive, but he was also confusing. I couldn't tell how he felt about me, and I couldn't decide if I thought he was a good person or if everything was an act."

He nodded his head. "What were the other reasons you wanted to be a guard?"

I was surprised for a moment that he picked up on that detail after everything I'd just revealed. "I didn't want to be weak anymore. I didn't want anyone else to kidnap me." I let out a dry laugh, thinking of all the times I had been taken against my will after that. "I didn't want the night my parents were killed to be repeated. I thought if I trained and if I became a guard, I wouldn't feel helpless anymore, I wouldn't be weak, but I was wrong."

"Scotlind, you know that your body may physically be weak right now because of what the dungeons did to you, but you were never weak. Your mind and soul were never weak. Not for a moment in your life. You are brave and strong. And absolutely no one can take that away from you."

"You don't think it's weak to fear water and fire?"

"Everyone fears something. What makes someone weak or strong is what they do with those fears. You turned yours into motivation. Look at yourself right now. You are in the pool. Last week you didn't even want to get near it, and you walked so close to the wall I thought you were going to blend in with it. Now, you're swimming with me."

"I'm being carried in a pool, and I'm too scared to even bathe," I replied dryly.

"Things take time. Give yourself that without the resentment. Your fears don't define you, and they definitely do not stop you."

His eyes met mine, and I inhaled sharply as I felt his breath against my neck. Had he leaned in or did I? His hands slowly drifted lower, making idle circles against my abdomen in the water. His fingers were so soft that I hadn't realized it at first, but now I couldn't think of anything but his touch. His eyes were near glowing as he gazed at me. His wet locks pushed back, revealing both scars. His fingers trailed lower, his eyes never leaving mine as they traveled down and down. A warmth crept up in my core as a new kind of burning took hold.

His nostril flared. A low growl escaped him as his lips parted. I watched as a water droplet traveled over his scar and rested on his bottom lip. I couldn't stop staring at his lips. I couldn't stop thinking about the fact that I wanted to lick the water droplet off of them. I wanted to taste them, taste him. What was wrong with me?

I shifted away from his touch, remembering how he could scent my emotions. I did *not* want him knowing what I was feeling right now, even though I was pretty certain by the growl it was too late.

"I need to get out of the water," I snapped abruptly.

"Rumor, I'm sorry if I—" he said, his hands immediately withdrawing.

"You didn't. I need to go."

SIXTEEN
SIE

I FELT WORSE THAN DEATH. Worse than when I was beaten to a pulp in that warehouse by Kole's men. I'd never been so exhausted and weak before in my entire life. I finally got up to taking the max dose of the poison, but my body hadn't adjusted to it yet. It was like getting hit by the monorail over and over again. My hands wouldn't stop shaking, and it was an effort to continue standing. Every vein in my body felt like it was on fire. I was burning from the inside out, slowly, agonizingly. I needed a cold bath. I needed to be submerged in ice until my fever broke, but I didn't have time for that. I had to do this, and I had to do this now.

It didn't help matters that I had used almost all of my power to teleport out of the castle. I could have requested a car to take me to the monorail, but I didn't want the Council to know where I was going.

"Sie, what are you doing here?" Greyland asked once he saw me standing in the foyer of our family home. His dark eyes assessed me, scanning my body. "What's wrong? Are you okay?"

"I'm fine." I attempted to smile, but judging from my brother's frown, it wasn't convincing.

Our mother came into the foyer and halted as if she saw a ghost.

Maybe she had. "I wasn't aware you were coming home today. No one notified us of your visit," she said as she started shooing the servants away.

"They wouldn't." I leaned against a pillar for support. My entire back was drenched in sweat. "The Council doesn't know I'm here. I didn't use the monorail."

"You teleported all the way here?" my brother gaped.

I nodded, letting them both think that was why I looked like death right now and not the poison running through my veins.

"Why?" my mother asked.

"I wanted to see my brother," was all I said out loud, but I entered Grey's mind at the same time, *I need to talk to you in private.*

Greyland smiled. "Come on, let's go to my room. I'll get you some water."

She looked between us, aware we were talking in our minds. She used to yell at us for it, but it never stopped us as children. "Fine, but you will stay for dinner. I'll have the servants prepare your favorite."

It wasn't a question. I used all the energy I had left to lift off the pillar and walk over to her. Kissing her on the cheek, I answered, "Yes, mother," then followed Greyland up the stairs.

Neither of us said anything until he closed the door to his room. Our father had our rooms on opposite ends of the house because he claimed Grey was a distraction to me. Most of our conversations consisted of speaking to each other late at night. When we couldn't sleep, I used to enter his mind, and we would talk for hours. Besides Peter, he was the only person I cared about growing up.

Greyland locked the door and turned to look at me. "What's going on?" he said. "You don't look well."

I shook my head. "Not here." I grabbed his wrist, the skin on his arms silky and smooth without his rank burned into him yet, and then I teleported one more time.

Greyland and I both hurled up our guts when we arrived. Him from the vertigo of teleportation and me from my body yelling at me to stop. When he finished, he wiped his mouth with the back of his sleeve. "I forgot how much teleporting sucks." Then he looked at me, and concern flashed across his face worse than before. "Shit, Sie, what's going on?"

"I had to speak with you without anyone overhearing," I managed. We were outside the cabin I brought Scotlind to after the warehouse. I was leaning against the wood flanks, trying not to collapse.

"Are you ill?"

I shook my head.

"Then what's wrong because you look like you're on the brink of death, and you're scaring me."

"I'm fine, Grey—"

"No, you aren't," he cut me off. "You're acting weird, and you're so pale you look like a ghost. Not to mention that you haven't stopped shaking or sweating since you arrived. And you lost weight."

"Let's go inside, and I'll tell you everything," I said. I had been coming here a few times since Scottie was taken prisoner by Lux.

"The hunting cabin," Greyland said as he looked around, noting where I had brought him for the first time. "I forgot about this place." He grinned. "You fixed it up."

I nodded my head, not bothering to answer, then used all my strength to push the door open. The inside now had multiple bedrolls rolled up in the corner of the room, chopped wood stacked and ready for the fireplace, fresh water, some canned food that wouldn't expire for a long time, and a small table and chairs.

Grey strode over to the fireplace. "I'll start a fire, but you better start talking now, starting with what's wrong with you."

I sank into one of the new chairs I had brought. "I've been taking poison every day."

"Why," he asked as he threw another log into the fireplace, trying to remain calm. I didn't tell him that a fire was just about the only thing that could make me worse right now. I thrived in cold temperatures, but I knew he needed the warmth. He didn't have time to grab a jacket before I teleported him here.

"Because King Lunder was murdered."

Greyland stopped just as the pile of wood burst into flames. "But I thought he died eating—"

162

"No. He was *murdered.*"

"By who?"

"Synder, I'm certain of it, and I think he's trying to take me out too." I filled him in on everything that had happened with Scottie and how Peter and I believed it was a setup to get me off the throne.

"Do you remember Moli?" I asked when I finally caught him up on everything. He was now sitting with me at the table, the heat of the flames making me want to pass out.

"The healer that was assigned to you growing up?"

"Yeah, she's at the castle with me. She's the one that told me how Lunder was murdered, and she's been giving me the poison every day."

"There's no lasting side effects that could hurt you, right?"

"No," I lied. Moli told me that she didn't know what taking it every day would do to me, but I didn't care. I needed to be in control of my own future, and if this brought me closer to it, then I'd do it. "I'm going to be fine. My body just needs a couple more days to adjust. That's all. But that's not the reason I needed to talk with you. Do you remember how to get here on foot?"

"Yeah, I think so."

"I need to know for sure, Grey. I can mark some trees for a path for you, but that leaves this place vulnerable to being tracked."

"I can get here on my own."

"Okay good, because if anything happens to me, I need you to bring mom here. Take Lilia and Peter's parents too. Don't wait, don't hesitate. The moment you suspect anything, you leave everything behind, and you come here. Tell no one about it."

"Sie, you're scaring me." His eyes were starting to water, but the tears didn't roll down his cheeks. "If things are really bad at the castle, if you think they're trying to kill you for the throne, you need to step down."

"I can't."

"Yes, you can. Nothing is worth your life, not even being the King."

"It's not about being King," I said.

"Then what? Is it Father? Because we will deal with him together."

"Grey, stop." The tears were pouring from his eyes now, and it was fucking breaking my heart. "It's not about Dad."

"Then what? Because I don't understand what's so important that you're willing to go through all of this for? Come home, please, brother."

"It's her." I said it softly, but from the silence that stretched out, I knew he heard me.

"You can't get her back. She's gone, Sie. She's—"

"I know, Grey. I don't need you reminding me that she's gone and that I've fucked the only good thing in my life, and the chances of me getting her back are slim to none. I fucking know." I didn't mean to snap at him, but hearing him say it felt too real, and I wasn't ready to believe it.

"Okay," he said softly. "If you think she's worth all of this, I'll stand by you, but I don't like it. Promise me that you'll fight back. Promise me you'll win."

"Thank you." I reached over the table and clamped my sweaty palm over his. "And I promise."

Greyland wiped his tears. "Is Peter still in Lux looking for Scottie?"

"Yeah."

"Okay," he nodded. "Lilia has been going crazy. He didn't tell her he was going, and she's been worried sick, thinking the worst."

"I know. I'm sorry for that. I haven't been able to come here until today, and Peter didn't have time to warn her. Everything happened so fast." I didn't tell him that I hadn't been strong enough until today or that I was terrified for Peter. He should have been back by now and the fact that he wasn't was eating away at me, but I didn't want to scare my brother. "How is Lilia?" I knew if—*when*—Peter returned, he'd ask me about her, and I wanted to know.

"She's managing as best as she can... no help from me," he murmured the second part under his breath. I didn't comment even though I had no idea what he meant by that. "She pretends she's doing fine and completely ignores the fact that everyone knows she's going to be a zero." He paused and took a breath. "I heard rumors that they're thinking of forcing everyone to go through some sort of compulsion. Is that true? Are they really trying to do that?"

"It is." The expression on his face broke me. I knew he cared deeply for Lilia. They had a love-hate relationship. He liked her, even if he would never admit to it and treated her worse than dirt. "I know, it's fucked," I said. "Synder wants to find out who is a zero right away and not let them have an education. Since only an un-ranked Tennebrisian can be compelled, he's trying to pass a law that would make compulsion a requirement to get into school. It hasn't happened yet, but there is a chance that it might."

"That's messed up. Everything's going to shit."

"I know, Grey." I didn't want to think about all the other plans Synder had. I knew I couldn't let him keep the crown, but things were only going to get a lot worse from here.

SEVENTEEN
SCOTLIND

I COULD FEEL myself growing stronger. From my daily workouts with Tezya to regularly eating and sleeping again, I was already starting to gain some weight back, and new muscles were forming. I woke up for the first time and wasn't sore. I was eager to start training again. After spending the past couple of days just getting comfortable with being in the pool, I wanted to start practicing my water ability. I wanted to see what I could do.

I still couldn't get myself to go underwater in the pool or take a normal bath in my room, but I was making progress. Yesterday was the first time I was able to get into the water without Tezya's help, and I wanted to keep pushing myself further and further. I wanted to put this behind me.

I was surprised to see another bag packed for me when I spotted Patricia. "What's that for?" I asked her as I stretched in bed.

"You're going to the hut again with Tezya," she said, frowning at the bag. I perked up. The hut meant that I got to see the ocean again.

"Really?" I asked. "How many days?"

"I'm not sure, but I was informed to pack an outfit for you for two days just in case." She noted my excitement. "You need to be careful, dear. I don't trust him," Patricia said tautly, her eyes narrowing.

"Trust who?"

"Tezya."

"Why?"

"Oh never mind, dear, just be safe. Hurry up, you must be on your way, or you'll be late. Just be safe," she said again as she wobbled over to me and patted my back awkwardly.

I took the pack from her, which was significantly heavier than last time. I prayed that meant there were normal clothes in it and not just skimpy swimwear. "I will, Patricia."

Once in the hall, I halted. Kole was standing outside my door. I tried to turn away from him, but he grabbed my arm before I could flee. He was waiting for me. "Let go," I growled.

"That's not how you treat an old friend. Haven't you missed me, little nix?" he hissed as he dragged me further into the hall, away from my maid. He pushed me against the wall, my back slamming hard into one of the diamond frames that decorated the place. I winced as a throb ran up my spine.

Kole's eyes glimmered, lingering over my chest. "I see you aren't wearing your Alluse necklace anymore."

I cowered, hating that I did. My body began trembling in his presence. I tensed, anticipating his compulsion.

"Let go of her *now*." Tezya's voice was sharp and authoritative that even I shivered at the menace laced in every word.

Kole straightened, not quite reaching Tezya's full height. "We were just chatting," he replied coolly, but he dropped my arm immediately.

"I don't care what you were doing. You aren't allowed to talk to her. You aren't even allowed within a hundred-foot radius of her."

"Says who?"

"Says *me*," his voice lowered with the command. "If you try again, I will make you regret it." Tezya's hard gaze remained fixated on Kole. I stopped breathing as Kole looked at me one more time, then sauntered off.

"Are you okay?" Tezya asked once Kole was out of earshot. When I didn't answer, he raised his voice, slightly shaking me to attention. "Rumor, are you okay? Did he hurt you?"

I still couldn't speak. I shook my head once in answer.

"He's a prick," he said after a moment. "I can't believe the King is still allowing him to roam the castle, especially after knowing his role with you. I'll make sure he doesn't come near your room again. I promise." Tezya wrapped his arm around my waist and pulled me toward him. "Come on, let's get out of here."

———

WHEN WE GOT to the hut, Tezya immediately wanted to go into the water. I didn't protest as the humidity clung to every crevice of my body. I was eager for the coolness of the water's embrace.

"I brought you to the hut because I want to work with fire today, and I don't think doing that in an enclosed building is safe," Tezya said.

"How?"

Tezya produced a small ball of flames in his hands in the blink of an eye. The ball was so tight and closely compacted, no flicker of smoke escaped its embrace. The control he had to possess in order to wield such a wild, untamed element was impressive. Fire begged to travel, it wanted to encompass everything in its path, but yet he kept it tightly bound.

"I possess fire, so I want you to use your water to douse my flames," Tezya shifted the flaming ball from one hand to the other. "You need to learn to use your abilities with purpose. With practice, you'll be able to move water at your will."

"But I can't create. I can only manipulate."

"That's why I brought you here to practice first. You can use the ocean today, but eventually, you shouldn't need it. Water is everywhere. You might even be able to shift the fluid inside of an Advenian. You can do a lot with water once you know where to look. So today, we're going to work on two things at once. You will practice your water abilities, moving the water to where you want it to go, and at the same time, you will work on overcoming your fear of fire."

"How is your flame supposed to help me overcome my fear?" I asked as I shifted in the sand, my feet slowly sinking into the hot, fine grains.

"I'm hoping that once you learn to control your own ability, you will realize that the flames can't hurt you. Water is powerful and puts out even the strongest of fires." He nodded toward the ocean and the crashing waves to my back. "You ready?"

"Yes," I answered, and I was. I wanted to master my ability. I wanted to control the water and expel the flames, to extinguish my fears. I was sick of being terrified of them.

"Good," Tezya smiled as he sent the flaming ball of fire past me. It landed in the sand just out of reach of the waves, burning through the golden shells and small rocks. "Move the water toward the flames."

I turned to stare at the ocean behind me, then at the ever growing blaze. I watched as it grew and grew. "Now, Rumor."

Turning back to the ocean, I took a deep, calming breath and called to it, envisioning myself becoming it. Stretching and manipulating the water as I would a limb. I curled the wave over the flame like I was bending my arm.

The flames flickered out.

"Good. Now get in the water. I'm going to produce bigger flames."

I nodded as I followed Tezya into the blue. He halted once the waves reached my waist. "This will do. You ready?"

I nodded as a flame the size of my head floated over the water. Concentrating, I created a wave of my own, sending it splashing over Tezya's fire. Sprays of water hit our faces as he smiled down at me. I could just make out his marking that stopped at the bottom of his scar from the water droplets that splashed onto him.

"Good. You're improving. You're able to move the water more easily, and your reaction time has gotten faster. Now, I want you to try to create certain shapes instead of just a wave. Picture what you want in your head first. I'm going to use a bigger flame now too, so you'll have to use more from your reserve. If you feel yourself crashing, tell me."

"I don't know what that would feel like," I admitted.

"I know. Once you get evaluated by the King, they will run tests to determine how large your reserve is. For now, try to look for signs that your body is drained. Using your ability is taxing. You will start to feel physical effects when you use too much of it. Everyone's warning signs are different. I get headaches, Rainer's entire body trembles, Brock's vision blacks out, Kallon's nose bleeds. It could be anything for you, so just tell me if something feels off, okay?"

"Okay," I said.

Tezya's fire erupted, expanding past me. I felt the heat from the flames as they danced around the waves, but they never touched me. They weren't going to touch me. Tezya confined them to their spots, but it felt too real as the flicker of colors swam, closing me in. I could feel the burn they produced. I started to panic. Lavender eyes flashed in my vision, and I heard the same menacing laugh on the cold beach as my mind brought me back to when I was seven.

"Put it out, Rumor," Tezya called, but his voice was muffled, distant over the roar inside my head.

I called to my ability, but my eyes were glued to Tezya. I studied him. He was watching me over the flames, giving me time to douse them on my own. My eyes drifted over his markings, matching the flames he produced. The small scar above his eyebrow crinkled as they furrowed together.

Closing my eyes, I tried again and again. I kept trying to call to the waves, but the heat of the flames kept drawing my attention. I couldn't focus on anything but the fire and the male yielding it. His powers were feeding my soul. My eyes jutted open when I heard him curse. Flames were everywhere, expanding for miles, like a mist settling over the vastness of the ocean.

"What are you doing?" I asked, panic rising in my voice.

"I'm not doing anything," Tezya yelled as he called to the flames, bringing them into his body. In seconds, the dancing hues of orange were gone. A light smoke lingered over the crashing waves. I hadn't realized how ragged my breathing was. We were both panting as we stared at each other.

"Holy shit," he breathed as he ran his fingers through the sleek hair at the top of his head. I watched as he stopped just before his hair tapered to his shaved cut toward the bottom of his scalp. He was staring at me in disbelief.

"What?"

"Rumor, you just did that," he said softly. His chest was rising up and down, expanding with each breath. The way he was assessing me was unsettling.

"No, I didn't. I can't. I don't have any other elemental abilities," I whispered as I took a step back. My foot rammed into the tip of a broken shell.

"I know," he said as his gaze pierced through mine. "I know what your other power is."

"What?" I gasped. *Please don't be fire. Please don't be fire.*

"You have enhancement." He ran his fingers through his hair again. I watched in fascination and horror at his unease. Something about the gesture seemed familiar, but I couldn't pinpoint it.

"Is that bad?" I asked because he certainly made it seem like it was a terrible thing.

"It's not bad, but it's powerful," he said slowly.

"What is it? What does it do?"

"You can enhance the abilities of anyone that you're around. I don't know your limits or how close you have to be in range to someone—those are all things we can work on, but—"

He paused long enough to grow my unease. "But what?"

"It's rare. There isn't much knowledge about enhancement in general because it hasn't been around since our kind was on Allium. It's been an extinct ability. But it would explain your back markings. You seem to have little bits of everything across your back."

I swallowed. "So I basically make people's abilities stronger?"

"Yes," Tezya paused for a second. "Rumor, after you and Sie performed the blood bond oath, what did you feel?"

"What do you mean?"

"Did things change for you? Did you feel a spark or anything different afterward?"

171

I tried to think back to that moment. "No, I didn't feel anything," I admitted. I remembered I wanted Sie to kiss me then, but I also wanted him to do just that in his bathroom before the bond was created, and I wasn't about to admit that to Tezya.

"I think you've been using your ability in Tennebris without realizing it."

"What do you mean?"

"Do you remember in your memories when Sie said he felt like his mind compulsion and telepathy were stronger around you?" I nodded my head as Tez continued, "I don't think it was because of the blood bond. I don't think you were ever blood bound to begin with. You should have felt something once you joined your blood if you were mated in that way. I think you were subconsciously using your enhancement around him. Anytime he made that comment to you, you weren't wearing your necklace, meaning your enhancement could have been gravitating toward him without meaning to."

My mouth gaped open. I replayed every memory I had with Sie. I had my necklace on during our wedding ceremony, but Sie took it off of me in his bedroom that night. It was also off the night Kole captured us and brought us to the warehouse. It would explain why bits of Sie's power was pushing past the Alluse. Why Moli was able to use her abilities on me so thoroughly the second time. She couldn't fully heal the gash on my leg the first time Kole cut into it. But the second time, when my necklace was off... I was in worse shape, and she healed me better somehow. It took me over a month to recover when she healed me with my necklace on, but that second time... I was walking fine at the lake with Sie.

I didn't know what to make of it. Sie and I were never blood bound? We didn't share any special connection this whole time. Was it really just my ability making him think we were?

"You can't tell anyone about this. No one can know you have this ability, especially not the King."

"Why?" I asked, looking up to meet his gaze. "I thought the whole point of you training me was to figure out my abilities. That I might be able to rejoin your society." I was terrified that if the King wasn't impressed with me, I'd be going right back into that cage.

"If the King learns that you possess enhancement, that you can make *him* stronger, he would chain you to his side and never let you go. You would spend the rest of your life as his prisoner."

EIGHTEEN
SCOTLIND

"THIS IS THE WATERFALL," Tezya said to me the following night. It took us an entire day to hike through the woods from the hut. Dusk was only a few hours from settling over the dense canopy of trees by the time we arrived.

"Beautiful," I breathed as I took in my surroundings.

He didn't say anything, but I could feel his gaze assessing me. We hiked along a river which he told me was the Sunindaya River. "It runs the entire length of the forest," he said. "Eventually, the Sunindaya opens up to the ocean on the west side of the island, but no one really knows about this place. It's too deep in the jungle. Most Luxians don't dare to hike through here."

The woods opened into a small clearing, where the river widened in response. Water poured from the rocky cliff edge, dumping into the river so violently that we had to raise our voices. I was surprised the current wasn't overflowing onto the ground. Empty lanterns were scattered throughout the opening, hanging from long tree branches. Tezya added a tiny ball of flame into each one. The fire was more blue hued, illuminating the entire place and reflecting off the water. It was the first time I saw fire and actually thought it looked pretty. It was the first time I saw beauty in the element instead of untamed death.

Maybe it was just the enclosed glass from the lanterns that gave a false sense of security or the fact that the blue coloring looked more like water.

"What took you so long?" Kallon shouted to us over the roar of the water. The side of her head that was dyed blue the last time I saw her was now a vibrant orange that contrasted against her yellow eyes. The other half of her hair remained shiny black. I looked up just in time to see Rainer standing on a large tree branch high above our heads. He was clutching the bark for dear life.

"We had another training session this morning, then we had to hike here from the hut," Tezya called out. It was true. My body was drained by the time we finally left. Using enhancement was more taxing than calling to water. Tezya still didn't think I hit the bottom of my reserve, but my muscles were limp and shaking by the time we finally stopped.

Kallon's lips perched as she cocked her head at me. "Well, you're just in time to see Rainer act like the total baby he is."

"I am not a baby," Rainer snorted from the limb but clutched the bark even harder. "I just don't see how jumping from this height into the water is fun. I actually enjoy my life, and I intend to live it for a long, long time." Rainer added, "On the ground."

Brock snorted. His body was glistening as the water dripped off of him. His short brown hair was a shade darker where the water touched it. Two black slashes formed a large 'x' over the center of his broad chest with four circles in between each line, and twin thick black bands encircled both of his forearms. I wished I knew what the Luxian markings meant to understand what abilities he possessed. I knew he was a healer—since he used his ability on me the first time I met him—but I got the feeling that wasn't all he had. He was sitting on the edge of a rock in the middle of the river, his legs still in the water. "He's not going to jump, Kallon. He never does."

Kallon's smile turned wicked as she glanced my way again. "Well, now he has a certain someone to impress. He won't back out now that Scottie is here."

I spotted a flash of silver to my left, and to my dread, I saw

Princess Dovelyn was here too. She intimated me more than I liked to admit. But luckily, she was too busy sunbathing on a patch of grass by the bank to acknowledge us, though I was certain she knew Tezya and I were here. The trees parted enough for the sun to shine down on the river, making the heat worse and the cool river sound more and more enticing. I stole another glance at Dovelyn. I assumed all citizens of Lux would be tan from the constant rays of the sun, but she was so pale that her iridescent skin seemed to reflect back.

Rainer glanced down at me. I couldn't tell if he was covered in sweat or water as he flashed his ample smile, but it didn't quite reach his eyes. "Hi, Scottie, I'm—" he started to say but didn't get to finish. One moment Kallon was knee deep in the shallow end of the river, and the next, I saw a quick flash of purple and black, and she was standing behind Rainer on the tree branch. She pushed him off before he could even register what had happened.

Tezya and Brock both let out husky laughter as Rainer screamed all the way down, his arms flailing. I couldn't help it as a smile crept over my lips as well. Once he came up from the water, spitting out a mouthful he must have swallowed, he cursed Kallon. His black markings were now shining over his onyx, slender chest. They blended so well against his skin that I couldn't decipher all the markings at first. Jagged, zig-zag lines started at the base of his fingers and trailed up his arms and chest, ending at the top of his neck.

He shook his long curly locks out like a wet dog, water splashing everywhere, as his amethyst eyes pierced into Kallon.

"What? You weren't going to do it yourself," she shrugged. "I just thought I would help." Then she dove into the water after him.

"You better watch it, or I'll electrify the water and shock you," Rainer warned Kallon once she surfaced. Her landing was much more graceful than Rainer's. She didn't take the threat seriously as she swam past him and gently pushed his shoulder back.

Tezya leaned in, and I could smell his scent—musk, pine, and something else that was entirely him. "Rainer has an elemental ability like us. He can create electricity. It's an extremely rare form of an air user."

"What about Kallon?" I was still baffled at how she traveled so fast from the river to the tree.

"Kallon is a portal jumper. She can create portals for herself and others, if she chooses, to go through. She has to have been to the location before in order to create the portal. Close distance portals like you just saw her use are nothing to her. But it becomes really taxing on her the greater the distance between the portals or if she's creating a new one."

I nodded, remembering having this conversation with Sie on the monorail when he first explained the differences between his teleportation from a portal user. I noticed all of Tezya's friends had a five branded onto their left wrists except Brock. His wrist held a four. "What's Brock's ability besides healing?"

He arched his brow. "What makes you think he has two?"

I shrugged. "A hunch." I didn't want to explain what I felt when I first saw him. I didn't know what to make of it. How one moment, I was scared of him, and then the next, I no longer had worries. I immediately trusted him, and I still had no idea why.

"Brock's other ability is called sensibus furari. He can steal someone's senses, which in turn, heightens his own when he does."

"Is that like your summa sensibus?" I asked. All the names of the senses abilities were starting to sound too similar and it was difficult to keep track of them in my head, but I wanted to learn. I wanted to know what the Advenians of Lux could do.

"No. I naturally have heightened senses all the time. Brock sees, hears, tastes, and feels normally. Only if he is actively using his power will he become enhanced by taking someone else's away."

"So if he takes away my sight? He can see twice as well?"

"Essentially, yes. Your vision will be added to his. Sensibus furari users also have a sixth sense in a way. He has an effect on someone's emotions. The same way he can take on someone's senses, he can do with your feelings, but in turn, he takes on whatever the person was feeling twice as hard."

I gulped. Was that what he used on me that day? "Does he use that a lot?"

Tezya scanned me, and I could tell he saw right through my question. "He used it on you?" he asked, genuinely curious.

I blushed. "I don't know. I think so. When he came to heal me, I tried to get him to leave. I was terrified that a stranger was at my door. I didn't know who he was or if I could trust him. But all of a sudden, I did. Can he do that? Can he alter my emotions like that?"

Tez frowned. "Not quite. There is an ability that can do that, that can completely shift what someone is feeling, and it's terrifying, but Brock probably just took your worry away. He can take away fear, pain, or any emotions that someone is actively feeling, which would leave the Advenian only with positive thoughts. He probably just shouldered your worry on himself, which would explain why it was gone. He can't create trust that wasn't there before. He can't randomly put a feeling into you. You have to have already had something there for him to use." He looked over at his friend. "I'm surprised he used it on you, though."

"Why?"

"Because he never uses that ability. The emotion part of it, at least," he clarified. "In battle, I've seen him take away the other senses with his powers, but he rarely messes with someone's emotions."

"Has he ever used it on you?"

"Only once," he paused as if gauging whether or not to tell me. "I didn't realize he had used it on me until my mother passed. I wasn't in a good place. I hadn't gotten out of my bed for weeks. I wouldn't eat. Then one day, I just felt better. It took me a while to realize that Brock shouldered my burden, that he was taking my pain away. I was furious with him. He's never used it again on anyone, I guess, until now."

"That seems powerful. How is he only a rank four?"

Tezya sighed. "The Luxian Council views his sensibus furari as a weakness just as much as it is a strength." I must have looked confused because he added, "Since he takes on the sense that he steals, it can be a negative thing for him. It's a balance. He has to make sure he doesn't take more than he can handle. And as far as his healing ability, his reserves aren't as strong as other healers. But he

178

should be a rank five, in my opinion. He is incredibly strong and uses his abilities well. He's valuable in the army. He's second in command, even despite being a four. Brock had to work really hard for what he has. Many of the soldiers in the army despise him for being so high up while having a lesser rank than them. He gets challenged to duels all the time by men wanting to prove they're better than him."

"Does that bother him?" I asked. I followed him to the edge of the bank as he dipped his feet in the water, gesturing for me to do the same. He didn't need to roll up his pants since they halted halfway up his calf already. The water was deep on this side of the river. The only shallow part seemed to be where Brock was sitting on the rock. I took a sodden seat on the grass next to him, gently rolling my pants as I listened, thankful that his friends were out of earshot, or if they did hear our conversation, they didn't show it.

Tez smiled. "No, he accepts the duels and then beats the living shit out of them. It's actually quite amusing to watch. No one will ever challenge him twice."

I looked over at Brock with newfound admiration. He was living proof someone could go beyond their rank. A chill went through me as I processed all of Tezya's words. "You said he's second in command?"

Tezya turned to face me, his expression hard. "Yes."

I swallowed. Once. Twice. "Does that mean he works with the Fire Prince?"

Before Tezya could answer, Kallon swam over to me and half dragged me into the water. "Come on, Scottie, I want to show you something." She turned toward Tezya and winked. "You don't mind, do you?"

I was about to fully lower myself in when Kallon stopped me. "Aren't you going to take off your clothes?" I looked down at my outfit. I was wearing thin pants and a loose white shirt. Tezya's friends weren't swimming naked, thank Pylemo, but they had on clothes similar to the Luxian swimming attire that Patricia packed for me.

Rainer turned to watch me, waiting for my answer. "Um, no, it's alright. I'll swim in my clothes."

I thought I heard Dovelyn scoff, but I didn't turn around to see. She still hadn't acknowledged that Tezya and I were here. Kallon pouted for a moment, then continued on into the water.

Tezya didn't take his eyes off me as I lowered myself into the water.

I was surprised by how deep the river became as we swam to the wider section. I had to tread water at the bank, but I couldn't even see the bottom floor here. Kallon looked back at me once before bobbing under the surface. I followed suit, and as I opened my eyes underwater, I saw her beelining toward the fall.

I could feel the water pounding against my back as I swam beneath it. When I finally broke the surface, my eyes widened. We were at an opening to a small rocky cave, just big enough for two people. Kallon hopped up onto the surface, her feet still dangling under the water as she patted the empty spot next to her.

"How are you holding up?" she asked me as I plopped down next to her.

"I'm fine, thanks."

She eyed me for a moment as if assessing if I was telling the truth. "I assume your training is coming along then? Tezya's a great teacher."

I nodded, feeling uncomfortable talking about Tezya for some reason. I bit my lip hard as the memory of him holding me in the pool flashed through my head, and my ears heated. I felt... guilty, which was ridiculous because Tezya made it very clear the first day he took me to the beach that this was just training. He was engaged for crying out loud.

"I love it here," Kallon murmured as she tucked the orange part of her hair back. "The waterfall feels like an entirely different place from everything else on the island. It makes me think we're not in Lux."

"Do you like living in Lux?" I asked.

"That's a loaded question."

"I'm sorry—" I started. I realized that it was probably rude and illegal for me to ask her that. I was just so curious about what it would have been like growing up here by the ocean, to have been able to swim every day and be out in nature without feeling like my body was going to freeze off.

"I hate Lux," she said softly, "but the hut and the waterfall feel more like home than the city does. I love anything that's far away from the politics of it all."

"How do you guys all know each other?" I asked her, trying to change the subject. They seemed like they'd been friends for a while, and she knew about the hut that Tezya took me to. I got the feeling that it was a private place that not many Advenians knew about.

"Tez and I have been friends since we were children." I looked over at her, noticing how her markings manifested into small circles that went up the front of her pale legs and then again on her spine. She had two larger circles over her shoulders. I guessed the circles indicated portal jumping.

"Tez met Brock next. He saved him, actually. He was supposed to be killed for a treason he didn't commit, but Tez convinced the Lux King to let Brock into the army. So now he's forced to serve. It's a long story and not really mine to tell, but they have been friends ever since I could remember."

"Tezya and Brock met Rainer fifteen years ago when he got placed in the army after his Trials. Rainer's young, and he isn't in control of his ability yet. When they first met him, his lightning was untamed. He accidentally electrified an officer in the army." My eyes widened because we were all now swimming with Rainer in a river. Kallon caught my train of thought and added quickly, "He has better control of it now. He can exert his electricity into objects like weapons or thrust it into water, but he can't wield it alone yet. He doesn't have full control over it. For now, he just infuses his lightning into things, but once he has full control, he'll be unstoppable. Brock and Tez both took him under their wings and have been training him to master it."

"And Dovelyn?" I asked, noting that she didn't mention the Princess' connection.

Kallon looked uncomfortable as she shifted on the rock. "You will have to ask Tezya about her. It's not my place."

I was about to respond when Rainer burst up from under the

waterfall, his long locks floating out next to him. His smile was truly dazzling as he looked up before he grabbed me by my legs and yanked me back into the water. "I'll be stealing her now," Rainer grinned at Kallon as he pushed me against his chest. "You can't hog her all night."

It all happened so fast. Before I could protest, Rainer sank under the surface to swim through the pouring fall with me in tow. The act of being dragged under the water, against my will, came spiraling out in waves of darkness. My eyes were slammed shut, and I couldn't coax my brain into opening my mouth. That familiar heaviness crept up inside me, filling my lungs, as I writhed out of Rainer's grasp.

Once he noticed I was squirming, he let go of me immediately. I darted toward the surface, using the water to propel me faster as I gasped for air. Rainer popped up a moment after me. I tried to steady my panting, tried to not give myself away that I was hyperventilating, but I couldn't. I kept wheezing through my mouth like I couldn't get enough air, my breath ragged. The water surrounding my body felt wrong and tainted.

Tezya's head snapped up immediately. He seemed to sense what just unfolded. He dove into the water and was by me in an instant, guiding me out of the water.

"Shit, Scottie, I'm sorry. I was just messing around—" Rainer started, but I didn't hear what else he said. My trembling body was leaning heavily into Tezya's embrace as he helped me out of the water and walked me past the river bank. His hand was warm and comforting against my back.

Once we were alone, he turned to face me. "Are you okay?"

I nodded sheepishly. "I'm sorry... I didn't... mean to... freak out." I kept staring into his pale blue eyes, finding the lack of brown comforting.

This isn't Kole. I'm not being drowned again. This is a waterfall, not the confined tile of a tub.

"You have nothing to apologize for. Ever," he said as a muscle in his jaw quivered, then clenched, his hands were resting on my shoulders. "It's my fault."

"How is this… your fault?"

"Because I shouldn't have brought you here, especially since they don't know about your past with water."

"They don't know?" I asked, trying to take a few calming breaths. I was surprised. Once I realized his friends knew who I was at the party, I assumed that meant they knew everything.

Tez shook his head, his moon-white hair tousled from swimming. "Only Dovelyn knows about you since she was there when they compelled you. It's up to you how much you want to tell the others. They are the only people in Lux I trust, so if you do decide to tell them, any of them, that information would be safe with them. But it's your call."

"Even about my ability? That I have enhancement."

"Yes, that information would be safe with them, but I have to beg you not to tell them about it."

"Why?"

"The less people that know, the better. I don't want to drag my friends into this. I don't want to ask them to lie for me." *Into this.* Was I a burden to him?

He must have sensed the shift in me. "What's wrong? Did I offend you?"

"No," I said softly.

He assessed me, studying my reaction before he finally said, "Come, we should get back now. We're an hour out from the castle, and we shouldn't be in the woods when dusk fully settles in."

NINETEEN
SCOTLIND

"I want to go," I pleaded.

"Rumor, you can't. If the King saw you there—"

"The King said that I couldn't go anywhere without you, and lucky for me, you'll be there."

Tezya ran his fingers through his pale hair, pushing the long strands off his forehead, exposing the top of his thick, jagged scar. "No. It's out of the question. I'm going to be busy at the Ball, and I won't be able to watch you."

I slumped onto my bed with a huff, folding my arms across my chest. "So I'm supposed to stay here alone? It's Yule."

He narrowed his eyes. "It's only for this year. You don't want to attract attention to yourself, especially around the King. Trust me, the less he thinks of you, the better."

"I don't care about the—" I started, but he cut me off.

"The answer is no, Rumor. You can hate me for it if you want, but you can't go. And don't even think about sneaking off because I will have my senses locked on you the whole night. I will know the second you open this door."

He stormed out of my room before I could respond.

"Prick," I called after him, knowing he could hear me. Patricia left to go home for the holidays, wherever her home was, so I would be utterly alone tonight. And I hated being alone—it left me thinking about Kole or Sie. Sighing, I hopped off my bed and sauntered over to the small table. Dinner was brought up thirty minutes ago and was already growing cold. I picked at some of the meats before frustration took over.

I wanted to go to the Ball. I was curious what it would be like at Lux. I wanted to know how their traditions for celebrating Yule varied from Tennebris. Luxians did everything more lavish and extravagant than Tennebrisians. If I got to see it, would it spark more memories from the seven years I spent here? Did my parents attend the Ball before everything happened?

In Tennebris, I'd spent every Yule with Vallie and Miles. Vallie always took me home with her, and we sat around the fireplace with her parents and had warm tea. Their house was close to the shield, that during cold enough winters, Vallie would convince me to build a snowman or have a snowball fight, but usually, I stayed inside with Miles reading a book. Yule was my favorite holiday because it was the only time I took off to enjoy living for once. I forced myself not to worry about the upcoming Trials or anything that had to do with me being Luxian. I forced myself to savor the moment. I read for enjoyment instead of studying fighting technique books. I didn't wake up to train, but stayed up late gossiping with Vallie for hours, then slept way past morning only to stuff our faces with her mother's dough balls until our stomachs hurt.

I imagined what it would have been like to be a Hartlin, and I often pretended I was a part of their family. I loved their simple traditions. They cooked together and went around the room saying what they were thankful for, and my answer was always the same—meeting Vallie. I wondered if they were celebrating without me this year.

My heart ached, and I tried not to think about her, which was another reason I wanted to go to the party instead of wallowing in self pity. I also desperately wanted to try the food. I overheard some of the maids gossiping in the halls about all the dishes they were preparing, and with all the training Tezya had put me through, and my new growing muscles, I was starving all the time. I was starting to put weight back on, and what Tezya put me through required me to eat... a lot.

But the real reason I wanted to go, though, the reason I was so upset that Tezya said no, was because I couldn't stand to be in my room. I knew I should be grateful I traded it in for the cage, but when I was alone and restless like this, it felt too similar. My eyes played tricks on me as the walls in my room seemed to shrink into themselves. The only saving grace was the electricity, which I kept the chandelier turned on at all times to ward off the darkness.

If I wasn't having nightmares about Kole finishing what he started —replaying what happened that night in the warehouse—Sie would work his way up to the forefront of my memories, which was so much worse. He would get stuck inside my head, and I would be forced to relive all of my interactions with him, attempting to sort through any warning signs, anything I might have misinterpreted, anything I could've noticed earlier to realize he wasn't on my side.

I hated knowing that I would be forced to see him again and *soon*. It gave me crippling anxiety whenever I thought about it. I couldn't sort through my feelings. What would it be like to have to look into his dark eyes and see Reagan at his side, his new bride...

And if I somehow managed to not think about my ex-husband or about how Tezya said the Lux King planned to use me to get Sie off the Dark throne, I was stressing about what would become of me. When I was alone my mind became a dark place, and my thoughts overtook any rational senses. I had no idea how the Lux King would use me or what his plans were, and I prayed to Pylemo I wouldn't have to find out.

One moment, I was alone, wallowing in my thoughts. The next, Kallon stood before me. She materialized out of thin air. A thick cloud of black and purple smoke lingered around her.

"Hey, babes," she said in her musically crafted voice and beautiful smile. She looked absolutely stunning. The side of her head that was orange at the waterfall was now coral pink. I got the feeling that she changed it frequently. The black half of her hair always remained the same—sleek and shiny. Now both halves were twisted up into a beautiful curly updo, exposing the lines of her face and her long slender neck. Her slanted yellow eyes were rimmed in coal that matched her translucent gown.

"Kallon, how did you get in here?" I dropped the piece of chicken I was holding onto the floor.

She shrugged. "I portaled." I gave her a look of confusion before she added, "I have portals in almost every room in the castle and various areas throughout the city. I don't like the feeling of being confined in a room."

I knew the feeling, but I thought better than to say that out loud. "What are you doing here, though? Aren't you supposed to be at the Ball?"

"Of course, but I'm not going without you. I honestly have been dying for Tez to bring a girl around. I *need* girl friends, and Dovelyn certainly does not count."

I smiled widely, thankful that she even thought of me. She reminded me so much of Vallie, always kind and thoughtful. Even though Kallon was still a stranger to me, she didn't treat me like one. She treated me like a friend, like I was someone she had known forever. Just as Vallie had the moment I met her. It was like the two of them would decide in their heads who their friends would be, and then that was that. You were friends, no questions asked. There was no going back. I missed Vallie. I desperately wanted to see her, to hug her, to know if she was okay, but I knew her life would be better off without me, safer without me. It was like Pylemo was blessing me with Kallon, knowing I had a void in my heart from missing my redheaded friend.

"Thank you, Kallon," I finally managed to say. "But I can't go. Tezya said he was monitoring my room. He's going to know if I leave."

"Oh, who cares about him. He won't know you've left until it's too late."

"I highly doubt that," I groaned, thinking about the time he followed me when I tried to sneak off. "He's going to know the second I open the door."

"Well, it's a good thing I can get you to the Ball in a second and without a door." She winked at me. I was about to ask her how that was possible when she added, "I already created a portal at one of the side entrances of the Ball. We'll get you dressed in here, and then once you're ready, we will travel through the portal I have set up. By the time Tez senses you are gone, it will be too late. And then once everyone sees you at the Ball, he can't kick you out."

"You are brilliant," I smiled as a giddy anticipation took over me. Tezya would be furious, but I'd deal with that later.

"Us girls gotta stick together."

Kallon snapped her fingers, then an exorbitant amount of maids came rushing through my door to help me get ready. Even when I was the Princess in Tennebris I wasn't this pampered. They worked fast, and I didn't get a glimpse of myself until they were completely done sticking and probing at me.

"Wow, Scotlind Rumor. If I could, I would steal you for myself. You look breathtaking. Every single male and probably most of the females aren't going to be able to keep their eyes off you," Kallon murmured as she eyed me slowly. Just that action alone reminded me of Vallie. It made me think of the prophecy Tezya mentioned, how it spoke of someone being born from both Lux and Tennebris. And right now, I wished it was true. I wished there wasn't a divide between the Kingdoms because I would have loved a place where Kallon and Vallie could meet.

I was about to open my mouth to protest her claim when I caught a glimpse of my reflection. My mouth dropped as I inched closer to the full length mirror Kallon insisted on dragging into my already cramped room. I hadn't felt pretty in a long time. I hadn't even looked in a mirror since the first day I was brought out of the dungeons. I was too scared of what I'd see, too scared that I'd still be that carcass of a girl I was when Patricia helped me during that first bath.

But I wasn't dead anymore.

The gown Kallon selected for me was a silky, thin material that clung to my newly formed curves. The dress itself was a flaming crimson and had two large slits traveling up both of my legs, exposing most of my skin, which was starting to tan from spending time outside with Tezya.

And the neckline—it was low and revealing and would not be helping in the whole not-drawing-attention-to-myself department, as Tezya kept saying. Kallon selected ruby drop earrings to match the gown and opted to leave my long hair down in soft waves, bellowing down my mid-back. I was thankful for it because it hid the worst of my scars.

The maids did my makeup to enhance my features. My freckles were popping out against my olive skin tone, and my sapphire eyes were bright and contrasting against the red of the gown. I no longer had to hate the color. For Luxians, my eyes were considered common.

"Kallon, I can't wear this," I gasped as I took a step away from the mirror, realizing, to my horror, that I had to be careful with how I walked to prevent the slits of the gown from riding up. It was way too revealing. I felt naked beneath the sheer fabric, which I was.

"Fine, suit yourself. You can stay cooped up in your chambers all by yourself then," she paused dramatically, eyeing her polished nails, which were neon green. "Or you can wear the gown and come celebrate Yule with me."

I huffed a sigh, realizing this was a losing battle because I wanted to go. I wanted to see the Ball and eat the food. I wanted to dance. I wanted to have fun for once. I wanted to feel like I belonged, and I was surprised as I looked at Kallon that with her, with Tezya, I was starting to feel that way again.

"Fine," I said as she smiled mischievously. Her cold, slender fingers wrapped around mine before I could second guess it. She swooped her free hand in the air, and a black circle materialized in the middle of my room. I gulped as I looked toward the portal. I'd heard of them, but I had never seen one before. When Kallon used it at the waterfall, she moved too quickly for me to glance at what she was doing. But now I was staring directly into it.

The materialized circle was a looming hole of darkness that had no end, at least none that I could see. Purple smoke entwined and danced around the outer edges of the border, mixing with the black.

It reminded me of the night sky. A terrifyingly haunting, starless night.

It was the darkness I'd been fearing, except this time, it was beautiful and calling me into its embrace.

"Are you ready?" she asked as she looked down at me.

I nodded my head yes. My throat was starting to feel dry, and my palms were already sweating.

"Good. Don't let go of my arm." Before I could ask what would happen if I did, Kallon lept into the blackness, her body disappearing into nothingness before mine was forced to follow.

My body cleaved in two as I felt a jolt of energy rush past me. I couldn't see anything as a cold wind overtook my senses. Not even Kallon's hand squeezing mine brought me back as my body whirled and spiraled through time. I was weightless. I had no way of telling if we were going up or down or to the side. A sinking, dropping feeling grew in my lower abdomen as nausea crept up fast and hard. I tried and failed to squelch it.

As soon as I felt the bile rise in my throat, we landed hard on the shiny marble floor. I covered my mouth with my hand, willing the meats I had eaten earlier to settle, but I knew it wouldn't help. I always had a weak stomach, and this wave of nausea was so intense that I was going to hurl up my entire guts in front of everyone.

But then it was gone. I felt normal. No, I felt better than normal. Brock came up behind Kallon, his brows furrowed, his hand outstretched, and it dawned on me that he was the reason my nausea left so fast. I didn't know if he used his healing abilities on me or if he took away the feeling with his sensibus furari. I hoped for the former as I remembered Tezya saying when Brock used his sensibus gift, he would feel things twice as hard if he took any senses away. I wouldn't wish that kind of nausea on anyone.

He gave me a soft smile. "It gets easier each time you portal jump. The first couple of times are rough, but your body adjusts."

"Sorry," Kallon said. "I didn't think about the effects it would cause you. I should have warned you. I'm so used to portaling Brock,

Rainer, and Tez, which they are used to it after decades and decades of jumping with me.

"No, it's fine. Thank you. Thank you both," I said as I looked between Brock and Kallon. A warmness crept over me, knowing that they went through all this trouble to get me here.

Before I even had the time to gawk at the Ball or how elaborately it was decorated, Tezya stormed over toward us, and he looked pissed. I caught a glimpse of the soldier he was within the Luxian army. We were positioned in the corner of the grand room, out of sight from most of the guests, but I knew that Tezya sensed my presence the moment I portaled here.

"What is she doing here?" Tezya glared at Kallon and Brock.

Kallon shrugged lazily. "I wanted to bring a date, and Goddess knows you are no fun at these functions. Plus, Scottie is much prettier to look at."

At that, Tezya finally glanced at me. I caught his furious expression faltering just briefly as he took in my gown. His lips parted, and his eyes widened, his pupils expanding and dilating. I swore he inhaled my scent, but then it was gone. His former livid expression was plastered back on. "This isn't a joke, Kallon. You shouldn't have brought her tonight."

"I can make decisions for myself," I snapped at him, furious that they were discussing me like I wasn't standing right in front of them.

Tezya turned his rage on me. "No, you can't, Rumor. You aren't a citizen yet. And you're walking a very thin line. A line that I don't want to snap. You are still considered the King's prisoner, his property. If he sees you here—" He stopped and turned toward Kallon. "Keep her hidden from him." His gaze found mine again as he added, "Even though that's going to be nearly impossible in that gown." Then he stalked off, disappearing into the crowd before I could think over what he said.

The room the Ball was held in was enormous. Large windows opened up to the sky, displaying the sinking sun, causing hues of colors to cascade onto the dance floor. And wherever a window didn't line the wall, it was met with lights, electricity flooding the room into brightness for when the sun descended.

A silver dais was positioned to face the open floor of dancers. It was raised high enough so it could be seen from anywhere in the room. There were four dark thrones on top of it that seemed so out of place compared to the rest of the open and airy decor. It was like the thrones were a reminder of the menacing ruling family who controlled Lux.

The three smaller ones weren't complex. No intricate designs were carved into the stone. They were simple and to the point. Prince Arcane filled the first seat. He was positioned so he could gaze out at the sea of flowing gowns dancing below. His eyes didn't seem to focus on anyone in particular but rather just watched the dancing unfold. He was striking in his cobalt blue robes and silver hair as he sat perched against the ebony throne. He resembled his father, a more handsome, younger, and slimmer version of the King. The only difference was that he didn't possess the same eerie presence the King exuded, and his hair was longer.

The other two thrones were left bare, presumably for Princess Dovelyn and the Fire Prince. My heart raced at the thought of finally seeing him. I had no doubt that he would be here tonight, and the three smaller thrones were indication enough. I just hadn't realized that coming tonight meant I'd be in the same room as him. I would finally be able to put a face to the male that haunted my nightmares.

His fire is so powerful that he leaves the battlefields in flames. There are no survivors—no bodies to bury. Just ash.

The last throne was the largest and almost took up as much space as the three smaller ones combined. It was broad and dark, with tendrils of charcoal vipers wrapping and snaking itself around the arms. It resembled a darker, deadlier version of the Goddesses' snake symbol. Large onyx wings looked to be wielded into the tall seat, but I couldn't fully make out the intricate details as the Lux King languished on the stone slab. His gaze met mine as a wicked, cruel smile peppered his thin lips. A shiver went up my spine from his assessment. Crap. So much for him not noticing me.

I felt glued in place, unable to move as his eyes roamed the thin fabric of my dress before meeting my wide-eyed stare. There was something about him that was wrong. My body screamed to run in his presence, begging me to put as much space between him as I could, but I couldn't move. He radiated power, too much power for one Advenian to control. I wondered if my enhancement could sense that? If that was why I hated his presence—that enhancing his abilities would be impossible. I didn't know what powers he possessed or what he could do, but I knew whatever it was had to be awful.

It wasn't until Kallon placed a gentle hand on my back that I finally pried my eyes away from the King.

Letting out a sigh of relief, I happily followed her toward one of the large buffets. Table after table after table was filled and brimmed with foods that lined the walls. My mouth watered as I took in the scents wafting through the air. I silently filled my silver plate to the brim with mounds of food I couldn't name. As we took a seat at the only vacant table left, I started digging into my helpings. I moaned softly as I took the first bite of something soft and flakey, the raspberry-filled layer coating my taste buds.

Dovelyn and Brock had already filled two of the seats as Rainer came up behind me and took the chair opposite mine. I was surprised that the Princess wasn't sitting on the throne next to her brother, but I figured that Brock had something to do with it. Her body was positioned and angled to face him as they shared a soft conversation. I couldn't help but notice the way Brock's eyes lingered on hers when she wasn't looking. The gaze was layered with longing and desire, but he never seemed to act on it. Whenever I saw the two of them together, they were professional. In fact, they never even touched. Was that even allowed? Could a rank four touch a rank five? I knew so little about the Luxian customs, and whatever was taught in the Tennebrisians schools weren't nearly enough.

Dovelyn looked like a fallen Goddess, but I guess that was expected of the Luxian Princess. Her flowing gown was silver to match her stunning hair and eyes. Jewels and diamonds were sewn into the threads so that it sparkled in the light as she turned and swayed. Her long hair was pinned up to reveal her small delicate neck. Her full lips were painted a light pink, at odds with her pale, almost translucent skin.

Rainer broke my train of thought as he said, "Wow, Scottie, you look gorgeous."

"I will take thanks for that," Kallon smiled as she sipped from a large glass of ale. I wondered if it was her own homemade one from the party. It smelled strong, with malt and hops instantly filling my nose.

I didn't know how to reply and was happy when Kallon chimed in. I couldn't deny that I felt pretty for once—or maybe I just felt alive again—but I didn't think gorgeous was the right word. I looked more like I was trying to seduce someone in bed rather than be at a ball. But judging by how a lot of the Luxians were dressed tonight, I didn't look that ridiculous. Regardless of the fact that the slits in my dress went up to my hips and that the flaming red color clashed against the silver in the room, the Luxian fashion seemed to consist of exposing the most skin in a delicate way with as little as possible.

"Uh-yeah. Whatever you say, Kal," Rainer stammered as he finally took a seat. He had two sparkling glasses in his hands, and he gestured one to me.

"Thank you," I said as I took it from him and tasted the sweet, fizzling contents. I moaned again. This was definitely my new favorite drink.

"Scottie, with how much you moan over your food and drinks, I don't even want to know how loud you are in bed," Kallon laughed. And it was at that moment that Tezya sauntered over to the table, no doubt hearing what Kallon had just said.

I blushed, and I swore my cheeks matched my dress as I cursed under my breath and set down the wondrous glass of alcohol.

"She has a tendency to do that," Tezya said as he slid into the seat between Kallon and Dovelyn. Then he added, "When eating," when all of his friends gave him a strange look. Yep. He definitely heard that.

"Well, I like it," Rainer said with one of his big white smiles. "It's adorable."

Kallon's laugh was deep and didn't match her slender frame and light voice. "Of course you do. You're a male. It's like she's having sex with the food."

"Can you stop," I gritted between my teeth as my palms clasped the silken material of my gown.

Before my embarrassment could sink to an entirely new level, the music in the Ball halted. On cue, the twirling swirls of color that were swishing and swaying on the glossy floor ceased.

A scrawny man who was profusely sweating stammered onto the front of the dais. Everyone turned toward him as he cleared his scratchy throat. "Would the Royal family please come forth and take their positions on the dais."

Tezya's tanned hands gripped the edges of the table so firmly that they turned white. Kallon looked wearily over at him. "Fuck," he murmured so low I thought I imagined it.

Dovelyn rose swiftly, her diamond gown flowing behind her petite form as she made her way to the empty throne next to Prince Arcane. My breath caught in my throat as I glanced around the room, searching for the Fire Prince. Movement stirred in my periphery as Tezya rose from the table. His jaw was set tight, his eyes pleading as they looked over at me for just a moment.

Then he sauntered up the dais and took a seat on the last empty throne.

TWENTY
SCOTLIND

No. No. *No.* He couldn't.

My lungs felt like they were collapsing in on themselves. My breath hitched and halted in my throat as my heart hammered against my sternum so fast I felt dizzy. My lips dried, and any heat from my earlier embarrassment left me. I felt empty.

All at once, the Lux King and the three Royal siblings rose from their thrones. I watched as Tezya stood next to Dovelyn. "All bow to our sovereign of Lux, King Arcane Xandrin the Seventh."

Dresses sifted, shoes scoffed, and chairs groaned across the marble as everyone rose from their own chairs to kneel on the ground. The King's domineering gaze was looming as he casually glanced around the room.

My own body moved without thinking, without me processing what it was doing. I thought Kallon might have gripped my elbow, might have ushered me forward. I couldn't feel anything until my knees slammed against the hard marble. The echoing thud sounded piercing to my ears, but no one turned their gaze toward me. No one heard it. The sound was an echoing box, only in my own head, growing louder and louder until everything would burst.

The ground was cold against my bare skin as the slits in my gown shifted, exposing too much of my thighs. The entire length of my scar, knee to hip, was on full display. I should have cared. I should have repositioned myself, but I didn't—couldn't.

I was frozen as the announcer continued to introduce the Royals one at a time. "Bow to Prince Arcane the eighth, heir to the Luxian throne," his wheezy voice echoed. Prince Arcane moved to stand next to the King. Princess Doveylyn was next. Then...

"Please bow for Prince Tezya, Commander of the Luxian army." Tezya's blue eyes met mine, pinning me to my spot on the floor as he moved from the blackened throne.

No, his eyes weren't just that beautiful crystal blue. They were lined in silver. I could make out the bare traces of it from my spot on the ground. His moon-white hair was so pale, only a shade off from Prince Arcane's and Princess Dovelyn's silver. He was broader, taller, more muscular, but he resembled them. Slightly.

He wasn't identical as Arcane and Dovelyn were to each other, but he still had Arcane's straight nose and angular jaw. He had Dovelyn's shaped eyes and the same thick, dark brows. His face was haunting, the difference being his nasty scar straight across it, defacing his beauty. No, that wasn't true either. I loved his scar.

My mind whirled on how he earned it. Was it in battle? Was it from the rebels that he left in ashes? *Commander.* He was the commander. Not just a Luxian soldier, not just someone who trained new recruits. No. He *commanded* them. He led them. Bile rose in my throat. I wanted to vomit. I felt like my life was an endless deception. I couldn't handle any more surprises. I couldn't fucking handle it.

"At this time, it brings me great honor to announce the selection for the Yule Carvot. The Royal Princes and Princess, would you please select your chosen Advenian for the night."

Tezya moved first. I refused to look at him as he made his way toward our table. My stomach shot up in my throat. My mind couldn't wrap around the events that just happened within a matter of minutes. Tezya Xandrin. He was a Royal. He was the youngest Luxian Prince. *The Fire Prince.* The Prince I feared. The Prince who murdered all the rebels with his flames, turning them to ash. The same Prince who burned my testing paperwork. The same Prince who claimed to hate the King and his rule. I gulped as he continued to make his way over to our table. Was he going to pick me? Would I say yes?

My body tensed when he reached his hand toward Kallon, and my heart stopped. "Kallon, may I have this dance?" His voice was colder, tension radiating off him.

"Always," Kallon said softly. A small smile appeared on her lush lips, but it didn't reach her eyes. She rose from her spot on the ground to join him. Tezya's own mouth was turned down. His presence was palpable, mere inches from mine, but now he was the one who wouldn't meet my gaze. I was forced to awkwardly gawk up at him. My mouth surely hung open. I was still on the cold floor, the slits of my dress hiked on either side.

I thought that he was engaged to Dovelyn. I thought that was his connection with the Royals, not that he was one. And his fiancé—I swallowed as I looked up at him again, at how he was touching Kallon's back lightly, leading her onto the dance floor. Tezya was engaged to *Kallon*.

Prince Arcane lingered on the stage as he shifted uncomfortably, searching the crowd, unsure of who to pick. Princess Dovelyn moved next. Her movements were elegant as she glided off the dais. But she didn't walk toward our table. She didn't even bother to glance once in Brock's direction as she chose an attractive ginger-haired male as her partner. He bore a five on his left wrist. Brock's face was emotionless and hard as he watched Dovelyn sweep to the dance floor with the male in tow. I wondered if Brock loathed his four as much as I did my two zeroes.

After Prince Arcane and the Lux King selected their partners, both beautiful females, the music began. I'd never seen the Carvot dance before, but it was mesmerizing. The way they moved across the now empty dance floor. I couldn't tear my eyes off Kallon and Tezya's form. They were a breath apart, his hand flat against her lower back. A wave of jealousy formed low in my gut and rooted itself there as Kallon's full breasts brushed against Tezya's chest.

I couldn't tell what I hated more—Tezya and Kallon dancing, or this new knowledge of him being the Prince.

He lied to me on the beach that day when I asked him if he worked with the Fire Prince. I asked him if he was as scary and awful as the rumors portrayed him. He probably was laughing about me to his friends, wondering how long it would take me to figure it out. I felt foolish for not piecing it together. All the signs were there—his closeness to the King, his relationship with Dovelyn, his abilities were fire for crying out loud.

Elemental abilities are really common here. A lot of people have water, fire, air, or ground abilities, Tezya had said when I first saw his flames.

The song changed into another, a slower dance than the one before, and other Advenians of Lux started to fill the dance floor along with the Royals. Tezya and Kallon didn't stop dancing. They remained pressed against one another and whispered briskly as they moved and spun around the floating newcomers. I was in awe. I couldn't stop staring at how eloquently he moved. How he and Kallon flowed in sync...

I jolted as a hand pressed into my shoulder. I turned to face Brock standing above me. "Come dance with me, Scottie," he said as he held out his hand for me. When I didn't take it right away, he added, "Trust me."

There was something about his tone and the look in his eyes that had me agreeing. I didn't know if I trusted him or if he was using his ability on me again. I took his hand anyway, not really caring. "I don't know the steps," I started as he led me to the floor.

"It's okay, I'll show you."

Tezya—the Fire Prince—finally glanced my way as if he was zoned in on my movements and knew now that I was on the floor. Good, let him look. I didn't care if it pissed him off that I came here tonight, now. I didn't care if he didn't want me dancing with his friend. He could burn in his own flames for all I cared. Anger boiled in me. Was this why he didn't want me to come? Why he insisted that I stayed in my room tonight? Not because the King would see, but because *I* would see. Because I would find out who he really was.

Brock twirled me in a circle before our bodies connected. "I know you are upset," he said gently, softly. "He should have told you sooner, but you need to calm down. Don't let your emotions show. If you need help, I can take them away for now."

"No," I gritted through my teeth, not wanting him to use his ability on me. I took a deep breath, loosening it. "I'm fine."

"Good because the King is watching you," Brock whispered into my ear so softly that I almost missed it. That did not help calm my nerves but instead did the opposite.

Brock was so tall that I had to tilt my head up at a sharp angle to be able to meet his gaze, and when I did, I found him already staring down at me. I didn't know how to respond or what to say to him, so we just danced. I tried my best not to think about how Tezya was holding Kallon throughout the whimsical melody of the song. Brock made sure to sweep me across the dance floor, furthest away from him.

Brock bowed to me once the song finally came to a close. "Come with me," he said over the round of applause. "I'll escort you back."

———

TEZYA FOUND me in my room, curled up on my bed, hours later. I couldn't fall asleep as my mind spun and processed everything that happened at the Ball.

"That's why you didn't want me to go to the Ball tonight, isn't it? You didn't want me to find out about you." I sprang up from my bed and stormed toward him the moment he appeared. Kallon must have portaled him in and then left immediately because he was alone, with only the misting black and purple smoke fading into nothing.

He flinched slightly. "I didn't lie. I meant it when I said I didn't want you to attract the King's attention."

"You mean your *father's* attention."

"He. Is. Not. My. Father." he said between gritted teeth.

I slapped him across his face. The sound reverberated throughout the room, echoing into a resounding silence. A red handprint was now painted across his scar. Tezya didn't move. Instead, he held my angry stare, his breathing deepening. "Don't lie to my face, Tezya," I seethed.

"Scotlind, I'm not lying to you. He isn't my father. That man will never be my father."

"You're the Prince. The Fire Prince, Tezya," I screamed. I tasted salt in my mouth as hot tears rolled down my cheeks. "I asked you about him. I asked if the Fire Prince was dangerous for crying out loud. I asked if you worked with him. You lied to me then as you are lying to me now. You made me believe that he was someone else. And for what? Was it some kind of sick joke between you and your friends? Betting on how long it would take me to figure it out?"

"What?" he asked as he pulled his hands through his hair, his voice raised and echoing now to match mine. "Of course not. I didn't tell you for this reason alone," he said as he gestured between us. "Look at you. You're looking at me like you hate me."

"Well, at least you got one thing right tonight," I snapped. "I do hate you."

He flinched at my words. "I'm sorry, Scotlind. I didn't intend to hurt you," he said quieter, deeper.

"Well, you did."

"I know." He sucked in a breath. Paused. "I just didn't want to lose you, lose this, I mean." He gestured to the space between us.

"And what is this?" I challenged.

"Friendship."

My heart sank, and I didn't know what I was expecting him to say. He was engaged to Kallon, who I wanted so badly to consider as a friend. I was mad at myself for even feeling disappointed in his answer. He lied to me. He was the Prince. I didn't want to be with him. I didn't want him to like me. He was who Sie warned me to stay away from, and I should have listened. I could still listen. I didn't have to get along with Tezya. I didn't have to care. All I had to do was get trained by him. So why was I disappointed?

Some deep part of me knew that I couldn't, that I didn't want whatever this was to end, that it wasn't only about the training. I just wasn't ready to think about it tonight.

"At first, I didn't tell you because I found it curious. And I know that is wrong and messed up. I get that now." He ran his fingers through his hair again. "But I loved that you didn't know who I was. I loved that you didn't look at me as the Prince. I wanted to just be that soldier in the army that you thought I was," Tezya said as he took a hesitant step toward me. "But then I knew. Once you told me the rumors you heard about me, I knew that you would hate me. That once you found out, things would change. I'm not sorry for not wanting that. I'm not sorry for wanting to keep things the same between us for a little while longer. But this doesn't change anything. This doesn't change how I feel about you."

This doesn't change how I feel about you. I tucked that into my memory for later. I couldn't decipher what he meant by it right now. My head hurt too much to even begin to process his words or the meaning behind them. "You're a coward, Tezya. A prick and a fucking coward."

I couldn't stand how much it all made sense now, how blind I was before. Why he was at my interrogation when I was compelled, why he was so high up in the army. I scoffed. He wasn't just high up. He was as high up as you could go. He controlled it. Then another thought washed over me. He killed the rebels that he claimed to share the same beliefs as.

"You told me you hated the ranking system. You made me believe that we felt the same way. But you don't. You murdered all the rebels. You burned them to ash. How could you do that if you believe in the same thing? They were fighting for the change that you claim you want, and you murdered them for it. How can you tell me that this changes nothing?" I was sobbing now, and my vision was starting to blur because of it. I hadn't even realized I started crying. Embarrassment clung to me. I tried to blink away the tears to focus on what was happening.

"They were my orders, Scotlind. I didn't want to do it, but I didn't have a choice, just like you don't have a choice now."

"What's that supposed to mean?"

"It means that we are all at the King's mercy."

"Please, just leave, Tezya," I snapped. "I don't want to see you." I was tired and sick of fighting for today. I wanted to sleep and just forget this night ever happened.

He looked at me with such sadness in his eyes. "I still have to train you."

"I know."

He sighed heavily before turning toward my door. "I'll see you at dawn."

TWENTY-ONE
SIE

A STRANGER WAS STARING at me during my training session. I didn't take my eyes off him as I went head to head with a Tennebrisian guard. My body was finally adjusting after Moli got me up to the max dose of the poison. I was still weak and was panting way too hard over something that normally would have been a warm-up. But I was alive, and my body finally stopped trembling from the dreadful concoction. It was nice to not be constantly perspiring from every orifice of my body. Now, I was only sweating from training, and I didn't mind because I needed to regain my strength. It's what I had been devoting my free time to.

Out of the corner of my vision, the stranger moved. Green eyes flashed as I saw a hand pull on an ear. Thank the fucking Goddess.

Peter was back.

I reached my abilities out toward him, thankful that with the poison's effects diminishing, I was able to use of them again. Although, I've been trying to save all my strength for teleporting in case I need to see Grey. *You're back,* I slammed my words into his mind.

The stranger, Peter, said back, *Meet me in your chambers. We have a lot to discuss.* Before I could push my thoughts into the stranger's head again, Peter transformed. The dark skinned, green-eyed stranger morphed into a fly and zoomed past me.

I threw my sword on the ground and sprinted toward my chambers. I didn't bother to explain to the shocked guard why I stopped sparring him.

Relief swelled inside me, knowing that my friend was alive. With every pounding footstep, a smile threatened my lips. I didn't know how damn long it had been since I smiled. Peter wasn't caught by the Luxians. He was alive and well and here in Tennebris. I knew I shouldn't have let him go in the first place. My exhilaration squelched as I rounded a corner. It was so fleeting that it almost seemed like I made it up.

Dread replaced my prior euphoria as one sweet, innocent name came to my mind. *Scotlind*. Shit. Shit. Shit. I sprinted faster, pushing my weakened body to its max. Did his return mean something had happened to her?

I was shaking by the time I finally pushed open my doors. A fly whizzed by my head buzzing impatiently. It wasn't until I forced the heavy doors to slam shut that the fly transformed into my friend. Golden markings faded from Peter's skin as his body adjusted back into himself.

Scottie? I breathed into his head, knowing that this wasn't a conversation we should be having out loud.

She's alive, Peter thought back right before he opened up his mind to me. I saw through his memories when he was a guard stationed outside her cage. A fucking cage. It was so small she could barely move. I watched as Scottie withered away into nothing. I watched as she was pulled out of that damn cage every day, then thrown back in hours later, covered in her own blood.

"Fucking shit," I breathed out loud as Peter's memories showed the Fire Prince coming to the dungeons. I watched as Kole compelled her to reveal everything about her past and about me. I wondered where the bastard ran off to. It twisted my gut knowing that he was in the same place as her. That he was still tormenting her, and I was stuck here, unable to do anything about it.

Peter caught me up on everything he saw during his time as Scottie's maid. I hated that she was spending all her time with the Prince. **Does she know who Tezya is?** I asked him.

Peter shook his head. *"At least she didn't when I left. I've been trying to spy and figure out what they want with her. Why the King is wasting so much time on training her, but I haven't been able to glean anything useful."*

We have to get her back, I gritted. I couldn't believe she was with the Fire Prince, that she was spending all her time with him, having no idea who he was. She was probably with him right now for fuck's sake. I bristled. Jealousy and anger flooded through me, and I couldn't do a damn thing to stop it.

"Sie, we can't. She's being monitored and watched too closely by the Prince himself. There is no way I would be able to get her out of there safely. Tezya is honed into her every movement and would track us down the moment we fled. Not to mention the interest the Lux King has with her. He saw through her memories, Sie. He knows you care for her. I came back to warn you not to do anything when the annual meeting comes up. I don't even think you should talk to her."

What? I snapped back. **How can you expect me not to talk to her? How can you expect me to just leave her there?** It was eating away at me that I never got to explain myself to her before she was taken. I had spent every waking moment thinking of some way to explain myself, to try and get her to forgive me, to understand. And now there was no fucking way that I wasn't going to tell her who she's been spending her time with all these weeks. I planned on telling her exactly who the Prince was and forcing him to stay the fuck away from her.

Because we don't have a choice. We are walking on a dangerous line. If you talk to her, they could kill her for it. She barely got out of the last treason accusation alive. What do you think would happen if she was caught with you again?

I hated that he was right, but I couldn't do nothing. There was no way I could just leave her there. Leave her with *him*.

Peter asked in my head, *What is happening here? I heard some gossip amongst the other maids, but I couldn't decipher what was real from the rumors.*

I filled Peter in on everything, from King Lunder's murder to Synder changing the laws to Moli giving me poison every day. When I was done, Peter looked as if he saw a ghost. I knew that Lilia flashed in his mind when I told him about the rights being taken away from rank zeroes. I knew he would be worried about his younger sister. And even though I assured him that my brother was looking out for her at school, we both knew it wasn't enough.

I'll go back to Lux for now. I'll continue to monitor Scottie, and I'll work harder on discovering the Lux King's involvement and what his plan is because something else is coming, Sie, I can feel it.

Be careful, I pleaded to my friend, unsure if I should let him go again. I swore to myself I wouldn't let him leave my side if I ever saw him again. But Scottie... she was with the youngest Prince. The one Advenian that was claimed to match the power of the Lux King. Even Prince Arcane wasn't as strong as his brother. *I need you.* I finally said to Peter, accepting that I had to send him again. Scottie needed him more, and there was no way in hell I was leaving her vulnerable now that she was with the Prince. **Synder threatened to name a second for me if you weren't back by my coronation. He plans to select himself, and then it will only be a matter of time before my death follows Lunder's. He plans to rule for good.**

I'm always careful. Peter tried and failed to smile. This was some deep shit we were in. *Sie, we have to stop them. We can't let Synder win. We can't let him do this to rank zeroes. I know you are worried about Scottie, but she is safe for now, trust me. We will bring her back to Tennebris eventually, but we have to get rid of the threat here first. We can't bring her back until Synder is gone. We have to make sure you become King.*

Peter hugged me tightly before he transformed in front of my eyes, and then the friend I knew and loved was something else entirely. I watched as the fly fitted through the cracks of my window, only to become a bird soaring in the wind the moment he was outside. My eyes never left his changing form until he was only a speck, disappearing into the clouds toward Lux.

TWENTY-TWO
TEZYA

FRUSTRATION AND RAGE plunged toward me as I kept my ability locked on Rumor's room last night. Her maid was still home visiting family for Yule, so I monitored her constantly. It didn't take much focus to hone in on her. Even though she was across the castle from me, her emotions were a palatable, living, breathing thing. It flung toward me, crawled under my skin, and settled there, making it impossible for me to forget what happened. Not that I would ever stop seeing the look of hurt and confusion on her face as I walked toward that stupid throne. The Lux King rarely forced his offspring to sit on the dais with him. Arcane does willingly, but then again, he agrees to anything and everything the King wants, not wanting to risk his disappointment. Dove and I never sit on the thrones, and we're rarely forced to. I knew the King only mandated it once he saw Rumor at the Ball. He probably guessed that I was hiding who I was from her and wanted to punish me for bringing her against his orders.

I sighed heavily, shaking away last night and trying to focus on the present. We were in the gym section of the training room, and she hasn't spoken to me throughout the entire morning. She didn't even look at me when I picked her up from her room at dawn. I walked her to the gym since her maid wasn't back yet. I could have easily assigned her to train with someone else, but I couldn't get myself to do it. Some sick part of me just wanted the excuse to stay connected with her. I didn't know where that put me. I was only assigned to train her for ten weeks. Then what would happen? I prayed to each and every Goddess that the King wouldn't discover that she possessed enhancement. I couldn't stomach to see her chained to his side.

Without meaning to, my senses reached out toward her throughout our workout. And every time I did, it came up blank. She was zoning me out and blocking me from her mind. She was emotionless, and it killed me. It actually fucking killed me. She wore her emotions on her sleeve. I could usually tell how she was feeling without using my abilities on her, but today she was empty. Void. Numb. Fuck, I did that to her.

"We're sparring now," I said after lunch, not giving her the opportunity to ignore me anymore.

She turned to look at me. Finally, and damn if those eyes didn't kill me. "Fine by me. I wouldn't mind punching you." I couldn't help but smile as I followed her back into the gym. She was getting stronger. Her body was corded with lean muscles, and I couldn't help but watch her from behind as she stepped up into the ring.

I tore my gaze away and smirked. "If you can manage to land a hit on me." She didn't hesitate to spring forward, aiming for my middle. I dodged her effortlessly. Again. And again. And again. She was good, quick on her feet, fast thinking and agile. She would have probably landed hits on many of my soldiers.

She grunted as I stepped out of the way, evading her next kick at the last second. I grabbed her still extended leg and pulled her toward me. My hand slid to her back as she slammed into my chest. My other hand inched up higher on her thigh to hold her leg in place.

She hopped on one foot and pushed, trying to break free from me but couldn't. "Get off me," she swore.

"Make me," I smiled, knowing full well I was pissing her off. Good. At least I was getting some emotion out of her. Even if it was a negative one, it was better than feeling nothing. She pushed again, but I tightened my hold on her and smiled as a small growl escaped her lips.

I laughed. "Come on, Rumor, you can do better than that."

"I'm trying," she grunted as she pushed again. I pivoted with her in tow as I saw her try to hop and slam her heel on mine.

"We can do this all day long, but you won't get anywhere. I'm stronger than you. If I have you in a hold, physical strength won't do anything," I whispered in her ear as I turned her around and held her back against my chest. Shit. This position wasn't doing me any good. I could feel her ass against me—

A flood of water came rushing toward the ring as my words dawned on her. The water was flattening and pouring in from under the cracks of the door. But once it reached the gym, it rose as she manipulated it into a wall.

She drained the pool.

I wanted to let the water hit me to test the effectiveness of it. So I turned my back to the threat just as the wall slammed against me, shielding her from the brunt of it. I grunted as I toppled forward with Scottie still in my arms. She tried to escape as we fell but only managed to turn herself around. I barely caught myself in time as I landed on my forearms, my knees on either side of her hips, hovering above her, careful not to crush her beneath me.

"Good," I breathed against her face. A jolt of energy went through me at her closeness. She was panting under my arms as I straddled her, her sapphire eyes wide and staring up at me. I couldn't tell if her ragged breath was from the effort she just used to move that amount of water or from the position we landed in. I was amazed by the speed at which she was able to make the water move and the power she was able to create with it. She still had a long way to go—I knew with practice she would be able to do so much more—but for such a short time training, it was impressive.

Scottie shifted beneath me, and the movement caught my attention. We were both drenched. Her hair was sprawled out around her, with some strands plastered against her neck and cheek. She pulled her lower lip into her mouth, biting it out of nervousness.

Without meaning to, I leaned into her, my hands now pressed against either side of her face. I was drawn to her. I had been since the moment I saw her. Her bottom lip fell out from between her teeth and parted slightly as her eyes searched mine. She wasn't breathing, and I didn't quite know if I was either. I expected her to push me off by now. But she didn't.

She was still, deathly still, and waiting. Before I did anything I regretted, I pushed up and stood, shaking my head to alleviate the excess water. She followed, her eyes were furrowed in concentration. Then the water was sliding off my skin. I looked up to see the same thing happening to her. Her dark wet hair was slowly returning to its light brown coloring as she manipulated the water off of us, drying us in the process.

I remained silent, watching her as she moved every drop of water back into the pool. She was panting by the time she was done. That was the largest amount of water she moved and the furthest she got it to travel. The concentration to move every last speck of water, to focus on each individual drop, was monumental.

"Come with me," I said. "I have something to show you."

She looked apprehensive. "What is it?"

"A peace offering."

I WATCHED Scottie as she scanned my room. She'd only been in here the first night she got out of her cage, and I honestly didn't know if she remembered the conversation we had on the balcony. She'd been so out of it...

"Why did you bring me here?" she finally asked, her gaze settling on me.

"When you had the testing done by the healer, Semadar, he also ran a blood sample on your DNA," I explained as I walked over to my desk and unlocked the top drawer. "Every citizen in Lux is required to give a blood sample when they are born. It's a way to keep track of everyone. Then after the Luxian Trials, their results, along with their abilities, are listed. You said you don't remember anything about your childhood, who your parents were, right?"

I waited until she shook her head before I continued, "Well, I took your sample and ran it through the tracking system. I found out who your parents are, and I know what happened to them."

She froze, her fingers hovering over an old book. "You found them? Are they alive?" The hope in her eyes fluttered and wilted away as I shook my head. "Oh... I figured. I just... Can I see?"

"Yes," I handed her the paperwork that I'd kept hidden ever since we got back from the hut. I honestly had no idea what possessed me to look into it in the first place, but seeing her reaction made me happy I did. Her eyes frantically scanned the pages, her lips parted and moved as she silently read. She slumped onto the sofa with a hand clutching her heart. I watched as she unraveled her truth, discovering everything she'd been told was a lie.

The only accuracy that was fed to her was that she was an orphan. Her parents were killed in a fire the night she was kidnapped. The fire was declared an accident and marked as classified. Her records indicated that the little girl that lived there was killed along with her parents. It claimed there was nothing left of her body, but the fire wasn't an accident. It was orchestrated.

"My name isn't even Scotlind," she whispered, her eyes still glued to the paperwork.

"No," I said gently as she finally tore her gaze away from the truth to meet my stare. "Your real name was Haevely Sirena."

"My parents..." she didn't finish. I knew what the paperwork stated. I'd read it over multiple times before I finally decided to show her. Her mother was Rosemilly Sirena. Her elemental ability was water. It was where Scottie got her power from, but Rosemilly didn't just manipulate water. She could create, making her a rank five.

"My water powers are from my mother," she said softly, her voice cracking. I hoped sharing this information would only strengthen her need to control the element. She was growing tremendously, but I prayed that maybe having this glimpse of her past would connect her more to her powers.

"She was powerful too," I said. "Your enhancement must be from generations back as it's an extinct power, or it *was* an extinct power. It's not uncommon for children to be born with different abilities than their parents, but the gene has to lie dormant somewhere in their line of genetics."

She nodded, her eyes once again glued to the papers.

"I don't understand my father's powers."

The first time I read about her father, Lincoln, I was shocked. He was a powerful rank five with the same ability as the King's second, Athler. With a single look, he could manipulate how anyone was feeling. He could make someone fearful, lustful, agitated, or confused without those feelings being previously there. It was chilling to know that she came from such power. "He possesses pheromone control," I said, not wanting to go into too much detail about how lethal the ability actually was.

"Is it common?"

I shook my head. "I only know of one of other person who possesses it."

A shudder ran through me as I recalled the times Athler manipulated my own feelings. I already felt everything stronger with my heightened senses, but when he messed with me, when he used his ability on me, I couldn't control myself. As a child, when I was too weak to undergo more physical punishments, the King liked to have his second instill an unending fear inside of me. It was so overwhelming that I wanted to end it all. He filled my head with so much terror and only stopped when I was sobbing, pleading, and begging for death. It was the second most frequent punishment the King requested done to me.

"You can't tell anyone you know about this," I said, wanting to bring the topic away from her father's abilities. "The world believes that you died that night. Whoever caused that fire and purposely left you in Tennebris is the only one who knows differently."

"Why are you showing me this?" she asked.

"I thought you deserved to know the truth."

"The truth," the words were soft leaving her lips as she looked up at me. "Tezya, just promise me that. Promise me no more lies. Promise me that you won't keep anything from me or lie to me anymore. Do that, and I'll forget about what happened."

I swallowed. "Okay." The word felt wrong leaving my mouth because I knew that I was already breaking that promise. I was keeping massive secrets from her. Secrets that I knew she'd never forgive me for. But I prayed that whenever she did discover what I was hiding, she would understand.

TWENTY-THREE
SCOTLIND

"ARE YOU SURE?" Tezya asked me the following day.

"Yes, I'm positive." We went through our usual routine of training in the private gym. "Besides, if I don't go with you, I would just be cooped up in my chambers with nothing to do."

He told me last night that he would be away for a couple of days. On top of being the commander of the Luxian armies, Tezya also oversaw the mortal territory and was in charge of monitoring the humans, whatever that meant, and he was leaving to go there.

"Alright, but I'm taking you to the training grounds where I take all of my soldiers before they go to the mortal territory. The land there isn't protected from the atmosphere like our Kingdoms are. There are no shields to protect you from what this planet unleashes. If you are coming with me, you're going to familiarize yourself with what could happen. You have two days before I have to leave, so we'll get started now."

"Deal," I grinned, knowing that Vallie would be jealous. She was fascinated with the humans and always talked about wanting to see their world and learn how they lived. I would be lying if I said it wasn't something I thought about too. I just never believed I would get the opportunity to even cross paths with one, and now Tezya was offering me to stay a night in their lands.

"Alright, enough training here. Save your energy for the grounds. Go eat lunch, and we'll head there after."

———

TEZYA MADE arrangements for the training grounds to be cleared for the rest of the afternoon. When we arrived, I was disappointed. Massive domes were scattered across a flat, muddy terrain, but that was it.

"Um, what is this supposed to train me for exactly?" I asked through pursed lips. If this was what the mortal lands looked like— endless muddy pits—I didn't care for them.

Tezya chuckled softly as he walked over to a control panel I hadn't noticed. He flipped a lever, and an instantaneous humming started pouring over the area. A quiet shudder made my feet quiver as the ground was shifting and changing underneath me.

"The training arena was set up by ground users. It's a simulation. They manipulate each dome to produce naturally occurring weather that happens on the planet. Once you leave our protective shields, the weather becomes unpredictable and unstable," Tezya said as he crossed his arms over his broad chest. He wasn't wearing a shirt again, and it took everything in me not to stare at his sculpted abs.

The rumbling grew louder and pulled my attention away from him. I snapped my head from dome to dome as they were changing before my eyes. My hair whipped against my face as I tried to make sense of everything. I walked over to the first dome, the slight humming encased whatever was stirring inside. A large mountain grew from the mud, but there was a hole on the top of it. Red, molten liquid spewed down the mountain, taking mud and ash with it.

"The mortals call it a volcano," Tezya said as he came up beside me.

"What is it?" I asked, "Is it fire or water?"

"A little of both, I guess. It moves and flows like water, but it's scorching to touch. It will burn everything in its path." It made me wonder what would happen if Tezya and I combined our abilities.

The next two domes I recognized. One had blazing fires burning all the trees that sprouted inside the circular mud pit. The other was a wall of water so powerful it knocked down the buildings that manifested on the dirt. "Wildfires and Tsunamis," Tezya remarked as I walked past each dome.

"I don't understand," I said as we made it to another one. This one vibrated and shook everything inside. I watched as the mud and earth cleaved into two right down the middle. "The mortals have no abilities, they are powerless, but the planet they live on has powers?"

It was odd to me how the mortals weren't anything special. According to our kind, they were weak, yet they lived on a planet that seemed like a living creature of its own. A creature that seemed angry with them, a creature that called to death. It seemed to possess every ability known to the Advenians and somehow made it more lethal.

Tezya smirked. "It's the weather here. The planet is strong and wild and can be unpredictable. At any point, any of these events can occur, but it's mostly calm on the mortal lands."

My eyes widened as we took in the last few domes. One was a moving, darkened spiral of debris. It looked like an air user was manipulating the wind itself, forcing it to hurtle together into a vertical wall of death. I squinted closer and realized that the grayish wind was spiraling around an axis, slowly moving to destroy everything in its path.

I jumped back into Tezya's hard chest as a bolt of lightning crashed from the top of another dome. A deathly roar crackled as rain poured and slammed into the mud creating a sloshy mess.

But the last dome gave me chills that wouldn't leave. It seemed to combine the weird twisted wind and water together. A beach rose inside the dome, but it was nothing like the calm, blissful ocean that Tezya took me to. The waves were tall and monstrous as they crashed into the sand, the wind was invisible, unlike that gray spiraling wall, but it was just as deadly. Roofs were thrown, trees were uprooted, and heavy rain poured down so thick that I could barely see through it.

"This one is called a hurricane."

"It's horrible," I breathed as I watched the destruction, unable to tear my eyes away. "How can the humans live on this planet when this happens to them? We've always been taught that they're frail and that they die so easily, so how does this not kill them?"

"It does kill them sometimes, but they don't have a choice. They don't know any better." Tezya tilted his head toward the dome that had me transfixed. "Hurricanes actually occur on our island too, but our air users thicken their shields and all work together, so it never breaches our city, but it can happen where I'm taking you." He turned to me. "Are you sure you want to go with me?"

"Yes," I said, and I meant it. I wanted to see the land. I wanted to see a mortal up close. Vallie would murder me herself if she ever found out that I had an opportunity to see one and didn't take it. Not that I would ever see my red-headed friend again. My gut twisted at the thought, and I quickly blinked away the tears before Tezya saw, focusing on the deadly waves. Would I ever be able to manipulate the water with enough strength to produce this kind of destruction? Would I ever *need* this kind of power?

"Alright, then you're going to be training inside each of the domes for the next two days. I want you here practicing up until the moment we leave. I have business to attend to, so Brock will be training you."

"Where are you going?" I asked, trying to hide my disappointment.

"I have to finalize some things for the trip. I'll see you before it's time to go. And Rumor..."

"Yes?"

"The mortals aren't weak."

Tezya left the moment Brock showed up at the domes. Kallon and Rainer were towing behind him. I was happy to see them, but some part of me felt hurt by Kallon. I wanted to be her friend so badly, but she, too, kept Tezya's identity a secret. Who her *betrothed* really was. I knew deep down that wasn't fair. She didn't owe me anything. I only met her a few weeks ago, and she knew Tezya for... I didn't even know how long, but probably close to a century. Was I really upset that she was more loyal to him over me? It was stupid. If anything, she should hate *me* for all the time I spent with her betrothed, but she didn't. She didn't seem to mind at all.

"Good morning," I called to the three of them once they were in earshot.

"Hey, babes," Kallon replied.

"Hi, Scottie," Rainer followed with a dazzling smile. His black curls were tied up in a high bun today that showed off the fine lines of his face.

I looked toward Brock, who was the only one not smiling. "We aren't here to socialize. I told you two that if you are coming along, you're joining the training," Brock growled as he made a point to look over each one of us. I shivered as I took him in. He was massive, slightly bigger than Tezya, but this was a different version of Brock than I had ever seen before. He wasn't the gentle male that danced with me at the Ball, distracting me so that I didn't have a meltdown in front of everyone. This was Brock from the army that Tezya told me about—the one who never backed down from a challenge and always came out on top. He was a born warrior, lethal in every way.

Kallon rolled her eyes. "I'm aware. You only reminded us ten times on the way over here. Besides, Scottie needs a girl to fight against, then she can really learn."

My smile was genuine as I looked at her. She wore skin tight clothes, showing off her thin and dainty frame, but I didn't doubt that she was a skilled fighter, that she had hidden muscles running up the length of her. It was like the Goddesses took a normal-sized Advenian female and stretched her out to make Kallon, leaving full parts only where a female would want them. Half of her hair was dyed a light lavender today, and it was pulled out of her face and wrapped in a tight bun, mixing with her usual shiny black.

"Fine then," Brock said, "Kallon, you fight Scottie first."

Brock's training was worse than Tezya's. So much worse. He didn't let me catch a break. I went from sparing Kallon, Rainer, to him, then all over again, back to back to back. They were all so powerful. Anytime I tried to land a hit on Kallon, she would use the portals she created to slip out of the way before I could blink. And her long, slender frame made her agile and almost impossible to land a hit on.

Fighting against Rainer was a different kind of difficult as my water only amplified his abilities. I had to fight him with just my physical strength. I learned the hard way that being electrified in water sucked. He was much slower than Kallon but just as skilled. Where she leaned on speed, Rainer went to strength. I was surprised by his powerful blow. He was lean, not a twig like Kallon was, but still smaller in stature for an Advenian male, but his throws... they hurt a lot. He worked with his body, angling in such a way to put all of his weight into each skillfully calculated throw. To make things worse, everything was electrified. He was wearing gloves that he infused his ability onto. Each time he hit me, he pulled back his power enough that I only felt a small pulsing shock. But I knew if we were truly battling, I'd be fried.

Fighting against Brock, though, was the scariest. I quickly learned that his ability was terrifying. I couldn't wrap my head around how he was only a rank four. He could cut someone but take away the feeling of pain to the area, so they wouldn't know that they were bleeding out until it was too late. He told me that he would normally blind and deafen his opponents, which he demonstrated on me, luckily, just not at the same time.

"Trust your instincts and listen to my movements," Brock said from behind me. I twirled out of the way, hating the feeling of the constant darkness. He was currently taking away my vision.

"It's kind of hard to do that over the thunder and constant down-pour," I gritted out as I strained to listen for his attack.

"You won't get a say in the elements around you, and you need to be able to fight under all conditions."

We were fighting in the dome Tezya called the hurricane, although Rainer turned it down to level one, stating it was just a small tropical storm. It didn't feel like that as I was soaked from head to toe. There was so much water sloshing around inside the dome that I couldn't manipulate it properly. It also didn't help that I couldn't see anything.

"Come on, Scottie, don't just dodge. Fight back. Use your ability on me. Even without your sight, you should have the advantage with these conditions," Brock said before he attacked again. From Kallon's gasp, I think I just barely stepped out of the way.

"I can't even see where the water is or where you are. How am I supposed to use it against you?" I snapped, frustration coursing through me.

"Just breathe and focus. You are one with the water. You don't need to see it to control it. Don't rely on your senses," Brock instructed.

"Says the guy that is seeing twice as good now," I ground out right before he landed a punch to my gut.

I toppled over, clutching my abdomen while wheezing uncontrollably. I cried out as Brock kicked my back, pushing my already half collapsed body over completely. I landed on the muddy ground with a loud thud. I didn't need my vision to know that every inch of me was covered in mud. The water rushed over to me the instant I was down, swallowing me whole as I cast my ability, attempting to manipulate the water away from me while trying to regain my footing. I couldn't hear him. Did Brock take away my hearing too? I got my answer with a loud crack of thunder. I knew he was going to attack again. He was so silent with his movements that it was impossible to glean when his attacks would come until it was too late.

The snap of bones crunched in my ears before my vision came flooding back to me. The dome stilled as the wind quieted and the pounding rain stopped. Brock fell to his knees beside me, cradling his wrist. But I hadn't attacked him. I looked down to see what caught his attention. Blood covered where I stood and was dripping from my arm around the jutted bone that pierced my flesh.

Rainer and Kallon came up beside me. "I don't understand," I started. "I don't feel anything."

"I know," Kallon said softly.

I looked over at Brock, whose brows were furrowed in concentration. His face was lined with agony. Then it dawned on me. Brock was using his ability to take away all my pain, feeling it for himself. But things were amplified for him. He would be feeling my pain twice as hard.

"Brock, you don't have to—"

He cut me off. "It'll only take a minute to heal it." Then he grabbed my shattered wrist in his. I felt nothing as Brock worked. Slowly my wrist was repairing itself. Agony flared on his face for just a moment as the bone snapped back into place. A bead of sweat dripped down his forehead as he grunted.

"Done," he panted and sank back into the mud. "Scotlind, I'm so sorry."

"It's fine. Thank you," I looked down at my wrist, able to feel it again, but I still had no pain. It was completely healed. Better than healed. "Your healing abilities can heal things completely?" I asked in astonishment as I turned my wrist over, bending it back and forth. My scarred zero that marred my flesh was still visible, but my wrist itself felt... great. The healers that were sent to Tennebris could only speed up the healing process, not completely reserve it.

Kallon answered for him. "There are many different kinds of healers in Lux. The ones that were sent over to Tennebris were usually only a rank one or two in healing and couldn't do much. Brock can heal completely if the injury is fresh, but it depletes his reserve fast."

And Brock was using both of his abilities at once. He was taking away my sense of touch to the area—taking away my pain—with his sensibus furari, and healed me at the same time. I looked over at him. He was still slouched in the mud, panting heavily. His face paled, completely devoid of color. I remembered Tezya telling me that Advenians reacted differently to their reserves being depleted, that Brock's vision blacks out. I watched in horror and fascination as the male knelt before me and blinked rapidly, not seeming to look at anything in particular. He was drained, his reserves gone.

"That's it for today," he finally said, his voice still breathless and ragged. I watched as he struggled to get up and left without another word.

Rainer started turning off all the controls, each dome returning to its original form of a mud pit. Kallon walked over to me, and it was the first time we'd been alone since the Ball.

"So," she said as we made our way over to an open spot on the grass away from the domes, "I'm sorry about the Ball and that you found out that way." Even covered in sweat and mud, she looked beautiful.

"I just feel stupid. I should have known—"

"Don't," she said quickly. "There is nothing for you to feel dumb about. You didn't grow up here like the rest of us."

"Why didn't you tell me?" I asked. "Not that you owe me anything," I added quickly. I barely knew Kallon, but there was something so familiar about her. It was probably just me projecting Vallie onto her, which wasn't fair to her. I'd been trying to fill her void since I left LakeWood, but I liked Kallon a lot. I desperately wanted to be her friend, and I was hoping that she felt the same about me.

"Tezya asked us not to. He wanted to tell you on his own terms, and I honestly didn't think about it when I brought you to Yule. The Lux King rarely forces Tezya and Dovelyn to sit on the thrones. The more spotlight he has all to himself, the happier he is. But for what it's worth, I'm glad you now know. It was really hard to not slip up."

"I am too." I was happy to know the truth, even if the idea of Tezya being the Fire Prince still scared me. "You and him are—" I still never confirmed what I thought when I saw the two of them dancing.

"Yeah, we're engaged."

"I'm sorry—"

"Sorry for what?"

I didn't know how to answer that. Tezya and I never did anything. I didn't even know how he felt about me. He told me in my room that we were friends, and I was coming up blank on how I could explain to her that I was sorry for everything that's only been in my head? That I've secretly been attracted to him all this time he's been training me, but it's one-sided... "I just didn't realize you two were a thing."

She turned her head to look at me. "Babes, Tezya and I are *not* a thing. Yes, we're forced to be engaged by our parents, but that's all it is. It's a transaction we have no say in. Neither of us like the other in that way, and honestly, half the time, I forget that we're engaged. We both try to push it very far out of our minds and avoid thinking about it."

"Oh," I responded because I didn't know what else to say.

"Trust me, babes, I don't like him. He's like a brother to me and has been one of my oldest friends. And Tezya feels the same way. If there's a way out of this engagement, he'd be the first to find the loophole."

"Are Dovelyn and Arcane betrothed?" I asked, genuinely curious if all the Royals had arranged marriages.

"They will be. The Lux King will take his time selecting a wife for Arcane. The longer he isn't married, the less of a risk he poses for taking the throne before the King's done. And as much as Arcane wants to rule, he isn't keen on marrying. He has no interest in taking a wife."

"Why?"

"He's in love with a guy."

"Is that allowed?" I asked because I had no idea what Lux deemed acceptable.

"Goddess, no," Kallon laughed, but I could tell it was laced with her own sorrow on the subject. "Any marriage that can't produce a strong offspring isn't allowed here. It's all they care about—breeding us to make Lux the stronger Kingdom."

"I don't really think that's allowed anywhere," I admitted. "Tennebris values birth and Lakimi too much to encourage that."

Kallon shook her head. "That's not true. It is allowed somewhere."

I couldn't keep the confusion out of my face as my eyebrows furrowed. "Where?"

"The mortals."

"I—" I went to open my mouth to respond, but I didn't even know where to start with that. It was illegal to breed with humans—banned by our ancestors when we first came here—but were Advenians still doing it? If it was with the same sex there wouldn't be a concern for a pregnancy, making it easier to hide.

"It's one of the many reasons I love going there. You can be whoever you want and love anyone. I like both genders, so that kind of freedom is appealing to me."

"Have you ever..." I couldn't get myself to ask it—to ask if she's ever been with a human.

But she seemed to understand what I wanted to say. She shook her head. "I've thought about it, but I never went through with it. It's too risky. I often dream that I'm human, though. I wish I had been born there. I wish I was mortal instead of an Advenian."

"Even with their short lifespans?"

"Yes. They actually get to live, Scottie. Even if it's just for a small blip of time. What's the point of our long lives if we can't even do what we want? If we can't love who we want?" She paused for a moment, looking at me longingly like she was begging me to understand. Maybe I did. Maybe I would give up our stretched immortality and powers in exchange for that kind of freedom.

"Anyway, as for Dovelyn, the King likes to use her future betrothal as blackmail," she said, bringing me back to what we were talking about, but it was hard to forget what she just revealed. "He threatens to marry her to his second in command, and that usually gets her to do whatever he wants. The King probably isn't in a rush to lose that kind of leverage over her."

"And Tezya?

She shrugged. "He's the youngest, so the least valuable to the King, even though Tez's powers are the strongest. He married him off in exchange for my powers. Portal jumping is really rare to Luxians."

"And did you get something in exchange for it?"

"Goddess no, Tezya and I had no say. My parents were the ones who made the bargain with the King. For a shit ton of money, they gave up their only daughter. The only good thing about it is that the document my parents signed stated that the King can't have access to my powers until I'm wed to Tez, and the only saving grace my parents gave me was not putting a timeline on the contract, so Tezya and I have been pushing it off, making excuse after excuse to delay the inevitable. Which, Arcane being the heir and not wed, has been working in our favor for postponing our own marriage."

"I'm sorry, Kallon."

"It's alright. Things could have been worse. I could be in Dovelyn's position with the threat of marriage to Athler." She shuddered, and I wondered who could possibly be worse than the King himself. "But Tezya is a good guy. Even if I'm not remotely interested in him in that way, he's my friend, and he's kind."

I nodded, not sure what to say back to that.

"Come on, let's get you back to the castle before nightfall. Maybe we can have dinner together?"

I smiled. "I'd love that."

TWENTY-FOUR
SCOTLIND

"I AM NOT WEARING THIS," I snapped at Patricia. I was happy she was back, but I did not miss her lack of fabric when it came to my clothes. Not that I thought she had a choice. Luxian fashion was limited and skimpy to begin with.

"These are the clothes Tezya gave me. If you don't want to wear them, then don't go," she retorted. She was furious when I told her that I was traveling to the mortal territory with Tezya and spent the entire night trying to talk me out of it. She was even more furious when Tez said that she couldn't come with us when I asked him.

I snatched the questionable fabric from her hands and stormed into the bathing room with it. Eyeing the tub, I knew I should try to bathe. I had dirt caked under my fingernails from the past two days of training in the mud with Brock, and I knew my cloth bath wasn't really cutting it. I had been thinking about it more and more, trying to coax myself to just try. But every time I thought I might, I chickened out.

Whatever Tezya had to do to prepare for this trip kept him completely occupied. I hadn't seen him since he first showed me the domes. I had no idea if he knew anything about what happened during my training with Brock, if he knew that his friend had broken my wrist and healed it immediately. I was still impressed with the fact that I never felt anything. I hadn't even realized the bone broke. If I hadn't heard the snap, if I hadn't stopped and looked at Brock, I wouldn't have even known. His abilities were terrifying and amazing. I could see how he was second in command of the army. He was really powerful—all of Tezya's friends were.

It was refreshing to hang out with them. I actually enjoyed the training, despite the fact that it made me feel incompetent. It was noticeable how far behind I was from all the years I lacked using my ability. But it only motivated me, only made me want to learn and master it faster.

I was in awe of all the Luxian powers, fascinated by each of them, and I knew I was only just scratching the surface of all that Lux possessed. It was so different fighting with elemental abilities. It was exhilarating to be able to incorporate my own for the first time in my life. In Tennebris, I could only spar using my own body, but mixing my water powers with my fighting was something else entirely.

The Luxian abilities seemed more evenly matched too. At least inside the domes, I could see how depending on your surroundings, you had the upper hand. Each element and ability had its advantages and weaknesses. Whereas the Dark abilities weren't as evenly matched. Compulsion and illusion overpowered everything there.

I stripped down and quickly put on the clothes Patricia gave me. The shirt was torn halfway across my abdomen, exposing half my stomach, and the pants—if you could even call them pants—seemed more like a second layer of skin. It took me forever to pull the tight material up my calves and over my thighs.

"Patricia, the shirt is ripped," I yelled through the door as I walked back into the bedroom. She was mid-drink and spit out her water all over her own dress once she saw me. "And these pants are so tight that I can barely move properly."

She let out a husky laugh as she eyed me. "I was told those are called *leggings* and quite popular amongst the humans."

"The shape of my butt is completely exposed. This is no different than not wearing anything at all," I huffed as I turned around to show her. I pulled at the material of the shirt. "And how is this even a shirt, and what the heck is on it?" I pointed to my half-ripped shirt that was all white except for this ugly green-goblin-looking-man-thing on the center of it. The print read *Yoda one for me*. I did not understand mortal fashion.

"Well, like I said, dear, if you aren't going to be comfortable blending in with the mortals, then don't go." She didn't bother leaving the sternness out of her voice.

A knock sounded on my door. I ignored my maid as I went to open it. Tezya was wearing his usual black baggy pants that halted down his calves. His shirt was white and extremely thin. I swallowed hard, trying not to notice the way I could see his muscle cord and move beneath it.

When I finally looked up, I noticed he was eyeing me too. I suddenly felt very uncomfortable in my barely covering clothes. "You look very *mortal*."

"I think you got the size wrong," I said as I stifled a yawn. Staying up all night bickering with Patricia was weighing heavily on me. "It doesn't even cover my stomach."

Tezya's eyes widened as they drifted to where I was pointing. "No, I didn't get it wrong."

"Yes, you did. It's ripped in half. Even the questionable swimming attire covered more than this."

He laughed. "Well, if you would rather wear the black swimsuit, I wouldn't object."

Patricia bristled behind me. I could tell she was fuming without turning to look at her. I crossed my arms over the ugly green man as Tezya added, "It's mortal fashion, Rumor. We need to blend in."

"Well, it's awful."

"I disagree entirely," he smiled as he looked me up and down again. I heard a swishing of skirts as Patrica started wobbling toward us.

"Let's go," I said quickly. I didn't bother turning around to say goodbye to her. I knew she would only scold us, and I wanted to leave before she could say anything to Tezya. I didn't want to risk her talking him out of bringing me.

Tezya and I walked down to the docks on the bay where Kallon was supposed to meet us. She had already created the portal that would transport the two of us somewhere off the coast of what the mortals called Florida.

"You ready?" Kallon turned to ask me. Half of her hair was sage green today. I nodded as Tezya wrapped his arms around my waist, pulling me into his chest. A jolt ran through me at his closeness. At the feel of his breath brushing the top of my head. I could hear his steady heartbeat through his chest.

"Okay, great," Kallon said, her eyes glued to the portal she was unfurling. "Because I have to leave as soon as I portal you two in. I'll reopen it tomorrow at the same hour to bring you guys back to Lux."

Only now did it dawn on me that she wasn't staying with us, and I would be spending the night alone with him. Again.

Kallon grabbed onto both of us as the darkness came a moment later. Bits of purple and black smoke surrounded us, casting the only light as Kallon navigated us through the portal. I expected it to be over in a heartbeat just like the one I went through to get to the Ball. The nausea came back the longer we traveled. I closed my eyes and buried myself into Tezya's chest, focusing on his smokey scent. It was a mixture of leather and pine and something else light and airy. I wanted to get lost in it, for it to completely engulf me, and if it was all I ever smelled for the rest of my life I'd be fine with that...

"You can open your eyes now," Tezya murmured into my hair. Kallon was already gone, with only the black and purple mist in her wake.

I slowly pried my eyes open and found that we were on a private balcony overlooking the ocean. My face was still pressed into his chest, and my fingers were cramping around his shirt. It took me a moment to realize that he had let go of me, but I was still gripping onto him like it was my lifeline.

I quickly stepped out of his embrace, embarrassed that it took me longer to do so than it should have. A coy grin was plastered across his smug face, making me utterly aware of how I reacted to being so close to him.

I finally took a moment to glance around at where he had brought me. I needed a distraction and wanted to focus on anything but the silver eyes still gleaming into me.

The first thing I noticed was the sticky humidity. It instantly clung to my neck, curling the loose strands of hair that fell from my braid. I could feel the sweat linger under my knees and between my elbows, and I had no idea if it was from the heat of this territory or the proximity I just was to Tezya.

I backed away from the drop below, only just now noticing how high up we were. The balcony stood twice as tall than Rainer's apartment. A glass railing was the only thing preventing our fall. There were tons of balconies that went up the length of the building, all identical to the one we were currently standing on.

"Aren't you worried about the mortals seeing us randomly appear on the balcony?" I asked, trying to ignore the fact that I wanted to close the distance between us again.

"No. Kallon created this portal decades ago, and Dovelyn used her air ability to create a cloaking shield over the balcony so it will always appear vacant to any onlookers. It doesn't matter what we do up here. No one will see us."

"That's very convenient," I muttered as I glanced around. "And where are we?" The balcony was small. It just barely fit one table with five chairs and had a small wicker sofa tucked in the corner. Lights were hung along the glass railing, adding to the glow and illuminating the view. Massive buildings that reached the sky were scattered on either side of us with the ocean looming in front. I tried to make out the mass of humans congregating on the sand, but we were too high up to see anything in clear detail. They all just looked like tiny moving specks.

"This is my residence," Tezya said. "I travel to the mortal territory a lot, and it was easier to buy a condo than constantly renting from a hotel with mortal cash."

"I don't really know what any of that means," I admitted.

He smiled as he slid open the glass door behind us, leading us inside. "Come on, I want to show you something I think you might like."

I followed him into his condo—or whatever he called it. Everything was bright. The place had plank wood flooring with cream walls to match. A weird light fixture with points that spun in a circle supplied a cool breeze against the heat. We entered into a wide living room with a kitchen against the far wall.

"Come on, what I want to show you isn't in here," he said as he walked me through one of the two doors in the place. It opened up into a bedroom with one large bed.

"You wanted to show me a bed?"

"No," he laughed. "It's in here." I followed him as he walked into another section of the place, this time opening up into a bathing room. I was horrified when I noticed there wasn't a door and that whoever was using it would be completely exposed. The room looked similar to the ones in Lux. I recognized almost everything inside. There was a toilet and two sinks with a large mirror hanging over them both.

"It's called a shower," Tezya said as he pointed to a porcelain open area that I hadn't noticed at first. A large faucet hung from the ceiling.

"What do humans do in the shower?" I asked, still not quite getting it.

"They wash. It's like a bath, but you can do it standing up. It's an open concept and not enclosed like a tub, so I thought maybe you could give it a try... only if you're up for it."

"Is this your way of telling me I smell?" I asked as I gawked at the shower. It was open, airy even. I didn't think I would feel claustrophobic in it. I expected Tezya to laugh or make a joke back, but he didn't. When I glanced up at him, he was already staring down at me.

"Rumor, I don't care if you never bathe for the rest of your life. But I know it bothers you. I can sense it. If you feel up for trying it out, you can. If you don't want to, that's fine too. I have to go out so you'll be alone for a little bit. You'll have privacy if you want to try."

"Where are you going?" I asked.

I watched his scar travel up his face as he smiled at me. I couldn't tell if he once had a single dimple on that side. "Believe it or not, I didn't just come here to have a nice time with you. I actually have to work. I'll be out, but I won't be long. When I get back, I'll show you around the city. We can walk to the ocean if you want to. We just can't swim in it, obviously."

Right. Humans didn't have markings, and it wouldn't be normal for them to see our black designs magically appear once water hit our skin. "How does this work?" I asked Tezya, turning back to the shower. He was right. I wanted to bathe. I wanted to feel normal again, and the thought of a proper wash was exhilarating, and one without the slimy, tiled walls of a tub was even better.

Tezya leaned forward and turned a silver bar to the right, "Red is hot, blue is cold. Whatever temperature you like, just turn it towards that color. The water comes from the ceiling. Soap is over there. Dovelyn and Kallon keep it stocked, so you should have everything you need." He pointed toward a shelf that was carved into the wall as the water started pouring from the square faucet hanging above us.

Steam instantly followed as the water splashed Tezya's arm. Black flames immediately appeared where the water had touched him. He looked at me, his mouth parted. "I'll be back, Rumor." I thought he was going to say something else, but then he stalked out of the bathing room, leaving me alone.

I stared at the pounding water for a long time. It wasn't until the mirrors completely fogged over and the steam was so heavy that it floated into the bedroom that I decided I wanted to go in. I was sweating in my horrible mortal outfit and still had mud caked on me and a stench that only a proper wash could cure.

I stripped out of the tight pants and ripped shirt, making sure to turn the green man facing down so the creature wasn't staring up at me as I undressed. Then I stepped hesitantly into the shower. My leg hit the water first, right over my calf with my mangled skin from my burn. It was scalding, but I embraced the heat as I fully entered into the steam.

It felt better than what I remembered from a bath. It felt like I was washing away everything negative and bad that ever existed, cleansing and healing me with each water droplet that hit my flesh. In a bath, whatever filth that came off me lingered in the water, surrounding and clinging to my skin even after I scrubbed it off. But here—in the shower—the dirt and grime disappeared, entering small holes in the bottom of the floor, leaving no trace behind.

I washed my body five times and my hair twice by the time I got out. Lavender wafted throughout the entire room. I inhaled a sense of calming. It had been way too long since I was properly cleaned. I felt whole again, like a new person, like I was leaving the old Scotlind behind.

I wiped away the film of water that lingered on the mirror to look at myself. I hadn't seen myself naked since Patricia helped me with my first cloth bath, and besides the Ball when Kallon helped me dress, I avoided looking at my reflection altogether. My freckles were becoming more prominent against my now tanned skin, and my blue eyes seemed brighter, less dull than before. It was like life was coming back into me. The dark circles under my eyes were gone as if the shower washed the coloring away.

"Haevely," I said out loud to myself in the mirror. "My parents named me Haevely." I wished I had known that girl. I wanted nothing more than to change the past I had been dealt. But some part of me felt like I was piecing myself back together just by knowing my real name. I could ask to be called that. I could go by Haevely, forget Scotlind altogether, but I couldn't. I was Scotlind whether I wanted to be or not, and the thought of Haevely seemed too pure to mix with the mess that was my life. I wanted to keep that part of me hidden. I wanted to protect the name. I wanted to savor it and lock it away for the happy little girl who played in the waves with her parents.

I called to my ability, moving the water down and off my body and into the hole in the bottom of the shower. Concentrating, I kept moving the water, droplet after droplet, until I was completely dry. I didn't really want to put back on the creepy mortal shirt again. My body felt too clean to wear dirty clothes, but I had no other ones, so I grabbed them, tugging them on before walking back out onto the balcony to wait. The only thing that kept me from coming out here naked was the fact that I had no idea when Tezya was going to come back.

It was thrilling thinking about how no one could see me from up here. I could do anything I wanted, and no one would know. I had complete privacy, no one watching my every move. No one I had to hide parts of myself from. I was surprised by how peaceful it made me feel.

The sun was slowly sinking into the sky, but there seemed to be a lot of day left in the night. I narrowed my eyes and tried to focus on the life happening below without getting too close to the edge. I wanted to see what a human looked like. I wanted to see how they acted, but they only looked like tiny bugs from up here.

I leaned over the railing a bit further, the height still bothering me, but my curiosity with the humans was getting the better of me. "Be careful," Tezya's smooth voice startled me, "I can't conjure wings like my siblings, so I can't catch you if you fall." I spun to face him, his nostrils flared, and his eyes widened as he took me in. "You showered."

It wasn't a question, but I answered anyway, "Yes." He was quiet as he studied me, probably gauging my emotions, so I added, "It was really nice. Thank you."

"I'm glad," he said as he schooled his expression back to normal. "I can bring you here anytime to shower if you want."

I bit my lip, unsure what to say back. I had never felt awkward around him before, but I honestly didn't know what to do. We weren't here to train. I didn't really know why he agreed to bring me. I assumed the Lux King wouldn't have approved of me coming here. He probably didn't even know that Tezya had brought me with him.

"And if I wanted to come here everyday?" I asked, surprising myself. I liked it here, even if all I saw so far was his one bedroom condo. It felt freeing to be out of Lux, to be so far from the King.

He smiled, taking a step forward onto the balcony. "I would love nothing more than to give you a permanent place here."

The air in my lungs left me, and all I could think about was the fact that no one could see us with Dovelyn's shield. I kept staring at his lips, imagining what it would be like to have him kiss me, to feel and taste him…

He was looking at me like he was waiting for my response, and I realized I didn't hear what he had said. "What?"

"I asked if you wanted to see the city."

"Oh, yes," I nodded as I followed him back inside, happy to stop thinking about him kissing me. Tezya locked the door once we were in a hall. It resembled the hall to Rainer's place as we walked by multiple identical doors until we stopped in front of a large metal one. My eyes widened as it opened up on its own.

He turned around to me. "Rumor, it's an elevator. It takes you up and down. You are going to have to pretend like everything doesn't fascinate you so we can at least blend in a little bit."

"Right," I said as my cheeks brightened. I remembered Tezya telling me something about a moving box when we went to Rainer's place, but we left in complete, awkward silence that I didn't say anything to him when he took the long flight of stairs back down. Soft dinging sounds rang in my ears as the silver box lit up and flashed across every single number. I started to watch the lights change over the numbers as it lowered us, flashing over forty, thirty-nine, thirty-eight, and down and down and down.

Tezya chuckled as we finally got out of the thing, and my legs were shaking. He held out his hand for me. I stared at it wide-eyed, my vision narrowing in on the five that was exposed on his inner wrist. "It's crowded here. I don't want to get separated."

A jolt ran through me as I put my zero hand into his five. I felt him run a finger along the scar in my palm from where I was cut to perform the blood bond, and my thoughts immediately went to Sie. I'd been thinking about him less and less, and I wanted to keep it that way.

Tezya's grip tightened around me as he showed me the mortal city. I was surprised by how much it resembled Lux's golden one. Tez told me that Lux's architecture was inspired from here, but the similarities still shocked me. And the mortals themselves—

They looked exactly like us. The only difference was a few of them were overweight, and most showed signs of aging, but Tezya and I blended right in with the youths of the humans.

A male human smiled at me as he noted my shirt. "May the force be with you," he said. I stared wide-eyed at Tezya as I had absolutely no idea how to respond or talk to a human. I had no idea what the *force* meant but figured it was a way of greeting.

"Nice to meet you, too," I said back to him. Tezya chuckled as he led me away from the confusing mortal.

The food, perhaps, was my favorite part about being here. "You have to try the tacos from this food truck," Tezya said as we walked past a parked box-shaped vehicle that had wafts of cooked meats inside. "I think Kallon would have my balls if I didn't get you a taco. It's one of the main reasons she visits so often."

It was messy and hard to eat, but I knew immediately that I would miss it as soon as we were back in Lux. Hot meat and cheese mixed with—I honestly had no idea what was in the weird taco thing—but it was amazing and melted as soon as it met with my tongue. I had never tasted so many flavors before in one bite. I moaned loudly before I stopped myself. Tezya laughed, then turned his head to shove the weird cylinder burrito thing into his mouth—eating his less sloppily than I was, and in two bites.

We walked around the mortal city as we finished our tacos, the heat remaining long after the sun sank into the sea. Tezya and I didn't talk much, but it never felt awkward. He kept holding my hand, claiming he didn't want to lose me in the crowd, and I could see his reason. There were so many humans, and they all seemed to be rushing somewhere. I was happy to hold Tez's hand and pretend to be one of them. I loved watching them, seeing how they interacted with each other. How simple and happy they seemed. And there were so many children mixed in with the adults and elderly. It was actually beautiful to see such a blend of ages.

"Without our markings and the numbers on our wrists, I don't think I'd be able to tell an Advenian from a mortal. They look a lot like us, or we look like them," I said to Tezya. We were walking further from the ocean now, more inland toward the crowds.

He was about to answer when I screamed. A creature was lurking in a small body of water in the middle of the city. Four meaty legs that ended in sharp nails held up its thick, low-lying body. A long tail flicked once to the side as it swatted at the water. Its neon green eyes seemed to glow as the thing remained in its spot, lurking. A long jaw extended from its green, bumpy head, with two rows of sharp teeth.

"Tezya," I panicked as my eyes widened on the green creature. Why weren't the humans scared of this? Why weren't others scream-ing? Why wasn't anyone running? Tezya followed my gaze and laughed. *Laughed.*

"Rumor, you need to calm down," he said softly, but he was still smiling. "It's an alligator. They're really common in this area." Tezya leaned in closer to whisper in my ear, "And a human doesn't normally scream at the top of their lungs when they see one."

I looked around and saw that all the mortals had paused to stare at us, to stare at me. Right.

Tezya laughed again as he steered me away from the alligator, but he squeezed my hand in reassurance.

"So that thing was harmless?" I asked once we were out of earshot from all the humans that heard me scream. "It doesn't ever kill anyone?"

"No, they kill sometimes, just not often."

I looked around in disbelief at the humans, at how they lived with so many deadly things. Luckily, we didn't see another alligator for the rest of the night.

My feet ached, and my jaw hurt from smiling by the time we finally made it back to Tezya's place.

He didn't drop my hand until we were back in his condo. A cold lingered where his fiery touch had been all night. I flexed my fingers, forcing myself not to think about it as he made his way toward the only bedroom... and started undressing without shutting the door. I didn't know if I should be flattered that he felt comfortable with me or annoyed that he didn't think it was a big deal. Or maybe in Lux, in the mortal territory too, it wasn't a big deal. Maybe only Tennebris made a fuss over the naked body.

"What are you doing?" I asked as I nervously twirled my hair around my finger. My voice had an undertone of a squeak that I hated myself for.

"I'm going to shower." He said it so matter of factly as he continued to strip down, and Pylemo damn me, but I couldn't look away. I gawked from the kitchen, a clear view into the bedroom, as he shrugged his shirt over his head. Scars were scattered across his formed stomach. There were thick and jagged ones, raised just like the one on his face, but others were smaller, some only thin, white lines against his tanned skin. Did he get them all during battles? How many had he fought in? I swallowed.

His pants came off next, and his undergarments were tight against his massive thighs. The muscles bulging as he took a step closer to the still open door. A noticeable *protrusion* was—

"Like what you see?" he grinned with that half smirk, raising his scar.

Well, that got me to look away. I forced myself to go sit on the sofa —that was positioned away from the still open bedroom and to the bathing room that had no door—while I waited for him to wash. I couldn't stop focusing on the water. It was calling to me, begging me to manipulate it, to become one with it. I could sense every droplet, feel it slide against his skin as it traveled down and off his body.

"Rumor," Tezya called through the wall. The shower was still pouring water, muffling his voice.

My chest tightened in anticipation. "Yes?" I asked breathlessly.

He chuckled. "You're making the water in here go haywire."

And thank the Goddess that he couldn't see my face because I felt like it turned the brightest shade of red. I flung myself toward the nearest object next to me, attempting to occupy my mind with anything so that I stopped thinking about him naked and in said water.

I was surprised that I picked up a book. A mortal book, by the looks of it. I didn't pin Tezya as a reader, but I guessed there was a lot

I didn't know about him still. I flipped through the flimsy pages of the novel. It was soft and the spine was broken in, indicating that it'd been read and loved many times. I couldn't remember the last time I read for pure enjoyment. Since LakeWood maybe? Once I was in the Tennebrisian castle, I forced myself to use the Royal Library for research, only selecting books they had on Lux. I opened to page one and lost myself in the words, thankful that Advenians had adopted the mortal language so that I understood the text. Some words were foreign still and didn't make sense, but I could understand the gist of what was being told.

The more I flipped through the pages, the more envious I became of the free world that was described on them. The characters could love anyone they wanted. They could do anything. Be anyone.

I was so engulfed in reading that I didn't hear Tezya come out of the bedroom until he opened a cabinet to fill a glass with water. He was dripping wet with only a towel wrapped around his waist. His black flame markings were now on full display, covering and hiding his scars beneath. I did my best not to look at the way his muscles moved while he walked or how dangerously low his towel sat. The fact that he had a small line of dark hair just above said towel... I whipped my head up to his face, knowing my own was reddening. With his hair wet, it was pushed back off his face for once.

"Tezya, can I ask you something?"

"Sure," he said as he padded over with the glass of water. He took a sip as he slumped into the cream sofa, water instantly soaking through the spot he took up.

I squealed. "What are you doing? Aren't you going to dry off first?"

His grin was devilish. "I thought you could do me the honors."

I swallowed and stared at him in disbelief. But before I could say anything treacherous, he added, "You can practice your ability and shift the water back into the shower."

Oh—OH. I'd never been so happy in my life that I hadn't responded right away because that was *not* what I thought he meant by that.

I shifted next to him, trying to focus on the water only and not his half-naked body. Taking a deep breath, I pulled the droplets off him, shaping it into a tight ball in the air in front of us, and guided it back toward the bathing room. I couldn't see the shower and had to trust my instincts on where to direct it.

"Good," he smiled when I released the ball, and we both heard the splash. He took another long sip of the water. "What did you want to ask me?"

"Oh, um… I wanted to ask why you came here. What business did you have to do earlier?"

"The King is fascinated with the mortals. He usually sends me here for information for himself. They have many technological and scientific advancements. He likes to learn from them and adapt."

"But that's not why you came this time?" I took a guess.

He shook his head, one strand of white—now dry—hair fell into his eyes. "No, it's not." I waited for him to say more, but he didn't, not right away. He sighed. "Rumor, I don't mind telling you. I trust you. But are you sure you want to know? You can't do anything with the information. You can't tell anyone. And once you start learning things, there's no going back."

"I want to know."

"Okay." He shifted on the sofa to face me, and I tried my best not to pay attention to where that left his towel. "I believe the King plans to overthrow the mortals, and I think he will soon. He wants to conquer everything. Being the ruler of Lux isn't enough for his greed. I think he plans to make them slaves, much like the rank zeroes are in Lux. He wants to expand from the island we live on. He wants the whole damn planet."

"Could he really do that?" Everyone knew that the humans overpopulated the Advenians. Even though we were the stronger species, there were much more of them. It's why our history books said we had to remain hidden. They reproduced far greater than we could and didn't need Lakimi to be blessed with a pregnancy.

"It depends if Tennebris gets on board. If the two Kingdoms work together, there's a chance that the Advenians could win," Tezya replied.

"I don't think Sie would agree to that," I said softly, and meant it. I knew Sie didn't care about changing our current society, at least, he wasn't motivated enough to act upon it. He would never get rid of the ranking system. But I didn't think he'd make things worse either. He would never agree to slavery.

"I know that. The King knows it too. That's the reason they do not want him on the throne. I already told you that I think the King is planning on using you somehow to do it."

"And you don't want that?" I asked, hoping it was true, but I wanted to hear it from him. He spoke one time of not agreeing with the ranking system. Of wanting everyone to be treated equally, so I couldn't believe Tezya would want to overthrow the mortals too. But I also had to know if Tezya had some part in planning to overthrow Sie.

"No, I don't want that. We need to leave the humans alone. They're innocent. We don't deserve to take over their planet because ours died." He paused for a moment, then added, "I envy the humans. Their worth isn't measured by their rank. They aren't categorized by some ability and then told what to do in their society because of it. They can love whoever they want, marry who they want. They have true freedom. I would give away all my powers to have that. A world of peace is what the humans have, and the King wants to rip that freedom out from under their noses. The abilities we possess makes our kind turn dark. It has the potential to fill us with greed and hate and a lust for power. But power isn't fulfilling. It's a void that, in the end, leaves you empty and alone. It leaves you starving, such a gnawing hunger that turns anyone in its path into a meal to be devoured. Power can never be quenched."

They were my orders, Scotlind. I didn't want to do it, but I didn't have a choice, just like you don't have a choice now, Tezya had said to me about fighting against the rebels. Did he really have no choice in that? Did he even want to be a soldier? Would he get a choice if the King forced the Luxian army to attack not only the rebels but the mortals too? Would Tezya go into battle? "Do you think that kind of a world could exist for our people someday?"

"It existed before on Allium, so I don't see why it can't happen

242

again. But our people are so brainwashed into tradition, it would be near impossible to convince them of it."

"What are you going to do then? What did you do today?" I asked.

"Another night, Rumor. I'll tell you everything another night. For now, let's go to bed."

Bed. Right. There was only one bed. In the hut, Tezya had grabbed a bedroll and slept on the deck, claiming he did it often when he was there to gaze at the stars. So I had the whole hut to myself, but here, the balcony was too small. "Do you have an extra blanket?"

"No, why would I need that?"

"Because... I am... I am going to sleep out here. You only have one bed." My hair knotted around my finger.

He smiled. "Take the bed. I'll sleep out here."

"No, it's okay—" I started.

"Rumor, I sleep naked, so unless you want to see everything tonight, I suggest you go to the bedroom." For emphasis, he stood, gripping his hand over his towel. I didn't wait to see what he did after that as I slammed the bedroom door shut.

TWENTY-FIVE
TEZYA

A HIGH-PITCHED SCREAM jolted me from my sleep. Fear swallowed me whole as I sprinted into the bedroom, terrified of what I would find, praying the King hadn't realized I had brought her here.

But she was alone, thrashing under the covers, fighting her mental demons. She was having one of her nightmares. I knew she had them. I'd heard enough of her screams, felt her panic stir as I monitored her room each night in Lux. I was grateful when they became less and less frequent. But tonight, I felt her panic in my bones, and I didn't think it was the proximity of where I was sleeping that had me running toward her.

"It's okay, you're okay," I breathed into her ear as I knelt over the bed. "You were just dreaming." My hands gently grabbed her shoulders, trying to stop her profuse shaking. Despite being slick with sweat, she felt cold.

"Tezya?" Her voice wavered.

"Yes, it's me. I'm here. It was just a dream," I said as I brushed aside the strands of hair that were plastered to her face. I stiffened as she reached over for me, one of her hands clutching my upper arm. I definitely should have grabbed some clothes before running in here. Thank the Goddess, it was still dark, and barely any moonlight was shining through the window. "Do you want to talk about it?" I asked when she settled back down against the pillow.

There was a long pause, and then softly, "No." Her voice was barely a whisper as her shaking started to subside. I nodded and started to get up to head back to the living room. "Wait," her clammy hand slid down my arm and wrapped around my wrist, over the five that was branded into me. "Please, can you stay?"

I stilled. Only Pylemo knew how badly I wanted to. How I'd fantasized about those words leaving her lips countless times. Dreamt a million different scenarios of spending the night with her. I should say no, I knew that. This was a terrible fucking idea. Things were bad enough with her being the King's prisoner and Sie's ex. I shouldn't confuse it more. I should say no. I *need* to say no.

But I couldn't stand the thought of leaving her, of going back to the sofa alone.

This felt like a finality, a threshold that we shouldn't cross, and this moment was the line drawn in the sand.

Fuck it.

"Okay," I breathed. I could convince myself later that it was just for tonight, that I only said yes because she needed me. This could just be a one time thing, a tucked away memory from our time in the mortal territory. A time we could both pretend I wasn't the Prince and she wasn't the prisoner.

In the morning, when we returned to Lux, I wouldn't say yes again. It would kill me, this little bit of temptation would make it near impossible to sort through the grains of sand, to once again find that line, build the divide back up. But we didn't have a choice.

She scooted over as I crawled under the blanket. My one arm slid under her pillow as the other rested across her stomach. Her dress was hiked below her breasts, probably from tossing and turning, and I let my hand travel under it. Slowly, I spanned my fingers out across her abdomen, feeling every inch of her soft skin. She tucked her head into the crook of my neck, and fuck, it just felt right.

Lavender was mixed with her scent as I inhaled. The top of her hair bristled against my nose. Without meaning to, my senses crawled over her, wrapping and winding around her like a second layer of skin. I didn't know if it was her enhancement reaching out, trying to connect us, or if it was all me, but I caught a drift of her residual terror from her nightmare. It was mixed with a new easing comfort as she settled her head against my chest. Her heart was racing, and I told myself that it was just from her dream. I honestly didn't know if I would be able to peel my ability away from her either. It seemed too far connected, too entwined to separate, but that was something I'd worry about in the morning too. I'd push everything off until then. If this is all we got, I wanted to embrace it.

She sighed as she sank further into my side. I shifted so the lower half of me wasn't touching her, so she wouldn't discover that I was still naked. "I'll stay until you fall back asleep."

"I don't want to have any more nightmares." Her voice was soft, dream-like, and I wondered if she'd remember any of this. I knew without asking that her thoughts were probably filled with that bastard of a compulsion user that tried to drown her.

"Then don't. Think about something happy. Think about something you want to do," I whispered as her fingers curled around my wrist. She stirred in my arms and mumbled something unintelligible in acknowledgment.

It didn't take long for sleep to find her. Her body warmed under the blanket, against me, and the sound of her breathing was my favorite melody, one I wanted to hear over and over again. I listened to it until sleep finally found me too.

When I awoke in the morning, we were tangled against each other. I didn't know where I ended and she began. She stretched her arms above her head as the morning sun flickered through the window.

I froze as my senses were still wrapped around her. I usually yielded to my ability effortlessly and was able to pick and pinpoint what sense I wanted to hone in on. It was something I had to learn at a young age, or I would have gone insane with sensory overload. I could focus and narrow in on one thing during a fucking battle, but this... I couldn't block her out. I couldn't control it around her. It was like some invisible string reached out to her on its own accord, probably her enhancement working against me. But… what I scented from her was… *arousal.*

Fuck.

My nostrils flared as I instinctively hardened against her back. I knew she felt it because she jerked away from me, pulling the blankets with her.

"Why are you clutching the blankets like it's a lifeline?" I asked as I sat up to lean against the white headboard, deciding to mess with her. I wanted to see her flustered at not knowing what to say, to watch her cheeks heat, and her blue eyes blaze like the hottest part of a flame.

"I'm not."

"Uh-huh. Then why won't you look at me?" I teased. At that her freckles did redden as she pulled the blanket closer to her chest even though she was the only one in clothes.

"When I asked you to sleep in the bed with me, I didn't realize you were naked."

"I told you last night that I didn't sleep with clothes on," I smirked, happy that she remembered she asked. Then added, "I'm jealous of whoever you were dreaming about just now."

"I don't know what you're talking about. I wasn't dreaming about anyone," she snapped way too quickly.

"If you say so," I said as I rose from the bed and walked over to the dresser to claim a clean pair of clothes, knowing that she was adamantly avoiding looking at me right now. "But I thought you would know by now that I can tell when you're lying."

"I'm not lying."

"Rumor, I can smell the emotions coming from you."

I turned around to face her, having pulled on a pair of pants. Her blush spread to her ears as she gnawed on her lower lip.

"And," I added, "besides smelling your arousal, I heard you last night."

"What do you mean you *heard* me?"

"After you fell asleep, you moaned. Loudly, might I add. I always wondered what you would sound like when getting fucked." I tossed a shirt over my head. "Well, now I know. And it was nothing like you eating a pastry." And damn, if that sound she made wouldn't haunt me. It was part of the reason I couldn't fall back asleep.

"I. Did. Not." she gritted through her teeth, which only made me smile more.

I shrugged, enjoying rattling her. "I was just saying I was jealous of the guy."

"Well, I didn't," she retorted back.

"Whatever you say, Rumor. Come on," I laughed as I held my hand out to her. "We need to go back now, or Kallon will close the portal."

———

"WHY CAN'T you just let her live the rest of her life in peace?" I seethed at the King. "She's seen enough of both courts to last a lifetime. Just let her go."

"It's unsettling that it bothers you what I do with her," the King retorted. Once Rumor and I returned, I was summoned into the council room. I left Scottie to train in the private gym by herself until I got back. "But, no matter. It would work in my favor if you did develop feelings for her."

"What's that supposed to mean?"

"This year's meeting is being held in Lux, and Prince Noren will be arriving by the end of the week. You will be her escort throughout the meeting."

"I'm aware of the meeting and that he's coming to Lux, but what I don't understand is why you are forcing her to be present for it." My gut clenched as I prayed it wasn't what I thought.

"Because I want their Dark Prince to see her in your arms. You will make him jealous, and based on his desire for the girl, I believe he will act irrationally, which is precisely what we need in order for this to work."

"You asked me to train the girl, not seduce her." I was trying my best not to fume, trying to keep calm so I could figure out a way out of this. I had guessed that he wanted to use her. He wouldn't have let her

248

out of that cage if there wasn't a purpose, some ulterior motive, but this...

"You will do whatever I tell you because I am your *King*."

A long moment of silence stretched between us before I tried another tactic. "In case you don't remember, I am betrothed by your request, and now you want me to openly court another female in front of our entire Kingdom? Kallon's parents will not take that lightly."

"Oh, save your breath for someone who will believe it. We both know you and Kallon are going to push off your wedding for as long as you can, and her parents are paid handsomely, so they won't be a bother." He paused. "I honestly thought I was doing you a favor, son. I know you aren't happy with the future wife I selected for you. And well, our little prisoner isn't bad on the eyes. I thought you'd be pleased."

Little prisoner. My teeth ground together as I tried to mask my hatred for the male in front of me, tried to stop myself from punching him in the throat. It took every ounce of self-control I possessed over the past century to master my rage, to will my emotions back. It only landed me with a visit from the King's second, Athler, if I didn't.

"And what is it that you hope to gain by me escorting Scotlind to the annual meeting?" No way in hell was I calling her a prisoner. He seemed to notice.

The King looked at my clenched jaw and smirked. "Once Prince Noren is crowned, there won't be much we can do to stop him. From my reports from Synder, he isn't as on board with my plans for our society as I would have liked. He is a strong rank five and, therefore, a threat to Luxians. We must keep the Tennebrisians weaker than us in order to maintain control. So I struck a deal with Synder a long time ago. He helps me get the Prince off the throne, and I allow Synder to rule Tennebris, modeled directly after our own Kingdom."

"And how exactly are you planning on getting him off the throne?" I asked as I threw my hands in my pockets to keep him from seeing them fisted.

"Our little prisoner's memories aren't enough to condemn Sie and commit him of treason. Even if we displayed them for the courts to see, the Dark Prince could claim that they were tampered with. Since she is still being seen as a nix in order to facilitate the changes for the ranking systems over in Tennebris, we can't argue with that. We aren't able to kill him as that was how King Lunder was dealt with. Too many deaths would raise suspicion. So we need to catch him committing treason. He needs to make a move on the girl again. Then, when he does, Tennebris will come out with the news of her being a claimed Luxian. It would be enough to imprison him for life." He paused as he assessed me.

I let out a deep breath, trying not to think about the fact that he actually considered displaying Scottie's memories for both Kingdoms to see.

"You only have two chances to do this, Tezya," he continued. "This week, when Sie and the Tennebrisian High Council come to discuss the further development of the ranking system, I expect Scotlind Rumor to be all over you. I want to use this as a test, as you will, to gauge the Prince's reaction and confirm he still has feelings for her. If he doesn't react, we need to know so we can initiate the backup plan. But I'd rather not have to use it as it means getting my hands dirty, and I can promise you that you won't like the consequences, so I expect you to not fail me."

He paused for a moment, letting his gaze settle over me as his threat lingered. "That being said, based on her memories of him, I don't think you two will find it difficult to make him jealous. Use your heightened senses to gauge how he is feeling. I expect a full report. Then the night before his coronation, we are to attend a ball in his honor. We will set up a trap for them to be caught. It will be your last chance, so you better make it count."

"And what makes you think Scottie will agree to this?" She would be caught in the crossfire. She would be equally as guilty as Sie would. But they probably wouldn't spare her a life of imprisonment. They'd just kill her when the two of them were caught. Fuck, I couldn't let that happen.

"Scottie?" He huffed a laugh. "My, my. You did let her get under your skin. I knew it would work in my favor to have you train her personally. Good, it will make this all the easier if you aren't faking it. Because if you can't do it with your looks and charms alone, I'll have Athler mess with her pheromones, and I highly doubt that is something you want. Athler will find great pleasure in making her go out of control. So for her sake, I hope you can manage." He smiled, watching my face closely.

"And she will agree to this," he added. "You will make her, because if not, she will find herself a permanent place in the dungeons, and I will be even less kind than I was before."

I bristled, thinking back to how I found her in that damn cage. How she was tortured for information... It was a power move then, just as it was now. He knew that she wouldn't talk and that Tennebris was sending a compulsion user. The King just liked to elicit fear whenever he could.

"And our Council has approved of this?"

"Both of our Councils have agreed upon this, at least those important enough to know. Sie has different views than us. He sympathizes with nixes and doesn't seek to claim the human territory as our own. It's revolting. Synder is set up to rule once we can eliminate the Prince. The first act he will do as King is abolish their stupid King's Tournament, and then he will run their Kingdom by bloodlines like ours."

"What else are you planning for the Dark Kingdom?" I knew he wasn't motivated enough to help Tennebris just because they now wished to make their ranking systems more ruthless. Regardless of how much he hated nixes and humans, he wouldn't risk treason and murder for just *helping* their society. There had to be something in it for him.

"Ah, yes. I forgot how observant you are. You and Arcane are so much alike in that regard. It's why I originally wanted you to rule over your brother. You both have the strategic mind and attention to detail needed to rule, but your brother lacks the willingness to see it through. He's too obsessive over his stupid lab to get anything done."

"You benefit greatly from Arcane's lab."

He smiled. "That I do. As do I with your skills yielding a blade. I will let Tennebris rule for a while. Let them think that they won. Together our Kingdoms will unite our forces so that we can finally claim Earth. It is time we accept our fate on this planet and make our presence known. Then, once things have settled and we claim Earth and rule over the pathetic mortals, we will take Tennebris back. We will rule over everything. I won't only be the King of Lux, but the King of this planet. The Kingdom of all the species. Once Tennebris is weakened after battling the mortals, that is when you will attack with your army."

"I won't help you. I won't bring my army to attack innocents."

He looked me in the eye, a smugness to his glare, as he said, "I'm afraid, son, that you don't have a choice. This is an order."

The King smirked as he sauntered out of the council room, leaving me to dwell on everything that he had revealed. This was a fucking disaster. I figured out his plans a while ago. I had a hunch that he wanted to take over the humans, but to hear him speak them out loud, to have him confirm them. I swallowed. Everything was banking on Sie being dead or imprisoned. They needed him off the throne in order to have the power from both Kingdoms to attack the mortals, and I planned to keep him on it.

I just prayed that he wouldn't act with his cock and could see through what was about to unfold... I would be forced to publicly seduce Scottie one way or another, and Sie would be forced to watch.

TWENTY-SIX
SCOTLIND

TEZYA CAME BACK to the gym just as I finished my run. It was becoming easier. I could run faster and for longer. I started to enjoy the pounding in my ears and the racing of my heart with each step I took.

"What's wrong?"

"We need to talk," he swallowed hard, and I watched his Adam's apple bob in his throat.

"Okay," I said as I descended the stairs towards him.

"It's about the upcoming meeting with Tennebris." He looked at me, and I didn't know what to say as I held my breath, waiting for him to finish. "Do you remember when I told you the King wanted to use you to get Sie off the throne?" I nodded. "Well, I just found out how. He gave us orders for the meeting. He gave us *roles* to play."

"He wants me to be with Sie?"

Tezya paused for a long moment that I wasn't sure if he was going to answer. "No," he finally said. "He wants you to be with *me*. He wants me to seduce you in front of Sie. He wants us to make him jealous."

"Oh." I didn't know what else to say. That was so much worse than I thought. Tezya's thick brows furrowed as he assessed me.

253

"I'm sorry, Rumor," he said, his voice softer. "The King threatened to put you back in the dungeons if you disobeyed."

The word seduce kept ringing through my ears. I didn't know what that meant for us, what we'd have to do...

"We don't have a choice," Tezya added, sensing my unease. "If we don't willingly agree, Athler, the King's second, will force us onto each other, and it will be so much worse."

I tried to slow my breathing. I knew things were too good to be true. I knew it was only a matter of time before the King tried something. "Force us how?"

"Do you remember reading about your father's ability?" I nodded. "Well, Athler has the same power. He can alter our hormones, making it impossible for us to keep our hands off each other. Knowing him, it would probably be equivalent to us fucking in public."

"He would really do that? For what purpose?"

"They want Sie to commit treason and they think he will if he sees you with me. They're hoping he will get jealous or pissed off and act upon those feelings."

"That's stupid. I told you it wasn't like that between us." My voice was soft, not confident. I wasn't sure if I even believed what I was saying.

"Let's pray you're right. Do not be alone with him, Scotlind. It's the first time you two are seeing each other since he sent you away. He probably will want to speak with you, especially once he sees us together, but you can't let him. This meeting is only a test. They want to gauge if he still has feelings for you. It's important that you don't give anyone any ideas that you two still care for each other."

"We don't," I interrupted. "Sie's engaged to someone else. He doesn't have feelings for me anymore."

"Rumor. Sie still has feelings for you, trust me. And you and I won't have a choice with how they want us to act, but maybe if Sie doesn't show interest in you, this idea will blow over."

"And if he does?"

He blew out a breath. "If he does, whatever we are forced to do at this meeting will be nothing compared to what they'll make us do during his coronation."

"When does he come?" I asked.

"By the end of the week."

———

Patricia was in my room setting up my dinner as I entered. She did her awkward half curtsey and went to leave. "No, please stay," I begged. "Have dinner with me."

"My dear, I don't think that's a good idea. Not tonight," she stammered. Sweat was beading into her brow, and she looked pale, sickly even.

"Patricia, what's wrong?" I asked as I rushed to her side, pressing the back of my hand against her forehead. She was burning up. "You aren't well."

"I'll be fine, dear. I just need to go back to my chambers."

"No, I insist. Rest here, you can have my bed. I'll go fetch you water."

Patricia ripped my hand away from hers and sprinted toward the door faster than I thought was possible on her wobbly legs.

I didn't know if I was ill myself because it looked like she was growing. Her rolls were disappearing, stretching to a taller height, and her ankles were now showing underneath her long skirts. Hairy muscular legs were staring back at me. I looked up and saw a beautiful, messy mop of blonde hair.

Peter.

He turned around slowly. His green eyes—the same as Patricia's, the same as the nice guard who gave me bread—met mine. "Surprise," he said with a smile, flashing his dimples.

My mouth dropped open. I went to speak. Stopped. Tried to start again. Then stopped.

"Well, I did tell you that it would be more fun for me to show you my ability than to just tell you. So here it is. I can shapeshift." Peter shrugged, tugging awkwardly at the dress.

I sauntered over to him, my mouth still fully gaping open, as I slapped him hard across the cheek. He went to speak, but I slapped him again.

"Ouch. I was expecting more of a warm welcome. *Peter, I missed you so much. Peter, oh my gosh, you are here. Peter, you're so cute. Peter, I love you,*" he mocked.

"You saw me naked." It was all I could register at the moment. My first night here, Patricia—no Peter—helped me bathe with the rags. He, at least, had the decency to flinch now.

"Scottie, I had to make sure you were safe. *We* had to make sure," he admitted softly.

"And now?" I asked, gesturing to him wearing a dress that was falling off his lithe frame. "You saw that I was safe. Why did you keep parading around like a girl? Why didn't you just tell me? Why are you even here?" The questions were rolling off my tongue.

"I wanted to tell you, but I couldn't, not after I saw Kole was here. I couldn't risk the King going into your memories again and finding out."

My anger, although still there, was being overpowered by worry for him. "They will kill you if they catch you."

"Ah," he smiled, "there is the adoring, concerning Scotlind I know."

"Peter, I'm serious. You shouldn't be here. Why did you come?"

"We needed to make sure you were going to be okay." His smile fell, and my heart ached. He kept saying *we*. All those days of thinking Peter abandoned me, that he didn't care… But he had been with me this entire time. I reached into my pocket, holding the note that he gave me. It was something I found myself doing often ever since Tezya gave it back to me.

"Sie and I were worried. We didn't want to send you here, but Synder was going to kill you. He was going to force Sie to be the one to do it too. He didn't have a choice, so I offered to watch over you. We didn't know what the Lux King would do with you, and when I saw you in that cage…" He stopped talking. I looked up at him. Agony and anger were written across his normally fun-loving face. "I just couldn't leave you."

I rushed over to him, flinging myself into his arms for a hug as the tears swelled and rushed down my cheeks. "I missed you." I hugged him tighter. "I love you, Peter."

"I love you too, Scottie," he said into my hair as he squeezed me back, not letting go.

We talked all night. I filled him in on what Tezya told me about the Lux King's plan, and Peter told me about his time meeting up with Sie.

Peter didn't mention Sie's engagement to Reagan. He either didn't know or didn't think I wanted to hear. Either way, I was thankful. I wasn't ready to discuss that. It was hard enough to wrap my mind around the fact that Sie sent me here to protect me. No matter how many times Peter explained what happened, it was hard to believe. I saw the distant look and hard demeanor Sie gave me the day he annulled our marriage. He could barely stand to look at me. He *didn't* look at me.

I also knew I couldn't afford to sort through those feelings right now. We had bigger issues to deal with, so I buried them deep inside me and locked them away for later. King Lunder was dead, and Synder was now ruling over Tennebris. If Tezya and I succeeded in our roles, Sie would be off the throne, leaving only Synder to remain.

"When are you going back?" I asked my friend as the morning sun was starting to fill the sky. We were sitting on my bed together—as we had been all night—with a plate of mostly eaten croissants in front of us. He turned back into Patricia once his reserves were refilled, in case anyone walked through my door, but now that I knew it was him, I had no idea how I never noticed before. At least now, he didn't mask his voice.

"I don't know yet. I have to be back by Sie's coronation. I mainly came to watch over you, but when I'm not with you, I've been snooping around. It's the reason you caught me last night. My reserves were low from shifting too much. It's draining to completely take on a new shape."

"That's why you leave some things the same, like your eyes?"

He nodded. "The less I have to change, the less of my power it uses."

"And your voice?"

"Unfortunately, that doesn't change. I can only alter my looks, and let me tell you, trying to talk like a girl this past month has been *hard*."

"How did you do it? How has no one noticed that you aren't Luxian?"

"To be honest, I'm surprised I've been able to get away with it. I swore a couple of times that Tezya noticed. I thought I was going to get caught by him, but then nothing happened. I got the feeling he let me go, which I know sounds ridiculous."

"Probably not knowing your way around the castle was a dead giveaway," I teased. I didn't want to offer up my opinions on Tezya... That maybe if he knew about Peter, he would keep it. That he wasn't on the Lux King's side.

"This castle is a freaking maze," he groaned, "and you aren't much better than me."

"For real though, how did you become my maid? Is there really a maid named Patricia, or do they just not keep track of the servants here?"

"Umm, yeah. It's a little of both."

"What does that mean?" I asked. I had a bad feeling about what he did. "Where's the real Patricia?"

"She's fine and extremely cranky for an old lady. Seriously, you two would not have gotten along. I did you a favor."

"Peter, what did you do?"

"I just told her that she has some time off, just kind of permanently... that's all."

"Peter—"

"All I said was that the Lux King doesn't want someone so haggard working for him anymore and instructed her to never be seen near the castle again, or she'd regret it."

"How did you pull that off?"

"I kinda shapeshifted into the King and told her that myself."

My mouth dropped open. "What if you got caught?"

"I didn't, and she's fine. She's enjoying just being with her family and not working here." I gave him a look that said I didn't believe him. "What? I'm telling the truth. I checked on her just the other day."

"And no one suspects anything? Everyone believes that you're really Patricia?"

"Well, like I said, the old lady is a complete bitch. I made sure to do my research before I picked her. All the other servants hate her because she's crabby."

"And how did she become *my* maid?"

"Well, that was the easy part. No one else wanted to be your maid. You're kinda like the walking dark cloud of death because you're tainted with the Dark Kingdom and all."

"Poor you." I shoved his arm. "And thanks for that. That really helps with my confidence."

Peter laughed, but it didn't reach his eyes. "I should get going," he said, his smile diminishing. "I won't be able to stay in Lux much longer, and I need to use all my free time to try and snoop."

"Thank you, Peter."

"For what?"

"For never leaving me."

He smiled. "Always, Scottie. I'll warn Sie before the meeting. I'll tell him what the Lux King's plans are and make sure he doesn't react to seeing you with the Fire Prince. If he isn't bothered by you guys together, their plan won't work. Just make sure you stay away from him during the meeting."

"I will. Thank you, Peter," I said. It was a massive relief knowing that Peter would warn Sie. We wouldn't have to worry about the King's plan succeeding. It didn't help the fact that I still had to be with Tezya in some compromised way while he watched. I tried not to think about what Tezya and I would be forced to do, but at least we'd only have to do it once and not again during his coronation once they realized it wouldn't work.

I never expected to see Sie again, nonetheless, have him see me

259

with someone else. The whole situation was confusing and messed up.

Patricia stood up and straightened her skirts. "Oh, and *Patricia*," I said, enunciating the name, "I won't ever forget the fact that I saw you in a dress."

Patricia's smile was very Peter-like as she grumbled, "Shut up."

TWENTY-SEVEN
SCOTLIND

ALL WEEK I had been a mess. I couldn't stop thinking about having to see Sie again, about what Tezya and I would be forced to do in front of him. Even knowing Peter was going to warn Sie didn't take away any of my unease.

I knew Tezya was just as worried, and even though he didn't know or care for Sie, he wanted him to remain on the Dark Throne. So many times throughout training this week, I had contemplated opening up to Tezya about Peter warning Sie. But every time I went to open my mouth, I couldn't do it. I wasn't entirely convinced that Tezya knew about my maid, and I couldn't put Peter at risk, not when he was in the heart of a Kingdom he didn't belong to, not when he was so close to the Lux King.

It made training hard. I was barely able to focus, knowing that Sie was coming to Lux, and that I'd be forced to see him so soon—and now the week was up. I was barely able to look Tezya in the eye. I didn't fully know what the King wanted from us, but my imagination ran wild with all different kinds of scenarios.

It would probably be equivalent to us fucking in public. Tezya's words kept replaying over and over again in my mind, and I got the feeling that it wasn't as simple as us holdings hands. We didn't talk about it, neither of us mentioning what they might make us do.

And now, we were about to find out exactly what was expected of us as we made our way toward the King's chambers. The Lux King had selected my gown—if you could call it that. It was a black slip with thin straps intertwining into an elaborate pattern across my open back. It was so low that I was sure the top of my crack would show depending on how I moved.

It took me twenty minutes of messing with the strings, of trying to tighten them enough so that it held the thin silk up. I really could have used my maid's help, but ever since I found out that Patricia was really Peter, I refused to let him assist me in dressing. And now that he didn't have to pretend with me anymore, he used all his free time snooping around the castle.

I was pulling at the straps for the tenth time during our walk when Tezya finally broke the silence. "Do you need Brock's help?"

"For what?" I asked as I turned to look at him for the first time. The King made calculated choices on our outfits tonight. We looked like a pair. A match made in hell. His white hair and silver-blue eyes were striking against the black attire that was fitted and sculpted to his muscular frame. It might have been the first time I saw him in pants that actually covered his massive calves. And he looked—he looked like everything I'd ever wanted. I had never found someone so attractive before.

"He can calm your nerves, help you get through what we have to do..."

Oh—OH. A blush crept over my freckled cheeks as I definitely thought Tezya meant help with my gown now that it seemed to be falling lower, exposing more of my breasts. He stopped in front of two opulent doors that I assumed belonged to the King, but he didn't enter yet. He held my gaze, face astringent, and waited for my reply.

Was he serious? Would he really ask Brock to take away my nerves? Did Tezya think I dreaded being with him so much that I would need help to get through tonight? I'd be lying if I said I hadn't thought about Tezya touching me, about his hands roaming my body, and with this dress... it would be so easy for him to take it off of me. I just never thought we'd be forced to do it in front of a crowd.

"No, I'm fine. I can do this," I said back as I pushed my thoughts away, remembering that Tezya could sense my shift in emotions. No. It wasn't being with Tezya that had my stomach turning in knots, although I hated that we didn't have a choice. It was the fact that we would be put on display for everyone to watch... for *Sie* to watch.

Now, my mind was racing. Was Tezya dreading this? Did *he* need Brock's help to get through tonight with me?

There was no way I was letting Brock inside my head and exposing my confused and jumbled emotions to him. I could do this alone. I could get through this one evening. I was able to get through Sie annulling our marriage, so I could do this too. I could see him one more time. Peter left as Patricia at the same time that Tezya and I were called to meet with the King. I had to trust him that he could find Sie before the meeting started and warn him.

"You ready then?"

I nodded and looked back toward the doors in front of me, my heart hammering in my chest. Tezya took a steadying breath himself, then walked in with me in tow.

The room was a large antechamber. A mantle fireplace was positioned against the far wall. It was the first one I had seen since coming here. It wasn't the massive floor-to-ceiling pits that Tennebris used for warmth and light. This one was smaller, more decorative. Large windows framed either side, closed off to the outside, which again seemed at odds with the rest of the open, airy castle. I squinted, looking closer. No locks were positioned within the frame. The windows didn't open. A sinking dread washed over me, and I was trapped all over again. Tezya and I were standing on a large woven rug that covered most of the floor. A bump protruded in the center of the room, directly under the rug, alluring that it was hiding something.

This room felt and seemed more like a prison than the dungeons had, just a pretty one to cover the horrors inside of it. But maybe it was just the man in the room that had the alarms inside me going haywire.

"You're late," was all the King said. He was leaning against the mantle with his ankle crossed over the other. His position next to the flames was dangerously close, but he wasn't phased by the fire. He assessed his son and didn't hold back the resentment plastered over his cool, dead eyes.

Tezya didn't respond.

After a moment of palpable silence, the King's silver gaze slid to me, sending shivers down the length of my exposed spine. He arched a brow, waiting, and I realized that I was expected to bow. I sucked in my breath, taking my pride with it, and bowed low. Tezya remained erect.

"You should take some notes from our little prisoner, Tezya. You could learn a thing or two on how to show respect to your sovereign."

Little prisoner. I bristled. Still bowed, I noticed Tez's hand clamp down into fists. When I rose, it was gone. Just a flicker of anger.

"I presume there was a reason you requested Scotlind's and my presence?"

"Ah, yes," he said as he took a step closer to me. "I wanted to inspect her appearance. She needs to be dressed appropriately in order for this to work." I felt like I was already on display as he scanned my body from head to toe. "Come here, girl."

I glanced at Tezya before I closed the distance between me and the King. He spun a finger, indicating for me to turn around. "I want to see the back." My chest felt like it was in my throat as I waited with my back to the King. I'd never felt so vulnerable in my life. A shiver escaped me as cold fingers grazed over my shoulders, and I knew he must have moved from his spot by the mantle. But I hadn't heard footsteps.

Tezya's body tensed as I was forced to face him. The King gently pushed my hair over my shoulder, exposing the intricate straps of the back of my dress. It took everything in me to remain still as his fingers traveled down my spine. He hooked a finger through the straps and tightened the dress, making my breasts show through the fabric. "That's better, but you're not quite ready yet."

A heavy weight went across my neck, and I jolted before I realized what he was doing. "I am aware that the Dark Prince can speak telepathically. I don't very well want you ruining our plans by communicating with him," he said as he clasped the necklace around my neck. The Alluse ran through me, and I knew it was Complete as I felt all connection to water dissipate. Ever since I had been training with Tezya, I'd learned to sense the element everywhere, to know where to look for it since I could only manipulate. I was loving wielding it and getting better at it too, but now, with the Alluse blocking me, I didn't feel whole. I felt my connection to water snap, and I hated it.

"Have a servant fix her hair so that it's up. I want her back on display," the King ordered Tezya as he spun me around again, this time so that I was facing him. He leaned forward, wrapping his hands around my neck, choking me for a split second before the necklace was off again. The sensation of my powers immediately flooded back into me, leaving behind the numbness of the chain. He chucked it at Tezya, throwing it over my head. "Have Arcane make a different one. I want it tight around her neck, not dangling. Other than that, she's ready," he smirked, looking down at me.

A man crept out of the shadows. I jumped, almost twisting my ankle on the ridiculous heels I was forced to wear. I hadn't realized someone else was in the room.

"Hello," the stranger grinned, still half submerged in darkness. His voice was raspy and menacing, and I realized he was far worse than the King. When he finally stepped into the light, I noticed his skin was as pale as his opal eyes. "It's been far too long, Tezya," the man smiled as he eyed Tez from behind me. His voice felt like nails were digging into every part of my skin, grazing down my body, leaving blood tracks in its wake.

Tezya grabbed my arm and pulled me back toward him. The man arched a thin, red brow. His dull hair was nothing like Vallie's firecracker red. It was rough and coarse and lifeless. There was nothing alive or natural about him.

"Athler will be watching you throughout the night, making sure that you are both believable. If either of you do not act accordingly, he will see to it that it's fixed," the King remarked.

I inhaled, finally putting a face to the King's second in command.

"That won't be necessary," Tezya rasped through gritted teeth, his hand still gripping my arm.

"For your sake, I hope so."

Tezya's grip tightened slightly. "And what exactly is expected of us?"

Athler smiled.

―――

THE MEETING TOOK an eternity to finish as I waited for the second portion of the evening to start. I wasn't allowed inside. Since I wasn't a Royal or a member of either Council, I was forced to wait patiently outside until it was over. Tezya sent away the Luxian soldiers that the King ordered to watch me and had Brock stay with me instead. Neither of us said anything. I was too anxious to actually speak, and Brock, luckily, didn't seem to mind the silence.

The King demanded that my hair was styled up off my back, so I couldn't twirl the long, loose ends like I normally did when I was nervous. I had nothing to do, but sit, look pretty, and wait, which was not boding well for me. I couldn't *not* fidget. I didn't know what to do with myself as I waited and waited and waited for the meeting to be over.

Many times I contemplated asking Brock how much longer it would be before I thought better of it. They held this meeting annually. Both Kingdoms had a year's worth of things to discuss, so of course, it was expected to take a while. I just wanted this entire night to be over. I wanted it in the past. Even if that meant it was a bad memory, I wanted it behind me.

At some point, I started endlessly picking at the skin around my nails. I was filled with so much dread, with adrenaline too, that I didn't feel any pain as I took chucks of skin off. It was torture, just sitting here and waiting, knowing what was to come after. What we were instructed to do...

It wasn't until nightfall—when Tezya found us and took in my frantic, anxiety-ridden state and the skin I had just torn open—that I noticed what he saw. Blood dripped down from my nail to my palm before it disappeared, just vanished like it had never existed. It dawned on me then—why I never felt anything—Brock was taking away my sense of touch to the area while healing me at the same time. That's why it wasn't painful, why my fingers were still intact.

"I'm sorry," I gasped as I stared at my hands. New skin had already formed around each fingernail. How long had I been sitting here doing that? How long had Brock taken away the pain and healed me over and over, only for me to do it all again? He never said anything—hadn't complained once. He just let me, knowing I had to let off the tension coursing through me somehow.

I quickly shoved my hands behind my back so I couldn't pick at them anymore.

"No worries," Brock smiled softly. He looked at me with sympathy and understanding. It made my gut turn and had me dreading tonight that much more.

"Are you okay?" Tez asked once Brock stood and walked away, leaving us alone in the hall.

No—no. I wasn't okay. I wasn't ready, but I nodded, embarrassed at myself for not noticing what Brock was doing. For being so consumed in my own head that I hadn't paid attention to the pain he was taking on or the power he was using to heal me. "Yup," I said instead. Tezya didn't seem to believe me, so I diverted, "How was the meeting?"

"About as painful as that," he mocked, gesturing toward my healed fingers.

"Very funny." I blew out a breath, then stood from the bench I'd been sitting on all day.

"You ready?"

"I'm as ready as I'll ever be. I just want to get this over with."

Tezya squeezed the top of my right shoulder once. "Me too," he whispered, then pulled something out of his suit pocket. It was the new necklace the King requested. Silver flashed in the setting sun, and I saw glimpses of the necklace reflected in Tezya's eyes. It was a plain thick chain with no pendant or pretty designs on it. Just metal linked to more metal, and I got the impression that it was made to resemble shackles, just a prettier and less obvious version. I held my hand out, ready to take the necklace from him, but he shook his head. "Let me."

I turned around, having no idea why the gesture made me nervous. At least with the Complete Alluse on, Tezya wouldn't be able to sense my emotions tonight—he wouldn't know how his touch would affect me. That in itself had me feeling slightly better about what we'd have to do.

Tezya's knuckles grazed the top of my neck, and I got the feeling he was taking his time clasping the chain. Maybe he was trying to delay the inevitable. Maybe if we showed up late, we'd have less time to put on our *performance*. But somehow, I had a sinking feeling that the King's warning wasn't an empty threat, that it would be worse than the cage in the dungeons if we disobeyed him.

"Let's go," Tezya said. His fingers grazed the back of my arm until they trailed down to my elbow. He hooked his arm with mine as he turned me around. Then we started walking toward where the celebration would be held—toward where Sie was. My heart raced, and nerves tore through me so thoroughly that I felt like I was going to pass out.

The King must have calculated our entrance into the dining room because we walked through the doors at the same time as Sie and Reagan. The latter glared at me, took in my dress, my mostly bare skin, and sneered, "Whore."

Sie did nothing. He didn't utter a single word to me or react to Reagan's comment. I honestly didn't know if he even heard it. He just stopped moving and stared at me like he saw a ghost. He acted like he was surprised to see me, like he had absolutely no idea that I'd be here tonight.

His onyx eyes were wide as he gaped at me, unblinking. I couldn't see where his pupils merged with his irises, but I knew they were fully blown. His lips parted slightly before I forced myself to look away.

I didn't take a breath until Tezya unlinked our arms and placed his hand on the open part of my back. He was so deadly calm as he replied to Sie's new bride, "Be careful what you say on Luxian soil, or you'll find yourself without a tongue. I don't take people disrespecting others lightly, especially my date."

Reagan balked as if only just noticing that I was standing with the youngest Luxian Prince. That I was with the Fire Prince. Tezya didn't wait long enough to hear her reply as he led me through the doors in front of them.

I didn't know how I would feel when I saw him, but I was surprised to find mostly anger. Seeing him with Reagan on his arm had me seething. I kept wondering what he would say to me if we were alone. Would he even try to speak to me?

Sie's dark eyes never left mine as we entered the room, and I could feel him tracking us as we walked toward the table. My necklace felt like a shackle. It was so tight around my neck that if I started hyperventilating, it would choke me. It was a weight. A reminder that I was still a prisoner. That the Lux King could force me to do whatever he pleased. Would Sie have entered my mind if I wasn't wearing it? Would he say anything to me if he could?

He had plenty of opportunities to explain his actions while I was still on Tennebrisian soil, yet he didn't. I wasn't wearing an Alluse necklace then. Nothing was around my neck when our marriage was annulled, and he never once reached out to me. He never tried. This wouldn't be any different.

Tezya slumped into the chair, displaying a perfect image of arrogance, and I realized that they only gave us one seat, *one*. He grinned up at me. It was more of a sly smirk than his usual full smile, but it still made my breathing ragged. His legs were spread as he held his arm out—an invitation. Just like we were instructed to do.

I sucked in a breath as I sat on his lap. He was still grinning as I adjusted my weight on his legs, shifting, trying to find a way to sit without touching a certain part of him. Tezya gripped my hips and pulled me into him, right overtop where I was trying to avoid. There wasn't an inch of my body that wasn't now pressed into his. "We have to be believable," he whispered, "or Athler will make things worse for us."

My breath hitched. I hadn't been this close to him since I had asked him to sleep with me in the mortal territory a week ago. Mercifully, Tezya never talked about it, and I never brought it up. We both acted like that night never happened.

I scanned the room, and to my horror, everyone was looking at us. Tezya told me days earlier that he had never brought a date to the annual meeting before, not even Kallon. So showing up with me tonight was going to make a statement. He warned me that everyone would probably be staring at us, not just the Dark Prince.

And Sie hadn't stopped staring.

Tezya's hand cupped my bare thigh through the open slit of my dress as his other hand snaked up my neck. Gently, he pulled my head down so that I met his eyes. The silver was outshining the crystal blue tonight. His lips brushed my earlobe, sending shivers down my spine. "Look at me," he whispered so only I could hear. His voice was deep and throaty and had my stomach in a knot. "Don't look at him."

I could feel onyx eyes burning into me as Tezya and I were positioned in perfect view of Sie and his entourage, the strappy back of my dress on display for everyone to see. If Sie possessed fire, there would have been nothing left of either of us. I sank into Tezya ever so slightly, thankful that I wasn't alone in this. Thankful that, even though he did a better job at hiding it, he was suffering through it too.

"He looks like he's going to kill you," I replied bitterly to Tezya. Where was Peter? He was supposed to warn Sie not to react, but the future King of Tennebris seemed shocked, like he wasn't expecting to see me here, especially not in the arms of the youngest Luxian Prince.

"I can handle it," Tezya smiled as he gazed over my shoulder to stare at the Dark Prince, and I could only imagine the pure rage it caused Sie. Tezya's smirk widened as he drew me in closer.

"You're making it worse," I commented. "What are you doing?" Not that it mattered, we didn't have a choice in what was still expected of us tonight, but Tezya didn't need to look so smug doing it.

"I'm trying," Tezya purred as his hand traveled up my back, "to get him worked up enough to enter my mind."

"What?"

"I think we're beyond him not reacting, so if I can get him pissed off enough to speak with me, then maybe I can explain everything to him. He won't risk saying anything to me where others can hear, not on Luxian soil, not in front of the Lux King, but maybe he'll threaten me mind to mind. It's early enough in the night that if he stops looking like a jealous, pissed-off puppy, and he starts ignoring us, it might still work."

"You really think he'd threaten you telepathically?" I asked. I hadn't thought about the fact that Tezya wasn't wearing Alluse. All we needed was to get Sie to initiate a conversation with him.

"Based on the look of murder in his eyes, I'd say so. I wouldn't put it past him to tell me face to face if the Lux King wasn't openly watching us."

I sat up straighter, but it only caused me to accidentally grind against him. "Fuck," Tezya groaned. His cock hardened in the process, and we both stilled. Tezya's hand stopped midway up my back. I could feel the thick length of him growing against my thigh.

"Sorry," I blushed, and then I laughed. I actually laughed. It wasn't even remotely funny. Nothing about this situation was. I had no idea why I was laughing, but once I started, my emotions just kept spilling out, and I couldn't stop.

Tezya smiled at my reaction, his scar inching higher on his face. "I hadn't realized me being turned on was so funny to you."

That got me to stop laughing. Was I turning him on? I didn't know what to do or what to say back, so I said nothing. I just sat there as his fingers started to follow their path back up the straps of my dress again.

A servant passed out drinks, and I greedily took two.

"It's customary to have a celebratory drink after a successful meeting," Tezya said, watching me down the first glass of fizzy contents in one sip. I was informed by a servant that dinner was being held during the meeting. They brought a small portion of food to where Brock and I were waiting earlier, but I didn't touch it. I had offered it to Brock, but I couldn't recall if he had eaten it or if he just sat with me. I was so caught up in my own head to pay attention.

"We only have to stay a little longer, then this night will be over," Tezya whispered into my neck. His hand kept trailing up and down my back. Slowly. Agonizingly slowly. He really needed to stop touching me like that. I couldn't focus on anything but his touch.

"We didn't even do what the King requested yet."

"I know," he said, his brows furrowing. His hand felt electrifying as his touch got softer, gentler up my back. And now, I couldn't stop focusing on his other hand still gripping my upper thigh. "I'm sorry for that."

I met his silver gaze. "It's not your fault."

"I'm not doing anything to stop it either."

His words shocked me. "What could you do?"

"Nothing. I'm just… I'm sorry for this. That you have to do this." He gestured to me on his lap. My ankle had hooked around his calf without me noticing. My own hands were resting on his sculpted chest. When did I put them there?

"It's okay," I breathed. "With you, it's okay." His eyes widened in shock as I lowered my hands halfway down his abdomen, leaning forward. I had no idea what I was doing, but I didn't back down from his gaze, from his unspoken question.

His fingers embedded into my hair, causing some of the curls to fall down over my shoulders. He met my stare and held it, and I realized that I meant everything I said. Doing this with him made it okay somehow. Even though my body was on display for the entire room to gawk at, and I hated every second of this night, I felt safe around him. I trusted him, and I hadn't realized how badly I needed that—to be able to trust again. I felt like I truly knew and understood him. Like he knew me too.

"Rumor, I know you don't want to, but I'm going to have to kiss you at some point tonight. Athler won't let us leave here until we do."

I looked over at the red-headed male. He was seated to the right of the Lux King and was watching us with a cruel smile plastered across thin lips. His grin widened, his lips stretching even further, as he noted my eyes drifting toward him.

Tezya shook his head violently as a shudder ran through him. I whipped my head back to face him. His tanned skin paled as a bead of sweat dripped down his temple and rolled onto his scar.

"What is it? What's wrong?"

"Nothing."

But it wasn't nothing. His voice was strained. He shuddered again as if he was trying to fight something off. His grip hardened against my waist as a low growl escaped him. A low laugh echoed down the table, and I knew it was Athler's without having to look. Not that seeing him would indicate what he was doing to Tezya. Luxians could use their powers without their markings flaring to life. As long as they weren't sweating or covered in any form of liquid, their designs would remain hidden. But I just knew it was Athler's powers...

"Rumor, I'm sor—"

Something snapped in him. He inhaled my scent loudly as he stood, taking me with him. The chair we were sitting on clattered onto the floor. The resounding thud echoed into the now-silent room. Everyone turned to look at us.

"Tezya, what are you doing?" I whispered to him, but his eyes were glazed over and focused solely on me. He picked me up, my dress hiking to my hips as he walked, half carrying me, and slammed me into the nearest wall with no care for the eyes on us.

"You smell divine." His one hand gripped my ass, supporting my weight, while the other worked its way up my leg. His fingers trailing over the raised scar that was left from Kole. "I want you, Rumor. I've wanted you for so long now."

He moved his hand from the back of my thigh to my head. I didn't have time to answer as his fingers entwined in my hair, and he pulled hard, eliciting a moan from me. He grinned, purely satisfied, as he pulled again, this time pushing my head to the side before his lips met the sensitive part of my exposed neck. For a moment, I thought of nothing else but those lips as I surrendered myself to his touch. I was so taken aback, so shocked at what was happening. His aggression caused my own adrenaline to rise. The way Tezya was moving like he craved me, like he needed me, like I was the answer to all his questions. His lips were so full as they sucked along my throat. His tongue flicked over the spot he just bit into before he sucked again.

A chair groaned against the floor, drawing me out of my daze, and I realized that Sie was now standing. His hard gaze met mine from across the room. His black eyes darkened as pure as night.

Reagan glared at her fiancé, but Sie didn't notice. His attention was pinned to me, to the Light Prince whose back was now to him. Tezya was holding me up with his hips, my open back pressed into the cold wall. His one hand still held my hair, holding me captive while the other explored.

Sie was livid. His jaw was clamped shut, and his fists were balled up, ready to throw a punch. His eyes met mine, and my heart stopped from the deadliness of them. I swore I saw his golden markings flare up under his clothes, but then it was gone. I had a sinking feeling that Peter hadn't warned him. *Sit down,* I silently prayed to him, but I knew the Alluse was working against me. He couldn't hear me.

I scanned the room, desperate for anyone to help, but it was hard to focus with the way Tezya was touching me, with how he was making me feel. Athler now stood, moving closer toward us. His grin told me everything that I needed to know. He was possessing Tezya somehow with his ability.

Something else dawned on me. Tezya already had heightened senses, so if Athler was messing with him, it was probably making it unbearable. Tezya was feeling everything stronger.

It would probably be equivalent to us fucking in public. Crap. How far would Tezya go?

Tezya's lips were soft as they moved up my neck to my jaw, drawing my attention back to him. I whispered softly, desperate to break him from this spell, "Tez, you have to stop. Please, I know we have to kiss, but not like this. If you don't stop, Sie is going to flip out. Then their plan—"

Tezya growled as he pulled back to stare at me. His face was deathly still, feral almost, waiting to devour me whole, but his one hand never stopped moving. He trailed idle circles up my inner thigh, and it took everything in me not to moan and lean further into the touch.

Even without sensing my emotions with his abilities, he knew the effect he was having on me. He knew exactly what he was doing. I'd never seen him so terrifying. He looked like the commander of the Luxian army that I heard about. He looked like a warrior, no, like the Fire Prince, and I realized I wasn't afraid.

"Scotlind Rumor. I do not give a shit about the Tennebrisian Prince right now. And if I hear you say his name one more time, I'm going to fuck you so hard that you'll forget it."

I was trying my best not to pay attention to his hand moving further and further up my leg. His other arm was still entwined in my curls, forcing me to meet his stare. His words made my heart skip a beat even though the entire room definitely heard them too. He hadn't whispered them, and now Sie knew I was talking about him.

But despite the humiliation from everyone witnessing this chaos, despite knowing Sie was still watching, despite understanding the consequences, it felt right. Wrong and right all at once. The feel of his lips against my throat. The way he held me, pressing his body into mine, keeping me locked against the wall. His chest beat in time to my racing heart.

His lips were soft as he slowly leaned back into me, drawing my full attention so I could no longer think of anything else. He kissed me everywhere but my mouth, like there was some part of withdrawal he was holding onto. Tezya hardened against me as he moaned into my ear. The scar against his cheek scraped my face as he pulled me in closer.

His hand cupped my breast, and Goddess kill me, it was all I could focus on. I wanted his lips there instead, sucking and teasing. "You're so fucking perfect," he murmured into my mouth, his calloused hand brushing across my peaked nipple.

"Tezya," I breathed, stopping him right before he was about to finally kiss me. As much as my body wanted it, I couldn't let it happen. Not here. Not like this. Not when it wasn't our own choice. "You're only acting this way because of Athler."

"No, I'm not, Rumor," he growled. "I meant what I said. I've wanted to do this for a long time now. I've never wanted anyone the way I want you." His fingers finally released and let go of its death grip on my hair, but now his hand was gliding down my face, cupping my cheek.

More sweat dripped down his temple. He shook out his white locks in frustration, like he was fighting it. His eyes lost a bit of its glaze, returning to normal enough to say, "Fuck. You need to leave right now," he ordered. His voice was low, but he didn't release his grip on me either. My legs were still loosely wrapped around him, my back pressed into the cold wall as he held me up, pinning me. He closed his eyes. "Scotlind, please. I can't fight this much longer."

I lost my breath. The way he said my name... Everything left me but him. "I can't take this back," he panted into my mouth. "What I'm about to do... what I'm going to do to you in a matter of seconds... I can't... take... it... back."

"I don't want you to." I surprised myself. I hadn't meant to say it. I knew Athler wasn't affecting me too, not with his powers. I was wearing the Alluse necklace, but it felt like my emotions were jarred. I wanted Tezya. I wanted all of him.

His eyes snapped open, searching deeply into me. Moments passed, and I didn't know how long we stayed like that. My hands slowly found their way to his face. My fingers stroked the shaved bottom half of his hair. I was surprised that I could feel his scar wrap around the back of his head. How did he get a scar so brutal and survive? It looked like someone went to cleave his face in two.

My own scar from my palm was brushing against Tezya's. I pushed his hair back, exposing the full breadth of it. It was thick and raised over his skin. A piece of his dark eyebrow was missing as the smaller scar sliced through the dark hair there. An inch lower and he would have lost his eye. His beautiful silver eyes. I stared at him, studied him, as he did the same to me.

I pressed my forehead against his, inhaling his scent. Our lips were so close that I could feel a tingling charge in the air, egging me to close the distance. Tezya didn't move. We stayed like that, breathing shared air, lost in the moment.

Sweat no longer poured from his temples. His shaking subsided slightly. He was still panting, but his breaths were slowing, gradually returning to normal. He wasn't under Athler's spell anymore, but he still held me against the wall. I forgot about everyone around me. How long had we been lost in our own protective shield?

Then everything happened at once. Sie was a step closer to us. I hadn't realized he moved. He looked like he was one second away from strangling Tezya. His fists kept clenching and unclenching at his side as if trapped, contemplating what to do next.

Athler clicked his tongue and walked off, drawing my gaze from Sie back to Tezya. Tez's eyes flared to life as he realized what had just unfolded. He gently set me down and withdrew his hands from my body the moment my feet hit the floor. The straps to my dress were torn, causing half of it to hang off. The material that he pulled up my thigh slowly slid back down my leg. My hair was fully down now. Any pin that was used to maintain its updo was scattered on the floor around us.

The proof of his attraction still showed through his pants, but he didn't seem concerned about his own humiliation as everyone gathered around us to gawk. I could hear people whispering, but it was all too much to make out what anyone was saying. His eyes never left mine.

"Scotlind, shit. I'm so sorry," he whispered low enough for only me to hear. His trembling picked up again. "I never would have. Not like this—"

I reached for his neck and pulled him into me. I didn't know what drew me to do it. If I wanted to hide his boner from all the onlookers who weren't hiding the fact that they were openly gawking, or if I wanted to send him a silent message that it was okay, I forgave him. I knew this wasn't his fault. I knew Athler caused this. His tense posture relaxed as his chest hit mine.

I was on my tiptoes, hugging Tezya, when I saw past his shoulders, noticing the room around me once again. A head of black hair was storming in the opposite direction. I watched as Sie weaved through the crowd until he disappeared out of view.

And I realized in that moment I had picked Tezya, that when he spoke to me, when he said sorry... He looked so wounded, so hurt by what he was forced to do, that I was only concerned about him. I forgot about Sie, forgot that he was still watching, about how he must have felt to see all of that unfold.

I didn't know how that made me feel. I was still hugging Tez, his boner digging into my leg, when I saw Reagan glare at me from my periphery. She shot me a look that promised vengeance before she stalked off after her betrothed.

I had to remind myself to not feel bad for Sie, to let go of the guilt eating away at my insides. Sie chose this. Sie sent me here. Sie picked Reagan.

But I had never been so confused and conflicted in my entire life.

TWENTY-EIGHT
SIE

TONIGHT WAS TIED for the worst fucking night of my life, right up there with the day I sent Scottie to this Goddess-foresaken island. It took every ounce of self-control I possessed to not storm up to the Fire Prince and rip him off of her. My blood was boiling. I couldn't stop replaying the fucking entitlement he possessed to place his hands all over her and right in front of me. And the smirk plastered on his face as he pushed Scottie further into his lap... I wanted to give him another scar to match the one across his face.

I had contemplated using my abilities on the bastard so many times. I was so close to compelling him to never lay his hands on her again, but I knew the King of Lux wouldn't take it lightly if I used compulsion on his youngest son, and I was worried that he'd retaliate on Scotlind. I had no right over her welfare anymore. I knew that, even if my mind refused to believe it. Not to mention, attacking a Luxian Prince would be seen as Tennebris officially declaring war against the Light Kingdom.

I just hadn't expected to see her during the meeting. It caught me off guard and rattled me. I thought I'd have to go hunt her down afterward. I assumed they were keeping her locked up when she wasn't forced into training. I knew from Peter that she spent a lot of time with the Fire Prince and that she was forced to work with him, but I never imagined what I saw tonight. Not that I didn't put it past the Prince to try to put his hands on her. I just hadn't anticipated that she'd be so willing...

"What was that about?" The door to the room I was staying in flung open behind me. Reagan stormed in, her arms crossed over her chest as she glared at me.

"Get out," I spat. I really wasn't in the mood to deal with her shit tonight.

"Do you want to tell me why you left the celebration early?"

"I don't have to explain myself to you."

Her eyes trailed up and down my body as she scoffed. "It's embarrassing."

I seethed, trying my damn best to stop picturing him pushing Scottie against the wall... how his hands kept roaming her body, and why the fuck hadn't she pushed him off? Not that it would have done anything. The guy was too fucking strong for his own good, but Scottie didn't even try. She didn't seem bothered at all that he was touching her inappropriately. Instead, she looked worried for *him*. I couldn't wrap my head around it. Were they messing with her that much? Did they threaten to harm her if she didn't obey every fucking repulsive demand of the Prince? Was she his? Did the King gift her to the Fire Prince?

Fuck. That thought alone was destroying me. It was making me contemplate storming back into that room and murdering him. Fuck the consequences. I didn't care what would happen to me as long as he never touched her again. How many other times had he done that to her? How many times did she just have to endure it? Fuck. This was damn torture.

"She isn't your wife anymore, so stop pining after her like a sick puppy," Reagan said when I didn't respond. "She's clearly moved on, so why can't you?" Her words ate at me. Had she moved on? Or was she forced into doing that with him tonight? Did they make her sit on his lap? Did she have a choice that his hands were roaming all over her?

But then she willingly hugged him after whatever the hell that was, and somehow that was worse than any of the Prince's groping.

Fuck. I was losing my damn mind.

"We're leaving."

"Yeah, I know. The meeting is over, thank the Goddesses, and tomorrow we can go back to Tennebris and forget about all of this. We'll just pretend it never happened—"

"No. Tonight. We're leaving tonight." I needed to get off this damn island. I didn't trust myself for another second because if I saw the Prince again, I knew I wouldn't be able to hold myself back.

I'd kill him.

TWENTY-NINE
SCOTLIND

I WAITED all night for Patricia—Peter—to return to my room. He should have been back by now. I started pacing even though my room only allowed for a few steps before I had to turn around and start all over again.

I couldn't sleep. I had to hear from him to know that everything was okay, that he was okay. He was supposed to warn Sie about what would happen tonight, but if Sie got Peter's warning, he didn't heed it. He wasn't calm during the dinner at all and afterward...

His reaction was exactly what the Lux King wanted, giving me the sinking feeling that we would be forced to do it again at his coronation, but I couldn't think about that, not right now.

The Lux King had instructed Tezya to take me back to my room, then gave him instructions to meet him afterward. The King was livid, which didn't make sense because we did everything he asked us to do. Well, not everything. We didn't kiss, not on the lips, but I think what Tezya did was worse than that. Was the King pissed at him? Was he mad because Athler stepped in?

Tezya didn't talk to me the entire walk back. I had opened my mouth so many times to try and break the silence and was so close to saying something—saying anything—but nothing ever came out.

When we finally reached my door, he halted outside. "I'm sorry, Rumor. For everything." I was about to tell him it was fine. I wasn't mad at him. I wanted to tell him that I was sorry too, but he left before I could.

And now I was left anxiously pacing my room, worried about what the King wanted with Tezya and worried about Peter.

A knock sounded on my door after what felt like hours. I sprinted over to it, panting by the time I reached it.

"Peter..." I stopped.

"Hey, little nix."

No, no, no. I tried to slam the door shut in Kole's face, but his arm flew out and caught it. He tsked. "There's no reason to be rude. I'm here to fetch you." Before I could move, Kole ripped the Complete Alluse necklace from my neck. It clattered to the ground in time with his skin turning golden. "Follow me."

My mind screamed as my feet obeyed. I followed Kole's brown hair silently as he led me through the castle. I knew this walk. I knew these stairs...

He was taking me back to the dungeons.

———

A BLONDE MALE, wearing a dress that was too short for his toned legs, was hanging lifelessly from the ceiling. His arms were chained above his head, and his body sagged, struggling to support his weight. The back of the cream gown he was wearing was torn open. His back was just as destroyed as the dress. A whip drenched in blood was thrown to the side. The large grate carved into the floor was positioned directly under him, his blood dripping down his body and draining into it.

"Peter," I choked on a scream as I ran to my friend. He stirred, his green eyes flaring to life as he saw me. *He's alive. He's alive. He's alive.*

My feet leadened as Kole compelled, "Stop. Leave him there." Tears sprang from my eyes as I helplessly watched my friend. I needed to get to him. I needed to do something. "You aren't allowed to touch him,"

Kole said as he bent down to pick up the bloody whip. "I caught your *Luxian* maid trying to approach Sie before the meeting," Kole said as he lifted his arm again. "So I followed her, or should I say *him*."

"No. Please. Kole, don't do this." I pleaded. "Please," the word broke from my lips, sobs wrecking me. Kole paused long enough to look at me, and for a second, I thought he might give in. Hope swelled in me. "Peter did nothing. He's innocent. You're angry at Sie and me, not him, please. Please, don't do this."

Kole laughed only once, the whip still clutched in his hand. "He's not innocent, and even if I wanted to help, it's too late. The Lux King is already aware we captured Tennebris' second in command. That he's been pretending to be *your* maid. You'll be questioned too, you know," he said as he looked at me. "The King is on his way down here right now."

No, no, no. This couldn't be happening. Fear tore through me. I didn't know how Peter would make it out of this alive if the King already knew about him.

"Why?" Peter asked. His eyes fluttered open and closed, like even they were too heavy for him. His voice was too soft, too faint. I could hear the struggle and effort it took to say each word. "Why... are you working for... the Lux King." Peter spit as blood poured from his mouth. "You're Tennebrisian."

"The Tennebrisian High Council sent me here. I'm supposed to—" Kole stopped talking mid-way through. "Enough of this. I have my orders." I couldn't tell if Kole looked more defeated or furious. He lifted the whip. "Until the King gets here, I'm not allowed to stop."

His arm reached the sky as he threw all this strength against Peter's already flayed back. Peter screamed. The sound echoed against the dungeon's walls and vibrated against my chest. A pool of blood rested under his bare feet. There was too much of it that it was clogging, unable to flow down the drain, and his cream-colored gown was staining, changing colors before my eyes...

"Peter, shift," I cried as I watched Kole's hand strike down over and over again. "Shift into something. Break out of the chains."

His eyes were closing. He was losing too much blood without a

284

healer. My best friend was dying before my eyes. He was dying. I didn't know what to do. My feet were still frozen on the ground as I was forced to watch, forced to do nothing.

"I... can't..." he panted. "The chains... too much." He winced as the whip cracked his open flesh again. He no longer had the energy to scream. I watched as his body sagged further toward the bloody ground. He stopped fighting against the pain. *No, no, no.*

Anger rose in me. I would not let Kole take anything else from me. I would not let him kill Peter. A memory surfaced from the lake. *I'll show you mine when you show me yours.* He was so jovial, so free-spirited. Peter never stopped smiling, no matter what was going on, but now... Now he couldn't even lift his head. Tears poured from me. I was going to show my friend my ability. I was going to see him smile again. He would live. He had to—

I poured everything I had into him so he could work against the Alluse shackles he was chained to. I could feel his ability stir. The urge to transform, the urge to shift into anything. My skin tingled as Peter met my stare.

"*I. Said. Shift.*" I seethed at him. Peter's green eyes widened as he realized what I was doing, as he felt my power flowing into his. I gave him everything. He didn't hesitate as he used the last of our combined reserves to transform into something else entirely. I watched in awe as he grew. His wrists thickened, and the chains clinked off effortlessly, unable to support his mass. Fur replaced his bloody skin, and claws grew from each limb. His back arched, his teeth elongating. Green eyes narrowed in on Kole's brown ones, ready to kill.

"Make him pay," I smiled as I looked toward the beast. Only his eyes were left the same. I wanted to watch as he killed Kole. I didn't want to miss a second of it. I felt my reserve depleting as I used all of my enhancement on Peter, giving him all my strength, giving him everything I had. Blood dripped from my nostrils as I tasted the metallic liquid. My vision was starting to blur, and my body was shaking so profusely that it was an effort to stand upright. But I didn't care. My friend was out of the chains. He would escape. He would make it out of here. But first, he would kill Kole.

Kole retreated a step, fear taking over him as he abandoned the whip. Then his eyes flashed, and he turned to me. "Stop breathing, Scottie," he compelled.

The air left me. My chest tightened, and that burning fire in my lungs returned. My lungs wouldn't move—couldn't expand—they were stuck, frozen in place. I wanted to inhale, to gulp in air, but I couldn't.

"I won't let her breathe again until you shift back," Kole said, a tremor in his voice. "If you kill me, she dies."

I wanted to scream at Peter to do it anyway, to kill Kole, but with the air out of my lungs, I couldn't find my voice. I could do nothing but watch as whatever beast form Peter took vanished in a heartbeat. He returned to his normal body, still in the torn dress, still covered in blood. "If you try to attack me again, I'll compel her to stop breathing and not stop. Got it?"

"Yes. Just... let her go," Peter pleaded as he collapsed onto the ground, his knees scrapping against the bloodied grate. Kole released me. My lungs could finally expand, and I sagged onto the floor.

A loud clap echoed throughout the room as I greedily gulped in the air. The Lux King was propped against the wall, assessing us from the shadows like he'd been there the whole time.

"Well done, Mr. Sanders. Your presence here continues to amaze me. Not only have you caught us a very important Tennebrisian prisoner," he gestured his head toward Peter. "You also may have just discovered Miss Rumor's abilities." The King's icy gaze fell to my spot on the floor where I was still struggling to breathe. My hands were clutching my throat over the small scar from when Kole first attacked me back in Tennebris. I tried to crawl backward, away from him, still gasping for air as realization sunk in. The Lux King just witnessed me using my enhancement on Peter.

Kole bowed. "It is my honor, Sir."

The King smiled. "And you, Miss Rumor, are also proving to be beneficial in more ways than one." He turned to Kole. "Hook her up to the monitors. I want to access her memories from her training with my son—"

My body was shutting down. I couldn't hear what else he was saying. I used too much of my ability going against the Alluse Peter was wearing that I had nothing left. My vision was fading. The last thing I saw before I fully blinked away the light were two fully silver eyes.

THIRTY
SCOTLIND

"BRING HIM DOWN," the King ordered. My eyes lifted open. I blinked, adjusting to the light. I had been moved, but it still looked like we were in the dungeons, just a different section. I was chained to the floor and could feel the Alluse in the shackles, blocking my abilities.

Everything came back to me. Peter was captured. The King saw me use my enhancement. He knew...

With that, I jolted up, searching for my friend. He was nowhere to be found. There were no windows in here, unlike the cages I was kept in, so I had no idea how much time had passed. I sent a prayer to the Goddesses that Peter was still alive, that maybe somehow he still managed to escape.

At the King's command, the soldiers instantly fled the dungeon cell. It was large, but the lack of windows made it just as dark and damp. There wasn't a drain in the center of the room, and I couldn't tell if that was a good or a bad thing.

The King lounged back in a chair that was brought out for him as he waited for the soldiers to return. He was staring down at me with a smug smile on his lips, the silence vexing. The minutes felt like hours, days even, as I waited for what would happen next. I wanted to say something, to ask what was going on, but I was too scared I would say the wrong thing and make things worse, so I forced myself to hold my tongue.

I shifted on the floor, wanting to see who else was in the room with us. The chains didn't allow for much movement, but I saw Prince Arcane and Princess Dovelyn flanking my side. I craned my neck, trying to see if Tezya was here. I sagged, relief flooding into me when he wasn't. Kole stood in the shadows of the room, his brown eyes never leaving mine.

I tried not to shake as visions flashed before me of what torture he could deliver. My throat still burned from when he compelled me to stop breathing, and it felt too familiar from the night in the warehouse. I hated compulsion. I hated what Kole could force me to do— which was anything. No matter how hard I trained, I could never win against him without Alluse.

The door swung open as Tezya strode in with the two soldiers at his back. He took in the room, the damp, cold cell, and then his attention snagged on me. I cowered on the floor, still in my dress from the celebration, my toes curling into each other from his glare as he noticed the state I was in. His eyes roamed over the chains to the dried tears that streaked down my cheeks.

A pained expression crossed over his beautiful, scarred face before he recovered and turned toward the King. Tezya kept his expression blank as he asked, "What is the meaning of this? I told you already that it was all my doing at the celebration. Athler used his powers on me, not her. She doesn't need to be here for my punishment."

"Oh, she doesn't now?" The King's smile was unnerving. "Your little stunt at the celebration is only part of why we're here."

Tezya scanned the room again. "What else is there?"

The chair groaned as the King leaned forward. "I was hoping you would tell me." He smiled as he twirled and flipped a dagger around in his hand. The silver glimmered as it caught in the lone light swimming above him. My head spun as he curled the dagger into another meticulous circle, making me dizzy. "You see, we had a marvelous discovery today. It seems our prisoner here possesses enhancement."

The King's mischievous smile never faltered as he studied Tezya's face, gauging his reaction.

Tezya didn't miss a beat. "What makes you think that? Enhancement is a long forgotten ability. It hasn't been seen since before we came to this planet."

"I'm aware of the rarity of enhancement, son. What I'm not aware of is why you didn't report it."

"She doesn't have it."

"Oh, I wouldn't deny it if I were you. She proved it to us already. I saw her using her ability with my own eyes in order to spare her Tennebrisian friend from being tortured. The male had no reserves left and was chained in Alluse-laced metal, and somehow, he found himself able to use his ability—to shapeshift after being lashed, and this one," he paused and turned to me, "made that most marvelous comment. *Make him pay*, I believe. It seems the girl really doesn't like our new compulsion user."

Tez looked up for a split second, his eyes lingering on Kole, before he replied matter of factly, "It could just be a coincidence. I saw nothing in her training that would indicate that kind of power. Perhaps you are wrong."

Dovelyn flashed her brother a warning look, but Tezya didn't notice. His eyes were focused on his father.

The King laughed at him as he said, "I haven't brought you down here to seek your counsel on what kind of ability she possesses. You can stop protecting her now. I already looked through her memories of your time spent together. It's interesting though. I specifically remember telling you to only train her in abilities. Yet, you two have been rather busy, going on swims, parties, taking her to a waterfall. It seems you also decided to physically train her too. Not that I mind. She looks much better with a little meat on her bones." He paused to look at me again. "But my favorite memory that we shifted through was the two of you at a beach. It seems you discovered this little ability of hers *weeks* ago and then proceeded to tell her to keep it a secret. *To tell no one about it, especially the King*, I believe, were your exact words."

Dovelyn inhaled sharply as she glared at me, then looked longingly at her brother. Her fear was palpable. Tezya didn't move.

Bile rose in my throat, and it took every ounce of control I had not to vomit. While I was unconscious, they went into my mind. He saw my memories, ones that marked Tezya going against the crown, his own blood. Fear, unlike anything I have felt before, overtook me as I shook harder on the floor. The only good thing was that it seemed like the King hadn't seen our entire conversation. His focus for Kole's compulsion must have been solely focused on my enhancement.

Tezya narrowed his eyes. "What do you want then?"

The King let out a huff, his smile now gone. "I want to know why. Why did you keep it from me, and what were you planning on doing with her? Why protect her, Tezya? Surely it wasn't just so you could bed and fuck her?" The King rose from the chair now and stalked over to me. He crouched down to caress my cheek as he added, "Regardless of how pretty she might be." Tezya's jaw clenched as he stared at his father. His fists curled and uncurled by his side, flexing his fingers like he wanted to do something but was taking restraint to hold back.

Silence rippled through the damp dungeon. The only sound to be heard was my heavy breathing and a steady drip coming from one corner of the cell, leaking filth onto the cold floor. The King stood, dagger now firm in his hand, as he said, "No matter. I didn't expect you to respond. The answer to your question, my son, as to what I want is to lay out your punishment."

In one heartbeat, the dagger was in the King's hand. The next, it was flying across the room with such speed and accuracy. I screamed as it sank into its mark and lodged itself into the center of Tezya's left thigh. Tezya grunted from the pain but didn't falter in his spot. He remained where he stood, eyes piercing with disgust at his father as blood pooled around the wound.

"And Scotlind, this is as much of a punishment for you as it is for my son. You cannot interfere like you did with that Tennebrisian male. This is what you get when you don't put your own Kingdom first. You are to watch a Luxian torture. Watch Tezya go through his punishment and understand that *you* caused this. But then again, since you still seem to place Tennebris over Lux, maybe this won't be difficult for you at all." He smiled at me before turning his attention to Kole. As if he knew he was being requested, he stepped out of the shadows and into the light. "According to her memories, how many days has my son been keeping this information from me?"

Kole answered immediately. "It's been twenty-three days."

"Hmm. Twenty-three days," the King mused. "I'm feeling rather generous today. I'll combine this with your punishment from the cele-bration. I'm disappointed that you weren't able to complete the task without Athler's help. But since the outcome was the same, I'll go easy on you. After all, I am extremely happy with how successful the dinner was tonight." I held my breath, hoping that it was over with, hoping that the dagger in Tezya's thigh was enough—

"You'll only have to endure twenty-three hours worth of torture." He turned toward Tezya. "The soldiers will each take turns whipping you. According to Athler, he was forced to waste his ability on you for fourteen minutes during the celebration, so fourteen lashes for that." He looked at the knife still embedded into Tezya's thigh. "Then, Tezya, you will remove that dagger and re-pierce the exact same spot for the remainder of the time."

Tezya nodded his head. *Nodded.* Like he had known this would happen. Like he'd done this before. My stomach turned. This was supposed to be an easy punishment.

"Unless," the King added, "you want to complete the *task* to get out of it. It's always the same. Such a simple little thing, and you wouldn't have to endure any of this."

Tezya ground his teeth together. "I'll take the punishment."

The King laughed. "As you always do." Then he nodded to Kole. "Compel her so that she doesn't interfere and force her to watch the entire thing. She isn't allowed to look away. Then compel my son to make sure he obeys."

Kole walked over to me as I rattled in my chains. "You will watch the Fire Prince's punishment and not interfere in any way." I heard the musical hint in his voice and knew I could do nothing to stop it. I wanted to scream, to fight, to do anything, but I was in shock. My mouth kept opening to protest, but nothing came out. I couldn't move. Couldn't breathe.

Kole walked over to Tezya next. "You will let your own men whip you. Then, you will remove that dagger from your thigh and keep re-piercing the same spot until your time is up."

The two soldiers hesitantly walked over to Tezya. The larger of the two removed a whip from his belt as the cell door opened. Dovelyn stiffened as Brock entered.

Brock assessed the room, his eyes lingering on Tezya's bloodied thigh, on the dagger that was left there. "You sent for me?" Brock asked, dipping into a slight bow.

"You will heal him only enough so that he doesn't bleed out. If I find out that you took an ounce of his pain away, I will kill you. Do you understand?" the King said. Brock was a healer. They brought a healer in here because what they were about to put Tezya through could kill him. The amount of blood he would lose from stabbing himself for hours... I swallowed, unable to finish the thought.

Brock looked between the Princess and Tezya before he answered. "Yes, Sir."

"Good." Before the King strode out of the cell, he added, "And Tezya, if you miss that mark, just once, if you don't pierce the same spot, your twenty-three hours will begin again, starting with the whip." He chuckled softly, then added, "It's a good thing you are the best swordsman in Lux." He held the thick cell door in his hands and said over his back, "I'm leaving Athler in charge. He will oversee your punishment and will inform me once it is completed."

Athler crept out of the shadows, and I wondered if he lived in them. The darkness seemed to swallow his pale skin and opal eyes. It welcomed and consumed him. I hadn't even realized he was in the room with us until he stepped under the light. Tezya's jaw clicked once as Athler stopped in front of me. His thin lips stretched so far as he smiled that I thought they would crack. He glanced at Tezya before answering the King, "It would be my pleasure."

The horror of what was about to happen sunk in. What Tezya would have to do to himself for hours. For *twenty-three hours*. That was almost an entire day. In one fluid motion, Tezya swiped his shirt off his back and threw it on the floor. Two ropes propelled down from the ceiling as Tezya took a few steps toward them.

The dagger was still embedded in his thigh as he grabbed each rope and stood there, waiting for the whip. Blood now covered a good portion of his leg. How much would he lose? The realization hit me that Tezya would merely stand in that spot, holding the ropes with nothing to keep him upright as they tore his back apart. He would endure it. Kole compelled him to endure it. My heart skyrocketed as I begged for anyone to stop this. "Please," I pleaded with tears in my eyes, "I'll do anything. Please, don't do this."

Athler turned toward Kole. "Do you want to handle her, or shall I?" I was screaming now, and once I started, I couldn't stop. It dawned on me that this wasn't just a dream. I wasn't stuck in one of my endless nightmares. This was going to happen.

Tezya stiffened, but Kole walked over to me with a predator's gaze, his golden arm outstretched. "Shut up and watch. Don't speak until it's over."

Athler chuckled softly in agreement. "You should have been born in Lux, boy. You are ruthless."

My jaw snapped shut. I wanted to keep screaming. I wanted to stop everyone from hurting Tezya. I couldn't bear to see someone else I cared for suffer while I did nothing. But all I could do was sit on the floor, chained with Alluse, and watch.

Tezya turned to look at me, the muscles in his back shifting. His one arm was still outstretched as he held onto the hanging rope. "It's okay, Scotlind."

"No, it's not," Dovelyn snapped. "Just do the task, Tezya. It's only one life, then you won't have to go through any of this."

Tezya growled as he looked toward his sister. "I'm not killing anyone, Dovelyn. If you don't want to watch, then leave. You know where the door is."

Princess Dovelyn fumed as her silver eyes filled with tears. Brock took a step toward her. "I'll make sure he's alright. You should go now, Dove." Dovelyn's face shifted as she looked up at Brock. He gently wiped away a fallen tear. "Go. You don't have to stay and see this."

She glared at me, chained on the floor, before storming out of the cell. Prince Arcane looked between me and his brother. "You brought this upon yourself," was all he said to Tezya before he followed his sister out the door.

"Begin," Athler ordered. The two soldiers only stared at Tezya. I could tell they were conflicted with their task. They probably knew Tezya well from working with him in the army. He was their leader. Tezya glanced down at me one more time before he reached for the other rope and nodded toward his men.

Only then did they begin.

THIRTY-ONE
SCOTLIND

AT THE FIRST sound of the whip against Tezya's back, blood instantly seeped out. By the time the second lash ripped his skin open, I felt faint.

"Don't go easy on him," Athler croaked. "Or I'll make you start over, starting with whipping each other."

I watched over and over again as the soldiers took turns destroying Tezya's back. It seemed like each heave on his flesh was met with more force. With each lashing, the soldiers swung harder and harder like some sick silent game of who could produce more blood, and both were winning. They were probably just terrified of disappointing Athler, of what he would do if he wasn't satisfied, but Tezya paid the price for it. His knuckles were white as he gripped the dangling ropes, but he never once let go. He grunted with each blow, the sound rattled deep in my chest, but he refused to scream. His knees started to buckle as his breathing grew heavy. I watched as his beautiful tanned skin turned crimson red.

"Fourteen," one of the soldiers said as they let the whip fall. I sagged a little on my spot on the floor. I couldn't stomach watching anymore. Tezya dropped the ropes and turned to face Athler, who's face was twisted into a grin.

"Please make yourself comfortable. You're going to be here for a while." He waved a hand toward the chair that the King was sitting on earlier. It was positioned in the middle of the room, right in front of me. Tezya didn't miss a beat. His jaw was clenched as he made his way toward the empty chair and sat down with a surprising amount of steadiness to his gait.

Brock stepped up behind Tezya, readying to replenish his blood supply.

Tezya met my gaze as he reached for the dagger that was still embedded in his thigh and pulled out the length of it. The blade was in the air for a moment's breath before it went plunging back into that same spot. He didn't cry out, he barely grunted, but I noticed his fingers trembled and his thigh shook. He grabbed the handle to free the blade once more. Again. Again. Again.

I didn't know how long we sat in the dungeon cell together. The drip of Tezya's blood was intertwined with the drip of water from the corner of the room. I couldn't tell which was more steady, which was stronger. The once brown concrete floors were now stained red. The bottom of my slip was soaked in his blood as it started to make a path toward me. I could feel the blood turn from warm to cold as it penetrated through the silk and absorbed into my own skin. I wondered how long it would take for both of us to scrub off his blood from our bodies.

Athler didn't let me move, so I stayed chained to the floor in front of Tezya with nothing to do but watch as he was forced to perform his own twisted punishment. The soldiers left after the tenth time the blade slid into his thigh. Kole didn't last long after that, leaving only Tezya, Brock, Athler, and I to listen to the sound of the blade hitting flesh. Even with Kole gone, his compulsion lingered. I tried again and again to speak, to say anything to comfort Tezya, but no sound escaped my lips. And I knew it wouldn't until the time was up.

I didn't know how much longer that would be. There were no windows in here, no way to tell how much time had passed. No way of knowing what hour Tezya was at. It was another sick form of torture. How could a father do this to his own son? My stomach threatened to spill. I caused this. He was protecting me by withholding the information from the King, and look where that got him.

Athler crept back into the shadows at some point. The only thing that was visible were his opal eyes that never left us. I focused on Tezya to avoid the eerie, iridescent glow.

I started to count the number of times the dagger met his flesh. Within sixty seconds, Tezya stabbed himself twenty-two times. Two minutes he was at forty-four. Only ten minutes in, and he was up to two-hundred and twenty. I counted and counted, but I had to stop because the number got disturbingly high. I wanted to scream. I wanted to cry. I wanted to let my weariness and weak body take over and pass out on the floor. I wanted time to speed up. I wanted to rip out of my chains only to grab the dagger out of Tezya's hand, storm the castle and plunge it into his father's heart. But I couldn't. I couldn't do any of that. I couldn't stop what was happening. I couldn't even speak.

I studied Tezya as he studied me. He stopped looking down at the spot on his thigh as if he had memorized it. He had done it enough times to know the exact angle he needed. His gaze never left mine now. We looked at each other for strength to get through this, for a distraction, for something else to concentrate on—so I memorized him. I was transfixed on him. My gaze roamed everywhere, exploring every inch of his skin except where the dagger kept going in and out.

His crystal blue eyes were glazed over in pain but still looked at me with longing. I was left shivering in his cold blood as every inch of him was covered in sweat. The top of his white hair was slicked to his forehead. His chest was completely drenched. From the perspiration, I could make out the black flames from his markings. I memorized them, too, until I knew his markings so well as if it was my own skin. It was rare for markings to appear on someone's face, but his flames reached the tip of his scar. The symbols over his bare abdomen moved in time with his breathing, giving the illusion as if the flames were alive and moving.

I watched as a large bead of sweat rolled down his temple, to the thickness of his neck, and then down his muscular chest and abdomen. I watched until the droplet met with the small amount of hair at his pants line and disappeared within. Then I looked back up, scanning his face until I found another droplet to trace.

I was so delved into the next sweat droplet that I didn't notice Athler moving. He came up behind me and pulled on my chains. I tried and failed to escape his hold, but I couldn't. Another one of the straps on the back of my dress snapped as my slip fell lower.

"I was thinking," he purred softly, "twenty-three hours is a long time, and I'm growing bored."

Tezya growled at Athler as the dagger drove yet again into his thigh, unable to stop the action through the compulsion Kole left behind. Brock stiffened behind him but didn't say anything.

Fear, unlike anything I'd experienced, worked its way through me. Every pain I had ever felt amplified and flashed before my eyes. It cleaved my chest in two, taking away my sanity with it.

I wanted to scream. I wanted Tezya to burn everything around me so the world could feel this agony. But I couldn't. My mouth flew open. My breath left me, but nothing came out.

I heard Tezya talking, but it was muffled and distant. All I could focus on was the pain. It was devouring everything inside me.

Athler's laugh was vicious. "The fact that you don't like me messing with her makes it all the more fun."

"If you lay another finger on her, I don't care about the consequences, I will murder you right here."

"I'm not even touching her." His chuckle deepened. "Just messing with her pheromones a little. Giving her a little taste of fear. Nothing serious."

"I will kill you."

"I think you'll find it hard to do anything with that compulsion working through your system. I can do anything I want to the girl, and you wouldn't be able to stop me." I felt hands roam over my body, but my vision was still too consumed in the shadows and agony of Athler's ability. "You would just have to watch as you continue to stab yourself. I could do anything I wanted to her. Make her feel whatever pleases me."

"I will murder you," Tez repeated. I'd never heard his voice sound so low, so murderous.

Athler dropped the chains, and I fell forward. Dots peppered my vision, and my breathing was ragged. Tezya stopped driving the dagger into his flesh, leaving it lodged into him as he glared at Athler. His hand tightened around the blade so hard that his fingers turned white through the blood that coated it.

Athler smiled.

I looked at what Athler was inspecting. Tezya's thigh. The blade had nestled into his flesh in a different spot, about an inch from where his mark should have been. He tsked. "You've grown sloppy."

Tezya barred his teeth at the King's second, then looked worriedly over at me, scanning my face with such desperation.

"Well, it looks like you'll have to start over. You were five hours in too. What a pity. Your soldiers left, so I guess this one will do." He motioned for Brock to retrieve the whip. *No, no, no.* This couldn't be happening.

I couldn't stop my tears now. Only five hours. He made it only five hours. I took in the amount of blood on the floor and wanted to faint. He couldn't start over. I wanted to scream. I wanted to beg and plead and offer anything in return for Tezya not to have to go through this.

"He shouldn't have to start over if you were the cause for the slip up," Brock sneered.

"Really?" Athler grinned. "Do you think you get a re-do in battle if you are distracted?" His grin dropped as his attention tore through Brock. "Because you don't. If you are careless in war, you die. I would think you would understand what it means to lose someone, Brock-wich. I still remember the feel of your mother's pulse as I took her life. Then your fathers."

Brock hesitated for a moment longer before he picked up the whip. I tried to plead with my eyes to get Brock to notice me, to try to convince him not to do this. But he refused to meet my gaze.

"That's what I thought," Athler said. The whip flexed in Brock's strong grip, and I knew there would be nothing left of Tezya's back after this.

300

Tezya rose from the chair on shaking legs. I watched through blurry eyes as he was forced to hold onto the dangling ropes for a second time.

"Again," Athler said as he sunk back into the shadows, once again becoming a pair of glowing, opal eyes.

THIRTY-TWO
SCOTLIND

ATHLER GAVE Tezya a break only twice in the twenty-eight hours we spent in that cell. Just twice. He had five minutes to drink water and go to the bathroom, before he had to sit back down in that wrecked chair. He didn't hold me to the same standards. The only liquid I came in contact with was Tezya's blood, and Athler never bothered to unchain me to use the bathroom.

My mind was too foggy, too weak, to be embarrassed as I realized a pool of wetness on my lap. I was covered in filth, urine, and blood— mostly blood. But I didn't care. It was nothing compared to what Tezya was going through.

I kept wondering what was going through his mind. Did he hate me? Did he regret helping me? Did he wish he had never been assigned to train me? Because this was all my fault. He was going through this because of me. I deserved to be cold, starving, and thirsty, but not Tezya. He didn't deserve this.

It was the longest twenty-eight hours of my life. It felt like years, decades, centuries even. I sobbed when Brock announced that the time was up. Athler's form emerged from the shadows.

"There, that wasn't so bad," Athler crooned. Tezya still clutched the top of the dagger, the blade poking through his thigh. "Now get out of this cell so we can have the blood drained and cleaned."

Athler kicked my chains, causing me to fall face first onto the floor. Tezya's blood covered every inch of my body, splashing up onto the right side of my face.

"The keys—" Tezya grunted as he tilted his chin toward my chains. His voice was scratched and as raw as I felt. Athler dropped them, and I watched as they disappeared into the pool of red. I looked up at Brock. It was the first time I took my eyes off of Tezya. He looked pale and clammy. His brown eyes were dull, black circles were painted under them. He was drained, probably having used too much of his healing reserve to keep Tezya alive.

Athler followed my gaze to Brock. "Get some rest. The King has a presentation planned tomorrow morning with the army, and he needs your reserves replenished." He looked at Tezya. "You are both expected to be there."

Athler walked through Tezya's blood toward the door. The sound of it splashing against his boots nauseated me. Brock looked over at his friend once, then silently followed Athler out of the cell, leaving us alone.

Tezya fell to the floor in front of me the moment they left. He started to unchain me immediately. I hadn't realized he had even found the keys in the blood. "Tezya, I'm so sorry. It's all my fault..." I sobbed as he worked on the last lock. It felt weird to hear my voice again, to use it after wanting to scream for so long.

"Scotlind, this isn't your fault. Do not blame yourself for this. I knew the risk when I kept your ability from him." He pulled me into his chest and wrapped his strong arms around me. "It's not your fault," he whispered again because I needed to hear it.

I cried harder. "It is. If I hadn't interfered with Peter, if I hadn't used my enhancement in front of them... You warned me, and I didn't listen, and I hurt you."

"Scottie, it was only a matter of time before he found out. I knew the consequences if we were caught. I know who he is, what he is."

"Why?" I asked as I looked up at him. "Why did you protect me if you knew this would happen?" He barely knew me when he discovered I had this ability.

His jaw clenched. "I'm afraid you're about to find out. He collects Advenians like they are belongings." He paused and then said more softly, "I didn't want him to get his hands on you. I don't know how much I'll be able to see you after this. He won't have me train you anymore. I'm not sure what's going to happen now."

I couldn't think about that. I didn't want to think about what would happen next, now that the King knew about my powers. They had Peter. They knew their plans during the celebration worked against Sie. They punished Tezya. Everything was going to shit, and I didn't want to think about it.

"Scotlind." I looked up at him. "No matter what happens, I won't let him hurt you like this, I promise." I stared at him, at the intensity of his gaze. His scar moved slightly as a concerned expression crossed his face. How many of the scars on his body were caused by his own father? How much had he endured over the past century from him? I assumed when I first met him that every marred inch of his flesh was from being in the army, that he earned every scar during battles. But now... now I didn't think so.

"What happened to you," I whispered as I moved my fingers down the larger one—the scar that went from the bridge of his nose and disappeared behind his jaw. Blood followed where my fingers trailed, leaving a line of red over the raised area.

He shivered. Then swallowed before he spoke. His voice was hoarse. "When I was younger, I used to fight what was expected of me."

It unnerved me to know that Tezya went through these horrors. Based on his reaction to his punishment tonight, this wasn't the first time he'd endured things like this. He grew up with the King as his father, and I couldn't imagine what that was like. His hatred for him made sense now. Beyond not agreeing with how he ruled, beyond having to ensure the ranking system was enforced even though he was so passionately against it, his father was a sadist and tortured his own children.

"What were the King and Dovelyn talking about when they said you could perform a task?"

Tezya sighed as he leaned back against the cell wall. He was still shaking, and I was wondering if I needed to bring Brock back in here. I didn't think he'd be able to stand up right now if he tried. "The King punished Arcane and me a lot. Me more than my brother, but he always had the same rule for the both of us. Dovelyn, too, although she hasn't been subject to his cruelty as often. We could always get out of whatever punishment was thrown at us if we agreed to kill someone."

"Have you ever done that?"

"No," he shook his head. "I've killed lots of people Scotlind, but not like this. I refuse to kill for *him*. Arcane does, or he did in the past. The King rarely punishes him as he now makes it a point to not step out of line. He was forced to become the obedient son and follow without question. It really messed him up. My brother isn't a natural-born fighter. He isn't a killer either, although he's been made into one. He is still tormented by the men and women he was forced to kill."

"Who are they? Who would you have had to kill tonight if you said yes?"

"Anyone. That's the catch. We don't know until after we agree. The King selects someone for us. Usually, it's someone he planned to kill anyway. He has numerous assassins, but it wasn't about that. He wanted us to take a life. But there's been innocent people before too. I've watched Arcane have to take someone out of their home while they were eating dinner for no reason other than the King knew it would fuck with my brother's head."

I hated him. I hated the King more than I ever hated anyone before. How could someone be so cruel to his own children? I gaped around the room, shuddering with the realization that this was a normal occurrence for the three Luxian Royals.

"I'm so sorry," I broke down as I pressed into him, wanting to feel his warmth. He winced, and I stole a glance at his thigh—the dagger was still lodged in it. Tezya followed my gaze. I wrapped my hands around the handle and pulled it out in one swift movement. I couldn't stand to look at it anymore. I didn't want to watch Tezya yank it from his thigh one more time... I went to chuck it across the room when he grabbed my wrist and stopped me.

He gently opened my fingers and took the blade from my grip. Then he turned my palm over so that it was facing up. The scar from my marriage with Sie was staring back at me. Neither of us moved for a minute as we both stared at the raised skin. I inhaled, watching as Tezya dragged the blade over my palm, making a shallow cut right alongside my old one.

My breathing quickened, and my heart skipped a beat. Once he finished the cut, he took the blade against his own palm, mimicking the same exact cut. I looked up. He was already staring at me, his eyes never leaving mine as he reached for my hand, his calluses scraping against my fingers. I sucked in a breath as his lips met with my new cut, and he drank from me. Leaning forward, I grabbed his palm and did the same, surprised at how I wasn't repulsed by this.

Without saying a word, we reached for each other, mixing our blood, and created the first half of the blood bond.

Only this time, it wasn't forced. There was no one around to witness it—just us.

THIRTY-THREE
TEZYA

SCOTLIND HELPED me back to my chambers. Going up the stairs from the dungeons was torturous. My leg throbbed every time I had to put weight on it. I leaned on her more than I should have.

"You should sit down," she said, pointing to my sofa once we were back in my room.

I shook my head. "I'm alright. I've been sitting for too long." I was beyond exhausted, but standing kept my attention sharp. I also was covered in blood, and I loved my sofa. Dovelyn tried to get me to replace it decades ago, but I had always refused. I really didn't want to give her an excuse to throw it away now, so I wasn't about to cover it in blood.

"Stay with me?" I asked her. I knew this was a bad idea, and if we were caught... I'd probably get a worse punishment than what I had just went through, but I couldn't stand the thought of her leaving. I didn't want her to go. I didn't want her to *ever* leave my side. And some part of me was scared that the King wouldn't let me see her after this—at least until Sie's Coronation when he needed us to be together, and I tried really hard not to think about that. About how we'd be forced to put on a show all over again. I hated myself for violating her, for how I reacted to Athler's ability so strongly.

307

"Okay," she said softly. She looked toward my desk and noted the food sitting there. "You should eat something. I'll be right back." Before I could respond, she disappeared into my bedroom. I wobbled over to the food Dove left me. She always did this. Anytime the King punished me, she left a warm meal waiting for me when I was finished. It was always the same—carrot stew. It was absolutely disgusting, but I loved it. Our mother made it for us anytime we were sick. Dove tried for decades to replicate it, but I never had the heart to tell her it was terrible.

I managed a few spoonfuls before Scotlind came back into the living area. "Did you eat enough?" she asked once she saw me set the spoon back down. I nodded my head. I couldn't stomach food right now anyway, and my sister's stew was more likely to make me vomit than feel better.

"Okay. Good. Come with me." She looked nervous. More nervous than I'd ever seen her. She held her hand out for me to take. It didn't pass my mind that it was the hand I cut, the hand that was still bleeding. I took it in my own cut palm, furthering our bond as our blood continued to seep into one another. I felt the same electrifying shock that pulsed through me when our hands met. Scotlind's eyes widened, and without sensing her, I knew she felt it too.

I honestly couldn't believe that I had initiated the bond. I don't know what came over me, but I wasn't about to take it back. I couldn't explain the urge that came over me as I looked at her. That having her by my side made everything okay. That I'd go through hell worse than that if it meant I could keep her safe. I'd do anything to keep her out of the hands of the Lux King.

I followed Scotlind as she led me into the bathing room.

The bathing room.

Holy shit.

The tub was already filled. Water steamed and floated around the surface. I snapped my gaze to her and was surprised to find her own steady.

"Scotlind, we don't have to—"

She dropped my hand but didn't respond. Taking a step back, her eyes never left mine as she slowly undressed. The black slip fell off her body and onto the floor. The material was barely staying on to begin with. She had nothing on underneath it. I already knew she didn't from having her sit on my lap, but to see it... I swallowed.

A selfish need to take in her body came over me, and holy shit, she was so fucking breathtakingly gorgeous. I couldn't stop staring, scanning every inch of her. Every curve. Every freckle. Absolutely everything until it was engraved in me. Her breasts rose up and down as her breathing quickened.

She was going to get into a tub for the first time since the night she had drowned. "We need to wash off the blood," she started to say. My eyes traveled down the length of her and halted at her knees, where she'd been forced to kneel the entire time. Dark red covered every inch of her lower legs. My blood was so thoroughly matted onto her that I couldn't see her burn scar. Some of it was splattered throughout the rest of her, kinked into the crevice of her elbows, her fingers, the right side of her face, her jagged scar that ran from her knee to hip.

I closed the gap between us. "Scotlind, if you aren't ready—"

"Don't." Her fingers went to the button of my pants as she started to unbind them. "Don't try to talk me out of it."

Her eyes traveled down my body, lingering on the bulge of my cock before they slowly drifted back up. My shirt was already off. I never put it back on. It was lost somewhere on the floor of the cell. The idea of a stiff material against my back sounded awful. Brock healed me more than he should have, but everything still ached. If I didn't show up to the presentation tomorrow with wounds to attest for the past twenty-something hours, I knew the King would kill my friend. He would probably make Dovelyn watch too. It wasn't a surprise to anyone that the two of them longed for each other. Despite how hard they tried to hide it, everyone knew. The King knew, and that was more dangerous than anything else. It was why Brock never tried anything. Brock saw firsthand how the King punished us. He always feared it that it would be Dovelyn in that room instead of Arcane or me. They could never be together. Even if he wasn't a rank four and she wasn't a five, the King would never allow his only daughter to marry for love, would never give her that happiness. I knew Dovelyn frequented the Goddess temples on the far side of the island often, praying that the King wouldn't go through with his threats of marrying her off to Athler. He's been holding that over her head ever since our mother died, forcing her to do anything—it was the perfect blackmail.

I looked at Scottie, and I tried to not think of how absolutely terrified I was when I saw her chained in that room. I was so scared that he was going to do something to her that I was relieved when he gave me my punishment. But we were far from out of this because now he knew what she was capable of. The fact that her power was enhancement—that she could directly make him stronger—she would never be free of him. He would never let her go. It changed everything.

I looked into her blue eyes and saw everything she had been through and everything she would still have to overcome. I couldn't believe she was willing to do this, that she was willing to get into a bath with me right now. I had seen how fearful it made her. How fucked up in the head she had been because of that compulsion user. I honestly didn't think she'd ever get in a bath again. I assumed I'd have to keep taking her to my condo in Miami to shower.

I stepped into the bath once I shrugged out of my pants, allowing her time to back out of this if she wanted. We were still holding hands, mine extended as she lingered outside the tub. Her breathing halted, a small hitch before she inhaled sharply, then stepped all the way inside.

I sat down first, sinking into the steaming water. I leaned my back against the cold tile, stifling a wince as it met with my wounds. But that was secondary to this moment, to what she was overcoming.

The tub was massive. Large enough to accommodate multiple people. Scotlind could have sat anywhere, but she sat down on my lap, high enough to carefully avoid the deep cut on my thigh. Despite any lingering pain, I instantly hardened against her as her soft skin pressed into me under the water. She gasped as I throbbed over her center but didn't back away.

Her hands slid their way up my abdomen, dragging the water with them until she cupped my cheeks.

My breath hitched, and I stilled. Slowly, she bent down and pressed her lips against mine. It was featherlight, barely a touch, and not nearly enough.

I was about to kiss her back, to wrap my hands around her and tell her that I was hers and she was mine when she suddenly stood and leapt out of the water. For a brief moment, I was worried it was all too much. I thought the bath was too overwhelming for her. But she smiled softly as she looked down at me. "I'll be right back."

I nodded because I honestly couldn't find words right now. I watched as she lightly hopped out of the tub, leaving water marks on my bathroom floor. I hated that I knew they would dry. I wanted them to remain there forever, so I could remember everywhere she walked, so I could soak in this moment and never forget a second of it.

She started rummaging through my cabinets as I leaned back to watch, not really having the energy to do much else, except enjoy the hell out of the view.

"Ah-ha," she said, and the excitement in her voice was music to my ears. Seeing her happy and safe was all I ever wanted. My cock throbbed as she went up on her tiptoes and pulled something off the top shelf. I was too focused on her ass to notice what she grabbed.

She walked back toward the tub—toward me—with a bunch of fresh linen in her arms. I arched a brow, and she halted, biting her lip and pulling it into her mouth. I wanted her kissing me again. I wanted to taste her and devour her. I was so fucking thankful that I never kissed her on the lips during the celebratory dinner, and that the first time we did was this moment. Without an audience. Without being forced. She kissed me willingly, and I wanted her to never stop.

"I was going to wash you. Get the blood off. Is that alright?"

I nodded, completely mesmerized as I watched her climb back into the water. "You can wash me," I murmured as I leaned forward and grabbed her hips, "as long as I get to wash every inch of you after." I pulled her down onto me, stifling a groan as my thigh throbbed and the water meeting my back stung again. I sucked down the pain, forcing it out of my mind because right now, regardless of what had just happened, regardless of what else the King had planned... I was the luckiest Advenian alive.

THIRTY-FOUR
SCOTLIND

My hand was shaking as I reached for a cloth and dipped it into the water. Tezya was so still. I didn't even think he was breathing as I brought the wet material up to his face. He wasn't that bloody from the waist up—just his hands, forearms, and where I had touched him.

I gently cupped the back of his neck as I traced over his scar, my own eyes straying to his mouth. A bead of water fell over his lips as they parted, and I tried to not think about wanting to lick it off.

"Are you okay?" he asked when I finally started cleaning his hands. Blood was so matted onto them that it took fifteen cloths just to clean one arm.

I nodded. I knew he wasn't asking about what had just happened. None of us were okay after that. He meant me being in the bath. I let out a ragged breath. I didn't think about my surroundings much. I was too focused on him, too focused on the task at hand.

"I'm sorry," I whispered again because it wasn't enough. The last twenty-eight hours shouldn't have happened.

"I'm not," he said as he picked up my hand where he had cut my palm. He kissed it, his lips lingering on my skin, making me crave more.

"How can you say that?"

"It was worth it to have those extra weeks with you." He let out a breath. "I promise it won't last. I promise I'll fix things. I just need time, and I'm so fucking sorry for asking that of you."

The silence that followed was rippling. He was still holding my hand, but neither of us moved. I knew things would change. He hinted that the King would want to use me for my power on him. I just didn't know how, and I was too scared to find out right now. I didn't want to know. I didn't want to think about that yet. I just wanted to have this moment with him.

My other hand still held the bloodied cloth even though his arm was now clean. I dropped it, leaning forward to bring his fingers into my mouth one at a time.

He cursed under his breath as he shifted beneath me, and I couldn't hold back my smile.

"I'm also not sorry it happened," he groaned, "because if I wasn't in pain right now, I don't think I'd have any self control with you."

His finger came out of my mouth with a pop as I stared wide-eyed at him. I went to open my mouth and then closed it again, having no idea what to say. Part of me had butterflies stirring in my stomach, wanting to ask him exactly what he'd do to me. Part of me wanted that. Wanted him to lose control, to have his way with me without an audience, without being forced, but simply because he wanted to. Because I wanted to.

But another part of me kept focusing on his first statement. He was in pain. I was so fucking mad for him, for everything he, Arcane, and Dovelyn had to deal with growing up with that monster. "I hate him, Tezya," I finally said. "I hate your father so much."

Tezya stared at me for a moment, the silver shining through his blue eyes. Then, he wrapped his hands around my neck and pulled my lips to his. "Me too, Rumor," he breathed into my mouth before he kissed me.

———

I COULDN'T SLEEP. I had to see Tezya again. I had to make sure that he was okay. I lasted one hour pacing my bedroom before I found myself walking back to his chambers. After the bath, we sat on his bed for what seemed like hours, neither of us bothering to get dressed. We held each other for warmth as our bodies slowly dried. I could have manipulated the water off of us and dried us right away, but I chose not to. I felt my powers slowly rebuilding once Tezya had removed the Alluse shackles, but I didn't want the moment to end. Once the water was gone, once every remnant of that bath had evaporated, our time together would be over. I kept thinking about how he said the King would keep us apart now. How our training was over. I didn't know what any of that meant or where that left me, but I didn't care. I just wanted to be with Tezya, to soak in this moment with him. So I stared at his skin until his markings faded.

We didn't complete the bond—we didn't have sex—but I wanted to. An uncontrollable need for him kept seeping into me. I knew with certainty that this was real. That once we did sleep together, we would be bonded. Every time our bodies connected, an electric pulse raced through me. It wasn't painful but felt more like a wake-up call. Like my whole life had been gray and I was only now seeing everything in color.

All of my senses were in a furor that it was difficult to not complete the bond. But I didn't want it to happen like that, not with him still in agony. Not when he still had an open wound on his thigh. The dagger had pierced through the entirety of him. Brock had healed it enough to scab over on both ends, but I knew the pain lingered. I saw the way he stifled a wince every time he kissed me.

We stayed in the bath until I washed all the blood off of him. I emptied and refilled the water seven times and was surprised by how easy I found it. Each time I refilled the tub, each time I saw the bottom tile, I didn't freak out. I didn't lose control. The tub no longer scared me as long as I focused on him.

Once I convinced him to stop kissing me—temporarily, at least—he agreed to let me finish bathing him. I went through about a hundred rags, slowly dipping them into a soapy bucket I kept on the ledge. I gently pressed each cloth over every inch of his skin, removing the blood as if I could take away the horror from what he'd just been through.

The lower half of him was a lot worse. I wasn't sure how long it took for me to wash everything off. Especially when I got to his thigh. I tried to be gentle, to barely touch the area, but there was too much blood. He gripped the edge of the tub so hard that I was worried the porcelain would break. Besides his thigh, he remained still the entire time, watching me bathe him. Neither of us spoke until I finished, until every drop of blood was scrubbed off his body.

When I finally finished, he gently pressed a kiss to my forehead before finding my lips again and pulling me back down onto him. I felt him harden underneath me, felt him throbbing between my legs. I tried not to focus on the fact that we were both utterly naked. How all he had to do was lean forward and push the length of him inside me. The feeling went beyond a want. I *needed* it.

Tezya's hands rested on my sides, his thumbs moving gently over my hips. His kisses were light and soft and gentle, nothing like the aggression from when he was under Athler's abilities. This was our own doing, our own choice. He made it seem like we had all the time in the world together, like he would savor every second of it. My lips were swollen by the time I forced myself to pull away.

"Don't stop," he murmured, wrapping his hands behind my neck and trying to bring my head back down to his.

"We need to," I managed back, even though I didn't want to say it. His moans of pleasure were mixed with pain, and I knew his thigh and back were bothering him more than he was letting on.

Only I didn't get off of him right away. I was still straddling his good thigh, his arms wrapped around my back, pressing me into him. He leaned his forehead into mine as he whispered, "Be mine Scotlind Mae Rumor. In this life and in the next."

A smile broke my cheeks as I murmured yes. He kissed me again, capturing the word in his mouth with a longer, deeper kiss.

Tezya protested a bit more, but eventually, he helped me out of the murky water. Once we dried off, taking way too long to do it, he walked me back to my room, saying that it would be safer for me here, that if the King found us together, things would be worse.

But I couldn't do it. I couldn't be apart from him. Some invisible cord kept tugging at my center, begging me to be near him. With him gone, I felt as if half of me was missing. I couldn't explain it... why this feeling was so strong all of a sudden.

I stared at my palm. At the two lines across it—one a thin scar. One a fresh cut, just barely scabbed over—the blood bond. My finger trailed over the cut Tezya made. It hurt to touch, but I still felt a surge of energy through the pain. I hadn't felt that with Sie. When Tezya's and my hand clasped together... I felt him. All of him. For a brief moment, snippets of his life flashed before my eyes. I felt his emotions. I saw myself through his eyes. It was as if our bodies were joining. As fast as it came, it was gone. The only thing that lingered was the jolt and rush of energy each time our hands came together.

I halted outside his bedroom door, about to knock and tell him I didn't care about the risks, that I wanted to be together, when I heard voices.

"Tezya, what have you done?"

"It's none of your concern."

"None of my concern!" a female voice shouted. "Of course, it's my concern. You're my baby brother. How could you be so stupid? I told you to stay away from her, and now look at you."

"Dove, this isn't her fault."

"What do you mean? It's all her fault! If you hadn't lied to protect her, you wouldn't have been punished in the first place. I told you to tell the King the moment you found out that she had enhancement." There was a pause. "I was worried sick. I came looking for you in the dungeons afterward, but all I found was blood."

"I'm okay, Dovelyn."

Muffled cries sounded through the door. "Tez, one of these days, you aren't going to be. His punishments for you are getting worse and worse. What if he doesn't call a healer. What if he takes it too far? I can't lose you too."

"You won't. I promise."

"Don't make promises you can't keep. Just stay away from her. She's only going to bring you more trouble."

"Dove, please," Tezya winced. "Stop blaming her. I chose to lie. I chose to protect her. I made the choice myself. I will always protect her. I know the consequences of my actions. I lo—"

"Don't finish that sentence. Don't you dare say it, Tezya," Dovelyn snapped.

"Dove, we're bonded."

Silence fell, and I leaned closer to the door. I stared down at my own bloodied palm, assuming that he was showing Dovelyn his. Proof of what we had done.

"Don't you dare, Tezya. You know you can't be with her. The King will *never* let her go. Now that he knows he can use her to make himself stronger, she will always be his prisoner."

"I'm working on it. I have a plan."

She sighed. "You and your plans are going to get yourself killed." A long pause. "It's not just the fact that the King will want her now. I had another vision."

There was a long pause that I was worried they might have gone into another room, and I would miss the rest of the conversation, but then Tezya growled, "Tell me." His voice promised violence, and I shuddered at the authority in it. I'd never heard him speak like that to anyone. "Tell me now, Dovelyn."

"She will turn against you. I saw a vision of her working with the King as clearly as I see you now. I saw her standing with the King, making an announcement to the Luxians. She wasn't chained. She looked well even, not starved or tortured. She stood there willingly, Tezya. She condemned you. She condemned and ruined everything that you've been working for. She will destroy everything you've been trying so hard to build. I saw it. I saw people die right in front of her, and she didn't do anything to stop it. She didn't even blink or seemed surprised by it either. She just watched. She let it all happen—"

"Stop," Tezya said, but Dovelyn kept going.

"I know what you're planning to do. How you plan to save her, but you can't bring her there. She will bring damnation to what you've been working for."

"You're lying. You're just saying that because you don't want me with her."

"I wouldn't lie to you. Use your ability and read my emotions, Tez. Does it feel like I'm lying to you because I'm not. She will work with the King. She will turn against us, against *you*."

"No, that's not true. She wouldn't."

"Don't presume that you know her just because you are now bonded by the Goddess. She's a stranger still. You've only been training her for a few months. You know nothing about her."

"I said that's not true," Tezya growled. "Your last vision didn't come true, and this won't either. She wasn't who the prophecy was talking about."

"Tezya, my last vision was that she and the Dark Prince would marry, and they did. It came true, and so will this," Dovelyn remarked.

"It only came true because you made it happen. You told the King to send her! You are the reason that she was sent to Tennebris. You made it happen, Dovelyn. And whatever you're scheming now, I want it to stop."

"You know why I did that."

"GET OUT OF MY ROOM!"

"Tez, please..."

"I. SAID. GET. OUT."

I heard movement coming closer to the door, and I bolted, running back to my own room as fast as my legs could take me.

THIRTY-FIVE
SCOTLIND

A CRAMP TOOK over my calf, but I didn't notice. I kept pacing, too worked up to sleep. I'd been doing it all night, walking back and forth in my room, my mind whirling in a thousand different directions. I couldn't sit still. I couldn't relax.

I was currently in my room at Lux, but for how long? Would I be thrown back into a cell? Where was Peter? Was he in one of those cages that I lived in when I first came here? Were they torturing him too? Was he even alive? I tried not to focus on that. He had to be alive. He couldn't be dead. But I had no idea what had happened to him. The last time I saw him was when I blacked out before Tezya's punishment.

And then there was Tezya... There were so many things I overheard last night, and I didn't know what to make of them all. Dovelyn said that she saw me working with the Lux King, whatever that meant. I didn't know that her second ability was sightseeing, that she had visions, that she saw Sie and I marry before it happened. The revelation that she had something to do with why I was kidnapped all those years ago put an ache in my heart. I couldn't understand it. And Tezya knew about it. He knew...

I couldn't wrap my head around it. I was pretty sure I was still in shock, not able to process what I had heard, not able to make sense of it. Because I just willingly initiated the blood bond with Tezya and then spent the whole night with him, only to find out that he's been keeping this from me. He promised me no more secrets. He promised to be truthful. But if he really knew the reason why I was kidnapped... I couldn't let myself go there. Not yet.

Then Dovelyn said that I would betray Tezya, that I would turn against him. She said she saw me working alongside his father—the Lux King. There was no way. That couldn't be true. Tezya said he was trying to save me, that he had a plan. But Dovelyn told him not to do whatever it was, that I would be the damnation of everything he was working for. I had no idea what any of that meant. Would Tezya listen to Dovelyn? Would he heed the warning and leave me here? Or would he still do whatever he had planned, and if so, was what Dovelyn said true? Would I really turn bad? Because there wasn't a bone in my body that believed the Lux King was good.

If I was working with the King, if I was willingly standing by while he murdered people... I swallowed. That couldn't be true. I didn't care what happened, there was nothing in this world that would get me to side with him. Nothing.

It chipped away at everything I was on the inside. Would I not react as people died in front of me? Would I really work with the Lux King? I hated him. I hated everything about him. I couldn't. I wouldn't...

No. Dovelyn was just saying that to Tezya. She didn't want us together. That was all that was. But, she knew Sie and I were going to get married...

A knock sounded on my door as I made another lap around my room. I hesitated. Then, another knock.

"Open up," a voice I didn't recognize called from behind a door. It was low and soothing. I walked over to it, my heart pounding. I had nowhere to go. The only window in my room didn't open, and my door didn't lock from the inside. The knock was only a courtesy. Whoever was at my door could just break in if they wanted.

I opened the door. "Arcane," I breathed, surprised to see the eldest Prince at my chambers.

"I'm here to collect you," he said. That's when I noticed the chain dangling from his hand. It wasn't a necklace this time, but shackles. He moved swiftly, clamping it around my two zeroes before I could react, but my powers didn't sizzle out and die. They weren't Alluse shackles. "I apologize for the intrusiveness," he continued as he tightened the lock and pulled, "but these are the King's orders."

"So what? I'm a prisoner again?" I challenged. I needed some clue as to what was going on, as to what I was about to walk in on.

Prince Arcane paused long enough to meet my gaze. He looked so much like Dovelyn. They both had slim figures and always looked elegant and well put together. Their shiny silver hair was sleek down their mid backs, not a stray out of place. His eyes were the same piercing silver as hers too. They were both cold and missing the crystal blue of Tezya's. It was what separated Tezya from his siblings— his eyes and his brutal scar across his face.

"You were never *not* a prisoner. I don't know what notion my brother led you to believe, but you are not a Luxian citizen." He pulled on the chains and dragged me barefoot through the halls, not allowing me time to dress.

My wrists were raw from being held taut by the time we arrived at the King's chambers. Arcane stood straighter, taking a minute to collect himself before he gained the courage to knock on his father's door.

"Come in," the King bellowed behind the thick wood. Arcane shoved me in first. Flashes of silver caught my eye. First, the King's gaze, then the dagger he held in his hand.

I found myself searching the shadows of the room, wondering if Athler was blending into the dark. I shuddered as the feeling of being watched ran through me, and I knew he was here even if I couldn't see him. Maybe it was my enhancement finding his powers. Maybe I could train myself to see what abilities were calling to me.

"Bring her to me," the King ordered his son. Arcane pressed my chains into the King's waiting hands. I balled my fist together, attempting to hide my new cut. Did anyone other than Dovelyn see Tezya's scar? I didn't know what the King would do if he put two and two together and realized that we initiated the bond last night, and I didn't want to find out.

I winced as the King slowly dragged the dagger down my arm before replacing the blade with a goblet and, to my horror, rested it under the cut he just made. I watched as my blood poured into the glass.

When it filled to the top, he dropped my chains and brought my blood up to his lips. Slurping penetrated the silence as he downed every last drop.

The Lux King smiled, blood-stained teeth on full display, as he turned to Arcane. "Bring her down to the training grounds. We have a demonstration to make."

———

ARCANE HELD my chains as we were forced to walk behind the Lux King. And all I could do was stare at the back of his silver head and fantasize about murdering him.

I hated him. I hated him more than Kole, and if you asked me prior to Tezya's punishment, I wouldn't have thought that was possible. I couldn't fathom how someone could be so cruel to their own children, to everyone around them. How he was so sadistic and got away with it. And he's been running Lux for *centuries*. How many Advenians have suffered because of him? How did he treat his citizens if that was what he did to his own flesh and blood?

I looked over at Arcane, the chains were taut between us. He was walking next to me with a stiff back, appearance pristine, and his head held high—he didn't have a single hair out of line.

I had no idea where he was taking me or what the King meant by a demonstration, but a pit was already forming in my stomach. This couldn't be good.

I didn't attempt to make a run for it or try and break free. We were surrounded by Luxian soldiers. They formed a semicircle around us with the King leading the way. My chains weren't Alluse, I could still feel my powers, but I didn't delude myself into thinking my water abilities were strong enough. Not yet. I was determined to train even if these chains meant I was a prisoner again. I would find a way to practice, to get stronger. I just had to bid my time.

We left the castle through a side entrance. I had no idea where we were, but I knew it wasn't the back gardens by the jungle or the front gates that led toward the sprawling city.

We were walking on a straight, paved pathway with green grass on either side. The path was plain, not decorated in the bright colors of the city or the wealth of the castle. We were walking further and further from the city, further from the bay and the ocean, further from people, and it had my anxiety skyrocketing.

I was sweating. I was still wearing Tezya's shirt and pants that he tied for me with eight knots in order to keep them up on my hips. He'd given me his clothes after the bath—so I didn't have to put back on my bloody, torn slip. But I'd been so preoccupied that I never even thought to change. I was so worried about Peter, and what I overheard from Tezya and Dovelyn's conversation, that I never even thought about what I was wearing—until now.

Until I was tripping over the hem—even with the pants running short on Tezya's calves, they were dragging across the pavement for me—I was trying not to trip or have them not fall down past my waist.

Arcane gave me a side eye, noting my struggle. My breath halted as he assessed my outfit. I saw as he made the connection. He knew my clothes belonged to his brother. I thought he was going to say something to the King, but instead, he loosened his grip on the chains. With the extra slack, I was able to hold the top of my pants up so they didn't fall off.

I looked up at the King, his form now striding down the path. I was just starting to make out a large clearing ahead, hidden behind a thick line of trees in the distance. He was too preoccupied with drinking my blood earlier to notice my appearance, and I prayed that he never did. Would Tezya get in more trouble if the King found out? If he realized whose clothes I was wearing?

My heart stopped when we finally passed the trees and a large, grassy field was before us. It was a training ground, but there was no resemblance to the muddy, transformative domes that Brock trained me on.

The entire Luxian army was waiting for us, looking like they were ready for battle. I was overwhelmed by the sheer mass of them. Males in matching dark leather uniforms with the sun symbol printed across their chests spanned for miles. Only the outline of the sun wasn't golden like the soldiers stationed in the castle had on. All these men had black etchings for the design. It blended in so well against the leather that I could only see it if I was staring at their chests.

All the uniforms had the sleeves cut off right before their wrists, exposing their four and five brands, marking them as powerful. They were all lethal, not only in abilities but in strength. It dawned on me then—Tezya's status—that he trained all these men. Trained, commanded, and fought with them. These were the soldiers who killed all the rebels. I scanned them with a newfound scrutiny. Did all of them share the same belief as the King, or did some feel the way Tezya did?

My eyes halted on white hair. Tezya was already on the field.

He immediately turned to face me as if he knew the moment I arrived. His eyes scoured me, scanning me from head to toe. His jaw tensed when he saw the chains held by his brother.

He was dressed in the same uniform. And I realized I'd never seen him in it before. I had only ever known him as the Tezya who trained me in private and took me to the mortal world. I never saw him as the commander, as the Fire Prince. I could envision how his reputation started. Besides the fact that word spread that he left the battlefield in flames, he fit the part. He looked fearsome and ruthless and daunting.

I never would have known what he suffered through just hours before by looking at him now. He didn't show any outward signs of being in pain, but for some reason, I could tell. I had no idea if it was the blood bond we started or just the fact that I had been forced to watch him stab himself over and over again for twenty-eight hours that I studied him so thoroughly. I had learned what each of his facial expressions meant. I now understood what was behind his composed mask when he was in front of the King.

I could tell by the way he moved that his back was stiff, that he was holding back a wince every time he put pressure on his left leg to walk. How he leaned heavily on his right, overcompensating for his injury. But despite it all, despite the pain I knew he was in, he stood tall, defiant against his father.

The Lux King stalked toward the center of the soldiers. Males parted and bowed as he passed. "I have brought you forth today to join your training," he bellowed to the soldiers. "It has been a while since I graced your training grounds, and I want to make sure that my army is up to the standards I desire. So who wants to show me how well my son has been training you? Who wants to show me the might of the Luxian army? Who wants the honor of fighting your King?"

He turned in a slow, full circle, facing each and every soldier. The field was silent, all of them cowering under his gaze. No one stepped up to the challenge.

"No volunteers?" He tsked, still scanning the men, gloating when everyone cowered. And I had a sinking feeling it was all a setup. "I'm already disappointed. Tezya, care to do me the honors since your men won't?"

I noticed Dovelyn amongst the sea of men. She wore a white dress that clung to her dainty frame. She looked so out of place standing in the middle of the army, but I didn't doubt that she could hold her own. Did Tezya and Brock train her? Did she regularly attend their training, or did the King only order her to come today? Her eyes narrowed at her father.

Tezya bowed his head as he walked toward the King. He was in no condition to fight. Fear clung to me as Arcane tugged on my chains and positioned us in direct view of the oncoming fight.

"What are the King's powers?" I asked the Prince. This still had to be punishment for what happened. I was sure of it. Tezya was wounded and now was being forced to fight him at full power. I'd never seen the King fight. I didn't even know what he could do, but dread filled me as I watched him smile, noting Tezya's leg. He wouldn't have challenged Tezya in front of an audience unless he knew he would win.

Arcane's brows furrowed as he looked over at me before he finally answered, "Everything."

Fire erupted, and I realized that it wasn't coming from Tezya. The King made a ring around the two of them. It simmered low, destroying the ground beneath it. "Dovelyn," the King demanded, "a shield."

The Princess threw her hands out, casting an air dome over the two of them. Father and son. King and commander.

The moment the circle of protection was over them, every element shot toward Tezya. Water doused any flames he created. Wind ripped at his back and blew his hair away from his face. Lightning erupted, sending jolts into his chest right over the blackened sun. Roots came up from the ground, twisting around Tezya's ankles, traveling up his legs, and locking him in place. He grunted as the thick vines wrapped around his injured thigh. Tezya wielded his fire to burn the roots off of him, but he only managed to get free for a couple of seconds before the King created more to hold him in place.

The King kept creating from an endless well, a vicious cycle of producing and burning. He was drawing from all the elements, bringing them forward from nothing. It was so much, so overwhelming, it was hard to keep up, hard to even see what was going on within the fight.

The King screamed in rage, even though he was the only one who was attacking. He was winning, gaining the advantage, yet he was furious.

"Why isn't it working? Why am I not stronger?" He yelled it under his breath, but I could still hear the malice in his voice from across the open field.

Attack after attack came charging at Tezya. He braced himself for each blow and used his fire to dissipate anything he could. I didn't know how Tezya was holding up, but he was still standing and moving effortlessly on his injured leg. The shield Dovelyn created was faltering. Water sloshed up the sides as fire sizzled, leaving steam in its wake. The wind threatened to buckle and cave the invisible walls in, but Dovelyn kept everything contained, kept adding fuel to the dome.

I'd never seen such power coming from one person, so all-consuming. The King possessed *everything*, yet his mania revealed he wanted more, that it wasn't enough. The soldiers shuddered back as the King's rage soared. His last scream bellowed across the open field before he halted his attacks, his chest heaving with unspent fury.

The fire ceased, and Dovelyn rested her hands back down at her sides as the King's rage turned away from Tezya, his cold, dead eyes focusing entirely on me instead.

He stormed over to me, death promised on his face. Tezya swore profusely once he saw where he was heading and started burning through the remaining roots that were still holding him in place, trying to get to me, but the King kept recreating them without even glancing back at his son.

"The enhancement should make everything stronger, but my abilities feel the same," he seethed, closing the distance between us. My heart was pounding. My body locked up as his mania was solely focused on me. Even Arcane tensed next to me and backed up as far as the chains would allow without dropping them.

Dovelyn looked at me, her silver eyes flaring, as it dawned on her that the King was trying to use my powers. But how? Did it have something to do with him drinking my blood?

The King whipped the chains from Arcane, forcing me to stumble forward, tripping over my too-large pants. He slapped me across the face. The sound reverberated throughout the whole field. "Why isn't it working?" he spat. "You made that boy's abilities stronger. Why aren't mine stronger?"

The King was about to slap me again, his hand raised in the air, when Dovelyn stepped forward. "Enhancement doesn't work like that."

Everything stilled.

"What do you mean?" he fumed as he tore his gaze away from me to look at his daughter.

"Enhancement works with other abilities. Scotlind can make

someone else stronger. If you try to use her abilities," she said carefully, not disclosing exactly how the King's powers worked, "you can only make *others* stronger. Not yourself. Scotlind would have to actively use it on you if you wanted her to make you stronger."

The King panted in rage as he glared at Dovelyn. "Brock!" he bellowed, his gaze never leaving hers. Dovelyn tensed.

"Yes, Sir," Brock said as he stepped forward and bowed his head.

"Let's test my daughter's theory, shall we? Take away their vision. I want to see if I can force you to take on more," he ordered as he pointed to the soldiers before us.

Brock hesitated, then the five men before us fell to the ground, screaming in agony as they grabbed at their eyes. The King stepped forward and amplified Brock's powers—but I wasn't doing anything. The King now possessed my enhancement somehow. I still felt the powers within myself. I still had my ability, but it was like a kernel of my power was now gone, given to the King to bend at his will. I just had no idea how. Seconds later, the screaming intensified as hundreds of soldiers fell to their knees, screaming in agony.

Brock's cries were the loudest.

"Stop," Dovelyn yelled. "You're hurting him. Stop!" Everything fell silent as the screaming ceased. The males whose visions were temporarily stolen returned as they slowly stood back up and regained their spot in line.

Brock was the only one left kneeling on the ground. Blood was pouring from his eyes. "He can't take on that much sight," Dovelyn cried as she ran over to him. "It's too much for his brain to process."

Dovelyn fell to her knees before Brock, the grass turning her white gown green.

"Get up," the King demanded with disgust on his face. "You do not act like this for a measly soldier."

"He is second in command," Dovelyn sneered as she whipped her head to glare up at her father. Tears were pooling in her silver eyes. "He is not some measly soldier, and you just blinded him."

"Then, he *was* second in command." The King left Brock lying where he was and stalked over to me. I tensed. "It seems if I take your powers, it will only allow me to make others stronger," he whispered softly so only Arcane and I could hear. I knew Tezya was listening, too, with his heightened hearing. He was still cursing, burning through the roots, but the King's powers weren't stopping. They were trapping him there, and I was amazed at his focus and control. At the fact that he could hold a conversation with me while still actively using his powers on someone behind him.

The King sighed as he assessed me. "I guess I got myself a new pet. You will remain by my side permanently, actively enhancing my abilities."

"No. I'm not helping you." I said, surprising myself. At the same time, Tezya growled, "Get away from her." He glared at his father, struggling to get to me, but winced as the King wrapped a branch with thorns over his wounded thigh. Blood poured out and down his uniform, but the King still didn't pay him any heed.

"Oh, you will, *pet*, because if you don't, your Tennebrisian friend will suffer."

Peter.

He was alive.

The King's grin widened because he knew he won. I was at his mercy.

THIRTY-SIX
SIE

TOMORROW I WOULD BECOME the King of Tennebris. I should be celebrating. I should be fucking elated, but I wasn't. I had so many things to worry about, like why Peter hadn't returned yet, or what Synder had planned for tonight's pre-celebration, but all I could think about was my ex-wife. Things had already gone to shit. I knew my coronation meant nothing. Without my second, Synder would name himself the position, and I'd be following Lunder into the grave shortly after.

I couldn't have her and be the King of Tennebris, and I was a fool for letting Peter convince me we could get her back. Everything was lost. This would be my last chance to see her... If she even wanted to see me.

The Royal family of Lux were due to arrive in Tennebris any minute now, and I heard word that Scottie was coming. My stomach clenched in two as I recalled the last time I saw her in the Fire Prince's arms. Rage rose inside of me as images of her leaning into Tezya's touch sprang to the forefront of my vision, and she wasn't repelled by his advances.

I had planned to sneak off at night to find wherever the Lux King was keeping her in the castle. I needed to explain everything. The long time apart left me with nothing but regret. Regret that I hadn't explained everything to her. Regret that I let her be handed over to the Lux King. Regret that I didn't do more. I should have just run off with her while I still had the chance instead of playing the stupid long game, being delusional enough into thinking that I could fix everything.

The last thing I expected was to see her wrapped around the Fire Prince's arm. I was so dumbfounded that all I could do was stare as she and the Luxian Prince walked into the room before us. They were seated across the table from us—in one chair. One fucking single chair. She was sitting on his lap, his hands all over her. I had to watch over and over again as he possessively caressed her back, running his fingers over the thin straps of the barely-there dress they had her in.

They were exploiting her. I tried to reach out. I needed to get into her mind, to make sure that she was alright. I had to see if she was being forced to be with him, to make sure that she didn't really have feelings for the prick. But I couldn't. Every time I tried, it came back blank. She was blocking me with some sort of Alluse. And not only that, she barely even looked at me, too focused on the man holding her, leaning into his touch, and sharing a whispered conversation. I hadn't expected her to move on so quickly.

Reagan came up behind me in the mirror and snaked her long arms around my waist. "If you so much as look at her, I will cut you and eat you for breakfast. Do you understand?"

I pried her fingers off me and stalked over to my desk to fill another glass of red wine. I downed it in one gulp.

"I'm serious, Sie. Do not ruin this for me. Don't pine after her like last time. It's embarrassing. I am your Queen, not *her*."

"You may be the Queen of Tennebris after tomorrow, Reagan, but you will never be my Queen." All the pleasantries between us were gone, but I didn't care. It was hard to imagine a time when we used to be civil toward one another because, looking at her right now, I had never hated her more. Her red lips pulled into a thin line. She wore a black charcoal dress that clung to her curves and a metal crown that was nestled on top of her golden curls. She was the Queen of darkness. The Queen of my fucking nightmares.

She scoffed. "I'm serious, Sie. Don't look at her." With that, she stormed out of my room.

I threw my empty glass of wine at the wall and watched as the remnants of red and glass shattered to the floor, just like my breaking heart.

————

SCOTTIE WAS SITTING on his fucking lap again. Jealousy consumed me. It became a living, breathing monster that crawled under my skin and embedded itself there. I couldn't shake it. I couldn't stand it anymore. I didn't care that Reagan glared at me. I didn't care who saw. I had to speak with her. There was no way I was about to just let her sit on his lap in front of me without even trying to talk with her. I had no idea when I'd get to see her again after tonight. I wasn't about to wait another year until the next annual meeting—if I was even still alive by then—and I couldn't stomach her with the Fire Prince for another year, let alone another minute.

I downed another glass of red wine before I had enough. The Prince's hand was resting on her hip. His thumb made rhythmic strokes onto her bare skin that it took every bit of self control I possessed to not rip it from his body.

She was dressed in the skimpiest deep blue slip, and it showed *everything*. Half the men in the room took notice and didn't try to hide their gawking, which just pissed me off more.

She was leaning into the Prince, whispering something in his ear. They talked in hushed tones back and forth, sharing what looked like a rushed conversation.

Tezya noticed me first. He sat up straighter in his chair as I approached. I didn't miss the fact that he pulled Scottie closer to his chest in the process. "Prince Noren."

Scottie whipped her head around, and her beautiful sapphire eyes widened in surprise. The dress she was in was perfect for her, at least in color. It matched her eyes so perfectly, making them all I could focus on. Tezya's hand repositioned on her hip, tightening as it gripped her. The damn authority and possessiveness in the gesture had me picturing daggers cutting into his jagged scar across his face until he bled out.

"Prince Xandrin," I replied, using their family name. I didn't nod my head in recognition. I didn't even bother to look at him as I kept my gaze locked on Scottie instead.

"Call me Tezya. Advenians only refer to my brother by that title."

I ignored him, my eyes still focusing solely on my ex-wife. "Scotlind, you look well." And I was surprised by it. Her skin changed colors. It was darker, more bronzed as if she had spent time out in the sun, and her freckles were more prominent over her nose. Despite being in the hands of the enemy for the past couple of months, she looked healthy. Her bones weren't jutting out at odd angles. Her eyes weren't sunken into her head. She wasn't starved and on the brink of death anymore, but I didn't let that delude me into thinking they were treating her well. Maybe the sick bastard could only stand to be with her if she looked good.

She swallowed. Tezya's hand began the rhythmic strokes again over her hip. I caught a glimpse of a cut on his palm. Why the hell was she not answering me?

"Congratulations are in order," the Luxian Prince said as he leaned back into his seat. Scotlind sank deeper into his chest from the movement. Her blue eyes met mine before she quickly diverted. What was going on? Why wouldn't she look at me?

"Mind if I have this dance?" I asked.

Tezya's eyes narrowed. "Yes, I mind. She's staying with me."

I reached for her anyway and pulled her off his lap. "I wasn't asking you." I could tell the Luxian Prince wanted to fight. It took everything in him to bite his tongue and hold back. If he reacted, it would cause a scene, and he was on the Dark's soil now.

"Sie, this isn't a good idea," Scotlind whispered, speaking for the first time. But I didn't care. To hell with good ideas. It never worked in my favor before, and I was done with having her slip out of my grasp.

She glanced around the room, her eyes locking with some ginger-haired male before I dragged her onto the dance floor and ignored the Advenians who watched us.

The Luxian Princess crossed her arms as she came to stand behind Tezya. Her dress was made entirely of diamonds, making it impossible not to notice her as she moved. Another female, with half her hair black and the other half dyed green, flanked his other side. She wore a deep emerald dress that matched her sleek strands. The material was silky and fitted around her slender but tall figure. And she was tall, really damn tall, probably the same height as me with the heels she was wearing. I ignored both of their pointed glares and turned my attention back to Scottie, leaving the Fire Prince and his posse behind.

"Are you okay?" I asked her when we finally made it onto the dance floor. She *finally* looked up at me, and I swore I lost my breath.

"You shouldn't have done that."

"Done what?" I asked as I twirled her before closing the gap between us. A few other couples were on the dance floor, swaying to the soft music, but most spectated from their tables.

"Taken me from him. You can't make a scene, Sie. We aren't supposed to be together tonight."

"Would you rather be back on his lap then? Dangling yourself like his fucking whore for everyone to see?"

She bristled. "I am stuck in this position because of you, in case you forgot, and this isn't Tez's fault."

"Tez?" I spat, disgusted by the nickname, disgusted by the fact that she actually seemed to like him. "What? Are you friends with the enemy now?"

"He isn't a bad person, Sie."

I couldn't believe what I was hearing, what she was saying. "Isn't a bad person? He's the fucking Fire Prince. He murdered thousands of Advenians. Did you forget that small detail? And not to mention, he's the son of the Lux King. They're all bad."

She bit her lip as her gaze flew to the Lux Prince, still lounging in his chair. His legs were spread wide as he leaned back in the seat, like his lap was a fucking open invitation, waiting for her to sit on again.

His gaze tracked our every movement, his eyes never leaving Scotlind's. I wanted to punch that smirk off his face when he realized Scotlind had turned to look back at him.

"I can't do this," she whispered as she dropped my hand. "Sie, we can't be seen together."

She left me alone on the dance floor, forcing me to watch as she walked back to the youngest Luxian Prince and perched herself back on his fucking lap.

THIRTY-SEVEN
SCOTLIND

TEZYA WRAPPED his arms around me as soon as I sat back down on his lap, and despite the situation we were in, I immediately felt safe. Athler was close by, watching our every move. I didn't want to repeat what happened last time. I was terrified that the Lux King's second would mess with his pheromones again, and if he did, Tezya would be punished after this.

We were instructed to do the same thing—to make Sie jealous as hell—and that if we didn't have our hands all over each other, Athler would see to it that we did.

Tezya winced as I repositioned myself on his thigh. "Sorry," I gasped, jumping off of him, forgetting that his leg hadn't properly healed yet.

He pulled me back down. "Rumor, it's alright. I'm fine." He scanned the room. We were both on edge tonight. We didn't know what the two Kings planned for Sie. They didn't fill us in beyond making him jealous. With his coronation tomorrow morning, we figured whatever scheme they were planning would happen tonight. And Sie just made things a lot worse by openly dancing with me.

Tezya brushed my hair to the side, tucking a thick strand behind my ear. "Are *you* okay?" His hands traveled down my neck, then down my back, until he gripped my hip again. I nodded. "Did he hurt you at all?" I knew Tezya didn't mean Sie. He meant his father—the King. This past week I'd been shackled to his side, forced to follow him around everywhere he went. He had a custom manacle designed to fit around my neck with a long silver chain that he carried around. It forced me to stay close to him at all times, to be dragged around the castle wherever he went. It wasn't infused with Alluse, either. There was no point to it other than it being decorative, for me to remember my place.

I hated it. It reminded me of being choked as I was forced to use my enhancement on him every waking second of the day, even when he was alone in his room for no one to witness his power. He claimed that it was training to make sure that I could maintain my enhancement at all times.

The only rest I got was when the King was sleeping. It was the only time I wasn't actively using my abilities. I felt more drained this past week than I had in my entire life. My reserves were constantly running low, and my body was barely sustaining at its breaking point. By the end of each day, I went to bed shaking and on the verge of passing out. Using my powers to that extent was dizzying. It reminded me of how weak I was when I first came out of the dungeons. Even though I was still holding onto my muscle, my hands would develop a slight tremble by the afternoon. Sweat accumulated behind my neck and armpits, and the pounding headache seemed like it was permanently a part of me now.

The King was draining all my power and taking it for himself. By the end of every day, I felt like an empty husk. Sleep became marvelous. It was weird how it used to be the thing I dreaded, but now, my body craved it.

Using my enhancement on him wasn't the same as when he took my blood and drank it. That felt like he stole a glimmer of my ability instead of just temporarily depleting it. I quickly realized that he had a power complex, an obsession with it. I wondered if it stemmed from paranoia. If he was worried that someone stronger would try to overthrow him.

Not that anyone could even try. He was too powerful. Even his own guards seemed scared of him. My enhancement couldn't decipher what his abilities were. Arcane said he possessed everything, but I didn't know what that meant. Did he have all the elements? He created each one during his fight with Tezya. Or was it something more?

When the King was preoccupied, I tried to cut back on the enhancement I was using on him and direct it towards other Advenians in the room. It didn't help my low reserves, but I was determined to still train, to master my powers for myself and not just have them be used for someone else.

So I started experimenting, trying to figure out what each power of Lux felt like. I had mastered the elements. Water users were the easiest for me to pick out as my own ability seemed to be drawn to them. Fire also was surprisingly easy because it felt the exact opposite of my own powers. It felt hot and sultry, whereas the aura I picked up from water and air users were cold and biting. Ground users were warm and gentle. But the other abilities of Lux, the more rare ones, were harder to understand, and I still couldn't grasp what the King possessed. His powers didn't feel raw but wrong and erratic.

I shook my head again. "I'm fine," I whispered to Tezya. And despite being completely drained and exhausted, I was. The King never lifted a finger on me. He didn't need to, not when I did everything he requested. Dangling Peter over my head was worse than the chains he forced me to wear around my neck. I couldn't help but wonder if this would be my downfall. Would Peter be the reason I turned against Tezya? Was this starting my spiral that Dovelyn claimed I would go down?

I tried not to think about it. I never got the chance to ask Tezya about what I had overheard that night. I hadn't seen him since we were on the field, and Arcane had dragged me back toward the castle before Tezya could break free of the King's powers.

Tezya's hand grazed my arm, and I shuddered as I felt his scar over my skin. It was the only thing that convinced me I hadn't gone crazy and made everything up. I curled my fingers over my own scar, hiding it from view. I kept telling myself that I dreamt it, that it didn't really happen. I hadn't gotten sleep or had anything to eat after his punishment. Maybe I heard things wrong, maybe my mind was playing tricks on me, or maybe the entire conversation was in my head. Dovelyn couldn't have been the reason I was sent to Tennebris all those years ago, and Tezya couldn't have known. There was no way. I was delusional after not getting any sleep and watching Tezya for hours and hours. I wasn't thinking right.

But then I would look down at my new scar, the twin to the one I already had, and I knew it all happened. I planned to confront Tezya about it. I had wanted to ever since I saw him tonight, but I knew it wasn't a conversation we could have here. Not when everyone was staring at us, not when I was forced to sit on his lap, and we were, yet again, the center of attention.

I scanned the room and noticed I only recognized Dovelyn and Kallon. "Where's Rainer and Brock?"

Tezya tensed.

I sat up straighter on his lap. "What happened? Are they okay?"

"Rainer stayed behind. He's still in Lux. None of us have seen Brock since the incident... We've been told that he's recovering and that the healers expect him to regain his sight, but they aren't positive. We don't know where the King is keeping him."

My chest tightened as guilt formed low in my gut and rooted itself there. I still heard Dovelyn's ear-piercing scream as Brock's eyes poured blood. I could still see Tezya burning through the roots that kept him grounded in place as they twisted around his injured thigh. I felt responsible for his situation. Even though I wasn't the one who blinded him, it was still my power that did it, some part of me had caused this. But I thought he had recovered...

I swallowed. Not sure how to process what I was hearing. No one had seen Brock since he was blinded, and what was worse, they weren't completely positive that he would be able to see again. Fear ran through me as I pictured what would happen to him if he didn't fully recover.

"So Rainer stayed behind to search the castle for him while we are..." Tezya didn't finish his thought as Athler stalked closer to us.

I knew I had other things to worry about, that I needed to get through tonight and make sure that Sie and I weren't set up for some disaster. But I couldn't stop thinking about the people that were already hurt because of me. Peter was still locked up somewhere in Lux, and now Brock was too. It was leverage, I realized, to make sure we all stayed in line.

Athler slid into the chair beside us, his raspy voice twisting my stomach. "I couldn't help but notice that there's a lot of *talking* going on here," he said slowly, that cruel smile peppering his thin lips. "Do you need my assistance again?"

Tezya growled. "No."

"You have one minute," he crooned, "of convincing me that you don't." I expelled my breath as he rose from the chair, not realizing I was holding it.

Tezya's fists clenched over my gown. "We don't have to. I can walk you back to your room right now. Get you out of here."

"But they'll punish—"

"I don't care what they do to me."

I turned to look at him. I knew Athler was still watching. I knew what they were waiting for, what they expected of us, and there was no way I would let Athler mess with Tezya's pheromones again. There was an even lesser chance that I would sit back and watch him go through another *punishment*, not because of me, even though I knew that Tezya would. He wouldn't force me to do this. He would take whatever consequences they threw at him, no matter how awful.

My hands found their way to his chest, my fingers sliding under his open shirt as I leaned forward and kissed him. He didn't react at first, too caught off guard, but then he moved. His lips slowly devoured and consumed me whole. With the next stroke, his tongue slid into my mouth, and I willingly opened for him. I moaned, not able to contain it. He felt so right, so perfect. I craved him, needed him. I leaned forward, pressing my body into his so that it was flush against him. I wanted to meld together until we were one.

His thumbs found purchase under my chin as he tipped my head back, giving him better access. I obliged. I felt molten in his arms, not really sure where my body was resting anymore.

I forgot where we were. I forgot about everything else but him. His scent. His touch. His lips. His hands found their way behind my neck, locking my head in place so there was no escaping him. I didn't want to. I wanted to be lost in him, in his soul.

Dovelyn coughed. "That's enough." Her voice was ice cold, proof that she didn't approve of what we were doing. "Take her back to her room *now*."

We broke apart, and onyx flashed in my peripheral. I caught a glimpse of Sie's livid expression—wrath incarnate—before he flipped his chair and stormed out of the room.

Dread filled me as Athler and the King both smiled, the latter more malicious than I ever saw him before. It was too late. We played right into their hands.

THIRTY-EIGHT
SCOTLIND

TEZYA WALKED me to one of the guest rooms in silence. It was weird being back in Tennebris and sleeping in the castle that I once was forced to call home. I didn't miss the roaring fireplaces engulfing every wall or the dark rooms lit by hung torches. The whole place felt cold and damp and... dark. But I was no longer terrified of the flames I walked past.

"I have to go," Tezya said, "I'll come back in an hour or so. We need to talk. There's something I have to tell you, but there isn't enough time to do it now."

"Where are you going?" I asked as we walked inside. The room was small, with only enough space for a bed, a nightstand, and a fireplace that was already burning to life. There was a small window in the corner of the room, but it didn't provide much light. Tennebris was approaching its dark season, which I didn't miss one bit.

I looked up at Tezya as he shut the door. There were so many things I needed to talk to him about, things I needed to hear, needed answers on. I had to confront him about what I overheard.

"The Kings called a mandatory meeting, and everyone is waiting for me."

"Okay," I said as his hand reached for the door frame. "Tez," I pleaded. He halted in front of the door. "I hate this. I hate your father. I hate what's happening. I hate not being with you. And I hate that the only time I got to see you this past week was for this." I gestured to our matching attire, to the revealing blue dress I was forced to wear tonight, and the Alluse necklace clamped back over my neck. "To put on a show for everyone."

He walked toward me and grabbed my hand. Our scabs from our bond scraped against one another. "Scotlind, I promise you, this won't last. I have a plan. But I need more time to implement it. We just have to get through tonight and make sure Sie becomes King tomorrow. If he doesn't, if Synder remains on the Tennebrisian throne, things will become more difficult. I need you to trust me."

I didn't say anything. I just stared at our linked hands. "Do you?" he asked, his voice a little breathless.

I was happy I was still wearing Alluse. I didn't know what my emotions would read right now if I wasn't. Did I trust him? If I was asked that question a week ago, I would have said yes without any hesitation. But now, after hearing his conversation with his sister...

"I trust you," I finally whispered, realizing for myself that it was true. I would ask Tezya as soon as he came back what I had overheard, but I did trust him. I had to.

He closed the remaining gap between us in seconds. My breath hitched as he leaned down to kiss me. His lips were soft, but the kiss was rushed. "I don't want to leave you," he groaned.

"Then don't." I smiled through the kiss as I gently pushed him toward the door. I couldn't stomach Tezya pissing off the Lux King again, even if I didn't want him to leave right now. If both Kingdoms called a mandatory meeting, Tezya had to be there.

"Don't open this door for anyone, Rumor."

"I won't."

"I mean it. I'll be back in an hour." He paused. "Stay in here until I get back. You can't be caught with Sie. If you are—"

"I'll be fine," I said. He squeezed my hand and gently kissed my forehead.

"I promise I'll explain everything soon."

———

I SPRINTED toward the door and flung it open when a knock sounded hours later. I missed Tezya, which was stupid because we had only been separated for a little bit, but every time he left, I felt like a piece of me was going with him. The desperation of needing someone that badly terrified me, and I had no idea where it stemmed from. And after not seeing him for a whole week, I wanted to soak up every second I could with him before I was chained to his father's side again.

My breath was stolen from me when I was greeted by two black eyes instead of silver ones. Sie quickly glanced both ways in the hall before pushing into my room. He closed the door behind him before I could open my mouth or process what was happening.

"Sie, what are you doing here? You need to leave *now*."

He ran a hand through his dark waves. He looked flustered. His skin was paler than usual, more sickly than when I last saw him.

"I had to see you," he said as he took a step toward me.

"If anyone catches us together—"

"They won't," he interrupted. "I teleported here and made sure I wasn't followed." He paused as he assessed me, and I forgot how mesmerizing his gaze was, how intense it felt to have all his attention focused on me. "I missed you."

"You should have thought about that before you sent me away," I sneered. Anger rose in me instantly. He didn't get to miss me, not when he was the reason I was gone. I didn't know how I would feel seeing him again but being alone with him brought out too many raw emotions. Mostly rage and confusion.

"I didn't have a choice, Scotlind. I had to send you to Lux. If I hadn't, they would have forced me to kill you. I wanted to explain everything earlier. I had planned to tell you when I came for the meeting, but when I saw you in Lux, you were wearing Alluse, and you were all over *him*."

"I spent a month in the Tennebrisian dungeons before I was sent to Lux. I wasn't wearing an Alluse necklace then. You could have entered my mind and told me everything then, but you didn't. You kept me in the dark, Sie. I trusted you. I opened up to you. I told you everything about my past." A sob broke from me. "Then, the next day, your father came to the lake, and I woke up in a cell—had been left in a cell for two months afterward, and you did absolutely *nothing*."

"I know. Shit. Scotlind. I'm sorry. I fucked up. Don't you think I know that? It broke me to send you to Lux. I didn't know what else to do. I didn't know how to handle it. I can see now that it was the wrong move."

He stopped speaking and assessed me. It was unsettling, the intensity, the sudden silence, the stillness in which he was watching me. I stepped back as Sie walked toward me with a gleam in his eyes. "What are you doing?

"You look beautiful," he breathed as he cupped my cheek. His other hand reached out and found mine. His finger ran over my palm. Then he froze. "What the fuck is this?" he asked as he turned my wrist over, exposing the scabbed cut next to his old one.

"It's nothing," I said as I whipped my hand back.

Sie's nostrils flared. "Did you bond with him?"

I didn't answer. I didn't know what to say, but my silence was answer enough.

"I thought... I thought you were acting. That you were forced to be fawning over him. I kept telling myself not to be jealous. That it meant nothing—"

"Fawning over him?" I seethed, confusion and shock bubbling through me. "You have no right to be jealous. You are the one who's remarrying. You are the one who sent me away to begin with."

"Did he force you to do that?" He pointed to my hand in disgust. His tone lowered, going deathly serious.

"What?" I asked, more in shock.

"You and the Luxian Prince. Did he force that on you?"

I didn't answer. I just stared back at him in disbelief. He pushed his fingers through his dark hair again, the long waves tangling. "I just... you can't be with him," he added, his voice pained.

"You don't get to tell me what I can and can't do," I seethed. "You left me. You annulled our marriage. You sent me to Lux to be their prisoner. Do you know what that was like? What they did to me? They kept me in a dungeon and tortured me every single day." My hand idling traced the small scars from the tallies on my forearm before I covered them with my palm. "I was starved and beaten, and Tezya brought me back. He helped me. So you don't get to tell me that I can't be with him when he was only picking up the pieces *you* broke."

Everything Tezya did these past couple of months came crashing into me. How he protected me before he even knew me. How he trained me to overcome my fears. I clutched my palm with my other hand as if I could protect the scar he gave me, as if it could protect what we had. And Sie was here, having the audacity to blame me, to accuse me.

"Why did you even come here, Sie? Why are you in my room if all you want to do is yell at me? You criticize my choices when I barely had any. When all I was trying to do was survive." I choked back tears. I was not about to cry, not that I was ever adept at controlling my emotions.

"Fuck. I'm sorry. I don't want to yell at you, Scotlind. I want to be with you." He took a hesitant step forward, reaching for my hand again. "I'll forgive you—whatever you two did. We can both forget about everything. Please..." His voice cracked, "Please, just be with me. Tell me that you want to be with me... not him." His other hand cupped the back of my neck as he bent his head down. "Fuck," he cursed, but it seemed like he was speaking to himself now rather than me. "I need you to want to be with me. You're the only thing in my life that—"

"Sie, don't," I interrupted. I couldn't have him finish that sentence. I couldn't stomach to hear it.

Confusion crossed his beautiful face. "I thought you wanted to be with me. You said you were forced to be with the Fire Prince. When you talked to me earlier and told me that you missed me, I thought you meant..."

"What are you talking about? I never said that, Sie."

He took a step back, his legs faltering, causing him to almost trip.

"What do you mean? You found me. I left as soon as I saw your mouth all over him at the party, but you came running after me. We talked and…"

"Sie. Tezya walked me back to my room. I didn't go anywhere else tonight. We never talked. Other than you dancing with me, but that was it."

His eyes widened before he turned away from me, running his hands through his hair again. "Fuck…" A long pause, then. "Fuck. Fuck. Fuck." He pulled a piece of paper out from his pocket. It was crumbled and looked like it'd been read a hundred times. "You didn't write this? You never gave this to me?"

A tear rolled down my cheek that I was unable to stop at the same time as chills ran up my body. Confusion and some weird form of grief I couldn't quite place was taking over my anger. "No, Sie."

"I thought… You told me to meet you in your chambers—" he cut himself off. He started pacing the length of the room before he began speaking again. "They sent an illusion user. I thought I was talking to you. They made me believe that you wanted to…" He stopped and turned to look at me. Sadness filled his eyes. Longing and sadness and regret.

I took a step back, dread filling me as I realized what was about to happen. That it was breaking my heart. I was still furious with Sie, but seeing him break, seeing him so vulnerable, and having him tell me how much he wanted to be with me. It was all I wanted to hear from him before. For him to be open and honest, to get to know the *real* him, not the person who put on a performance for everyone. But seeing him in pain… I had no idea how I felt anymore. "Sie, listen to me. You need to leave right now. This is a setup."

He closed the distance between us, reaching for my hands. "Leave with me, Scotlind. Run away with me."

I was about to open my mouth to tell him why we couldn't do that when the door burst open.

THIRTY-NINE
TEZYA

SHIT. Scotlind stood frozen, only a breath away from Sie. This looked bad, really bad. I bit back my jealousy from seeing her with him and focused on the moment, trying to figure out how the hell I was going to get her out of this. I should have known that the meeting was a ploy. They kept me there long after it was officially dismissed, claiming they needed information from me regarding the latest rebel attack. I should have known it was all bullshit.

I didn't have the time to be hurt by the fact that Scotlind didn't listen to me, that she opened the door for him and invited Sie into her room when I warned her not to. I didn't understand. I couldn't think about it right now. I knew they shared a past. I knew it was probably torture for her to see him again. I knew she struggled with it, but I thought... Fuck, this wasn't the time for this. What was done was done. I couldn't change it. I just had to make sure she got out of this alive. My mind whirled, circling over every possible scenario on how I could make sure she wasn't to blame.

"What is this?" Synder asked. The current King of Tennebris made an effort to look appalled, but I knew it was all a facade. "This is how you treat your Kingdom the night before you are to be crowned."

Sie dropped his hold on Scottie. Another member of the Tennebrisian Council ripped a note from his hands.

"It's a love letter from *her*," the male sneered as he met Scotlind's wide-eyed stare. Her blue eyes looked depthless. He turned the note over in his hands. "It seems the two of them have been continuing their affair this entire time."

"I hope you two are aware of the consequences of this. An affair between the Kingdoms is treason," the Lux King said coolly.

"Take him away," Synder ordered. "Lock him up in the prison for now. We will discuss what will become of him later." Sie stiffened, but he didn't say anything.

"And the girl?" someone questioned.

The Lux King interjected. "I will deal with her. It's only fair, as she is from Lux, that she will be dealt with and punished in Lux. The boy is Tennebrisian. Do what you want with him."

The males didn't hesitate as they launched themselves at the Dark Prince. He willingly obeyed and went with them. Sie took one last glance at Scotlind before he held his hands up, allowing them to be shackled. Shit. This wasn't supposed to happen. Why the hell wasn't he fighting back? If he did, if he made an effort to stop this, if he tried to escape with Scottie, I could cover. I could pretend to go after them while making sure they made it out unharmed. But he did nothing. He just gave up. He was letting them take him away. Fuck.

The Lux King turned to me. "Tezya, watch her. Make sure she doesn't leave this room. We'll deal with her when we return." He tossed a pair of chains at me, inching closer to me so only I could hear. "Do not get any ideas."

Then everything happened at once. Commotion rippled through the room as they secured and led the Dark Prince to his doom. The rest of the Council filed out with him until it was just her and I left. The moment we were alone, Scottie fell to the floor. "I'm sorry. He came in here. I didn't know—"

"Shh. It's okay. This isn't your fault." I dropped the chains onto the floor and went to her, holding her close to my body.

"What's going to happen? What are they going to do with him?"

350

I wiped the tracks running down her freckled cheeks. "They'll take him to the prison. They won't kill him, not yet anyway."

"Will he be okay?" she asked.

I thought about lying but figured it wouldn't do any good. This was our new reality. There was no coming back from this. "No one escapes the prison once they are sent there."

"What have I done?" she sobbed further, rocking back on herself.

"This isn't your fault, Scotlind. He came here tonight knowing the risk. Do not blame yourself for this."

Her eyes drifted toward the shackles on the ground. "Those are for me?"

I hated this. I hated what was ahead for her. I shook my head. "We can leave right now." It would make everything ten times more riskier to do it now, but I didn't care. There was no way I was going to hand her back to the King in chains.

"What?"

"I can get you out of here tonight. We can leave together. I won't let them hurt you."

Her eyes flashed as she thought it over. A long moment passed, and then, "I can't."

"What? Why not? Scotlind, I don't think you understand. He will punish you for this. You will forever be his prisoner. I can't let that happen. I can't sit by and watch..."

"Tez, he has my friend," another cry broke from her. "If I leave with you tonight, he'll kill Peter. I can't—"

"Scotlind, what he has in store for you will be worse than death."

She continued sobbing, her mind made up, as she held her hands up for me to chain.

———

A WEEK HAD PASSED, and I hadn't seen her since that night. It was killing me, not knowing the state she was in, if she was okay. I cursed myself for listening to her, for allowing her to talk me into returning to Lux. I should have taken her away that night. Damn her

Tennebrisian friend. I knew by agreeing that it would make my job harder. I knew the King would keep her locked up, but I hadn't anticipated this. I thought I would have been able to find her by now, that I'd know where she was, and that the only challenging task would be getting her out. I thought I could use my senses to track her down, but everything was blocked. There was no trace of her throughout the entire damn castle. I narrowed in on her friend and knew he was alive, but I was going crazy not knowing where she was being kept.

I checked the entire dungeons at least twice a day, even the restricted section, and still, I never found where the King was keeping her. Every free moment I had, I used to look for her. And now, tonight, the Lux King requested a mandatory *family* dinner. It was bullshit. We didn't dine together, not unless he was hosting someone he wanted to either impress or intimidate. Whether I liked it or not, he made sure that his three children were feared throughout Lux, another power play he liked to flaunt.

I was pissed that my nightly check would have to wait. The thought of sitting down and dining with him while Scottie was suffering made me sick. But I knew if I refused, if I didn't show up for dinner, I'd be punished, and as much as the thought crossed my mind, I wouldn't be strong enough to help her then.

I halted at the door when I made it to the dining hall. "Welcome, Tezya. I'm glad you could join us," the King smiled. He took a sip from a goblet of red liquid that I knew wasn't wine. But my eyes flung to Scotlind. She was here, standing behind him, chained to the floor. A piece of tan fabric stretched across her breasts, leaving her entire abdomen exposed. Two slits of the same matching material were tied together at her waist, leaving her full legs on display.

"Do you like my new *pet?*" he grinned as he took another long sip of the thick liquid. I scanned her face, searching for any signs of injury, searching for any indication that she was okay. But her eyes never met mine. "Well, don't just stand there. Sit down. The food is going to get cold."

I didn't move—couldn't move. I could barely breathe as I took her in. I just kept staring and staring at Scotlind. Something was wrong, horribly wrong. I felt it deep in my bones. Her posture, the way she was pointedly ignoring me. Her emotions were radiating toward me now and mixing with mine, and I realized he must have kept Alluse on her until this moment to prevent me from finding her. Her pain flooded into me now, with bits of fear and frustration intertwined. I could feel her fighting against something. I just couldn't figure out what.

"Don't worry, she won't disrupt our dinner," the King mused as he noted where my eyes had drifted. He took another long sip from his drink. "She has been compelled not to look or speak to you. I do enjoy having that Tennebrisian boy around. If only compulsion was a Luxian trait. It's marvelous."

My fists clenched at my sides. They fucking compelled her to not look or talk to me. Rage surged through me. Dovelyn and Arcane were already seated. Dove was chewing her food pointedly, trying to remain calm. I forced my feet to move, to walk toward the table and sit down.

"Did you only call a family dinner to flaunt her in front of Tezya?" Dove asked coolly after she swallowed her bite of food.

"No, daughter. That's just an added bonus. I called a dinner to update you on the happenings at Tennebris." Scottie's chest rose slightly, but her eyes were still fixated and glued to the floor. "Sie has been sentenced to life in the prison, and Synder has officially accepted the role of King, *permanently*."

"That is only for the next ten years, you mean," Arcane spoke. "Since they have a King's Tournament every decade."

"Wrong. The first law he passed since becoming King is abolishing that stupid Tournament. Tennebris will now mimic Lux. They will rule by bloodlines just as we do here." He paused and turned slightly so that he could gaze up at Scottie. "They also eliminated everyone in their guard that isn't a four or five. The fact that they used to have two and three's serving is astronomical." I tensed, realizing that he didn't mean that they were dismissed. They were most likely all murdered. Fuck. This was so much worse than I thought.

No one spoke after that. No one dared. My siblings knew not to piss him off.

The King threw his knife down on the table when he finished his meat. The sound clattered and echoed across the dining room. "I'm done eating. Arcane, take her back tonight. I expect updates on your work soon."

My brother nodded his head as the King rose from his chair. "Goodnight, *pet*," he crooned as he stroked her cheek. My fists clenched at my sides. I tried to take steady breaths as I was forced to watch her flinch. Repulsion came to the center of her emotions, but she didn't respond. She couldn't say or do anything as he touched her.

Arcane stood as soon as the King left, none of us really wanting to eat this dinner. "Let's go," he ordered her.

"You aren't taking her anywhere," I seethed, knowing full well the kind of work Arcane dabbled in. He loved mortal practices and liked to mix our abilities with their synthetic magic, or *science*, as he called it.

Dovelyn stopped eating. "Tez, he doesn't have a choice."

"I know what kind of shit you do, Arcane. You aren't running any experiments on her."

Arcane cleared his throat. "They are harmless. He just wants to know if her blood can be manipulated in the same way I can make Alluse objects. If I can perfect it, someone would just have to wear it and their abilities could be enhanced."

"I said *no*."

Dove rose from her seat. "Tezya, what is the alternative? If Arcane doesn't succeed, this will be her life." She pointed to Scottie from across the table. "She'll be in chains following the King around like a puppet. Drinking her blood does nothing to his abilities, at least not in the way he seeks, so he will force her to use enhancement on him if Arcane doesn't figure this out. How is that any better?"

My gaze snapped to Scottie as I assessed her. She looked exhausted, similar to how I found her when I first started her training.

"And if he does figure it out, he will drain every fucking drop of blood she has. I'm not allowing it."

I saw Scottie wince at my tone, but she was still looking at the damn floor. I couldn't take it. I couldn't stand to finally be near her, and she couldn't even look at me. I had gone crazy all week searching for her, feeling like my heart was being ripped out of my chest every time I never saw those sapphire eyes. "Scotlind," I breathed. A tear escaped her eye and ran down her cheek. Her head bobbed like she wanted to meet my gaze, but she couldn't.

I couldn't take it any longer. I turned to my sister. "Dovelyn, it's happening now. Get Kallon."

Dove's silver eyes flared. "We can't. Brock isn't ready. He isn't healed yet. We still don't even know where he is."

"Then only her and I will go. Meet us when he is ready. If you stay, you can gather more information to help."

"What are you talking about?" Arcane asked, glancing between me Dovelyn and me. "This better not be what I think it is. You can't go to the mortal territory. You will put *him* in danger."

"Then come with us, brother," Dove said. "I know you love him. You don't agree with the King, so why do you obey him?"

"Because you guys want to go back to Allium. Father wants to stay on Earth. If we rule over the mortals, I can stay with him. Our kinds can mix, and once I take over as King, I'll change things. We can live together."

"Arcane," I said slowly, "all that mortal boy will be is a slave. If the King knew you loved a human, he would force you to kill him in cold blood. You can't pretend that what he is doing is good, that it will somehow work in your favor."

"Doesn't some part of you want that, Dove?" He pleaded as he pointedly ignored me and turned toward our sister. "To be able to fly anywhere we want? We are trapped on this stupid island. I want to explore. I want to be free. I don't want to live for forbidden moments, only enjoying life when I can sneak off to the mortal world. I want to live together. I want every second to be free."

"There is no living at peace with the mortals with what the King has planned, you know this," I said. "And Wells will never forgive you if you attack the humans."

"Do not mention his name," Arcane screamed, bending over and swiping the dishes off the table. They came crashing down and shattered around Scottie's bare feet. "Do not presume you know what he will do."

"Tezya, this is getting nowhere. He won't see our side. I'll fetch Kallon. Just do what you need to," Dove said. She walked over to me and pulled me into a hug. "Are you sure about this, though? I still believe my vision will come true."

I nodded, pulling her tighter into me. This wasn't how I planned it. We were all supposed to go together. It terrified me, leaving Dovelyn behind, but I knew she wouldn't go until she found Brock. But seeing Scotlind like this... I couldn't wait anymore. I had to get her out *tonight*. If I didn't, I had no idea when I'd get to see her again. It was now or never, and my opportunity was slipping through my fingers. I had to act fast.

"I won't let you," Arcane yelled. "All you two will do is get him killed. If you go against Father, he'll be caught in the crossfire."

Dovelyn ignored Arcane as she pulled out of my embrace. "Be careful."

"You too," I said to Dove before I walked over to my brother. Arcane tensed as I placed my hand over his neck, finding that soft spot until he passed out. When my brother's silver eyes rolled into the back of his head, I gently laid him on the floor, away from the shattered bits of plates and bowls he'd broken. At least it would make it look like he put up a fight. I prayed the King's punishment for him wouldn't be too severe because I was getting Scotlind out of here, and after tonight, he would be missing his favorite prisoner.

FORTY
SCOTLIND

I saw Tezya's feet step toward me. I wanted so badly to meet his gaze. Arcane was lying on the ground, away from the shattered glass. Dovelyn had already fled, and their whole conversation left me confused. I wanted to speak. I wanted so badly to just be able to look at him. I had so many questions, but Kole's compulsion was weighing heavily in my veins. I couldn't do anything but stare at the ground before me. Tezya crouched low, his white hair entering my vision as he started to unlock my chains from the bolt carved into the floor.

"We're leaving now, Scotlind," he whispered as he stood back up, the ends of the chains now in his hands. "I'm getting you out of here."

I nodded my head, still looking at our feet. He grabbed my hand, the chains rattling between us. "You can't stay any longer. Things are only going to get worse from here on out," he added as he started to guide me out of the room.

Peter.

I couldn't leave without him. I grabbed Tez's arm and frantically traced the spelling of my friend's name over his skin, praying he would understand. I couldn't leave without him.

Tezya stopped, realizing that I was trying to communicate with him. I could feel his gaze on me before he looked down at what I was drawing on his forearm.

He grunted. "Rumor, I know you care for him, but do you realize how dangerous that is? He is heavily guarded. Getting to him would be near impossible."

I kept tracing his name again and again. I didn't care about the risks. I wouldn't leave without him. Guilt already consumed me that Sie was suffering from my actions. I couldn't leave Peter to the same fate. I couldn't leave him with the Lux King.

Tezya mumbled a curse under his breath, then grabbed my chains and started walking me toward the dungeons. "You are going to have to trust me for this to work," he said, his voice low.

I nodded, just thankful that he listened to my request and was helping me.

As soon as we reached the entrance, Tezya stood straighter, reaching his full height. I never really paid attention to the doors leading inside the horrid place. I'd only ever stared at the inside walls. Four men were stationed at the door on high alert, armed with enough metal that it consumed them. The normally open, silver walls of the castle turned a musky gray. A hint of what horrors were behind the metal doors they were guarding.

"What is your business, Prince?" a soldier asked.

Tezya pulled my chains taut, causing me to trip into him. "I thought it was obvious. I'm delivering a prisoner."

"We weren't made aware of this," one of them said to the other. "We'll have to check with the King."

"This is an order *from* the King," Tez demanded, his voice booming with authority. "He was growing sick of her and needed a break. I'm just dropping her off for a little, giving her a taste of what to expect if she keeps disobeying."

The soldiers shared a confused look with one another, trying to decide what they should do. Do they risk upsetting the Fire Prince, or do they wager the wrath of the King? It dawned on me how easily Tezya fit into the role. He was daunting and lethal. Even I had chills running through me at his tone, at how similar he sounded to his father. The four soldiers stepped aside, allowing us entrance into the dungeons.

The floor was cold and wet as we walked through the damp halls. My bare feet were slowly turning brown from the filth. Muffled screams followed us as we traveled further down. The small windows I had in my cell didn't exist in the pure depths of this place. The deeper we descended, the more the darkness took over. I kept searching the shadows for Athler. My heart was racing. Tez switched his hold from the chains to my hands, and I rejoiced in the comfort it provided. I hadn't realized how numb I felt until his warmth seeped into me.

The dungeons were larger than I had realized. I was only kept in a small section of them near the entrance, and I had no idea they went this far below the ground. It spanned down and down, and I had a sinking feeling that they were larger than the castle itself.

Finally, he stopped in front of a door where three more soldiers were stationed. There was a dingy light hanging next to the cell door, the first one we'd encountered since we entered. "Let us pass."

"I'm sorry, Prince, but we have strict orders. No one is allowed to enter this cell under any circumstances."

Tezya had switched back to holding my chains. "I'm here to give her a reminder. She's been acting up for the King. She needs to see what happens when she disobeys. I'll only need five minutes."

A long moment passed as they considered. Then they nodded and stepped aside, letting us through. My heart pounded, and sweat was pouring down my back. I couldn't believe it worked, that we got in. It made me question the brutality Tezya portrayed as the Commander. I was happy it was working, but I figured getting in was the easy part. Leaving would be the challenge. I couldn't think of one excuse Tez could give that would explain why we were leaving with Peter.

But right now, I didn't care. I was finally with my friend. I hadn't seen him since Kole whipped him and the King captured us.

He was still suspended from the ceiling, just a different one than before. The little bit that was left of his cream-colored dress was fully red. He didn't stir at all. Tezya reached into his pocket and removed two sets of keys. First, he unchained me, then he worked on the locks around Peter's wrists and ankles.

Peter groaned as he fell into Tezya's arms. His eyes rolled in the back of his head. I had no idea what his plan was. How we were going to get out of here. The guards were just outside the cell, and we only had five minutes before they came to investigate. I wanted so badly to be able to talk, to be able to ask him what his plan was. I prayed he had one.

I could feel him looking at me. Tezya was hesitating. He sucked in a deep breath, then whispered, "I'm sorry," which made no sense. Why was he sorry if he was helping us?

Before I could trace the word *why* on his forearm, he opened the door to the cell. I wanted to scream. I wanted to yell at his stupidity. He just unchained us—the both of us—the soldiers weren't stupid. They were going to catch on to what he was doing. He was still holding Peter up, who was dead weight in his arms, and I had no choice but to follow him blindly.

For a brief second, I thought Tezya was going to hand us over. There was no other explanation for his stupidity. I couldn't breath, couldn't focus...

But then his markings appeared. Only it wasn't the black flames that usually took up his skin. It was golden spirals—Tennebrisian golden spirals.

Tezya turned to the guards. His voice was different. Softer, musical, light. I knew the tone too well... I stared in horror as I watched him *compel* them, "Don't scream. Don't make a sound. You aren't going to alert anyone about this." Then, he directed his compulsion toward the one furthest from the door, "Go get a healer."

I watched in disbelief as he immediately obeyed. I was thankful I couldn't meet Tezya's gaze right now because I didn't know what I would do if I could.

A minute had passed before the soldier returned with someone else. The healer's eyes widened as he took us all in. Tezya compelled them all, "Forget we were here. You never saw us. Continue to guard the cell like nothing happened. The prisoner is still inside. No one came down here." Then, he turned toward the healer, "Heal him. Then forget you were ever brought down here. You had to go to the bathroom and got lost. You never saw us."

The healer worked on Peter in silence, blue light radiating from his fingertips. Peter groaned but didn't open his eyes. "That's all I can do," the healer panted as his blue light began to fade, "my reserves are tapped out."

I could see white hair flash as Tezya nodded. My feet leadened. I couldn't move. I couldn't follow. I could distantly feel him pull at my arm, egging me forward. I heard his voice whispering my name, telling me that we had to move now, that we had to get out of here. But I couldn't do anything. I was in shock. Tezya grunted as he shifted Peter over so that he was only holding him in one arm and picked me up in his other.

Everything was a blur. I kept replaying what I saw. *Tezya had golden markings. Tezya used compulsion on the guards.*

I blacked out. I couldn't remember anything that happened from the dungeons to when we met Kallon on the docks. I thought Tezya compelled more people, but I couldn't be certain. My brain was stuck on replay, constantly rewatching what just happened. I briefly heard him having a rushed conversation with Kallon, but I didn't retain it, couldn't process anything.

"Hurry and come to us, Kal. Don't wait. It won't be long until the King makes the connection that you helped us. Once Brock is healed, follow us."

"I will, Tez. I promise." The purple and black portal flashed, and Tezya jumped into it with Peter and me on either arm.

I didn't think about where we were going or what would happen next. The only thing I could think was...

Tezya had golden markings.

Tezya had compulsion.

Tezya was from both Kingdoms.

Tezya was *Luxian* and *Tennebrisian*.

FORTY-ONE
SCOTLIND

THE MOMENT we portaled onto the shielded balcony of Tezya's condo in the mortal territory, he sat me down. His golden markings flashed across his skin again as he gently lifted my head to meet his gaze. "You can speak again," he compelled, eradicating Kole's prior compulsion. As soon as it vanished, my tongue felt heavy in my mouth.

But I still couldn't speak. I still couldn't find the words to describe how I was feeling. I didn't know where to start, what to think. Peter groaned as Tezya repositioned him in his arms.

"I don't understand," I finally managed. "How?"

"My mother fell in love with a Tennebrisian. He was high up and frequently visited Lux by a work visa."

Things were clicking in my head. Tezya said over and over again how the Lux King wasn't his father. He never referred to him as anything but the King. "Dovelyn and Arcane?"

"Are my half-siblings."

"Do they know? Does the King know?" I asked.

"Dove knows. She used to have visions about me, of what I could do. Arcane and the King don't know."

I thought back to when Kole compelled Tezya to stab himself. Compulsion doesn't work on someone with a rank in Tennebris. That meant Tezya had to act compelled, had to pretend. He had to willingly stab himself with that dagger.

His warning for me to stay away from Sie came to my mind next. "You told me about the prophecy. You made me believe it was about Sie and me, but this whole time—"

Peter's green eyes fluttered open as he adjusted to the light from being outside.

"Am I dead?" he croaked. He looked up at Tezya, who was still cradling him against his chest. "Damn, I was really hoping that red hair and boobs would greet me in the afterlife. This is highly disappointing."

"You're not dead, Peter." He stirred in Tez's arms and turned toward me, squinting against the beating sun. Tezya gently set him down on one of the other chairs. He sagged, barely able to hold his head up.

Tezya frowned as he slid the door open to the condo and disappeared behind the glass.

"If I'm not dead, then where the hell am I? And why is Prince happy-pants with us?" He grunted in pain as he pointed in the direction that Tezya went. I didn't answer. I still couldn't process everything.

Tezya came back with a platter of food. "You've been starved. Eat. You need to regain your strength because I'm not carrying you everywhere we go." I finally took a look at my friend and he seemed better. I was relieved because when I first saw him hanging from that ceiling, I didn't know if he was going to make it. I caught a glimpse of his back when Tezya helped him into the chair and it was mostly healed, but there were still a few open gashes going up the length of it. He looked bruised and beaten and had lost some weight from the two weeks he'd been captured, not to mention all the blood he lost from the whip...

"So," Peter drawled as he clapped his hands together, looking between us. "Who wants to tell me how we escaped?" When neither of us said anything, he added, "Because the last thing I remember was being chained in a dungeon cell by this guy's family," he gestured toward Tezya again. "And now I'm unchained and in broad daylight with him."

Tezya and I still didn't comment. I refused to look at him. I couldn't.

"I mean, not that I'm complaining," Peter continued as he took three croissants off the plate. "But a little information would be great. Like starting with where we are?"

Tez finally spoke up, not touching any of the food for himself, "We're in Florida. It's a place in the mortal territory, but we can't stay here long. It's only a matter of time before they figure out we are gone. We have to move fast."

"Uh-huh. Okay, so we are running away. Fugitives then, good to know, and who are we running away from?" Peter asked in between bites. His dress rode up his thighs as he crossed his legs. I tried not to stare at the blood staining his skin.

"The Lux King," Tezya replied. A piece of the croissant fell from Peter's now-open mouth. "When my brother wakes up, there's a chance he might go right to him, and this will be the first place he looks for us."

"Um, no offense, but if this is the first place he is going to look for us, why the hell are we here?" Peter asked.

"Because," Tezya growled, "you were unconscious and in horrible shape. We can't travel in the mortal world with you passed out and wearing a bloodied and torn dress without making a scene. The humans don't take that sort of thing lightly."

"Travel," I spoke for the first time. "Travel where?"

"We're going North to Maine."

"I'm not going anywhere with you," I snapped.

"Whoa," Peter drawled as he leaned back in his chair. Then winced as his back hit the cold metal before he readjusted. "I missed a lot. Since when do you hate him?" he asked as he nodded to Tezya. "I mean, I've always hated him, so I'm totally on board with this newfound information. Just wondering when this all happened."

Tezya glared at Peter, which wiped the cocky grin off his face. "Since I was saving your ass in the dungeons. Now go bathe. The both of you. This is the last time you will be able to for a while, and you can't walk around here covered in blood. We leave in an hour to go North."

Peter cleared his throat. "Okay, and then what? I'm gathering from whatever happened we are probably walking targets. What is your big plan then, Fire Prince? Are we going to live together in exile wherever this Maine place is? Will we sing songs while making dinner together as a new-found family?"

Tezya rolled his eyes. "No."

"Then what is the plan?" Peter challenged, his eyes narrowing, and for once, his playful demeanor was gone.

"I'm not walking away from our people," I added, thinking of Vallie and Miles and all the Advenians we were leaving behind in Synder and the Lux King's hands. With Sie now imprisoned, I feared a lot of things would be changing rapidly and only for the worst. "I'm not leaving them."

"I'm not suggesting that," Tezya said, growing annoyed. "I'm saying we fight back, but first, we need to move and not get caught. I have a plan. Just trust me."

"Right. Trust you. Trust you like I did before. Just like you promised me no more secrets," I cried as tears fell down my cheeks. I really didn't want to get emotional. I was trying to hold everything in. I hated that I was crying again, but it was all too much.

"Fine. Don't trust me, but you need to come with me," Tez snapped. "The King will find you here, and if you want to fight back, you have to be alive for that, Rumor."

Peter cleared his throat. "No offense, but I don't really think the three of us can take on an entire Kingdom."

"No, we can't," he said. "No more questions until we get moving."

Peter ignored Tezya and turned to me. "Where's Sie? I was caught before I could warn him."

"He's..." I started, more tears threatening to spill. "He's in the prison."

Peter set down the remaining croissants. "Shit." Pain shot through my friend's face, and I couldn't bring myself to meet his gaze. "How long?"

No one spoke. Peter's knuckles cracked as his fingers wrapped around the armrests of the chair. His blood was starting to seep and stain the metal. "How many days since Sie has been locked up? How long have I been out of it?"

"It's been a little over two weeks since you were captured and one week since Sie was imprisoned," Tezya answered.

"Good. Then he's still alive. I'm not going with you until we rescue him," he said. My head perked up.

"Then you're a fool, and you'll die."

"It sounds like we have a pretty good chance of dying anyway, and if you truly want to fight back, we need him. You know we need him."

"He's in the prison. He's as good as dead," Tezya snapped.

"But he's not dead," I added, surprising myself. I had to free him. I didn't know what he would be forced to suffer through, but growing up, both Kingdoms always claimed that an Advenian would beg for death if they were ever sentenced there. That there was no escape. Punishment there was always for life, and Advenians could live for a long, long time. I shuddered thinking of the damage the castle dungeons did to me and knew with certainty that the prison had to be worse. It was my fault he was locked up, and I couldn't handle the guilt that had embedded in my gut since he was caught. I focused on it, not ready to work through what I was feeling toward Tezya. This. This I could fix. We could rescue Sie. We could make things right.

"It's out of the question."

"We rescue Sie, then we follow you North," Peter said sternly. "We stand a better chance with him."

"We will all be dead. Do you even know what you are suggesting? Do you even know where the prison is?"

"No. I was kind of hoping you would help us there, *Fire Prince*."

Tezya fumed. "It's at the deepest part of the ocean. There is only one way in and one way out, through a small trench that would barely fit one of us. You have to ascend down slowly, then enter at the bottom. The prison is worse than death. If we get caught—"

I finally looked at Tezya and met his silver gaze for the first time since finding out his secret. "We rescue Sie first."

EPILOGUE

Sie

LUXIANS AND TENNEBRISIANS co-existed in the prison. And not just the prisoners, but the guards too. Everyone was intermixed. It was the one place where both Advenian Kingdoms were constantly around one another. There was no separation. Not that they got along, but they shared a common desire. The guards hated the prisoners, and the prisoners would do anything to stay alive.

The prisoners were sectioned into two groups. The trenchers and the loners. I was a loner, and even though the loners were the only type of prisoner to receive torture by the guards, we were considered the lucky ones. Not that the guards made us feel lucky to not be a trencher. They made it their life's mission to make us miserable, and ever since I arrived, they'd developed an obsession with trying to make me crumble. But they didn't know that I already came here fragmented. I was a shell of everything I hoped to be. The bits were too shattered to put back together. It didn't matter what they did to me. I was already broken.

They tortured me multiple times a day. Which, as long as they didn't perform the torture inside my cell, I was okay with it. I hated being in that cell, hated what lurked below me. The worst part about this place, beyond the asshole guards and the trenchers, was the fact that I was powerless, cut off from my abilities. I hadn't used my powers in so long that it felt like that part of me was already dead and my body was just waiting to follow. All the loners got injected with Vir Alluse daily, leaving us defenseless while the guards could still use their abilities on us. And they used every single fucking power that existed between the two Kingdoms and twisted it into a sadistic form of torture.

At first, I couldn't tell which abilities I hated more—the Light or Dark powers, but I had many encounters to determine which form of pain was the worst.

There weren't any rules down here from what I could tell. The loners were only given one measly meal—if you could call it a meal— and were rationed half a cup of water, if the guards were feeling generous. I honestly would have no idea about the frequency of anything here if I wasn't privy to the knowledge of the prison from being the Prince.

Time didn't exist this far below sea level. The prison rested at the deepest part of Earth, and it showed. Everything was damp and dark and desolate. I was given my own cell, but that was only because they wanted me alive... for now. The loners—the high esteemed prisoners —were isolated and only brought out during torture sessions. As long as we were kept alive, the High Councils of both Kingdoms didn't care what the guards did to us.

Everyone else, the Advenians who were not deemed as important, were known as the trenchers. It was something I wasn't aware of as the Prince. I hadn't realized that part of the prison existed until I was brought here in handcuffs myself. The trenchers were all thrown into one large cell called the *Puteus*. They didn't get torture sessions. They didn't need it. Once they were thrown into the trench, no one escaped.

The *Puteus* was below the normal prison. Each loner cell was made out of grates instead of floors, so we were forced to watch the horror that happened below. It was my own sick form of entertainment, wondering which Advenians would die today and if the guards would clear the bodies. They never did. At first, I avoided looking down. The *Puteus* was thirty feet below the cells and the sounds of the dying and fighting were unavoidable.

This place was my own personal living hell. It was so fucked up that I could never have imagined it, and my mind was a living nightmare to begin with.

And the guards were just as vile, the most immoral Advenians I had ever encountered. There was a Luxian guard in particular who possessed both fire and ground abilities and liked to burn my flesh while strangling twine over my neck so I couldn't scream. I named him Fuchsia because the guards never admitted to who they were. So I started remembering them by physical traits, and this one had the brightest shade of pink eyes I'd ever seen.

His smirk was menacing and radiated pure dominance as he stood over me today. "I have a present for you, *Prince*." I sat up in my cell, resting my back against the jagged edges of the cage. Agony shot down my arm, and I was certain that it was broken.

The Advenian in the cell next to mine crawled into the furthest corner of his cage, heaving up before the spewed vomit passed through his grate and onto the trenchers below. Fuchsia was one of the most sadistic guards I'd met so far. He liked to go to everyone's torture sessions and added impromptu ones whenever he grew bored, which was all the fucking time. And lucky for me, he seemed to be obsessed with breaking me.

He bent down and opened the hatch to the *Puteus*. The entrance was situated a few feet from the cell I was in. It was the most heavily guarded area of the entire prison, and I fucking hated it. I hated hearing the screams of the poor Advenians who got sentenced below. Most didn't even commit horrible crimes, but only became a trencher because they possessed a lower ranking, and the Council didn't want to waste resources on keeping them alive. No one survived long down there. Most Advenians died by the desperate hands of each other rather than starvation or whatever else they were neglected. I'd quickly realized that if you put a man in darkness and closed him off from the world, they would grow mad, impulsive, and irrational.

They became monsters.

I wondered what poor soul I'd be watching fall to their doomed death today when deep sapphire eyes met mine. *No, no, no, fucking no.*

"Look who we found." Fushia's grin widened as another guard threw Scotlind toward him. He grabbed her by her hair, the long brown ends matted in knots. Her eyes met mine, tears pouring from them and her body shaking profusely. "We found her escaping into the mortal territory with the *Fire Prince* of all people," he smiled. "Ironic how your love for her ended you a permanent residence here, and she didn't even return it."

"Please," I pleaded, my voice was husky from barely using it. "Please, let her go—"

"As you wish," Fuchsia cut me off by pushing Scotlind down into the hatch. I pressed my head against the crate that made up the floor, watching in complete horror as she fell into the *Puteus*. Her screams pierced my heart, hurting more than what anyone could ever do to me. "I thought you'd enjoy watching her die as a trencher. Though I don't think you'll have to wait long for the show to start."

The trenchers below started gravitating toward her, seeing what new Advenian was dropped into their satanic pit. Scotlind looked up at me for a second. One split second was all I got, her blue eyes briefly searing into mine, before she was forced to scramble to her feet. By the way she was limping, I was positive she broke her ankle from the fall, and I knew that she wouldn't survive long.

"No, no, no," I screamed as I banged my fists against the crate, not caring that my wrists and hands were bleeding from impact. I begged the crate to fall, trying desperately to rattle it from its hinges to drop me below. It was the first time since I came here that I wished I was a trencher because if Scotlind was going to die, I was damn well going to die with her.

Laughter filled my ears as Scotlind disappeared before my eyes. She was no longer thirty feet below in the hellish nightmare under the lined cages. She was nowhere to be found. I stayed with my head pressed against the crate, trying to calm my breathing.

Illusion users from Tennebris were who I hated the most. It was worse than any physical torture the guards could conjure. I could never tell when I was in an illusion and when I wasn't. I could no longer tell what was real and what was projected onto me... because it *felt* so real.

I stayed curled up on the crate, my wrists still digging into the rusty metal as I watched my blood drip onto the trenchers, hoping this nightmare would never become a reality. They couldn't bring Scotlind here. That alone would be the last bit of me to break. That would be the only thing that could shatter me completely.

No, she was alive, far away from this hell.

Not real. Not real. Not real.

But the more I tried to convince myself that she was safe, the less I believed it. We were both caught that day, and I had no idea what had happened to her.

I prayed to the Goddesses for the second time in my life, hoping that she was safe, even if that meant she was in the arms of the Fire Prince.

ACKNOWLEDGMENTS

Thank you to anyone who has picked up my first book and stuck around long enough to read book two. It means so much to me that you are invested in my story and love my characters as much as I do. Thank you, thank you, thank you!

To my Nana. Thank you for everything. This book is partially about finding your strength within yourself. *Even if you may be physically weak at times, you are never weak...* someone said that to Scotlind in this book, and I can't help but think of you. Because you are strong, and our family finds our strength through you. I love you, Nana. You have been one of my biggest supporters of this story, reading my book countless times and helping me edit it. Thank you so much for everything. Hugs and Kisses.

To my husband and soul mate, Anthony. Thank you for everything. Thank you for showing me what real love is. Thank you for helping me be *brave* when I had to, for letting me face my own fears while never letting go of my hand. I love you more than anything, and words can't even begin to describe how happy I am that you are my chosen family.

To my family. Thank you for supporting me throughout this entire process. You have all been my biggest cheerleaders, lending me words of encouragement when I needed it.

To my extended family. I am blown away by your love and support. I am the luckiest girl alive to have such amazing aunts, uncles, cousins, and grandparents. Thank you for buying my book, reading my story, and sharing it with whomever would listen. I am so grateful to have a large, loving family behind me.

To my parents. Mom, thank you for constantly being my rock. Whenever I have doubts, I go to you. Whenever I'm struggling with what to do, I go to you. Thank you for being my best friend and my constant. Dad, it meant the world to me that you picked up my first book and read it in two days. Thank you for your continuous support in everything I do. I love you. I love you always. I'll love you forever, Mom and Dad.

To the B.A.B. Book Club and my Aunt Robin. I can't even begin to explain how thankful I am for you. It was really surreal to be able to be a part of your first book club, and I'm so grateful and honored that you read my book. It has become one of my favorite memories as a published author. Thank you all for your support and encouragement!

To Lisa Worthy. Thank you for your continued support throughout my publishing journey. All your advice and tips have helped me so much, and I value your opinion and appreciate everything you have done for me. I can't express enough how grateful I am for you. Thank you!

Thank you to all of the beta readers that took the time to read my story. Every word you read and every feedback you gave meant the world to me. Whether it was listening to my ideas, reading a few chapters, or finishing the entire book, I can't thank you enough. Special thanks to Nancy Kohutka, Laura DiMauro, Cassie Stockwell, Ashlynn Caudle, Lana Gooch, Lisa Worthy, Lynn Christ, Lauren Ettaro, Katy Farrell, Natalie Hague, Stephanie Berardi, Kat Turner, Kelly Pepper, Kasey Benjamin, Trey Benjamin, Carter Benjamin and Mary Benjamin.

My list of thanks could go on and on. I feel so blessed for everyone in my life. Thank you with all my heart!

ABOUT THE AUTHOR

Mallory graduated from Penn State with her bachelors in nursing and works at a hospital, helping to bring tiny humans into the world. When she's not working, you can usually find her drafting stories with a coffee in hand or smothered in blankets with a book on her lap. And when she isn't completely consumed by fictional characters and imaginary worlds, she's traveling with her family, going on walks with her dog, or eating pizza.

Milton Keynes UK
Ingram Content Group UK Ltd.
UKHW041844291223
435208UK00010B/238/J